MAL

'FILTH UPON THE day we came here,' spat Gorvetz. 'This is no place to leave a good brother behind.'

The fire was dying down, the fast-burning fuel feeding a hot but short-lived flame. Lycaon walked through the burning detritus closer to the ashes and scorched bones that remained of the brood mother. He poked around in the debris, bent down, and came up clutching the scorched length of a chainsword. Golden paint still clung to it, and to the clenched fist symbol of the Chapter.

'Brother Lysander,' said Lycaon. 'You left your weapon in your foe.'

WARHAMMER
40,000
SPACE MARINE BATTLES

A WARHAMMER 40,000 NOVEL

MALODRAX

BEN COUNTER

BLACK LIBRARY

A Black Library Publication

First published in Great Britain in 2013 by
Black Library,
Games Workshop Ltd.,
Willow Road,
Nottingham, NG7 2WS, UK.

10 9 8 7 6 5 4 3 2 1

Cover illustration by Clint Langley.
Internal illustration by Helge C Balzer.

A CIP record for this book is available from the British Library.

UK ISBN 13: 978 1 84970 543 1
US ISBN 13: 978 1 84970 544 8

See Black Library on the internet at
www.blacklibrary.com

Find out more about Games Workshop and the world of Warhammer 40,000 at
www.games-workshop.com

Printed and bound by CPI Group (UK) Ltd, Croydon, CR0 4YY

It is the 41st millennium. For more than a hundred centuries the Emperor has sat immobile on the Golden Throne of Earth. He is the master of mankind by the will of the gods, and master of a million worlds by the might of his inexhaustible armies. He is a rotting carcass writhing invisibly with power from the Dark Age of Technology. He is the Carrion Lord of the Imperium for whom a thousand souls are sacrificed every day, so that he may never truly die.

Yet even in his deathless state, the Emperor continues his eternal vigilance. Mighty battlefleets cross the daemon-infested miasma of the warp, the only route between distant stars, their way lit by the Astronomican, the psychic manifestation of the Emperor's will. Vast armies give battle in His name on uncounted worlds. Greatest amongst his soldiers are the Adeptus Astartes, the Space Marines, bio-engineered super-warriors. Their comrades in arms are legion: the Imperial Guard and countless planetary defence forces, the ever-vigilant Inquisition and the tech-priests of the Adeptus Mechanicus to name only a few. But for all their multitudes, they are barely enough to hold off the ever-present threat from aliens, heretics, mutants - and worse.

To be a man in such times is to be one amongst untold billions. It is to live in the cruellest and most bloody regime imaginable. These are the tales of those times. Forget the power of technology and science, for so much has been forgotten, never to be re-learned. Forget the promise of progress and understanding, for in the grim dark future there is only war. There is no peace amongst the stars, only an eternity of carnage and slaughter, and the laughter of thirsting gods.

1

'My thoughts upon witnessing Malodrax for the first time were akin to those of a chirurgeon who, when opening up the body of a diseased patient, witnesses a growth of such incurable malignancy that his instincts are to sew the incision back up and flee the operating theatre.'

– Inquisitor Corvin Golrukhan

THE SCRAPING OF the coral against the spaceship's hull was a howling, as if a pack of wolves were clawing at the *Breaker of Darkness*. The whole ship shuddered, the churning of the outer hull's torn steel a cry of pain.

'Was it like this?' asked Chaplain Lycaon.

Captain Lysander's face did not change. His features were square and solid, and it seemed he had kept his jaw clenched since the *Breaker* had dropped out of the warp into real space at the edge of this remote system.

'It was worse,' he said.

'Good,' said Lycaon.

They were the only two Imperial Fists on the bridge. The rest of the crew here were servants of the Chapter, unaugmented men and women who served on the strike cruiser. The tension here was the kind that could only exist among those who had not ascended to the stature and rank of Space Marine, for it was based on fear. The *Breaker*'s bridge was a gloomy and arcane place, where the clockwork of the ancient difference engines and cogitator arrays were laid open, thousands of cogs and pistons chittering away in a constant background whisper. Bridge officers read the topography of space around the ship from reams of numbers spat out in loops of parchment from the cogitators, or fed punchcards into the command helms to coax tiny adjustments from the *Breaker*'s thrusters. The Malodracian Reef was hidden from them outside the hull, but it was picked out in zeros and ones, a terrible equation that changed even as it was solved. Upwards of fifty navigation crew were on duty for the approach through the reef, every one terrified.

The ship lurched. Some of the crew were thrown to the deck. Punchcards slewed across the floor and loose cogs pinged free.

'They will try to herd us closer,' said Lysander.

'They?' asked Lycaon.

'The reefs are haunted,' said Lysander. 'Predators. Wreckers. They will try to dash us against the reef and break us open.'

'But they will not succeed,' said Lycaon. 'You have seen to that.'

Compared to the Reclusiarch, the most senior Chaplain in the Imperial Fists, Lysander looked plain, if that could ever be said of a Space Marine. His armour was deep golden-yellow with no adornment except for the red fist emblem of the Chapter on one shoulder pad – he had returned to the Chapter lacking his own armour with its decoration of deed and rank. Lysander was captain of the First Company by right, the post he had held when he had been taken from the Chapter, but one glance told that he was not standing shoulder to shoulder with the great warriors of the Chapter now. Lysander's bolter was slung over one shoulder. Even in the short time he had spent back with the Imperial Fists he had acquired a custom model, with an enhanced scope array and an enlarged box magazine. The steel studs in his forehead told of his long service. There his ornamentation ended, compared with the skull-mask and dozens of Chaplain's honours worn by Lycaon.

He had been away for a thousand years. If he was to be what he once was, he would have to rebuild everything he had earned. He would have to start on Malodrax.

Another sound reached the bridge – a shriek, like that of someone in pain or terror, thin and wailing, yet strong enough to cut through the groaning of the ship's painful journey through the reef. The cogitators on the bridge reacted, spewing reams of parchment printout as if in alarm.

'That's the Red Widow,' said Lysander. 'It means we are close to the inner reaches, but close to danger as well. She dwells at the edge of the whirlpool in the heart of the reef. If she draws us in, we are done for.'

'Is she on the map?'

'She is.' Lysander carried a leather case on the belt of his armour. He unlatched it and took out a folded piece of hide, cured light-brown, and shook it open. It was the hide of an animal, hairless, and covered in the intricate contours of a detailed map. It was covered in illustrations of fanciful creatures – serpentine monsters with fringes of tentacles, huge fish swallowing spacecraft whole, swarms of winged creatures carrying off unfortunate sailors. The pictures symbolised real creatures whose true forms could not be drawn.

Lysander laid out the map on one of the cogitator housings. Flag-Captain Remor, the helmsman of the *Breaker*, hurried over from the heap of printouts he was reading. 'My lords,' he said.

'Here,' said Lysander, indicating a place near the centre of the map. It was a black spiral, a whirlpool, and at its edge was the image of a woman. Her body was elongated and thin, her arms long reaching talons, her face avian and stretched, half-hidden in lank hair. She wore a dress of rags picked out in red ink, one of the few splashes of colour on the map. 'If we skirt around the whirlpool we will be safe from her, but she will try to drag us into the currents. Once we are past, there is a way through.' He ran a finger along a canyon edged by sharp masses of coral, winding across to the edge of the map. 'It will be tight going, but it will take us out of the reef.'

'Can you do it?' asked Chaplain Lycaon.

'We can,' said Remor.

'Commander Langeloc said the same thing the last time I was here,' said Lysander. 'Remember that.'

'Of course,' said Remor. 'But in defeat the next victory is born. The Chapter learned from the *Shield of Valour*'s fate. Our crews are taught about its downfall. We will not repeat it.'

'To your helm, then,' said Lycaon. 'Bring us in safe.'

The bridge crew responded to the arguing cogitators, typing on valve-operated keyboards as cumbersome as church organs. Brass compasses skittered across diagrams of the ship and her engine arrays. A small body of crewmen were hurtling through calculations on abacuses with beads of ivory and jet.

'What is the Red Widow?' asked Lycaon as the two Imperial Fists watched the barely controlled chaos of the bridge.

'I do not know,' said Lysander.

Outside the *Breaker of Darkness*, something let out a shrieking laugh.

THE BREAKER WAS an old ship, a noble ship, her hull laid down in the fifth millennium after the ascension of the Emperor to the Golden Throne. Shipwrights of the forge-world Ruo's Hope had built into her hull and bulkheads strands of psychoactive metals, the secrets of their alloys long since lost, which were to the daemon and the spirit of the warp like red-hot wires that burned and dismembered. Clerics of the Imperial Creed had blessed her, and bathed the bolts of her construction in vats of consecrated machine oil. The Librarians of the Imperial Fists had reinforced her further with wards and protective circles of ancient and arcane origin, which forbade entry to beings of the warp.

For this reason it was a full thirty minutes before the damage control teams began reporting casualties. Stationed across the ship, on full alert as the currents of the Malodracian Reef dragged at the *Breaker*, they saw in the strobing light of failing glow-globes the remains of crew members smeared and torn across walls and ceilings. Some witnessed first-hand others lifted off their feet, twisted around and stretched until they came apart as if wrenched by giant invisible hands.

The order went out to break open the arms lockers, well stocked with autoguns and shotguns for use in the close confines of the ship's corridors. Crewmen shot one another in the darkness that rippled through the ship. Systems were strained – the lighting was always the first to go as power was driven to the plasma reactors and their coolant systems. More died, folded up and crammed into heating ducts or slammed over and over into the steel deck.

The *Breaker*'s psychic defences flared and the attackers became visible as flickering images, their spectral hands around the throats of the dead. They had long serpentine bodies like eels, skinny torsos, many-jointed arms that creaked and snapped as they wrapped around their prey, and faces that were knots of insectoid horror.

In the cells, where the battle-brothers meditated and trained away the days in transit across space, bells tolled to rouse the Imperial Fists to action. They threw on their armour and took up their weapons, with barely time for the most hurried blessings to make their wargear ready. First Sergeant Kaderic was the ranking officer on that deck, and he called for every Imperial Fist to hold the cells. They could not rush off in ones and twos to face down the enemy, to be separated and picked off. They could not assist the crewmen calling for help. That was how the enemy would defeat them, and the enemy could not.

Not now. Not when the Imperial Fists had yet to shed a drop of blood on Malodrax.

LYSANDER VAULTED DOWN a stairwell, dropping to the next deck down with a ringing impact on the steel deck. Screaming was coming from down the corridor, which led to several dozen crew cabins and storerooms. Pipes and ducts wound along the ceiling, hung with embroidered prayer-strips that were currently doing little good for the crew.

One of the enemy darted along the corridor, ducking into a side cabin. Lysander barely glimpsed it as it shimmered past – it was something like a sea creature, something like a scrawny, wiry, elongated man, with a dash of spider or diseased fly. Lysander swept his bolter after it but it was gone. In its wake was a screaming that turned to a gurgling howl, and then was cut off. A spray of gore spattered from the cabin doorway.

By the time Lysander was at the door only the creature's tail could be seen, sliding through the bloody steel of the cabin wall. The crewman who had hidden there had been dragged from under the bunk and ripped open, slit down the middle lengthways and almost turned inside out.

Lysander put a shoulder down and charged. He slammed into the cabin wall and it gave way, steel five thousand years forged buckling under his impact.

If the spirit could be said to have human emotions, it expressed surprise then, as Lysander burst into the mass of pipes and cabling inside the wall. It coiled back on itself and shrieked, its face opening up into a fan of extendable mouthparts coiled to strike.

Lysander took aim and fired, stuttering volleys of bolter fire into the spirit. Even halfway into the parallel world of the warp, the spirit's flesh had enough consistency to be mangled and torn. Bolter fire ripped it open and it came apart, the scraps of its spectral flesh dissolving back into the warp.

Lysander kept moving, forging through the machinery into the corridor beyond. Screams were coming from everywhere, and isolated bursts of gunfire, but he couldn't be distracted any further. He spotted the next stairwell and ran down the steps.

The deck below was clad in stone. It echoed the monastic cells that were a Space Marine's home. The Imperial Fists were based on their fleet, and many of their ships were fashioned to recall a planetbound fortress such as those Rogal Dorn was famed for building. On the *Breaker* the decks were dark and gloomy, lit by ribbons of burning gas from concealed jets in imitation of torch or candlelight.

'Lysander!' called First Sergeant Kaderic. He carried his chainsword in one hand and a single-handed axe in the other, a sparring weapon from the deck's training circles, and had donned his armour rapidly with the sketchiest of wargear rites. Kaderic was old, his face blunt and grizzled, the kind of man who served as the lynchpin of the veteran First Company. He was Lysander's second-in-command in the First – technically. 'The enemy cannot wait to die, they rush to meet us!'

'Malodracians call them the Grey Hungers,' said Lysander. 'Predators, like animals. All but mindless. They wait for ships to wreck upon the reef, and feed on whatever is inside.'

'Anything else?' asked Kaderic.

'Nothing more,' replied Lysander. 'They can be killed.'

'That will be enough.'

The First Company of the Imperial Fists was ready to make war. The elites of the Chapter, the veterans and specialists entitled to wear the white trim of the First, were usually spread throughout the Chapter and the various warzones in which it fought, lending their expertise and steadfastness where it was most needed. For Malodrax two squads had been gathered together, along with support troops, into a single strike force, because this was not a war like any of the thousands being fought across the Imperium, where the Imperial Fists answered the call of the Imperium's Warmasters. This was the Imperial Fists' fight alone. This was revenge.

They had not expected to fight until the strike force reached the planet's surface, but that did not mean they were not prepared. Already almost a hundred Space Marines were armed and ready training their bolter sights across the corridors and crossroads of the cell block, or clustered in the centre of the sparring circles covering every approach. The battle-brothers who specialised in close assault had their chainblades ready. Devastator Squad Gorvetz was gathered in the chapel beneath the black marble statue of Rogal Dorn, where their heavy weapons could fill the wide corridor leading to the chapel doors with chains of shrapnel and plasma fire.

'A good fight, captain,' said Kaderic. 'You must have missed those.'

Before Lysander could reply, a screeching sound tore through the cell block from every direction. The artificial torches flickered and shadows leaped.

'Break the foe!' cried Sergeant Gorvetz. 'Hammer and anvil! Thunder and sky!'

The Grey Hungers charged. They rose from the ground and descended through the ceiling. Others rippled along the corridors, lurching from cell doors, snuffing out the torch flames as they passed through the walls.

The volley of bolter fire was so vicious that for a moment there was nothing but the roar of gunfire and the howl of shrapnel. A steel gale blasted through and the warp spirits were shredded. One spirit made it through, slithering to the feet of Kaderic. Its mouth-parts shot out but Kaderic cut through them with his axe, driving the point of his chainblade down through its body with his other hand.

A fat bolt of plasma immolated one of the Hungers, dissolving it away into a spray of ash. Lysander snapped off a volley of shots of his own, and somewhere in the cauldron of fire another Hunger was destroyed, its head blown apart into a burst of translucent gore. All this seemed to take place in silence, the noise too brutal for any one sound to make it through.

But there was one sound. It wormed its way into the back of Lysander's head, its fingers running up the inside of his skull.

It was laughter. A thin, reedy cackle, something between glee and the crazed laughter of complete terror.

Lysander grabbed Kaderic by the shoulder. 'It's the Widow!' he shouted.

Kaderic dropped to one knee and leaned in close to hear. 'The Widow?'

'The Red Widow!'

'Where?'

Lysander tried to pick out the strains of the sound. The gunfire faltered for a fraction of a second and he could make out the strains of it again, high and grating.

'The apothecarion!' he yelled.

The *Breaker of Darkness* had a sickbay for the crew, but the Imperial Fists had their own apothecarion equipped for a Space Marine's unique physiology, and at that moment its treatment slabs were not empty. If the Red Widow was to feed, that was where she would find the most accessible meat among the Imperial Fists.

'Hold fire!' yelled Kaderic. 'Hold fire! Moving!'

Kaderic's squad halted firing long enough for Lysander and Kaderic to run past the chapel doors towards the apothecarion, situated at one end of the cell block. Ahead, bloodstained foot- and handprints glowed against the walls, iridescent drops of gore dripping from the ceiling. The door ahead was shut, banded iron sprayed with blood.

Lysander shouldered the door off its hinges. The shriek of laughter and the stench of spoiled blood hit him as hard as a bolter round.

A dozen treatment slabs were laid out in the apothecarion. Autosurgeons hung from the ceiling and glass cylinders of artificial organs and rolls of synthetic skin lined the walls. Medicae-servitors, their metal casings adorned with scalpel-tipped manipulators, were parked at recharging stations in the corners of the room. A chart of a Space Marine's body, including the many additional organs that helped turn a man into one of the Adeptus Astartes, adorned the ceiling like a fresco in a cathedral, picked out in ivory and silver.

In the centre of the room stood the Red Widow. The illustration of her had not done her justice. She was tall and skinny, her limbs malformed, her fingers long and probing, lank hair hanging down over a pallid body covered in scars and open wounds. She had no face, and where a face should have been was a black void, like a window into space. She turned that face to Lysander as he tore into the apothecarion, and he felt himself falling into it, time and space rushing past him.

Nebulae and galaxies rushed past. Stars boiled into existence from the heart of incandescent stellar clouds. Solar systems were cracked and shattered to dust, and swallowed up by endless maws of nothingness that opened up to devour them.

The warp. It was the warp, the dimension that ran parallel to reality, the dwelling place of the Fell Powers and the source of everything that was worst in this galaxy.

Lysander tore his eyes away. The laughter rang in his head. He shielded his eyes and tried to gauge what the Red Widow was doing without looking at her face.

In the Red Widow's hand was an arm. It was the oversized arm of a Space Marine. Lysander recognised the recent blister scars and surgical marks around the ruin of the shoulder. The arm had belonged to Brother Skelpis.

'This is your friend,' hissed the Red Widow, and somehow the laughter was uninterrupted. 'Your brother. Sworn to the same oaths. Born of the same battles.'

Lysander lunged with his chainblade. The Red Widow batted the blade aside with Skelpis's arm.

Sergeant Kaderic ran past Lysander and slammed into the Red Widow. A hand, impossibly strong, closed around one of Kaderic's legs and the Widow threw him aside. Kaderic crashed through one of the organ cylinders, falling to the ground in a heap of shattered glass and torn artificial flesh.

'You chose the wrong ship,' snarled Lysander.

'You chose the wrong god,' hissed the Widow.

Lysander slashed at her, the teeth of his chainblade shrieking. The Widow leapt up onto the ceiling, the joints of her elongated limbs cracking as they bent the wrong way and grabbed handholds in the image on the ceiling. Her face flared open, a great void threatening to drag Lysander's consciousness into it. As long as she faced him, Lysander could not look directly at her – he would be paralysed by the warp's assault on his senses and the Widow would tear him apart as she had done Brother Skelpis.

Nails as hard as diamond tore chunks from the fresco as the Widow scuttled across the ceiling, reaching down at Lysander's throat. His chainblade flashed in his hand, guided by reflex rather than choice, and sawed through the Widow's arm just below one of the elbows.

Blades of shadow slid from the torn stump. The light

of distant stars bled from the wound, and the sound of colliding galaxies roared in Lysander's ears. The stuff of the warp oozed from the Widow, pooling in masses of darkness where it touched the deck.

The Red Widow giggled, as if the severing of a limb was the most wonderful fun.

Lysander lost sight of her for a split second as darkness swirled around her. He heard her land on the deck behind him, and the shadow claws closed around his torso, grossly elongated. They dug in, biting through the ceramite of his breastplate and shoulder guards.

Lysander's chainblade arm was pinned. He drew his bolt pistol with his free hand and aimed blindly over his shoulder, loosing off three shots at the place he guessed her head would be. The Widow's other hand grabbed his wrist and wrenched it behind his back.

'I saw your god die,' the Widow whispered in his ear. 'I lapped at the liquor from his corpse.'

A tremendous crash cut her voice off and Lysander was thrown forwards, face down onto the blood-slicked deck. He rolled onto his back and saw the Red Widow reeling, shards of glass impaling her ragged skin.

Behind her was a Space Marine, stripped of his armour and wearing the simple half-robes of an apothecarion patient. His skin had been dark, but now it was a patchwork of new scars and synthetic skin. He was holding the remains of the organ cylinder he had smashed into the back of the Red Widow's head. His eyes were wide and wild.

Lysander stamped a foot down onto the Red Widow's back and drew back his chainblade. He plunged the blade into the Widow, its chain teeth grinding through spine and rib.

Darkness sprayed out, miniature fragments of a mirror reflecting the warp. Sergeant Kaderic had extricated himself from the wreckage of the organ cylinders and brought his axe down, cutting off the Red Widow's head.

A sudden flood of darkness blinded Lysander. He wrenched his chainblade free and stumbled for the door, finding the doorframe with an outstretched hand and making it out of the apothecarion. Kaderic followed him out, carrying with him the severed head of the Red Widow.

'Halaestus!' shouted Lysander. 'Skelpis!'

Brother Halaestus, still holding the base of the shattered organ cylinder, emerged from the darkness clinging around the doorway. 'Skelpis is dead,' he said. 'He was helpless on the slab. She killed him.'

'He is avenged,' said Sergeant Kaderic.

'None of us are avenged,' said Halaestus, 'until Malodrax falls.'

Lysander put a gauntleted hand on Halaestus's shoulder. 'We will have our revenge,' said Lysander. 'I swear.'

For a moment Brother Halaestus just stared at Lysander, his eyes looking far away as if focused on the Red Widow's glimpse of the warp. Then he refocused, and looked down at the head in Sergeant Kaderic's hand. The head was sagging and limp, little more than a hollow mask of skin with the window to the warp gone.

'That's the Widow,' said Halaestus.

'Just as in the map,' said Lysander. 'We were ready for her.'

'Not ready enough,' said Halaestus. 'You said you would lead us here, Lysander. You said you would be prepared for anything Malodrax had.'

'I did not say there would not be losses,' replied Lysander, his voice level. 'It is a lot for me to ask you to have faith, I know that. But that is what I ask of you now.'

Whatever reply Halaestus had, he never made it. Chaplain Lycaon approached from the cell block, both barrels of the storm bolter in his hand glowing dull red, the head of his crozius arcanum still crackling with its power field. 'The enemy is scattered, First Sergeant!' said Lycaon. 'What of the apothecarion?'

'Held, Chaplain!' announced Kaderic. 'The Red Widow it was, and this is what remains of her!' Kaderic cast the Widow's head onto the deck at Lycaon's feet. 'But one brother, Skelpis, was lost here. The daemon was vanquished by the captain and myself.'

'Rejoin your brethren,' said Lycaon. 'Sweep the cell block and launch patrols to clear the rest of the ship.'

'Of course, Chaplain,' said Kaderic.

'And captain, sergeant,' said Lycaon, 'and you, Brother Halaestus. Well fought.'

* * *

USUALLY THE CREW of the *Breaker* worked in two shifts, changing every fourteen hours. For the next twenty hours both shifts were awake and at station, guiding the *Breaker* around the Red Widow's lair of treacherous orbital currents and jagged masses of coral. Two thrusters were torn off the ship's stern, and a hole torn in her flank a hundred metres long that bled three decks' worth of air into the void. More died, added to the tally taken by the Grey Hungers and the Red Widow a few hours before. But the crew of the *Breaker* had known that they would not all make it home, not from this journey. They worked to exhaustion until the ship emerged from the reef into the relatively clear high orbit of Malodrax. They would have leave to mourn their dead when the mission was done.

In the new quiet that had fallen on the ship, Chaplain Lycaon was able to return to his art. In his fingers was a small piece of bone, and in his other hand a miniature drill with which he was inscribing illustrations onto the bone. Around him were mounted the arms and armour of a senior Chaplain of the Imperial Fists, a tattered banner stained with smoke from an old battlefield, shelves of books of battle-lore and a polished stone Crux Terminatus mounted on the wall like a plaque. His armour, painted in the black of a Chaplain instead of the gold of an Imperial Fist, hung from a rack against the wall.

Lysander watched Lycaon work. The Chaplain's hands were those of a Space Marine, huge and powerful even without gauntlets, but he worked with the fine dexterity of a watchmaker.

'Dorn himself scrimshawed the bones of the dead,' said Lycaon at length. 'He wrote that pursuits such as these separate us from other soldiers. Any savage can swing a club or fire a gun. But a Space Marine is better than that. He can turn his mind inwards, and channel what lies there into focus as well as rage.' The Chaplain blew dust off the bone, revealing the finely cut detail. 'I hope Brother Skelpis would agree, having unwittingly donated his finger bone.'

'He would consider it an honour,' said Lysander.

'Good.' Lycaon gave the bone a few more strokes with the drill, and held it up to the light of the cell's glow-globe. Dense knotwork wound around the clenched fist symbol of the Chapter, and through the wings of the Imperial aquila beside it. 'Brother Halaestus has lost his focus.'

Lysander did not answer for a long moment. Lycaon put Skelpis's scrimshawed finger bone on the table in front of him, and turned his gaze up to Lysander for the first time since the captain had answered the summons to Lycaon's cell.

'He has gone through much,' said Lysander. 'He wants revenge.'

'Every Space Marine wants revenge,' said Lycaon. 'All the time. With every breath. He wants revenge against the galaxy for daring to be so full of enemies. Revenge is not an excuse to lose one's focus.'

'Do you intend to leave him on the *Breaker* when we go down to the surface?' asked Lysander.

'I am not such a fool to shun the use of an able-bodied Space Marine when we face an environment like Malodrax. No, my concerns lie deeper. A man driven to extremes by rage might be just what this strike force needs. But it is not what the Chapter needs.'

'Brother Halaestus will be rehabilitated. What he underwent on Malodrax could never leave a soul unmarked, but he is an Imperial Fist and he is strong. The apothecarion and the help of his battle-brothers will fix him.'

'Perhaps,' said Lycaon. 'But I have another concern.'

'Chaplain?'

'Brother Halaestus is not the brother who compels the greater part of my attention. I had heard much of you, Lysander. Your loss was the cause of great sorrow. Even amidst the tragedy of the *Shield of Valour*, the death of Lysander was mourned most keenly, for they spoke of you as a Chapter Master of the future. When you returned to us, it was with great joy that we learned you lived, but among the Chaplains there was concern. A thousand years had passed and the men you fought alongside are not those who serve the Chapter today.'

'The Imperial Fists are the same,' said Lysander. 'Dorn saw to it that our principles were strong enough to weather the ages.'

Lycaon did not acknowledge Lysander's words. 'And then came the *Shield of Valour*,' he continued. 'Then came Malodrax. And I do not know if the First Captain of the Imperial Fists, the one whose death was among the greatest tragedies the Chapter has suffered, is the same man who stands opposite me now.'

Lysander did not respond. He stared down at the scrimshaw in front of Lycaon, which had once been a finger bone of Brother Skelpis. Skelpis had been crippled, unable to fight, and he had died a helpless death that no Space Marine should ever suffer.

'What do you have to say, captain?' asked Lycaon. 'Or have you nothing?'

'When we leave Malodrax,' said Lysander, 'Thul will be dead. That is all I have to say.'

'I pray that you are right,' said Lycaon. 'It was your intelligence that led us here. It is your experience that we hope will give us the edge on the surface. Much relies on you, Lysander, and you will be judged when it is all done. When we come to leave Malodrax, whatever has happened down there, we will know which Lysander the Imperial Fists name among their number. The Reclusiam stands apart from the Chapter, for even its heroes are not beyond our judgement.' Lycaon handed the scrimshawed bone to Lysander. 'You were down there with him. Carry him with you.'

Lysander took the finger bone, saluted, and left the cell without another word.

THE CORAL HAD grown up over millions of years, encrusted around flecks of rock and debris in orbit around Malodrax. Tiny organisms had woven microscopic calcific shells around themselves, and gradually, as the millennia ground by, enormous reefs had built up that cloaked the world of Malodrax in a shield of jagged coral that rendered it impervious to any attempt to land.

Any attempt, that was, without a map. Crazed scholars had mapped the reefs and the intricacies of their movement. Captains had braved the reefs to reach the forbidden planet inside. Who had first come to Malodrax, and why, was lost to the infinite histories of the Scattering, when mankind flew heedlessly to the most distant stars. But someone, to the woe of all, had made it.

The *Breaker of Darkness* emerged from the reef scored and tattered, dragging its own train of wreckage, chunks of shredded hull and the bodies of crewmen floating in her wake. Wide gashes laid open the latticework of deck and bulkhead inside. Half the golden fist emblem on her prow had been sheared off. But she could still fly, and her cargo was intact.

With a flare of engines the ship changed attitude, presenting the heat-shielded prow to the upper atmosphere of Malodrax.

It took a force of will to look on Malodrax itself. Like a void against a void, it forced the eye away from it, something darker than black. If an observer could compel himself to look at it he would see a discoloured orb, its southern hemisphere mottled and decaying like a tumour, its northern half parched and broken as if hammered into pieces. Its northern pole burned with purple flame, and near the equator an open wound oozed molten rock like infected blood. A tormented and suffering world, pulled apart by the unnatural forces that teemed on its surface, infested, befouled and rancid.

To this world the *Breaker of Darkness* descended, the flames of its upper atmosphere licking against the prow.

2

'My captain was a brave man. He had served me for six decades as personal pilot, and then master of my fleet. The only time I saw him weep was when he condemned his ship to the atmosphere of Malodrax, knowing she would never rise from that toxic cauldron of hate.'

– Inquisitor Corvin Golrukhan

IN THE COOL of the *Shield of Valour*, Lysander knelt to pray.

The ship was old indeed. It still bore the patina of Mars, deep red speckles on the blueish steel of her bulkheads and decks. Cold vapour clung to the floors and rippled down the walls. The archeotech engines, supplied by plasma reactors more efficient than any made for eight thousand years, required a deep chill to function and the whole ship was refrigerated.

Lysander's silent prayer came to an end. It was one

he had spoken to himself so many times before that it was as natural as strapping on his armour or the weight of his hammer in his hand. He asked the Emperor and the spirit of Rogal Dorn to lend him strength and wisdom. And he prayed for his own strength, because a Space Marine had to rely on himself above all. His soul cleansed, his mind rigid with faith, he stood and turned to face his battle-brothers.

The First Company stood to attention in the cathedral hall. One hundred Imperial Fists. They wore the white-painted armour trim and Crux Terminatus of the First. One carried the company banner, depicting Rogal Dorn, hammer in hand, straddling a crumbling fortress wall as traitors burned beneath his feet. It was hung with hundreds of battle-honours.

Lysander's breath misted in front of him as he spoke.

'Our mission is extermination,' he began. 'There is no word that suffices save that. Our mission objective is the extinction of a species. The Vorel are an immediate threat to the settlements of the Eastern Fringe and the only response the human race can make is to revoke their existence. I need not tell you of the hatred the alien must kindle in your hearts. You know full well the weight of the duty that carries you, as you carry it, unto death. You are men of the First Company and need no description of such.

'What I will tell you is that for all that we live in an Imperium of a million worlds, for all our lives shall encompass but a speck of time in the ten thousand years of our history, missions such as this give us our chance to leave a mark on that history. The galaxy is vast, and even a Space Marine may feel his role in it is vanishingly small. But we shall leave that mark. The Vorel were, and when we finish, they will no longer be. No human will ever suffer their predations again. How few men can say that the galaxy has changed with their passing? We can, we men of the First and of the Imperial Fists. That is our blessing. That is the legacy of the Emperor and of Rogal Dorn, their gift to humanity. Give thanks as you bring humanity's wrath to the Vorel. Praise their blessing as you anoint yourselves in xenos blood!'

The Imperial Fists of the First clapped their hands to their breastplates and cheered, a warrior's salute. Lysander hefted his hammer, the Fist of Dorn, over his head, and the men raised their chainblades in response.

They had studied the Vorel during the two months they had travelled through the warp on the *Shield of Valour*. The Adeptus Mechanicus had speculated that the Vorel had evolved from the airborne predators of a prey-starved world and had come to dominate that world in a civilisation based on floating sky-fortresses and eyrie-cities. It was inevitable they would look to the sky for more meat to hunt, and inevitable that they would come into contact with humanity as their eyes settled on sovereign Imperial worlds.

It was inevitable they would be exterminated in response. The Space Marines would seal that fate. The

Vorel, by one standard, were unfortunate. They dreamed of hunting the finest prey across infinite worlds, their civilisation coming to chase predators between the very stars – and yet they would be wiped out by the cruellest hammer blow from a species that hated anything not human. A Space Marine might comprehend such a point of view, but he had the mental discipline to set it aside and replace it in the forefront of his mind with the duty to wipe out the alien and preserve humanity's rule over the galaxy.

'To your duties,' said Lysander. 'Prayer and wargear rites. Make your souls ready today, for tomorrow the killing begins.'

The Imperial Fists saluted their captain and filed from the cathedral, the mist of their breath forming a pale haze in the refrigerated air. The cathedral was consecrated not to a god, as the common people of the Imperium conceived of the Emperor, but to the Imperial Fists themselves – to the spirit of their Chapter, the responsibility and power of a Space Marine. To the example of the Primarch Rogal Dorn, figurative and literal father of the Chapter.

Some would call it arrogant, Lysander thought as he looked up at the Chapter's fist symbol covering one wall, Dorn's gilded statue standing before it. Those who said it, though, would have failed to understand the place the Space Marines occupied – at the pinnacle of the Imperium, and the front line against extinction.

Rogal Dorn's statue shuddered as an impact rang

through the ship. Lysander felt it through his feet, running up the segments of his armour.

'Report,' he said into his vox-link, opening a channel to the ship's bridge.

'We've taken an impact,' came the reply from Commander Langeloc, the captain of the *Shield*. Lysander did not know her well, but she was valued by the Chapter as a dependable, if unimaginative, spaceship captain. 'Starboard ventral. I have dispatched damage crews.'

'Was it a meteorite?'

'There was an accompanying energy signature. Could be a weapon hit.'

'Bring the ship to battle stations.'

'Already under way, captain.'

Lysander felt himself shifting into the state of readiness, the physical and mental routines, of battle. The Imperial Fists of the First Company were doing the same, breaking off in squads to man the sections of the ship allotted to them in the event of an attack – important defence points like the apothecarion and the bridge, the fighter deck in case of evacuation or deployment on a boarding mission. Though it would be difficult to explain, it was a good feeling, a sense of purpose. A Space Marine knew battle. It was where he was designed to be.

Drevyn, Skelpis, Halaestus and Vonkaal were his command squad, his honour guard. Lysander had chosen them from the men of the First because they were solid and trustworthy. They made their way through the other Imperial Fists to join him before the image of Dorn.

'We may be under attack,' said Lysander as they approached, 'so we will act as if we are. Halaestus! Lead us in the prayer.'

Halaestus bowed his head. Lysander did not insist on any one of his squadmates leading the rest in prayer, and instead selected them all equally. This time it was Halaestus's turn.

'The eve of battle burns bright,' began Halaestus. For this occasion he had picked a lesser-spoken prayer from the corner of one of the Chapter's works of collected battle-lore. 'The sword and the bullet burn brighter. The shadow of the enemy looms dark. Our wrath and our sorrow rise darker. When the enemy soars above us, we will stride over him. When he goes far, we go further. When he kills we kill more, when he lives we live…'

The next impact threw Lysander off his feet. Rogal Dorn fell too, the golden statue snapping off at the ankles and crashing into the front rows of the cathedral's pews. Slabs fell from the ceiling, the artificial stone falling away to reveal the chill steel of the ship's structure.

'Langeloc!' yelled Lysander into the vox.

'That was a lance strike,' came Langeloc's voice. Over the vox came sounds of commotion as the bridge crew reacted to the sudden impact. Someone was yelling for a medical team to attend the bridge. 'We are pursued. Sensorium teams are trying to identify the enemy.'

'What is our integrity?'

'Major damage to the ventral weapon bays. Geller field fluctuating. We may have to drop out of the warp.'

'Keep me updated,' said Lysander. 'We're heading to our post.'

Lysander and his squad were slated to take up position where the main body of the spaceship met the engine block. The engines were one of the principal weaknesses of the *Shield of Valour* in the event of a boarding, for its plasma reactors were an eminently sabotagable design that could be the target of a suicidal boarding party. Enough damage to the reactors or their coolant systems could cause them to breach and vaporise half the ship. Lysander might be the commander of this mission but when the ship came under attack he and his command squad had their defensive duties just like everyone else.

'Someone wants a fast death,' said Brother Skelpis as the squad moved from the damaged cathedral sternwards. 'And one they don't deserve. Attacking the Imperial Fists in the warp is a very special kind of suicide.'

'Is it the Vorel?' asked Halaestus. 'Can they do this?'

'Unlikely,' said Lysander. 'But they have hurried their extinction if it is.'

The whole ship shuddered. Lysander braced an arm against the cold steel of the wall. Crewmen were running in every direction, damage teams with fire extinguishers, engine-gang men running to supplement the engine crews who must have already sustained casualties as loose gear and coolant leaks made the block a lethal place. 'Report!' voxed Lysander.

'The sensorium crew has a profile,' came Langeloc's voice. She sounded in pain. 'There's only a forty per cent...'

'Who is it?' demanded Lysander. Up ahead a crew member supported another, almost dragging her along the corridor, trailing blood as he headed for the sick bay.

'It's the *Carnage*,' Langeloc replied.

IF YOU WERE to ask a spaceship crewman what was the worst thing that could happen on a ship, his answer would be 'fire'. Unless he was one of the old guard, the voidborn veterans, ancient by Naval standards, who had indeed seen just about everything that might happen on board a spaceship and heard tell of everything else. In that case, his answer would be 'the warp'.

A human mind could not properly describe the dimension that surrounded the *Shield of Valour* as it hurtled through the warp. No human tongue could describe it. The Geller field around the *Shield* kept it intact from the insanity of that endless ocean, but when that field failed (as happened in countless sailors' yarns) the warp took the ship, plunging its crew into the sea of madness and warping the ship, its inhabitants and their souls into something different and awful.

The concept of attacking another ship in the warp

was as impossible to comprehend as the warp itself. Time and space did not mean in the warp what they meant in reality – that was why the warp could be used for faster-than-light travel in the first place. But legends were passed between the old guard of the space lanes of opponents who would try just that, to dive from the warp's black maelstrom to maul their prey when they were most vulnerable.

As impossible as it was, as insane as anyone attempting it had to be, that was happening to the *Shield of Valour*.

The enemy was a tarnished, age-pitted shark, its long nose knife-like as it sliced through the thunderheads of the warp and broke through the Geller field envelope around the *Shield of Valour*. The enemy ship was longer than the *Shield* but narrower, a sleek, acute-angled predator. Its flanks were serrated with sloping banks of gun batteries. Dorsal vanes crackled with power, drawing in the surrounding warp energies to power the nova cannon slung beneath the ship's armoured prow.

The symbol carved into its flank, scored deep into the steel of its hull armour, was an open gauntlet. The heraldries of a hundred commanders covered the hull around it. Banners of segmented steel flowed from the sternwards batteries, etched with battle-honours in the languages of the warp.

The Imperium's older battleships had machine-spirits that remembered old foes. The *Shield of Valour* was one of them. It recognised that profile, the prow coolant vents like narrowed eyes, the triangular flare of its stern engines like the fins of an undersea predator. It was known as the *Carnage*, and the Imperial Fists fleet had a particular reason to hate it.

The rear-firing guns of the *Shield* opened up, spraying the prow of the *Carnage* with enough fire to shred a smaller ship. The *Carnage* rode the fire, turning the denser armour on the side of its prow to absorb the worst of it. Explosions stripped off sheets of armour, throwing out a glittering cloud of debris. The enemy ship rolled onto its side, bringing the sternwards section of the *Shield* into the arc of its nova cannon.

The *Shield* responded, venting a great cloud of frozen gas from its coolant systems to lend strength to the thrusters that bucked its stern upwards, bringing the engines out of the firing arc.

The nova cannon fired. The dense yellow-white beam, as hot as the heart of a star, hit a glancing strike against the *Shield*'s stern. In the void it would have been silent, but in the warp the sound was a very human scream, a sound of anger and jubilation, as if the *Carnage* were crying out in ecstasy to see such destruction brought to bear.

The two ships were within close range now, within the kill-distance of their defensive guns. Prow-mounted gun batteries opened up on the *Carnage*, peppering the stern of the *Shield* with explosive rounds that ripped through the sections exposed by the glancing nova strike. Clouds of vapour and flame sprayed from the gashes, throwing out fountains of debris that burned brightly for split seconds in the void within the Geller field. The *Shield*'s turret-mounted guns replied, everything sternwards of the ship's midpoint blazing directly into the prow of the *Carnage*.

The *Carnage* did not care. She was built for murder up close.

The *Carnage* weathered the fire, angling for another shot. The nova cannon recharged, spilling waves of supercharged particles from the glowing aperture beneath the prow.

Every thruster on the *Shield* fired at once, tearing the ship around to bring herself out of the cannon's arc. Debris rained against her, secondary explosions rippling through her hull. The *Shield*'s armaments were broadside laser batteries and torpedo arrays, and with a single decent broadside volley she could knock her assailant spinning into the warp, lost and out of control. It was her one chance, but thousands of years of naval doctrine said it would work.

The nova cannon charged. Another thirty seconds and the *Shield*'s broadside would be unleashed, and even the armoured hull of the *Carnage* would be blistered and torn by the thousands of impacts. Those thirty seconds never happened as the nova cannon fired again.

This shot was not glancing. It hit the *Shield* amidships, spitting her through on a bright lance of incandescent fire.

* * *

'BRACE FOR FIELD collapse!' came Langeloc's voice through the din of the impact. 'We're coming out of the warp! All hands brace!'

Lysander had felt the nova cannon hit home and he had heard the sound, like an impossibly loud tearing of paper, of the energy beam shredding the steel of the *Shield*'s internal structure. He knew war, space war included, and a hundred battles of instinct told him the damage was massive and catastrophic. It was a crippling shot, spearing the *Shield* right through and catching Throne knew what critical systems in its path.

'We are brought low!' yelled Lysander as warning klaxons blared from every direction. 'But when our guns are called upon, we shall rise!'

'What senseless animal hunts us down?' snarled Brother Skelpis, dropping to a knee and grabbing on to a wheel lock to steady himself. 'Do they not know what we are?'

'When do we board them?' said Brother Drevyn.

Lysander had chosen his command squad because of their mix of aggression and discipline, the epitome of the Imperial Fists way of war. He also felt the urge to jump into the nearest saviour pod or shuttle and storm the enemy ship, and it took an effort to resist it. 'Hold, brother,' he said instead. 'Man our post and do our duty. When the time for vengeance comes we will be the first in, that I swear.'

'We shall hold you to that, captain,' said Drevyn. 'If it is as Langeloc says, if it is the *Carnage*...'

The *Shield of Valour* changed as it shifted out of the warp and into real space, violently ejected by the helm crew before its fields completely collapsed. The colours became duller, the light less bright, even the chill of the refrigerated air less biting, as if the senses were covered by a frosted layer that removed the mind a single layer from its surroundings. Lysander's stomachs jumped with the lurch from one reality to another.

'We're out,' gasped Halaestus. 'Now we can fight.'

'Helm report boarding torpedoes in the void!' came Langeloc's voice. 'Boarding imminent! All crews armed and make ready to repel boarders!'

Spaceship crews dreaded boarding actions. There were few military actions that were more brutal, more unforgivingly random in the death they dealt. A Space Marine, however, was made for them – in once sense literally, for ship-to-ship combat was one of the roles the Emperor himself had in mind when he created the first generations of Space Marines for the Great Crusade. Drevyn whooped as Lysander led the way sternwards, through clouds of vented coolant vapour and gaggles of crewmen rushing to arms lockers and medical posts.

If the enemy were indeed aboard the *Carnage*, and it was their intention to board, the Imperial Fists had a far better fight on their hands than the Vorel would ever give them.

THE SHIELD OF *Valour* was battered and bloodied, but she was not dead yet. She was made of old stuff, structures and systems laid down in the millennia directly following the Horus Heresy, when the most powerful secrets of ship design had yet to be lost to time and ignorance. Her broadside guns, though off-centre of their target, blasted a fearsome volley into the forward sections of the *Carnage*, stripping away more hull armour and exposing silvery wounds underneath, where the spaces between hull layers were exposed. Raw, like bones with the skin stripped away, they bled vented atmosphere and torrents of wreckage like bright drops of chrome blood. This time the backdrop was real space, the bleak sanity of the vacuum and its speckling of stars.

The nova cannon on the *Carnage* was charging again. The *Shield of Valour* continued its painful slow pirouette out of its killing arc, but the *Carnage* was executing a feint. Its main weapon, the one with which it sought to bring the *Shield* to heel, was not a gun or a torpedo tube at all. It lay deep inside the spaceship, in the minds of the thousands of souls who made up its crew.

As one, a sacrifice was torn from their minds. Their memories, their loves and hates, the countless layers of their personalities, pledged to the dark gods of the *Carnage*'s masters. Five thousand cultists crewed the *Carnage*, with five thousand stories of sorrow, desperation and the promise of salvation. They had given everything they had to the gods to whom they had turned in their bleakest moments and pledged everything that was left, but none of them had truly understood what that meant. The sacrifice of their minds was guzzled up by the powers of the warp, syphoned through the ship's archeotech according to pledges drawn up with countless petty gods of the warp.

In return, the warp reached through into real space. It could only do so by burning away the greater part of the spiritual energy drained from the crew of the *Carnage*, but that was the deal.

The space around the stern of the *Shield* bent and warped, forming a lens through which distant stars grew into wide smudges of cold light. Trails of debris were looped around and sucked back into the whirlpool sinking through spacetime behind the *Shield*. Glistening, slithering shapes writhed in the heart of the anomaly as the shape of the *Shield* itself lengthened and warped, a deeper darkness than the void spreading out to stain this patch of reality.

THE SHIP TWISTED violently and Lysander was thrown against the wall. A crewman fell past, the corridor he was heading for suddenly wrenched into a vertical shaft. He heard the man's body breaking as he fell. Then the gravity shifted again and was gone completely, Lysander spiralling away without any force to hold him down. He grabbed the frame of a doorway as he drifted past.

'Keep going!' ordered Lysander. Brother Drevyn clambered up out of one of the side corridors that had suddenly become vertical. The rest of the squad were behind Lysander, propelling themselves along in the zero gravity with whatever handholds they could find. The freezing mist intensified and visibility was almost gone, Lysander still navigating sternwards by instinct.

He came up against a bulkhead door, large enough for two men abreast and solid enough to contain an explosion. It was set into the wall of the engine block, part of the reinforced cell separating the ship's engines from the rest of the vessel. In times of crisis the engines and their crews were expendable, the requirement to contain leaks and fires from the reactors more important than the lives of those inside. It was the lot of the engine-gangs to be forsaken when the ship was in peril, and once the call went out for damage control stations they were on their own.

Lysander put a hand against the door. It bowed and rippled under his touch, the steel becoming pliable. From beyond it came a groaning and crashing, the sound of metal and equipment torn free.

'We're too late,' voxed Lysander. 'The engines are lost.'

'Saviour pods online,' replied the ship's captain. 'Abandon ship, Captain Lysander. There is nothing more for you to do on board.'

'Emperor be with you,' said Lysander, but Commander Langeloc's reply was lost in the static and din.

It had happened so quickly. The Imperial Fists were ready to repel boarders, Lysander preparing to face anyone who tried to force their way into the engine blocks to destroy the reactors. Then, in an apparent heartbeat, the whole engine section had gone dark and the battle had transformed into something very different.

'Brothers,' said Lysander to the men of his squad. 'The *Shield of Valour* is lost. Our duty is to get to the saviour pods and survive. Stay together and do not pause for anything.'

The bulkhead wall behind Lysander bowed away from him, and the sounds of destruction were replaced with the dense, ripping noise of reality itself tearing open. The bulkhead disappeared, the whole stern of the ship collapsing away from Lysander, plunging into an endless dark shaft lit by billows of plasma flame from the ruptured generators. The substance of the engine room, its turbines, generators, its crew of engine-gangs and tech-seers, were twisting and churning into a single twisted shaft falling into the warp like a great water-spout of liquid steel.

Lysander grabbed a shard of the deck that peeled up beside him. Brother Skelpis fell past and Lysander grabbed him by the wrist. Skelpis's feet kicked out over the shaft as the flame billowed brighter, great plumes of vented plasma burning as hot as the surface of a star. In its harsh white light, crewmen were ground into red slivers and the shape of the enormous engine turbines were lost as grinding masses of deformed metal roared past.

'This is our stand, brothers!' cried Lysander. 'We did not ask for it to come like this, but it has, and as Dorn at Terra we will face it like Imperial Fists!'

The maelstrom was reforming by the second, islands

of turbines melting down into the churning mass, new forms reaching up in liquid spires, winding into new shapes in the chaos.

Gravity was shifting again, this time to match the structure appearing where the engines and reactors had once been. The ocean of steel became a level floor, inlaid with swirling glass mosaics echoing the nebulae of the void in a riot of colour. A section of the floor sunk down, a pit ringed with stairways, and gold spiralled across the surfaces. From the gold rose the bodies of misshapen things, clothed obscenely in finery and jewels.

Daemons. Lysander's soul recoiled. Men had gone mad just imagining that such things could exist, and where they found an unprepared mind daemons could turn a servant of the Emperor into a craven dedicated to the warp's Dark Gods. They came in infinite forms – these were crouched and lolling, slack jaws hanging to the gilded tiles of their pit. Every one carried a musical instrument – a harp, a horn, a drum – and as one they struck up a terrible atonal sound that rose and fell like a heavy sea. Lysander's stomachs knotted at the sensation hammering into him.

The scene was still transforming. The ballroom floor spread out around the daemons' orchestra pit, walls soaring up alongside it, curving silvered columns meeting overhead to describe a great dome open to the endlessness of the warp. Meteors shot past, trailing burning clouds of souls lost in the warp and condemned to hurtle through its reaches forever. Incandescent clouds boiled out of nothingness and hardened into bright diamonds of young stars, bursting into dark red flame as they were forged, grew old and died in seconds as if to flaunt the plasticity of time in the warp.

Daemon-giants were forged into the walls, enormous barrel chests and massive crushing hands restrained by the layers of gold and marble that held them. Their jaws gnashed and fingers clenched as they fought to escape, but they were part of the entertainment here, mighty lords of Chaos enslaved and turned into mere decorations for this monument to the warp's opulence.

The song roared up a tone and Lysander dropped to one knee, the sound a wall of mental noise trying to shut him down. A man would have broken down and curled up on the floor – or, worse, danced to their tune, writhing and spasming until his body came apart with the fury of it. Lysander glanced at Brother Skelpis lying on the floor beside him – Skelpis's jaw was clenched and blood ran from his nose and ears. His eyes were bloodshot, the strain of staying conscious and sane rupturing his body.

These Imperial Fists would follow him. They were his squad, men chosen because they would not falter even in the face of the foulest provocation. Lysander planted a foot, cracking the glass tile beneath it, and forced himself up to his feet. He was bowed and shaking, but he was upright. He would not kneel to this, no matter what might face him.

A fountain of marble and glass spiralled up from the floor before the orchestra pit, and from it flowed a torrent of molten gold. Trapped souls writhed through it, their faces distorted with pain as they flowed from one bowl to the next, their crying out mingling with the music in terrible harmonies. The gold spilled over the last bowl and crystallised into scuttling things like golden crabs that glinted as they scurried, a host of tiny daemons underfoot.

The madness of it would have been enough. This was not a place in reality but of the warp, conjured from the mind of some madman who had given his imagination over to the powers of Chaos. It was one heretic's tribute to the warp, where the rantings of a diseased mind might become reality. But that was not the only danger that would face Lysander and his squad. It was not an accident that the *Shield of Valour* had fallen to this fate. The warp had been waiting for her, and for the Imperial Fists.

Grand doors congealed from the blazing finery of the walls. They burst open and from the glaring light behind them emerged a host of shapes, ugly where the ballroom had its terrible beauty, brutal where it had grace in its madness. Even in silhouette Lysander recognised a make of power armour such as had not emerged from a Mechanicus forge for thousands of years, since the days of the Heresy ten thousand years before.

Lysander knew his duty. He raised his bolter and loosed off a round. In the assault on his senses his aim was off, and the shot blew a shard of gold from the wall behind the lead figure. Lysander held down the firing stud and half the bolter's magazine thundered off.

Space folded, and the leader of the newcomers was suddenly shifted out of the firing line and right in front of Lysander, an arm's length away. Lysander knew before his eyes focused on him what he would see.

There was an awful inevitability about that dark gunmetal armour, similar in form to the Imperial Fists own power armour but of a more ancient and baroque make with exposed cabling and bulky reinforcement panels. He had known, perhaps even before the figure had entered, that he would see the yellow and black warning stripes at the joints and on the knuckles of the wearer's enormous clawed power fist. Lysander knew the story of the markings – they were added by the first tech-priests to test the armour. They had been kept by the wearers to remind all onlookers that this was gear for war, not show, brutal and functional like the men inside.

'Iron Warrior,' spat Lysander.

The Iron Warrior knocked Lysander's gun hand aside. The brothers behind him jumped up to fight, for they knew their duties too. An Iron Warrior had to die. Lysander had been chosen for the diplomatic mission because he was able to compromise his hatred, if those were his orders, but this was one hatred that could never be permitted to die down. Dorn himself had decreed the Iron Warriors to be blood foes of the

Imperial Fists, and every time the Chapter had crossed paths with them that decree had been proven correct.

The *Carnage* was part of the Iron Warriors fleet in which they had fled justice after the Horus Heresy. It was as much an enemy as any Iron Warrior, and the Imperial Fists had sworn to destroy its like as well as the Iron Warriors themselves. But when the time had come, when Lysander had been put face to face with that ancient machine, the *Carnage* had won.

Brother Skelpis jumped to his feet. Before his bolter muzzle was up, another Iron Warrior lashed out with a chainblade and sawed through Skelpis's leg just below the knee. Skelpis toppled to the side, armour clattering, the glass mosaic floor cracking.

Everything was unfolding in slow motion. Lysander counted a whole combat squad of Iron Warriors, ten Traitor Marines, the remaining eight of them turning their guns towards Brother Drevyn. Drevyn did his duty by charging the Iron Warriors, drawing his own chainblade as he went, and was caught by a volley of fire that cut him clean in half at the waist and tore what remained into flailing shreds of armour and flesh.

'Hold!' yelled the leader of the Iron Warriors. 'Thul will have them alive! Hold your fire!'

'Better a corpse than in chains,' said Lysander.

'You will know what it means to be both,' said the Iron Warrior, aiming a backhand at the side of Lysander's head. Lysander's mind was still ringing from the assault on his senses, still recoiling from the impossibility of the place that had coalesced in front of him, and his reflexes were slow as a drunkard's. He brought up a hand to defend himself but he was much too late and the blow slammed into him. Everything was black for a moment and when it returned as before, Lysander was sprawled full length on the ballroom floor.

The Iron Warrior planted a foot on the backpack of Lysander's armour, pinning him down to the floor. Another Iron Warrior, the one who had mutilated Brother Skelpis, kicked Lysander's bolter and hammer away. Lysander hadn't even been able to raise it in anger, such was the effect of this daemon-born place.

The other Iron Warriors were among the surviving Imperial Fists, disarming and knocking them to the ground. Skelpis fought on and an Iron Warrior stamped on the back of his head until he stopped moving. Another Iron Warrior wrestled Brother Halaestus and threw him to the ground, down in the pool of blood and gore leaching from Brother Drevyn's remains. Brother Vonkaal was shot through the thigh and fell.

'You killed one of ours,' said Lysander. 'We remember our fallen. Though it take ten thousand years, we avenge every one.'

'Kraegon Thul will give you plenty more to avenge, whelp of Terra,' replied the lead Iron Warrior.

'You face the First Company,' said Lysander. 'We will scour you from this ship. You can never stand before us in battle.'

'I'm not here to fight the First Company,' replied the

Iron Warrior. 'I'm here to take you alive.' He spread out his arms as if proudly showing off the insanity that surrounded him. 'The Dancing-Place of the Lesser Gods,' he said. 'More ostentatious than my Legion is used to, but a place that will come at our beckoning and deliver us to our enemies. It disappoints me that you were so addled, Imperial Fist. I would have fought you champion to champion. Perhaps that will be the means of your execution when we are done with you, but that will not be for a while yet.' The Iron Warriors leader turned to one of his squadmates. 'Khaol! Inform the fortress that we are done here. Our haul is one captain, three battle-brothers and a corpse, all Imperial Fists. Have them make ready for our return.'

The Iron Warrior saluted and began relaying the order through a field vox, an archaic device of tubes and valves. The daemons in the orchestra pit changed their tune, the music now rising and falling like the waves of a stormy sea, the highs piercing and painful, the lows a bass rumble that made the whole cathedral blur as it shook.

The dome overhead peeled open. Darkness bled in. The gold turned to mottled brass, lit as if by a fire from far above. The orchestra pit was a shaft of blackness, the daemons cavorting through it as if they were breaking the surface of an inky ocean. Through the darkness overhead could be glimpsed a scattering of stars and among them one grew closer, a bloated red star near the end of its life, scattered with black sunspots and bursting out flares of red flame. Around it was a system of worlds, shattered and grey, any life on them long since drunk dry by the anger of their sun. But one world was different. Discoloured and foul, it had survived not because of some celestial accident but through a force of malevolence. So beloved was it of the warp's gods that their favour sustained it and it could not die.

Impossible detail reached Lysander's eye, time and distance meaningless through the lens of the warp. He could see the shattered continents, splintered like broken glass, slowly swallowed by oceans of decaying gore. Gashes in the crust laid the mantle open, seething and bubbling with heat. Endless rotting badlands rolled around half the world, broken by mountains of bone.

And he saw the fortress. A great black steel jaw breaching the border between the broken continent and the lands of rot, its teeth enormous towers and its jawbone a rampart of gnashing spiked rollers. The semicircle bounded by the fortress wall was studded with a thousand fires, each one manned by a thousand labourers. Black and yellow banners hung from the battlements and the watch was held by more Iron Warriors, each one a nightmare of archaic pitted steel.

In violation of time and space, the structure of the Dancing-Place of the Lesser Gods melted and reformed into a bridge span linking its pocket of the warp with the fortress. Light years were compressed and warped as the Iron Warriors clamped a set of chains around Lysander's wrists and ankles, and dragged him behind them onto the bridge. It was of tarnished gold and rust, worn by thousands of years' worth of marching feet. The fortress loomed closer and Lysander could make out the filthy ragged vultures that roosted in its spires and fed on the labourers who collapsed at the forges. In the forge fields below, enormous segments of armour and gun barrel were hauled out of the fires by hundreds-strong mutant gangs. Daemons shambled among them – loping monsters of the Blood God with red skin and slavering fangs, writhing flesh-knots, drooling sacks of pestilence, shadowy things that slithered into the bodies of the dead and walked among the living, eye sockets burning with purple fire.

The Iron Warriors, it was said, called no single Chaos God their patron, and instead were pledged to them all. Lysander's fevered perception made out the hallmarks of many gods, from the bloodstained spiked rollers grinding away beneath the battlements to the ecstatic agony of the mutant labourers driven to dance in the flames. He could smell the fires and the cooking flesh, he could hear iron against iron and the ringing of the forge hammers. The lens of the warp magnified it all, filling his head so full of appalling sensation that there was no room left for sane thought.

'Look up, Imperial Fists!' said the Iron Warriors leader, and in spite of himself Lysander did so.

Above him was the orbital space of this world, choked with vast reefs of gnarled coral. Spaceship hulks hung there trapped, the coral grown over them so only the odd stern or sensor mast broke through the encrustations. The awful distortion, which brought the fortress beneath into such detail, rendered the whole orbit of the planet visible, the view arcing between horizons so maddeningly that Lysander feared the sight of it would throw him unconscious.

He saw the *Shield of Valour*. It had been brought along the bridge behind them and deposited in the upper reaches of the coral maze. Fire bled weakly from the nova cannon wound in its side and its engines were gone, distorted and torn off by the reality-warping weapon deployed by the *Carnage*. Lysander did not know how the *Carnage* had inflicted such destruction, but he feared to imagine the magnitude of the blasphemy brought to bear to make such a thing happen.

Through the reef loomed three great dark halos of battered steel, crunching through clouds of shattered coral. Lysander recognised ancient marks of space stations from illuminated histories of the Heresy, bristling with ancient guns and bedecked with the heraldry of the Iron Warriors. Three star fortresses circling the crippled *Shield of Valour* like scavengers on the wing.

In silence, a rain of white fire streamed from the three space stations. In spite of all his training and discipline Lysander found his thoughts turned to a desperate prayer, begging fate to turn the fire aside from the *Shield*. He all but cried out aloud for mercy as the bolts of fire hit the *Shield of Valour*.

The three Iron Warriors star forts poured their flame

as one into the Imperial Fists strike cruiser. Secondary explosions rippled along the sides of the ship, billowing out huge sections of the hull plating. The image loomed closer, brought right into Lysander's face by the warp-distortion, a willing presentation of the ship's death.

He could see the ship's entrails laid open, the warren of corridors and hallways deep into its heart. Bodies tumbled everywhere.

The First Company spilled from the ship. They struggled to find handholds to steady themselves and keep from falling into the void. They had donned their helmets, and their power armour was proof against the void, but that was the only advantage they had over the unprotected crewmen. The Imperial Fists of the First Company were fighting on because they were Space Marines, but there was nothing they could do – the *Shield of Valour* was dead, dying behind them, and the star forts were pouring waves of fire into it with impunity.

Space Marines were supposed to die in battle, the bodies of their enemies crushed beneath their feet. They were not supposed to struggle through the warp, crushed by spinning debris or frozen in the void. Not like this, hammered to dust by an enemy leering from behind the pict-screen of a space station's gun battery.

Then something within the *Shield of Valour* went critical, an ammunition store or a remaining plasma reactor pushed past its tolerances by the barrage of fire. A white blossom bloomed in the centre of the ship, expanding outwards in a shimmering sphere. It threw off flares like a miniature sun, flinging arcs of blue-white flame that sliced through what remained of the ship's structure.

Almost a hundred Imperial Fists, irreplaceable veterans. The crew and the ship were a grave enough loss, but the First Company of the Imperial Fists were among the best soldiers humanity had. And as quickly as it took for the explosion to reach from the heart of the ship to the tip of its bow, they were gone, extinguished, ash.

Lysander's head was wrenched back down. He got a glimpse of the other captive Imperial Fists being dragged along – they had seen it, too. They knew the enormity of that crime.

They knew what the Iron Warriors had given them to avenge.

The bridge through the warp bowed and shifted, the malformed planet ahead rushing closer. The Iron Warriors leader hauled Lysander another few steps and suddenly they were on the battlements, the Iron Warriors sentries saluting their officer as he passed. Lysander was dragged through armouries of bolters and archaic halberds, past shrines to obscure gods heaped with rotting offerings of severed heads and animal bones, beneath statues of beings so foul Lysander's eyes refused to focus on them.

This was a place built to withstand a siege. The stairways were too narrow for more than one Space

Marine abreast, the doorways had gun ports and the floorboards could be pulled up to reveal a grid through which spears could be thrust into attackers on the floor below. No Imperial Fist was blind to such things, for Rogal Dorn had been a master of siegecraft and the brothers who called him their primarch all learned how a fortress could kill anyone trying to force their way in. While Dorn was a builder of fortresses, the Iron Warriors primarch, Perturabo, had been a besieger, to whom the mightiest fortification was just a puzzle to be unlocked. This fortress was a product of siegecraft at the same level as Dorn's own, a vast and brutal deathtrap.

The Imperial Fists were dragged down through the layers of the fortress. Lysander glimpsed Brother Skelpis, his face pale and bloody, trailing the gory stump of his leg, each arm held by an Iron Warrior dragging him along. He saw Brother Halaestus spattered with Drevyn's blood, struggling against the Iron Warriors holding him, and Lysander knew Halaestus would tear himself apart rather than submit willingly to his Chapter's enemies.

Beneath the fortress, beneath the walls and the forges they encompassed, was another structure entirely, the seat of the Iron Warriors on this world protected by the fortifications above. It was shadowy and infernally hot, what light there was coming from yet more forges fed, it seemed, by the heart of the planet itself. Great shapes loomed in the vast underground hangars, half seen in the darkness, some still glowing from the heat of their forging, others moving like giants stretching their limbs after waking.

At the very heart of it was a crucible, a great spherical chamber half filled with molten fire bubbling up from beneath the planet's crust, hot enough to scorch the lungs of an unaugmented man. It was accessed through a huge gate of iron, its two halves meeting at an enormous lock. A circular platform suspended over the fire held up a great anvil and from the domed ceiling hung countless weapons and segments of armour.

Lysander's senses had come back to him a little. His head still whirled but he could tell, even from here, that the pieces suspended over this great forge were masterpieces. They were sized for Space Marines, and among them were sections of rebuilt armour from marks long lost to the Imperium, power weapons matching size with balance, pieces inlaid with precious stones and metals as well as brutal machines created for industrialised killing.

'Lord Thul!' cried the Iron Warriors leader, removing his helmet. Beneath was revealed a pale and pocked face with jet-black eyes and a cruel twist of a mouth. Black hair clung to the scalp. 'We have returned! The scryers told the truth. We found the dogs of Terra, and praise the pantheon, they are destroyed! And more than that. For the continuation of our Legion, we bring these ones to you alive!'

Over the anvil stood a figure taller than any Space Marine. It was encased in armour so gnarled and jagged it looked like it had accrued over thousands of years rather than being forged by any hand. Beneath it somewhere was an ancient mark of armour, but Lysander could not recognise it from any of the illustrations he recalled depicting the days of the Horus Heresy. The shoulder guards were masses of grinding cogs and pistons and its weight was supported by pneumatic rams that hissed as the figure turned towards the crucible entrance.

'Your return was well omened, Captain Hexal,' said the creature that had been called Thul. Its voice was thick and deep, welling up from inside the armour like the crucible's fires welled up below. Its face was a mass of corroded steel with two large clouded lenses for eyes. A single air hose ran down the centre of the face and spurts of greasy smoke surrounded Thul in a filthy halo. 'And you.' The lenses turned to Lysander. 'Would that I could make you understand why you are here. That you could see through our eyes, we who were abandoned by the same Terra you swear by. But I can see by your face, by the hate in it, that no words of mine can ever sway you. I can see that honour is not for you as it is for us.'

'Do not speak of honour,' spat Lysander.

'As I said,' replied Thul. 'Hexal, this one's weapon.'

Hexal motioned forward one of the Iron Warriors, who handed Lysander's hammer to Thul. 'This is the Fist of Dorn,' said Thul weighing the weapon in his hands, feeling its weight. 'A relic from the age of the primarchs, no less. Then you are Captain Darnath

Lysander of the First Company. A man much feted by the lords of his Chapter. A future Chapter Master, some say. How distant that fate looks now. You and this hammer have much in common, captain. They are both in my possession, and they will both serve in my armouries one way or another. Hexal, you have brought a corpse with you, I see?'

'But one,' said Hexal. 'I knew we would value prisoners over the dead.' Lysander knew they were referring to Brother Drevyn and the mention of his battle-brother on their lips made his skin crawl.

'Good. Bring it to the observatory. Isolate the others. Bring the captain to the sanatorium. He is the greatest risk. Best he is processed immediately.'

Hexal's Iron Warriors hauled Lysander off his feet again.

'I will see you at Dorn's side!' cried out Brother Skelpis. 'At the end of time! At the final battle! I will see you there, my brothers! My captain! At Dorn's side!'

'Still they understand so little,' said Thul. 'They think they are to die.'

The great doors of the crucible were hauled shut behind Lysander as he was dragged off into the depths of the fortress.

LYSANDER'S SENSES HAD returned to him by the time he was wheeled into the sanatorium's anatomy theatre. He had been stripped of his armour and chained to an operating slab, which had been pushed into the observatory by a gaggle of hooded, hunchbacked creatures that stank of corrosive chemicals and machine oil. Their faces, half-glimpsed, were of grainy grey skin wrapped around elongated snouts, like animal skulls inexpertly covered in spare flesh. Their fingers ended in hypodermic needles and medical saws.

Lysander was looking up at a glazed blister rising above him, the glass dome clouded as if by cataracts. Half-glimpsed shapes were assembled in audience beyond him like students awaiting an anatomy lecture. Perhaps, Lysander thought, that was exactly what they were.

Lysander fought against his restraints. He knew they would not give, but the principle of it forced him to move. A Space Marine was a prideful creature, Lysander could not deny that, and his pride was inflamed. He had been unarmed, unmanned, his armour stripped away. Mutant hands had clawed at him as they pulled the armour's segments away. The uncleanness clung to him, and the eyes looking at him beyond the glass were unclean, too, as if whatever they saw became defiled.

He could see cracked tiles, stained and filthy, hung with cabinets of deformed bones and shelves of rusted medical implements. The hunched creatures shuffled around him.

The audience were not Iron Warriors, or at least Lysander could see none of them among the indistinct shapes. Lanky, huge-eyed things watched there, long grey fingers touching the glass. Mutants, or aliens, perhaps. Unholy things, gathered to learn at the feet of the Iron Warriors.

Lysander was aware of a door opening somewhere behind his head. An elongated shadow fell over him. A greyish figure hovered indistinctly above him. Its eyes were large and without whites, watery black lenses set into grey skin. Its nose was a vertical slit and its mouth without lips, and its head was framed by a frond of tattered tendrils that looked like they were rotting in place. Discolouration ran down its skin, weeping from sores and pits in its flesh. A hand reached over Lysander, with three very long fingers.

'The subject is human and yet not human,' someone said. It was not the alien surgeon, Lysander thought. The voice was level and soulless, as if sleep-taught to someone who was not a native speaker. He thought it was coming from somewhere in the gallery.

'Witness the external signs,' continued the voice. 'The surgical scars around the ribcage and abdomen. These are indicative of a systematic series of operations performed in strict sequence. Note the subcutaneous panels concealing the topography of the ribs. The Black Carapace, the final implant of the Space Marine, both armour plating for the central organ tree and a seat for the interfaces that connect the nerve-fibre bundles of the power armour to the subject's own nervous system.'

Lysander could make out the speaker, he thought. It wore elaborate armour, scalloped and bladed, its silhouette distinct among the shapes in the audience gallery. Its shoulder guards rose like the horns of a half-moon around its plumed helmet and its shape was obscured by the cloak that hung from one shoulder. A clawed gauntlet gestured as the speaker continued. 'The Black Carapace lies outermost of the enhancements of a Space Marine, and is the final to be added. Thus the means of his creation can be observed by paring away the layers, as with an ancient ruin where the passing of the ages can be seen the deeper one digs.'

Lysander did not care about the pain. He had suffered pain before. A Space Marine learned to set it aside, to recognise it as a signal from the body that could be interpreted and understood like anything else. It was the humiliation that dug deep, the knowledge that he would be a curiosity for these creatures, as if he were an animal dissected by some student in the schola progenium.

That was not how a Space Marine should die. Not just unarmed, not just helpless, but being used as an aid to the enemy. Whatever these allies of the Iron Warriors were, they would learn a little more about their enemy in the Space Marines of the Imperium, and they would learn it from Captain Darnath Lysander.

Lysander could not have ceased fighting his restraints if he had wanted to. His teeth gritted and the muscles of his neck and torso stood out like coils of rope as he tried to bend his back, fold the operating slab in two underneath him, spring up and tear this place apart.

'Note the muscular development,' the speaker

continued. 'The result of the operation of the progenoid organ, the gene-seed, which we shall see in good time.'

The gene-seed organ, the organ cultured from the flesh of Rogal Dorn himself, implanted in Lysander's throat, that sacred flesh which made a Space Marine more than a man. Lysander's bile rose to think the alien even knew of it. For one of them to hold it in his hands would be a blasphemy, the desecration of a relic, the despoiling of holy ground. But worse than that – if Lysander's gene-seed was not harvested and returned to the Chapter on his death, it would not be implanted into an initiate to take his place. That speck of light, that part of the primarch, would be snuffed out forever, and the galaxy would be a little darker.

If it was in his power, he would not let them. He would fight them to the end. Even if he merely blunted their needles or forced their blades to slip, if his every effort was nothing more than an inconvenience to them as they cut him apart, he would fight. It was his duty, and he would not die with his duty undone.

A surgical saw whined and its circular blade descended over him, towards the scar that bisected his chest. Lysander's joints cracked as he strained against the shackles holding him, and the audience leaned closer to watch as the first blood flowed.

3

'Upon landing, I instituted a strict moral quarantine over my acolytes lest this world have a baleful influence on them. In the days to come I would regret permitting some of them to join the landing party at all, for Malodrax erodes the principles of the mind as the shrieking gales erode its rocks.'

– Inquisitor Corvin Golrukhan

LYSANDER'S SKIN CRAWLED as the smell of Malodrax hit him. Rust and smoke, and dried blood, heavy and metallic. It was a taste in his mouth, and he knew he would not get rid of it until he left this place again. Perhaps even then it would stay, the taste of metal and blood always on his tongue.

He jumped down from the shuttle's embarkation ramp onto the parched, cracked earth. Waves of heat washed off it from the shuttle's landing jets. First Sergeant Kaderic's squad jumped down around him, bolters scanning in every direction.

The sky was the colour of copper. The clouds were a dark murky green. The earth was red-brown, dry and cracked, broken up into ridges and valleys from one horizon to the other. In the distance were shapes something like buildings, but lopsided and decrepit. Flocks of airborne predators wheeled in the distance.

And it stank. It stank like old blood. Lysander lifted the faceplate of his helmet and spat on the ground, like a ritual.

'Secure, by sections!' ordered Kaderic. The strike force had trained for the landing on the shuttle decks of the *Breaker*, and each Space Marine had his section of the perimeter to scan and secure. In seconds it was done, and within half a minute the shuttle doors were being hauled shut behind the strike force. Thirty-four Space Marines – Squads Kaderic and Gorvetz, and Chaplain Lycaon's command squad, plus Brother Halaestus, Lysander, and Techmarine Kho and the Imperial Fist who served as Kho's pilot. A pair of Land Speeders, rapid scouting skimmers under Kho's command, had been dropped off by the gunships that accompanied the two personnel shuttles. The gunships had low enough orbital signatures that the chances were, no one on Malodrax was aware the strike force had landed.

The gunships, compact and sturdy Stormtalons, had fuel requirements too costly to guarantee they could function for long on Malodrax. The Imperial Fists had no friendly supply lines to count on and Lysander's information on the planet suggested there was no abundance of fuel sources to capture. The gunships would be easy to spot, too, larger and less nimble than the Land Speeders that could cling to the terrain. The Stormtalons took off back for their berths in orbit – the strike force would have to walk.

Lysander spotted Halaestus. He was at his part of the perimeter, and looked back from his bolter sights once satisfied that his angle was clear. There was nothing that could be said, not with what had happened the last time Lysander and Halaestus had been on this world, not with Brother Skelpis not being there. Halaestus glanced at Lysander, but said nothing either.

'Good choice, Lysander,' said Chaplain Lycaon, looking around the valley. 'Defensible and sheltered. When the gunships clear we will leave no silhouettes.'

'We cannot stay long,' said Lysander.

'Indeed not. We move out once the Land Speeders are on the move.'

'Keep a watch on the skies,' said Lysander. 'Most of the predators are just animals, but the powers of Malodrax have airborne spies. Daemons.'

'Kho's guns will keep us hidden,' said Lycaon. 'How keen is your sense of direction, now you are down here?'

'We head north-west,' said Lysander. 'Two days' fast march. The ground levels out closer to the fortress but we should still be hidden well enough. We may have to leave the Land Speeders once we get closer.'

'The sergeants have misgivings about your plan once we get there.'

Lysander did not rise to the comment. Lycaon was testing him. That was why he led this strike force – for Lysander was the captain, the position was still honorary in practice. Lycaon was in charge down here. 'There is no other way,' said Lysander. 'Either we take this path, or we leave Malodrax alone and our brothers unavenged.'

'Then our duty is clear,' said Lycaon. He spoke into the strike force's vox-net. 'Brothers! Brother Kho has the point, he will range ahead with our Land Speeders. The rest, keep good pace and keep our profile to a minimum. This world has eyes everywhere. Move out!'

THE STRIKE FORCE came across the first war machine within the half-hour. They made good time even over the broken earth and through narrow crevasses, with Techmarine Kho always just around the next bend. The drone of the Land Speeders' engines mingled with the thin whistling of the wind that hissed across the shattered landscape.

Lysander rounded the rock forming the next bend to see the Land Speeders hovering, the mounted guns trained on the hulk of rusting metal that towered just ahead.

Each Land Speeder was a large enough vehicle to carry a crew of two Space Marines and an array of weaponry, with a nose-mounted assault cannon as well as the mounted guns, but each looked like an insect next to the enormous bulk of the structure in front of them. It resembled a siege tower, its sides clad in bands of rusting iron and hung with the threadbare remains of war banners. The desiccated remains of countless corpses were hung around the tower's battlements like a shrivelled necklace, and many more had fallen into a drift of skin and bones around the enormous spiked wheels at the tower's base. The tower leaned heavily to one side where it had apparently toppled into the valley, and its ramp hung open like a jaw studded with spikes resembling needle teeth.

A flock of airborne predators, something like winged lizards, shrieked as they flew from rusted holes near the top of the tower, alarmed by the approaching drone of the Land Speeders. They hacked and spat as they dissolved off towards the horizon, spiralling around the guns mounted on the top of the tower.

'Do we go around, Chaplain?' voxed Techmarine Kho. He was sat in the gunner's seat of one of the Land Speeders, the articulated manipulator arms mounted on his backpack visible outside the lines of the cockpit.

'We go through,' replied Lycaon. 'Watch our backs, Techmarine.'

The strike force approached the many openings around the base of the tower. It had sunk into the earth so there was no way under, but the partial collapse of the structure had forced open great rents in the steel, exposing the metal beams and darkness within.

'What do you know, Lysander?' voxed Lycaon.

'These are proving grounds,' replied Lysander. 'The Iron Warriors make war machines. They pit them against one another across these lands, and those that survive are sent to join Black Crusades across the galaxy. This machine did not survive.'

'These are plasma blastguns,' voxed Kho from his Land Speeder, which was ascending the slope up near the guns that crowned the siege tower. 'Would that I could get a better look at the induction coils.'

'We have not the time,' said Lycaon.

'Of course, Chaplain,' voxed the Techmarine.

Inside the tower was foul-smelling and dark. The floor was spongy underfoot and Lysander looked down to see it caked with dried remains, whether human or not he could not tell – a crust of parchment skin, stringy muscle fibre and brittle bones that crunched as the strike force's squads moved through the gloom. The walls were plastered with it and twisted limbs hung from the low ceilings like stalactites.

'What manner of obscenity is this?' voxed Devastator-Sergeant Gorvetz.

'Witchcraft,' said First Sergeant Kaderic.

Lysander moved through the lower floor of the tower alongside Squad Kaderic. His augmented eyes could see through the dark but even so the place seemed fuzzy and indistinct, as if his mind did not want to acknowledge the sheer number of bodies needed to create the carnage in which the siege tower was steeped. He saw a fully-formed body in the centre of one wall, spread-eagled, the chest and abdomen pared open. He saw distorted faces and familiar bones – pelvises, vertebrae, femurs.

Lysander caught movement from the corner of his eye. A Space Marine's peripheral vision was excellent but he couldn't give the shape form as it flitted out of view. Lysander's bolter was in his hand without him having to will it.

'The multiplicity of hearts means cardiac arrest is not an issue,' said a voice that knifed right through Lysander's memory.

Lysander broke into a run. The voice had come from the shadows up ahead, which clung to an archway leading deeper into the body of the tower. Lysander crunched through the bodies and through the archway, and in a shaft of light falling from a rupture in the side of the tower he saw a silhouette.

It wore ornate armour with curving shoulder guards, a high helm with just the gleam of twin eyeslits to suggest a face, and a wide cape hanging from one shoulder.

'So restraint, not anaesthesia, is the only concern,' came the voice again.

Lysander opened fire. He did not send the thought down to his trigger finger. The signal came from somewhere in the animal hindbrain that even a Space Marine's training could not fully erase.

Half a dozen bolter shells ripped across the chamber. In the strobing light the interior was revealed – a

chapel, the pews forged of shoulder blades and crani-
ums lashed together with ropes of dried sinew. Severed
hands hung in their hundreds from the vaulted ceiling,
and on the altar at the head of the chapel sat a statue
of some warp-spawned lesser god, squatting like a toad
with a face that dripped with spiny tentacles. It held
up four webbed hands with an eyeball in each palm.
Stray bolter shots burst against its green stone, blasting
chunks of its misshapen skull onto the floor.

The silhouette was gone, as if it had been nothing but
smoke blown away by the gunfire.

Squad Kaderic stormed into the chapel behind
Lysander, bolters sweeping every angle.

'What have you seen, brother?' demanded Kaderic.

'Movement,' said Lysander, lowering his bolter. 'It is
gone.'

'Chaplain!' came a vox over the strike force channel. It
was Sergeant Gorvetz. 'We are picking up phantom signals
on the auspex scanner, but we may have found the source.'

The strike force gathered one floor up, where Gorvetz
had found the origin of the signals his auspex scanner
had registered. A great mass of brains, old and decayed
but human in size and shape, hung from one wall like a
huge bunch of rotting berries. A thin sheen of moisture
covered them and each brain pulsed, almost impercep-
tibly, as if veins received blood from somewhere.

'Tech-heresy,' said Chaplain Lycaon when he saw the
obscenity. 'This must have been what controlled the
war machine. Lysander?'

'Without doubt,' said Lysander.

'Gorvetz!' ordered Lycaon, and the Devastator-Sergeant needed no further elaboration. He ordered forward Brother Antinas, who carried his squad's heavy flamer. The weapon was hooked up to a pair of fuel canisters on Antinas's backpack, and required a Space Marine of Antinas's training to carry and use while minimising the risk to his fellow Imperial Fists of such a weapon. The other Space Marines stepped back as Antinas sprayed the cluster of brains with a gout of flame, the burning fuel coating them and instantly causing them to shrivel away, their mass disappearing in the sudden yellow glare.

The darkness seemed to lift – not just because of the light, but inside Lysander. He saw in full clarity now, and the seething shadows that clung to everything receded.

'Can you feel it?' said First Sergeant Kaderic. 'The shadows die away.'

'We have exterminated a moral threat here,' said Lycaon. 'It will not be the first we find. Brothers, we move on. Kho! Are we clear on the far side?'

'Clear, Chaplain,' voxed Techmarine Kho in reply.

'Then we leave this place,' said Lycaon.

The strike force forged through what remained of the siege tower, sticking close as they forced through the far side of the tower, out among the spiked wheels embedded in the ground below.

Brother Halaestus sought out Lysander. 'What did you see, captain?' he asked.

'Nothing,' said Lysander. 'And what did you see?'

Halaestus did not reply, and the strike force moved on out of the shadow of the siege tower.

4

'An inquisitor must respect his acolytes. He must care deeply for them, as if they were members of his own family, for he has a responsibility for them that goes beyond that of a master and his underlings. But he must also be willing to pitch those acolytes into the worst peril that a human mind can imagine. Few can do it. Fewer still do not fall prey to malice, tossing aside human lives for amusement or to prove superiority. My acolytes, then, must sometimes be sacrificed in the name of something greater than any of us, but it is always with sorrow that I cast them into the path of danger. I trust that each understands that, when his time comes.'

– Inquisitor Corvin Golrukhan

THE FORTRESS OF Kulgarde was haunted. They were old ghosts, as ancient as Malodrax itself, and they remembered the times when the planet was not a deformed plaything of the warp. They remembered its beauty and purity, and the glee with which the dark gods despoiled it.

They clustered around Lysander like flies around decay. They sensed the desperation in him. A Space Marine was created to know no fear, but he could still recognise hopelessness when it came, he could still feel the black hole of a future cut off with no way to get it back. It was not fear that Lysander felt, but something equally cold. Every push against the restraints was a hollow gesture, every curse he voiced was like spitting into a bottomless pit.

He could see the ghosts of Malodrax now, hovering around the anatomy theatre. They were a hollow-faced, spindly species of xenos, wearing the tatters of finery that spoke of a proud and wealthy civilisation. Perhaps they were cousins to the thing that prepared to operate on Lysander now, a thousand generations removed, debased and enslaved by the lords who had taken over Malodrax after it fell.

Lysander's body tensed, his spine arching, as the circular blade bit into his sternum. Pain meant nothing, but weakness did, and as his body was mutilated he would lose the strength that made him a Space Marine.

'You will witness shortly that a Space Marine possesses two hearts,' said the xenos leading the demonstration from the viewing gallery. 'The multiplicity of hearts means cardiac arrest is not an issue, so restraint, not anaesthesia, is the only concern.'

The surgeon peeled back a patch of skin from Lysander's sternum, revealing the slab of bone that made up his internal breastplate. It was made of fused ribs, created among the bone and muscle changes caused by the action of the gene-seed organs. The circular saw was withdrawn and the alien now wielded a long, sharp blade, like a stiletto with a double edge.

The alien aimed the point down at one of the joins in the breastplate, where two plates of bone joined. The blade was forced down into the joint, the blade twisted to force it open a little. Blood flowed, obscuring the white bone.

Lysander drew in his breath in a sharp hiss. His arms were manacled above his head and he forced his head round, trying to find some way of getting at the lock holding his wrists. He could almost reach it with his teeth, but the lock was just beyond his reach and he couldn't touch it without dislocating his neck. And what if he could? He couldn't bite through it. If he could reach it he would try, but he knew it would do no good.

Black pits of eyes looked down at him. The ghosts were watching as intently as the mutants and the xenos in the viewing gallery, as if this was the only entertainment they had in their half-lives.

Lysander had to try. That was its own reward. He would make them work at killing him, and he would fight to the end.

The blade was drawn up his chest. He felt it paring the skin away. Here and there it juddered as it met a particularly dense patch of bone.

It was almost at Lysander's throat.

'Removal of the internal breastplate,' the lead xenos was saying, 'will reveal both the organ tree and the seat of the progenoid gland. The fabled gene-seed, seat of a Space Marine's prowess. In all the galaxy there is nothing so valuable, there is no weapon so potent.'

With a tiny metallic sound, the blade snapped off its handle. The surgeon hissed annoyedly and turned to a rack of implements behind it to find a replacement.

Lysander forced his head forwards. He could just see the blade sticking out, just below his collarbone.

His neck muscles strained as he bent his head further. His windpipe was compressed and he could not breathe. He felt the sharp metal against his lower lip and closed his teeth around the broken stub of the blade. Wrenching his head back, he pulled the blade from his chest, the sliver of pain he felt there a welcome reminder that he still lived.

The ghosts looked on. One tilted its head a little, as if in curiosity. Another opened its mouth, revealing the black void inside, perhaps in surprise, perhaps that species' equivalent of a smile.

The blade slid into the manacle's keyhole. The key would be simple, the manacle made for strength not complexity. A child could pick it. Lysander told himself this as he forced his head around to twist the shard of metal in the lock.

It wouldn't budge.

The surgeon looked back round, its eyes and nose-slit widening in alarm.

The metal twisted. The lock snickered open.

Certain assumptions could be made about a xenos which was largely humanoid. For instance, very few such creatures could live without whatever organ was protected inside its cranium. A Space Marine knew this, because he had to possess all the knowledge necessary to make him the most efficient killer of any foe, including a xenos of a previously unknown species.

Lysander put this knowledge to use when his newly freed hand closed around the surgeon's throat and lower jaw. He squeezed, his augmented strength giving him a grip powerful enough to splinter the alien's jawbone. Its upper jaw cracked and its face distorted and narrowed.

The alien struggled in his grip, flopping around from its neck. Lysander crushed its throat, his hand now balled into a fist, and dashed the alien against the ground.

Shrieks rose from the viewing gallery. The alien orator leaned against the smudged glass, and Lysander could make out the stylised, inhuman features of its faceplate, the emerald eyepieces and the dark-green marbled substance of its armour. Lysander met the alien's gaze.

'I will come back, alien!' said Lysander as he forced himself into a sitting position and grabbed the chain that held his ankles with both hands. 'And I will find you first!'

Lysander ripped the chains out of the operating slab, the sundered links falling to the tiled floor.

Alien mandibles were clicking in alarm. Audients were fleeing the viewing gallery. Lysander swung off the slab and his bare feet touched the floor.

He ached all over. It was good. His body still worked. It was the only weapon he had. That changed a second later as he grabbed the most vicious-looking implement off the rack of medical tools on the wall. It was an autopsy knife, long, straight, double-edged, flimsy in a fight but definitely capable of killing. It was still next to nothing compared to the power armour, hammer and bolter that he wielded by choice. But it would have to do.

Lysander gave the operating theatre one last look before he shouldered his way through the only door. The alien surgeon's blood was warm and sticky under his feet.

The medical wing of the fortress stretched around him. Ceiling-high tanks contained creatures the shape of adult humans, naked and half-developed, features soft and skin translucent, wound around with cables and hoses. The orderly creatures, hunched and robed, with their elongated faces like masks of gnarled bone, were working on wall-mounted racks of bloodstained steel where alien and human bodies were chained up in various stages of dissection. The place stank of old blood and rang with the reedy moans from waist-high cages stacked up in the corners, issuing trickles of filth collected by the drainage channels cut into the stained floor.

Lysander grabbed the closest orderly, yanking it off its feet and hurling it into the nearest glass tank. It crashed through the glass and into the wall, the half-formed body inside spilling out onto the floor. Its face was barely there, as if made of clay with the features just pushed in by a sculptor's fingers. Its musculature, however, was that of a Space Marine, as were the scars of puckered white skin that ran across its back and chest. The implications were too grave for Lysander to give them any thought now.

The orderlies ran in every direction, recognising the escaped prisoner who should have been dissected on the slab. One snatched up a flensing knife and ran at Lysander, who knocked the blade aside with his forearm, the red line of pain along his wrist barely registering as he jammed the autopsy knife up into the orderly's throat. The tip broke through the bony exoskeleton and punched through whatever passed for the creature's brain. It shuddered and fell still, and Lysander dropped it to the ground.

The medical wing was madness. Brass-cased engines belched smoke as they rendered alien and human down into fat and paste. Prisoners, whether human or not Lysander could not tell, shrieked and rattled their cages as he ran through the wards and laboratories. The few orderlies who got in his path were beaten out of the way, necks broken or skulls crushed, and Lysander found a heavy wrench-like implement to fight with when his autopsy blade broke. He could hear the sounds of alarm in the distance – news of his escape had surely reached the Iron Warriors, who would be moving every spare Traitor Marine to intercept him.

The Iron Warriors were disciplined, but the opposite reflection of their orderliness was in the areas of the fortress left to their underlings and xenos allies. It was chaos down here, in its purest form. Lysander saw aliens of the surgeon's lanky, diseased species, and realised they must be what remained of Malodrax's natives. He saw the ghosts of their fallen civilisation, clustering around the corners of the ceiling among the shadows and spiders' webs.

The exoskeletoned creatures, artificial serf-constructs made by the Iron Warriors to tend to their fortress, teemed in the winding corridors and fled from him as he approached. In side chambers, humans with more scar tissue than original skin lay among heaps of trash and rags. A great cauldron of body parts churned, tended by skinny, filthy humans with their eyes and tongues torn out. Shrines to lesser powers of the warp were heaped with offerings – raw meat, broken pieces of gold, bones, weapons, organs in glass jars. Some stretches of this wing were pitch-black, or ice-cold, or scorchingly hot, and every corner seemed to have some broken-minded and insane inhabitant whose mutilations and insanity crossed the border between alien and human.

LYSANDER SURVIVED THREE days in the sweltering filth that lay beneath the medical wing. The blood and gore that dripped into the drains of the wards and operating theatres ran down here, into a great sump of decay. An underground sea of bubbling black-red filth stretched along a wide, low natural cave, and here the lowest scum of Kulgarde had been banished. Shanties of trash and scrap metal sat on pontoons of worm-eaten wood that would sink or capsize, throwing another handful of diseased mutants into the filth. Blind serpentine predators nipped at dangling legs and hands, and in the half-light of bioluminescent fungi these subhumans lived out short, brutal lives of dark madness.

Lysander's stature as a Space Marine meant that he could not pretend to be one of the skinny, malnourished creatures that had presumably once been workers in the Iron Warriors forges. But some mutants were hulking as well as deformed, with massive shoulders and hunched bodies that, if they stood upright, would have caused their heads to brush against the cavern ceiling. Upon arriving in the sump Lysander had seen one such brute-mutant devouring one of normal human size, while others lay prostrate and watched, and surmised that the brutes were the leadership caste in what passed for a society down here. He found filthy rags to wear and went hunched. Regular mutants scattered at his approach and he avoided the brutes, but even so, it was only a matter of time before he was recognised as something other than one of this place's mutant dregs.

And it was unclean. As foul a place as he had ever been. This place did not just house mutants – it made them, the accumulation of effluent and chemicals enough to warp even a Space Marine's genetics until he was one of the accursed, given enough time.

On the third day there was a great commotion, a shrieking and gabbling among the mutants. They gathered on shanty roofs to watch a collection of lights approaching from the cave's darkest reaches. Lysander watched from a distance, feeling the flimsy boards under his feet churning as the filth was stirred up.

The lights were lanterns hung from a flotilla of a dozen boats, carved and ornate, painted with gilt and bright colours. They were punted through the mire by figures in hoods and robes dyed deep crimson, and among them moved things that resembled the medical servitors that Lysander was used to seeing in Imperial medical facilities. A servitor was a machine created from human parts, such as from condemned criminals or pious souls who bequeathed their remains. Its brain was imprinted with a simple set of commands and its limbs augmented with mechanical devices appropriate to its purpose. The servitors on the flotilla had human torsos, wheeled or tracked motivator units in place of legs, and several jointed metal arms tipped with syringes, blades, saws and other implements of surgery or dismemberment. The biological parts were discoloured and blistered with disease and the steel was stained with old blood.

Lysander looked around him. He had taken shelter in a large shanty that had, by the size and smell, been inhabited by a brute that was now absent. No lesser mutants had dared to squat there and Lysander reasoned that if the owner returned he could deal with him – a good hiding place was worth that risk. Outside the shanty, at the corner of the pontoon, knelt one of the sump's countless mutants. It wore a loincloth and its skin was pallid, covered in purplish rashes from which tiny white worms hatched in a weeping of pus. Lysander darted out of the shanty and grabbed the mutant by the scruff of the neck.

It had four eyes, arranged around a mouth in the centre of its face. Lysander hauled it off its feet and held it level with him.

'What is this?' he demanded of the mutant.

The mutant's eyes rolled in fear. Lysander raised it up higher and held it over the churning gore. 'What is this?' he asked again. 'Who approaches?'

'Prisoners,' squealed the mutant. 'Taken from above! Thul's prisoners! Some he sends to the Bone Sculptors to be used. The Sculptors' isle is across the black ocean. The ferrymen take them there.'

Lysander looked again at the flotilla. The boats were painted with the eyes and teeth of monsters, like fanciful versions of the predators that snaked through the gore.

The ferrymen stopped pushing the flotilla forwards and turned to haul ropes and chains attached to wooden contraptions in the centre of each boat. The mutants began to cheer, wailing and clapping as if they were watching the return of a great hero.

A pole, like a mast, was drawn upright from inside each boat. To each was tied a body. Some were clearly dead, and they were unmutated humans as far as Lysander could tell – their skin an odd pale-pink colour, wearing straps of red leather in place of clothing, their faces – where they had faces – obscured by dark blue tattoos. One had been disembowelled, another's skull stove in. Some others were alive, and their heads lolled as if barely aware of their surroundings. Another was like the brute-mutants of the sump, and a great cry of glee went up from the mutants when it was raised. Its skin was scaly, its face a brutal blunt snout, and it roared as the ferrymen goaded it with barbed pikes. Other mutants included one with the lower body of a snake, another with clusters of vestigial heads bulging from its stomach, and another with vividly patterned skin and curving horns.

The last three prisoners made Lysander's stomach churn, though he had known somehow he would see them. Three Space Marines – three Imperial Fists.

Brother Skelpis, the stump of his leg bound with filthy leather strips.

Brother Halaestus, still conscious, beaten and bloody, patches of his skin burned or pared off. Lysander could see his mouth moving as he yelled and though he could not hear the words, he knew they were curses from the limits of a Space Marine's vocabulary.

Brother Vonkaal, with iron spikes impaled through both thighs and upper arms, unconscious like Skelpis.

And one who did not live – Brother Drevyn, the two halves of his bisected corpse hanging like obscene decorations from a crossbar nailed to the mast, entrails hanging in red ropes.

It had not been enough to wipe out the greater part of the First Company. No, the Iron Warriors had to take their trophies, and parade them as if they were banners captured in war.

The flotilla passed by Lysander's vantage point, and he saw the crew jabbing at the Imperial Fists prisoners with barbed polearms, to the shrieking delight of the onlookers.

'What happens at the Sculptors' isle?' demanded Lysander of his prisoner. The prisoner squirmed and whimpered, and its eyes rolled back to their whites.

'What do the Bone Sculptors do?' he asked again.

The mutant was insensible with fear. Lysander threw it aside and it clattered through a wall of his shanty.

Lysander watched the flotilla's lights pass by the settlement in the sump. Then he dismantled the shanty, selecting one wall that seemed wide and sturdy enough to support his weight on its own. Going by the length of the punting poles used by the flotilla's crew, he found a length of wood long enough to reach the bed of the sump. He pushed off from the platform on this makeshift raft, poling in the direction the flotilla had gone.

As the light died and his vision struggled to pick out the shifting murk in monochrome, Lysander became aware of the predators that lived in those filthy waters oozing along in the wake of his raft. When they strayed too close, he batted them aside with a strike of the pole, and they gave him a wider berth for a while. Great dark shapes loomed by, segments of war machines that had fallen down from above in some long-ago collapse. Chunks of the fortress's foundations lay half-submerged. He even passed a shipwreck, a barge something like the flotilla's in design but far larger, its bow reaching up above the surface, a few gnawed bones still lying on the stone blocks where it had foundered.

Far above, through a tear in the cavern ceiling, glowed the dull fires of a forge. Acidic rain stung Lysander's skin. The low, titanic moans reached him of the fortress above settling lower into the sump.

Lysander saw lights ahead and slowed down. The lights resolved into lanterns hung about a rocky island in the filth, on which was built a temple of standing stones smooth with age. Enormous bestial heads carved in stone loomed over the temple, staring out across the black sea. The flotilla had moored and its crew were taking their prisoners down off the masts and carrying them onto the island.

As Lysander watched, from the temple emerged the first of the Bone Sculptors. It bore some resemblance to the exoskeletoned orderlies in the fortress's medical wing. But where those were hunched and feeble, this was far taller and glided with a strange elegance as it approached the prisoners being unloaded. Its head resembled three long animal skulls attached base to base, with three sets of eye sockets, mandibles, and rows of white teeth. Additional limbs, half mechanical and half bone, reached from beneath its heavy black robes, each tipped with a syringe or blade. Others followed it out, each a different form of the same horror.

And flanking the Bone Sculptors were a pair of Iron Warriors Space Marines, in the functional gunmetal of their Legion's livery, armed with bolter and chainsword. Lysander knew that even with arms and armour, it would be throwing his life away to storm the island alone. He would die and his battle-brothers would lose any chance of escape.

It wrenched at him to leave them there. Perhaps they would be executed the instant they passed the temple threshold. Perhaps, once he left this place, he would never find a way back in. But his fellow Imperial Fists would benefit nothing if Lysander died there.

Lysander pushed the raft away from the island into the darkness before he was noticed by the Iron Warriors guarding the temple.

He swore silently that he would return, soon, and on his own terms. And when he did, for whatever evil they planned to inflict on his brothers, the Bone Sculptors would die.

5

'My intention of authoring a natural history and sociology of Malodrax, and charting of its various lifeforms and inhabitants and the relationships thereof, was scuppered when I understood for the first time the nature of life on this world. On a sane planet, one species predates on another, one nation conquers its neighbour or is conquered. Peoples wax and wane, empires rise and fall. Not so on Malodrax. Malodrax resists even the simplest attempts of holy logic to govern its histories. In fact, I will say that it has no history, instead an infinite tumult of conflict and death that started at its birth and stretches to the Time of Ending.'

– Inquisitor Corvin Golrukhan

THE FIRST SIGHT of the enemy was the glint of Malodrax's sun off the lenses of their rifle scopes.

It was an alien sun that rose suddenly, a small, hot orb whose light burned through the discoloured clouds, picking out the broken land in a chemical white light while leaving the shadows even darker. The strike force could do little in response save bring Techmarine Kho's Land Speeders in even lower to the ground, to keep the skimmers' telltale movement from giving them away at a distance.

But in spite of their precautions, the Imperial Fists knew they would be found. It was the Emperor's own fortune that they had made it this far, the better part of a day and a half, without being seen.

'I have contacts, brother-Chaplain,' voxed Techmarine Kho from ahead of the strike force. 'Several, half a kilometre north-west of us.'

Chaplain Lycaon held up a fist and the strike force halted, suddenly ready to open fire or charge any enemy that showed itself. Lycaon gestured to Lysander and scrambled up the side of the shallow valley through which the strike force had been moving. Lysander followed Lycaon and dropped onto his front, crawling up the slope until he reached the crest and could see what Kho had reported.

White glints flickered along a ridge several hundred metres away. Lysander focused on one and saw the form of a head and shoulders – a figure, sighting down the barrel of a gun. One rose slightly to change position, perhaps aware the strike force had suddenly stopped. Lysander caught a glimpse of pale-pinkish skin, and a partially shaven scalp which had a fringe of feathers instead of hair. The gun was an ornate hunting rifle with a scope. The owner was wearing leather straps wrapping around his torso and upper arms, and goggles obscuring his face.

'Do you know them?' asked Lycaon.

'Yes,' said Lysander. 'Cultists of Shalhadar.'

'The daemon prince?'

'The same.'

Lycaon spat into the dark earth. 'Is he a threat?'

'If he learns of us,' said Lysander, 'then yes, he definitely is. These lands are contested between Shalhadar and Kulgarde. Shalhadar will see us as invaders as much as Kraegon Thul would.'

The cultist scouts were moving now, disappearing from view behind the ridge.

'Kho!' voxed Lycaon. 'Bring your speeders down and pick up Lysander and I. We are to the hunt!'

KHO'S LAND SPEEDER bore the name *Dorn's Dagger*, and was the oldest such machine in the Imperial Fists armoury. It was therefore the fastest and most reliable, with a machine-spirit housed in an archeotech core that compensated for wayward piloting and kept the vehicle arrowing straight and fast as it flew. Kho occupied the pilot's seat, his mechadendrites folded back behind him to reduce drag, sub-manipulators in his gauntlets clattering across the complex dashboard while he concentrated on banking and throttling. Lysander sat beside him in the gunner's seat, the heavy bolter in front of him on its mountings.

The wind shrieked as *Dorn's Dagger* rode up to the

crest of the slope and accelerated, the anti-grav units underneath letting out a deep hum to complement the hollow roar from the jets at the rear.

'The *Dagger* has not hunted for many a month,' Techmarine Kho said. His face was hidden behind the faceplate of his red-painted artificer armour, and the cogitator array of valves and circuits on his chest whirred rapidly as it calculated endless angles of approach and attack. 'Let us get her blooded, captain. It is time this world began to suffer.'

The landscape ripped by, the *Dagger* rising and falling barely enough to keep it from barking its underside on the rocky ridges hurtling below. Lysander knelt up on the gunner's seat, leaning into the bulk of the heavy bolter, cycling its action to check the load and playing its sights across the horizon.

Movement glimmered below. A creature ran in long, loping strides, a tail swinging out behind it for balance and a tapering head angled out in front. A rider, one of the cultist scouts, clung on, pressed low against the beast's back for stability with his rifle slung on his back. The creature was galloping towards a knot of rocky outcrops, a miniature mountain range with passes and valleys running through it, surrounded by tilting slabs of shattered ground.

'I see it!' said Kho, speaking over the vox as the howl of the wind and the engines made normal speech inaudible. 'Rain steel, brother!'

Lysander squeezed the firing stud as he held the sights

steady just in front of the beast. The weapon bucked in his grip and he leaned into it harder, keeping it steady as another chain of shots ripped off. The beast was struck in the shoulder, blasting a ragged hole right through it. Its head pitched into the ground and it cartwheeled, throwing its rider spinning out of the saddle to crash broken against the rocks.

The second Land Speeder, the *Talon Blade*, swept around from the other side of the outcrop, its nose-mounted assault cannon hammering at a trio of scouts scrambling on foot up a rocky slope for the cover of a cave. Chaplain Lycaon was in the *Talon*'s cockpit alongside Kho's fellow pilot, Brother Gethor, operating the multi-melta the *Talon*'s gunner used. While it was better for boring holes through tanks than chasing down fleeing infantry, a multi-melta's concentrated heat beam was just as effective at ending a pursuit if it hit home. Assault cannon shots blasted one cultist apart, sending a shattered leg spiralling away in a spray of blood, while a beam of superheated particles carved a deep molten furrow across the rock that bisected a second cultist through the mid-torso.

The last cultist dropped to a knee and fired off a shot at the *Talon Blade*. Perhaps he hit, perhaps he didn't – it mattered little because the armour of the Land Speeder and the Space Marines crewing it were enough to turn aside the shot, and the cultist was punched through by a half-dozen assault cannon shots an instant later.

'Brother-Chaplain, do you see any more?' voxed Lysander.

'None,' said Lycaon. 'Fly a tight sweep, and watch for them doubling back. None can be permitted to reach Shalhadar.'

The two Land Speeders circumnavigated the outcrop. The *Talon* shot down two more riders as they fled from behind a couple of fallen boulders. Lysander spotted a cultist on foot, and Kho shot him down with the *Dagger*'s assault cannon before Lysander could bring his heavy bolter to bear.

'There,' said Lysander pointing to a ridge a couple of hundred metres west of the outcrop. A cultist rode up over a ridge and disappeared down the reverse slope.

'We pursue,' said Kho, and the *Dagger* arrowed at full speed in the direction of the fugitive.

Lysander held the heavy bolter level as best he could. Below him the assault cannon on the Land Speeder's nose stitched a spray of gunfire along the ground just behind the rider. Lysander could make out the rider was not just another cultist. Perhaps he was a leader of their kind, going by the headdress he wore with silk pennants rippling in the wind behind him and the large wicker panniers on the beast he rode. Lysander squeezed off a ranging shot of his own and it fell just short.

The rider's path took him down into the kind of narrow broken valleys the strike force had used to conceal their march. Each time the rider passed through

Lysander's sights he vanished behind the slope of a rise or a finger of shattered rock.

'The *Dagger* does not lose her prey,' said Kho, his voice calm even though he was sending the Land Speeder jinking a few metres above ground level, swinging between outcrops of rock.

Lysander caught a flash of pallid skin and bucking animal between the rocks. Instinct forced his finger down on the firing stud. The heavy bolter kicked and Lysander saw the broken limbs of the riding beast flailing as it flipped over and smacked into a boulder. Bright red spray painted the side of the rock.

'He's down,' voxed Lysander. 'Bank us around to confirm.'

Dorn's Dagger swept up and banked, looping around to approach the downed rider from the other direction, slowing as it did so.

The rider had sprawled onto the ground, and was crawling back towards the broken remains of his beast. Lysander opened fire and caught the rider in the shoulder, blowing an arm clean off.

The rider reached the beast. With his remaining arm he unfastened a clasp on the side of a pannier and pulled the lid open.

A cloud of dozens of tiny bright shapes fluttered upwards, billowing towards the sky.

Birds, trailing bright plumage as they flew.

'Shoot them down!' voxed Lysander. 'All of them!'

He fired his heavy bolter into the flock. The assault

cannon did the same. Tiny bodies burst into nothing. But there was so many of them and they flew off in every direction, too small and numerous to pick out with the Land Speeder's weapons.

The *Talon Blade* reached them a moment later, but the single beam of the multi-melta was even less use. Fully half the flock dispersed into the air, beyond the strike force's reach.

The two Land Speeders rejoined the rest of the strike force, dropping back down near ground level to reduce their profile. Lysander vaulted out of the gunner's seat, hands still tingling from the heavy bolter's recoil. Chaplain Lycaon dismounted the *Talon Blade*, his gauntlets scorched by the heat coming off the multi-melta. 'What did they release?' he asked Lysander.

'Messenger birds,' replied Lysander. 'It is how Shalhadar's forces communicate over a distance. He will have news of our arrival before the sun goes down.'

Lysander walked up the slope and looked west towards the horizon. The strange sun that had lit the hour was setting and its harsh light glittered against the distant hills. Among them it picked out tall slender towers and minarets, high walls cutting through foothills and mountains, thousands of banners fluttering. 'There,' he said. 'The city. It dominates this land along with Kulgarde. It has an army hundreds of thousands strong, so it was said. Cultists and daemons, all answering to the city's master.'

'Can they overtake us?' asked Lycaon.

'We are on foot over broken ground, and swift though a Space Marine can march he cannot outpace the outriders that will be sent to hunt us down. Yes, Chaplain, they can overtake us, and the daemon prince is jealous of this land. I imagine they will send out their cavalry to force us to stop and face them, and then seek to crush us with their main force following up behind.'

'Sound strategy when you outpace the foe,' said Lycaon. 'I read nothing in the Codex Astartes demanding that we give the enemy such courtesy as to fall in line with his plans. First Sergeant Kaderic!'

Kaderic hurried to Lycaon's side. 'Chaplain?'

'A small, swift force pursues us from the city you see on the horizon. They wish to force us to give battle to a larger force marching in its wake. How does a Space Marine fight?'

Kaderic smiled. The question might have been sprung on a novice in the training halls of the Phalanx, an elementary puzzle which every recruit would be expected to answer swiftly. 'He turns around and marches on the city,' he said. 'We will punch through the enemy's vanguard and fall upon him when he is not ready. And Emperor willing, we will walk into his city when his army is elsewhere and impale his head on the battlements. Such Dorn would say.'

'Such he would!' agreed Lycaon. 'If the ruler of the city is the one whose destruction we seek. Lysander? Would it be straying too far from our mission's path to bring the Emperor's wrath to this Shalhadar?'

Lysander looked towards the city again, and in the failing light gold glittered among its spires. 'He will hound us until we are dead or gone,' he said. 'Now he knows we are here, Prince Shalhadar will be our enemy until the end. He must die.'

'Then he will die,' said Lycaon. He switched to the strike force's vox-channel. 'Brothers! The forces of the city of Shalhadar do not take to intruders such as ourselves, who have so rudely intruded on their lands, so we shall introduce ourselves like gentlemen! A friendly bullet will be our calling card! A kindness of chain-blades will see they remember the Imperial Fists!'

A low ripple of voices ran across the strike force, murmurings of good battle finally approaching, for the Imperial Fists had been too long on this world without a fight.

'Techmarine Kho, scout the way,' voxed Lycaon. 'There are damned souls between us and our objective. We will go through them like a spear to the gut. Lead on!'

THE CITY DID not have a name. It was the City of Shalhadar, or simply the City. Some referred to it as Shalhadar, the city and its ruler becoming one. Most had no need to name it anything because the majority of its inhabitants were born there and died there, and never left.

It was surrounded by walls that served not just to protect it from invaders, but to remind its population how blessed they were to live inside. The walls were of enormous blue and rose marble blocks, inlaid with whorls of gold. The skins of past exiles hung as banners, covered in obscene tattoos of entwined limbs and tormented bodies. Below the walls were the exile grounds where those banished from the city clawed at the base of the walls and wept that they would never again look on the face of Shalhadar. A few of them were kneeling there now below the wall, pale and shaven-headed, wearing the torn and stained silks of the city's castes. Whatever their crime, there was only one punishment – to be cast out of the city of pleasures and condemned to starve, incapable of surviving without the city around them.

The Imperial Fists strike force had passed an army from the city on their way towards the marble walls. Several thousand cultists, armed with flintlocks and clubs with obsidian blades, wrapped in silks around gilded armour. The riding beasts carried outriders at the army's flanks, and up close Lysander could see the beasts' flickering tongues and asymmetrical black orb eyes, daemon-bred and warped by the influence of Malodrax.

Lycaon had brought the strike force swiftly to the shadow of the city, evading Shalhadar's troops on the way. At Lycaon's command the strike force broke out of the cover of the low hills around the walls, across the open ground towards the nearest gates.

The exiles looked around from their weeping-places at the wall to see thirty Space Marines rushing towards the gates. Some whimpered at the sight, some did nothing. One stood and took a couple of faltering steps towards Lysander as he ran alongside Squad Kaderic.

'You,' said the exile, a man whose face was streaked with grime and tears, and bearing the marks of a recent beating on his pale skin. 'You will end it. I knew it would be you…'

The deep lowing of alarm horns sounded up on the walls as Lycaon brought the Imperial Fists within a pistol shot of the gate. The gate itself was almost the height of the wall, purplish wood banded with iron – sturdy enough, but not designed by a fortress-builder like Dorn.

'Gorvetz!' ordered Lycaon. 'Bring them down!'

The Devastator squad halted and braced their weapons, aiming up at the great hinges holding the enormous doors. Techmarine Kho's twin Land Speeders thundered overhead, nose cannons spraying the top of the wall where defenders were gathering to fire down at the attackers.

The art of the siege was beloved of Rogal Dorn. He had written volumes on the subject that still guided the Imperial way of war to that day. But Dorn knew that there was one way for the endless armies of the Imperial Guard to take a city, and another way for the Space Marines. The Imperial Guard would spend months moving men and machines into position, setting artillery positions to bombard the target city and gradually forging closer to the walls in trenchworks and tunnels until demolition squads could rush forth and bring the walls down, or until artillery could be brought close enough to shell the city within at will. It was a bloody and drawn-out business, where the will to stay the fight was of greater importance than skill or experience.

What the Imperial Guard did with big guns and endless manpower, the Space Marines did with shock and with speed. In the kind of battle for which he had been created, each Space Marine was worth an army. Once through the breach he could visit the kind of violence on an enemy-held city that a whole regiment of Imperial Guard might wreak. First he had to get in, and to do that he used all the speed and ruthlessness the Emperor's own teachings and the blood of his primarch had given him.

Squad Gorvetz's plasma cannon and heavy bolters blasted chunks out of the doors, blowing the fittings free that held them to the marble pillars on either side. One door sagged in, the final hinge giving way under its weight, and it crashed to the ground with a sound like a peal of thunder. Choking masses of rubble dust flared up where it fell.

'Onwards!' ordered Lycaon, before the echoes had died. The Imperial Fists followed their Chaplain through the gate, ignoring the pattering of fire from the few defenders who had reached the walls in time to see the gate fall.

It was a terrible familiarity that Lysander felt as the dust around him cleared and he emerged into the grand road that led from the breached gate. There was gold and silver everywhere, plating the slabs beneath his feet, swirling up the walls of the pleasure domes and temples lining the road. Fat emeralds and rubies studded the marble walls.

Down the thoroughfare roared the daemon host of Shalhadar, the prince's handmaidens and viziers, the courtiers who danced around him eternally. They were things of the warp just as much as the Grey Hungers or the Red Widow, but where those were horrific, Shalhadar's host had an appalling beauty. They were humanoid in shape, but elongated and sharp-featured, as if the shape of a human being had been stretched and tapered by a sculptor on a futile quest to make it perfect.

They wore the features of male and female, jumbled together on the same daemon as if to further divorce them from a sane concept of beauty. Their torsos were snakelike and muscular, their eyes enlarged black pools, skulls elongated to accentuate their swept features. They wore silks and harnesses of black leather, claws of glinting amethyst chitin, black talons for toes, vestigial wings, tentacles in place of hands, ridges of waving fleshy protuberances along the spine or breast-bone, smiling mouths inscribed into their flesh, purple tattoos or raised pinkish scars – each was different, each the work of a mad artist's lifetime.

Shalhadar's court had its dancers, musicians, scribes and advisors. All of them were there, sent from Shalhadar's palace to intercept the intruders who defiled his city. They might have been gifted by the warp to beautify the court, but they were still predators, still killers filled with the warp's own malice.

One, clad in a spectacular construction of silks that flowed behind it like the fronds of a sea creature, threw its head back and screeched. The others took up the cry. Claws snapped. Tongues lashed, long and spiny. Lysander's battlefield instincts told him the Imperial Fists faced more than a hundred daemons. His oaths as a Space Marine told him the galaxy would soon be a hundred daemons less.

Lysander drew his chainblade. The Fist of Dorn, his power hammer, was in Kulgarde somewhere in the hands of Kraegon Thul. He would rather have the hammer in his hand now, but a chainblade was the weapon he had trained with and he put faith in what he knew it could do.

'The enemy shows his face!' cried out Chaplain Lycaon. 'And he but begs us to cut off his head!'

The Imperial Fists charged as one. The daemons rushed to meet them. Lysander ran alongside the brothers of Squad Kaderic. Brother Halaestus was beside him, firing his bolter from the hip with one hand as he drew his combat blade with the other. Halaestus's eyes were blank, as if he were focusing on something far away. Lysander barely had time to register the look on his face before the first of the daemons was within a lunge of his chainblade.

Lysander waited a split second more. His target was

sprinting right at him on legs with knees bending the wrong way. It had a claw for one hand and a jewelled dagger in the other, its gilded blade sheened with greenish venom. Its face was a horror, noseless and with a round lamprey-like mouth. Its ugliness was only enhanced by the pink and purple silks wrapped around it, too thin to hide the slithering knots of its muscles and the pallid expanse of its skin.

A thrust with the chainblade would have impaled the daemon through the gut but left Lysander open to a dagger in the back of the neck, and perhaps the point would find a seal or gap in his power armour and hit home. As the battle around him seemed to slow down, Lysander's mind automatically accessed the years of battle-lore a Space Marine learned from the moment he was chosen to join the Adeptus Astartes.

Lysander let the daemon come within the arc of a chainblade's swing. He swept the blade in front of him, squeezing on the activation stud to send the chainteeth churning. The daemon was caught in the midriff, skin and bone chewed up by the blade.

Lysander ducked to one side and caught the dagger on his shoulder guard. It rang off harmlessly. He brought his free hand up to block the claw snapping down at his head, and for a moment was face to face with the daemon.

This thing of the warp, the abomination, had about it a grace that Lysander could not deny. A man could go mad to look at it, captivated by the movements of its sinuous body, obsessed and desiring. It was in this way that such a daemon corrupted and destroyed. Perhaps lesser minds, already broken down by the galaxy's cruelty, had fallen to it. Not a Space Marine.

Lysander clamped his hand around the back of the daemon's head, where its skull erupted into a crown of fleshy feelers, and rammed it face-first onto the paving slabs of the road. He drew back his chainblade and stabbed it down through the back of the daemon's neck. The chainteeth ground through spine and sinew, and the daemon's head came free in a spray of blue fire.

Lysander tore the chainblade free and took stock of his surroundings. Imperial Fists and daemons were duelling, glowing blood sprayed across the gilded pavements. Beside him Halaestus wrestled with a daemon with four tentacles in place of arms. Halaestus rolled on top of the daemon and drove his combat knife down into its face again and again until it was a smouldering ruin.

Lysander grabbed Halaestus's shoulder guard and pulled him up. 'There are plenty more to kill!' he shouted over the gunfire and the screeching of the daemons.

For a moment Halaestus looked at Lysander with that same blank look. Then a light went up behind his eyes and he nodded his understanding.

There were more daemons than Imperial Fists, but these creatures had never faced Space Marines before. Chaplain Lycaon threw one aside and lunged at another, slicing it in two from shoulder to hip with his crozius. The discharging of the power field was like a lightning bolt falling into the middle of the fight and the Imperial Fists surged forwards as if it were an omen sent from Dorn himself.

Past the daemon ranks, beyond the closest spires and domes of Shalhadar's city, rose the pyramid of its palace. Lysander recognised the patterns of blue and gold covering its sides, picked out in precious stones and silver filigree.

If the Imperial Fists were to do what they came to Malodrax to do, if Lysander were to do his duty to the brothers he had left behind here, the palace would have to fall. The man knew this, and looked ahead to storming the bejewelled walls. The soldier kept fighting, focusing entirely on tearing apart the enemies that fate had put in front of him.

6

'I spoke with one of them, the creatures indigenous to this world, evolved or mutated, I surmised, from human stock an aeon ago. His people were nomads, travelling the hidden paths between Malodrax's perils. I told him that I was from the world beyond his planet's sky, and it was then I realised he had no concept of a planet at all. To him his world was a gallery of hells, linked by the paths his forefathers had forged, and beyond them could exist nothing.'

– Inquisitor Corvin Golrukhan

IT WAS, BY Lysander's reckoning, rather more than two days since he had crawled into the effluent channels leading to the fortress's sump. Forging through the filth had helped hide him among the dregs of the fortress's lower levels, catacombs, tunnels and half-collapsed cathedral domes that maintained a society of mutants and xenos. From what Lysander had seen they served little purpose in the fortress except to survive there, like colonies of fungus or nests of vermin, with the most able of them skimmed off to serve in the forge levels above. The uppermost fortress, the battlements themselves, were the barracks and sparring halls of the Iron Warriors, but beneath them was the bleak anarchy of these malformed dregs.

Lysander had made his way upwards, towards the forges and assembly vaults. The place was a factory as well as a fortress, with its forges producing parts for war machines assembled by armies of menials. The only way out of the place was to go up, even though that would bring him closer to the Iron Warriors who would even now be scouring the fortress for him.

There had been close calls. Lysander had broken the necks of mutants who paid him more than a glance. In any other company his size would make it impossible to hide, but the mutants included plenty of the huge muscular brutes among them and Lysander, hooded in rags, could pass for one of them. No Iron Warrior would be fooled, even at a distance, and Lysander had seen patrols of them marching through the mutant hovels looking for him. It was in a ruin of a previous city, crushed among the fortress's foundations, that they had come the closest, and Lysander had lurked in the plentiful shadows as a five-strong squad played the sights of their bolters across the hosts of mutants that cowered when they passed. If one of them had broken off from the squad and poked around in the heaps of rags that passed for the inhabitants of the hovel where

Lysander had hidden, he would have been found. And he would have been shot down where he stood, because Warsmith Thul could only have ordered that Lysander be executed out of hand rather than risk him escaping again.

It was in the forges that Lysander realised he could rise no higher and still hope to stay hidden. He found himself in an enormous stone vault where gangs of menials and mutant labourers hauled massive segments of armour and machinery towards the half-finished war engines that dominated the vast space.

Lysander counted a dozen engines in various states of completion, some little more than enormous metal skeletons, others looming hulks that looked ready to ride on massive grinding wheels or spiderlike legs. One was shaped like a steel dragon rearing up, its shoulders supporting massed batteries of cannon. Another was a turtle-like hulk, countless layers of armour surrounding sally ports to deliver hordes of troops into the heart of an enemy army. Still another, apparently complete, was a mobile idol of a lizardlike god-figure on an altar that moved on spiked rollers. Steel cauldrons held mounds of bones and skulls, and fuel tanks on the figure's back were hooked up to an enormous flamethrower wrought into the god's mouth. Hundreds of guns studded the shoulders and torso like spines.

It was a weapon of terror, the image of a power of the warp to terrify the defenders of a besieged city as it rumbled towards the walls spewing fire and crushing fortifications. Dozens of menials scrabbled across it, hammering its final armour plates into place.

Lysander took all this in as he waited in the shadows, away from the light of the fires used to bend the plates of armour being prepared for installation on the steel skeletons. The idol-machine was the most complete war machine, possibly ready to roll out from the gates of Kulgarde and into whatever waited in Malodrax beyond.

Lysander worked his way closer to the idol machine. It was several storeys high and the workers on it looked like insects scuttling across its surface. As Lysander watched one fell from the idol's shoulder, his death going unnoticed by the workers who laboured around the rollers where he landed. Taskmasters, brute-mutants like the ones Lysander had tried to resemble, laid into the workers with whips and prods. One spotted Lysander and trudged towards him, a slab of muscle with the features of its face barely discernible. It wore random segments of armour, plain gunmetal like the armour of the Iron Warriors, strapped to its grotesque body.

'You!' it growled. 'Who is your god?'

Lysander did not know the answer. Presumably there was some power of the warp he could name that would satisfy the taskmaster, but a sane man did not seek to know their names.

'I am here to work,' said Lysander. 'I am strong.'

The taskmaster drew a barbed whip and lashed it at

Lysander. The bladed tip cut a deep gash into Lysander's shoulder and Lysander dropped to one knee. The pain was like nothing to a Space Marine, but Lysander knew that tyrants loved to see supplication from those they made suffer.

'To work?' demanded the taskmaster. 'You who have no brand upon him? What creature is this that knows not his place! Overseer Gortz will cut out your guts and twist them into ropes for the catapults!'

Lysander glanced up at the closest mutant worker, who was deliberately focusing on his work and not watching the taskmaster berating Lysander. Lysander could just spot the raised skin on the worker's face, almost lost among the fronded gills around his neck. A brand was scorched deep into the mutant's features. Lysander had no such brand. It was the mark of the taskmaster's work-gangs, and anyone without it was an intruder.

'It was Gortz who sent me,' said Lysander, invoking the name of whatever creature he hoped was lord of this forge hall.

The taskmaster spat a wad of bloody phlegm into the floor. 'If your body is as weak as your lies,' he said, 'you could lift no hammer for me. And I have no use for the weak.' The taskmaster gripped Lysander's chin and forced his head up, so he had to look into the taskmaster's bestial face. 'Except,' it said, 'as food.'

Lysander knocked the taskmaster's hand aside and grabbed it by the throat. He stood up to his full height, lifting the massive mutant up off the floor. For the first time the taskmaster was able to appreciate Lysander's full size, as his feet kicked out half a metre above the flagstones.

The taskmaster drew its whip hand back and lashed the weapon at Lysander, who caught the strip of leather with his free hand and threw the taskmaster down to the floor. Before the mutant could get back to his feet Lysander planted a foot in its back and looped the whip around its neck.

Even as he was hauling on the whip to tighten it around the mutant's throat, Lysander was looking up and gauging the consequences. The mutant workers were well aware of what was happening, but they did nothing – most of them wouldn't even watch. They were so used to being the slaves of the taskmaster, so used to being punished for looking it in the eye, that it did not occur to them to defend the mutant. Even so, the taskmaster fancied itself important, and it would be missed sooner or later. Lysander had played his hand. He had to get out of the fortress now, here, before the Iron Warriors learned of the Space Marine-sized intruder killing their underlings in the shadow of the war machines.

The taskmaster had fallen still. Lysander dropped the whip, kneeled down and wrapped an arm around its throat, wrenching its neck and snapping its spine to make sure it would not wake up.

Lysander hurried towards the war machine ahead of

him, the enormous siege-idol. He ignored the workers around him as he reached the foot of the idol, where the huge spiked roller had sunk into the flagstones of the floor. Lysander found a handhold among the battered steel plates and began to climb towards the war machine's idol.

He climbed quickly. It was not a usual mode of transport for a Space Marine, but an Imperial Fist had to be ready to climb, leap, swim and crawl as the battle demanded it. The idol was easy to climb, with plentiful handholds among its armour plates and carvings, and in a few minutes Lysander had reached the altar. The surface of the altar was already scored and stained with evidence of past sacrifices, and doubtless many more would be required before this war machine could be permitted to rumble out of the fortress into Malodrax.

There was, realistically, only one way out of the fortress of Kulgarde. Lysander had known from the start that he would not simply walk out. It was a risk, this way, but less of a risk than staying in the fortress waiting to be hunted down by the Iron Warriors. If he died here, he would die seeking to escape, because only by first escaping could he avenge whatever happened to his battle-brothers at the hands of the Bone Sculptors.

The idol itself was a more difficult climb, with its overhangs and smooth expanses of stone. Lysander made for the head, for he knew the conceit of the builders would probably have put any command systems there. Whoever drove it would look through the eyes of the idol so they could fancy themselves the equivalent of that huge stone god, and see the fear of the soldiers in their way as they looked up at its hideous face. He was aware of a commotion below him as word finally spread of the taskmaster's death and workers from other gangs were gathering at the foot of the siege idol to watch the intruder whose death would surely win them a higher status in the forges.

Lysander reached the face, finding useful handholds among the fangs and twisted lips. Above him was an eye socket and sure enough it was glazed with the winking lights of a cockpit or bridge beyond. Lysander forced his way up into the eye socket and kicked at the glass, feeling it crack and bow under him.

Gunfire stuttered below him and shots flew wide, pinging off the stone face. The glazing collapsed and Lysander fell through into the interior of the siege idol's head.

In the cramped bridge were four or five human forms, merging with the baroque technology and ironwork of the siege engine's interior. It was difficult to tell how many there were for they were fused with the metal and the machinery of the siege idol's command systems. Their faces, glazed-eyed and barely conscious, rolled towards Lysander as he fell down on top of them, their brittle bones crunching under his weight.

'War machine!' demanded Lysander. 'Answer me!'

More gunfire was spattering up at the shattered eye socket. Lysander could see through the banks of machinery to the cavity beyond the second eye socket, similarly crammed with fused human forms. Gunshots punched through the glass. Lysander could hear more shouting voices below. Soon the Iron Warriors would know, and then Lysander would be trapped here.

'War machine!' he repeated. 'Whatever you are, however you were created, I am Lysander of the Imperial Fists! I can lead you out of this place! I can give you freedom!'

The siege idol lurched. Lysander planted a hand in dried, stringy flesh to find a handhold and keep himself upright. Machinery ground deep within the war engine with a sound like an avalanche. The eyes of the fused corpses opened, revealing their dried-out eyeballs, their mouths working as if trying to speak.

The rear wall of the cockpit split and receded, revealing a dark maw of iron beyond. Shards of metal split off from the wall, hovering in front of Lysander as they spun and converged.

Lysander's stomachs recoiled. He was in the presence of witchcraft. The whole fortress of Kulgarde was a foul place, corrupted right down to the stones of its foundations – but this was pure darkness, warp-magic worked right before his eyes.

The metal formed twin pits, where bright silver shards glinted in place of eyes. The lips of a mouth. Two slits in place of a nose. It was an inhuman face, somehow more grotesque for being an indistinct result of the metal fragments as they spun and flitted.

'Freedom?' said a voice that took its form from the grinding of the siege idol's engines far below. 'There is no freedom. What is this thing? A dream? A lie? Nothing of the warp is free. You cannot offer me that, strange fleshy thing, Lysander of the Imperial Fists.'

'Daemon,' said Lysander. He tasted bile in his mouth and his skin crawled such that it was a wonder it did not tear itself from his back.

'What,' replied the siege idol, 'did you expect?'

'Move from this place,' said Lysander. 'Start your wheels and break out of this fortress. Seek your own destiny on Malodrax. Do not serve the Iron Warriors.'

'And in doing so, save you from Kulgarde?' replied the daemon. 'So you might ride me to your own freedom as a bird rides the wind? And why would I do such a thing, Lysander of the Imperial Fists, when Warsmith Thul can give me a thousand years of war? A million bodies ground beneath my tracks? An ocean of blood in which to wallow? What is it that you can grant me that I might desire?'

Lysander forged his way back to the idol's eye socket and risked a glance down. Hundreds of menials were surrounding the siege idol, jostling to get a look at the strange intruder who had killed the taskmaster and forced his way into their war engine. There were other taskmasters among them, cracking menials' heads to make their way through the crowd, or arguing with one another about what to do.

'You don't know, do you?' taunted the daemon, the

note of its engines rising in amusement. 'This slave of the dead god, this whelp of mankind. Your tiny mind cannot comprehend what one such as I could possibly desire.'

Lysander turned back to the daemon's face. 'You want blood,' he said.

'Blood?' The daemon laughed, the sounds of pistons falling and engine chambers thundering. 'I have all the blood I could want! A thousand men already have been butchered on my altar! My very steel was quenched in blood when it was first bent upon the anvil! Blood? What need have I of blood? Before Warsmith Thul commanded me forth, I presided over a great arena in the warp, where the blood of a million gladiators filled the place to the brim every night!'

'An arena,' said Lysander. His mind was working fast, trying to outpace his revulsion at being in the presence of such a being.

'The greatest altar of the Blood God!' cried the daemon. 'A great ocean of hate in the warp! I stood upon the parapet and at my signal half a million men slit the throats of the other half, and at my word the survivors battled for the glory of having my eye fall upon them! And you, fleshy thing, will never know that glory, to see two great champions butcher one another in your name. Your imagination cannot stretch to such wonders.'

'And you prefer this tomb of steel,' said Lysander, 'to ruling as lord of your arena?'

'You cannot give me what I once had,' replied the daemon.

'You have doubt, daemon,' said Lysander. 'There is more human in you than you would admit.'

The daemon's face loomed larger, its metal components shuddering and spinning with anger. 'I am not like you. My kind were ancient before your existence was even possible. Do not compare us, Lysander of the Imperial Fists.'

'And yet we are in the same situation. We both want something. I want to get out of this fortress, and you want to be lord of the arena again. There might be nothing else in common between us, but we both desire. Tell me I do not speak the truth, daemon.'

The daemon's face receded. It did not reply. Its engines thrummed angrily, a low growl of frustration.

Lysander knew it would do him no good to argue with this being further. He would only give it the chance to spin lies, or waste his time until the Iron Warriors came to oversee the storming of the siege engine and the execution of Lysander. He pulled himself back through the idol's shattered eye socket and out onto the stone face.

A cry went up from the labourers gathered to watch. Gunfire stuttered up at Lysander, wide and ill-disciplined, sparking stone chunks out of the idol's face. Lysander let go of his handhold and fell down past the face and chest, landing in a heavy crouch as he slammed into the stained surface of the altar.

'Overseer Gortz!' yelled Lysander. 'Lord of this vault! Will you stand by while this intruder defies you? Or will you take his head and throw it at the feet of your Warsmith?'

A bellowed order split the crowd below. One of the huge taskmaster mutants, who could only be Overseer Gortz, shouldered his way to the front – a massive creature, bound in muscle sliding beneath skin that was a mass of scar tissue. One of its hands had been replaced with a mechanical steel claw, more like an industrial tool than a weapon, and in its other it carried a club almost as long as Lysander was tall, a length of steel square in cross-section studded with spikes and well-stained with the blood of menials.

Gortz reached the base of the siege idol and began to climb. The crowd began to chant his name as it got closer to the altar where Lysander stood.

Lysander was very aware he was not armed. There had been nothing in the cockpit that would have made a passable weapon. One of the bone cauldrons was within arm's reach and Lysander grabbed the largest bone there, perhaps a femur from a pack beast or oversized mutant, long and heavy enough to serve as a club.

Gortz reached the altar to a cheer from the crowd. Up close his face was a horror, a mask of torn and hanging skin through which could be seen the bloodied bone.

'You dare?' growled Gortz. It was all the introduction Lysander supposed he would get.

Lysander dropped back half a step and Gortz took the

BEN COUNTER

bait, swinging with his club. Lysander ducked it and the
club smashed shards of stone out of the idol. Gortz followed up with his claw, stabbing it down as it snapped
shut, aiming to grab Lysander around the shoulder so
its blades would cut down into his upper torso.

Lysander rammed the femur up into the claw, jam-
ming it for a moment. The blades of the claw crunched
through the bone but by then Lysander had swivelled
out of the way and was face to face with the mutant.

Lysander matched him in height. Gortz's musculature was grotesque, more massive and powerful than
a Space Marine's build. A Space Marine was trained to
see such things as an advantage in his favour instead
of a weapon in the enemy's hand. Gortz was stronger,
perhaps, in a raw and brutal sense, but that slowed
him down. It meant he could not react quickly enough
when Lysander drove the heel of his right hand up into
Gortz's massive jaw, splintering bone as it snapped the
mutant's head back.

Lysander rammed his knee into the mutant's groin,
not pausing to wonder what might actually be there.
His left hand hooked Gortz's forward leg and threw
Gortz onto his back. The mutant sprawled onto the
altar and Lysander was on him, both knees dropping
into the mutant's abdomen, right fist punching over
and over down into his face. The ravaged face was a
mask of gore, the bone of the eye sockets and jaw open
to the air, bloodshot eyes rolling.

Gortz's only move was to snap the claw at Lysander's

neck. Lysander knew it was coming before Gortz did. He leaned back and the claw passed over his face. Lysander grabbed Gortz's elbow and wrenched it, feeling the joint part and the tendons snap, the claw hanging useless.

Gortz roared as the claw clattered to the surface of the altar. The mutant tried to raise his other arm, dropping the club to claw at Lysander's face with his fingers. Lysander caught Gortz's hand in his own, forcing it back down to the altar. A philosophy of unarmed combat that Space Marines learned – one among many – stressed the isolation and neutralisation of an enemy's individual joints. The sleep-taught technique came to the front of Lysander's memory as he forced Gortz's wrist around and placed his palm down on the elbow, and put all his strength into forcing the hand up in the wrong direction.

Gortz's forearm snapped with a sound like a gunshot. Lysander took his weight off Gortz and turned him over, kneeling now in the small of the mutant's back. He wrapped an arm around Gortz's neck and forced his head back, so he was looking up at the stone face of the mutant looming down above the altar.

'Here, daemon!' yelled Lysander. 'Here is the champion of your arena laid low! Do you want his head? Shall I hold it up as a trophy? Give me what I want, daemon, and you will live your glory again!'

The crowd were silent below. They had expected to see Gortz victorious, as he must have been countless times before while rising to the rank of overseer. Now one of them cried out, a long, keening howl of sorrow and disbelief. Others joined him and in a few moments the sound filled the vault.

The sound of the siege idol's engines growled and thundered, and resolved into a low, grinding laughter. It echoed the cries of the menials below, mocking them even as they fell to their knees and tore at their skin in distress.

The siege idol lurched forwards on its rollers, and menials scattered to keep from being crushed. The idol moved forwards towards the back wall of the vault, crunching through segments of armour and equipment laid ready to be installed on the half-finished war machines.

The siege idol accelerated towards the back wall of the vault.

Lysander had given it what it wanted, in return for a chance of freedom. It was a deal with a daemon – there was no way he could pretend it was anything else. But this was the way it had to be. This was the way he would avenge his lost brothers, and give himself a chance to save those who still lived down there in the guts of Kulgarde Fortress.

The thought was broken as the siege idol gathered speed. Standing on the altar mounted on the front of the war machine, Lysander would be crushed when the idol hit the wall and the huge chunks of masonry started to fall. Lysander threw Gortz to one side and jumped off the altar, grabbing the idol's arm and swinging to the side of the war machine.

Lysander clambered along the armour plates covering the machine's side, where gun ports shaped into grimacing daemons' mouths made for some easier handholds.

With a deafening grinding sound the rollers at the front met the wall and the siege engine rode up as blocks of masonry shifted and split. Enormous slabs of it fell and kicked up clouds of pulverised rock. The siege engine forced its way through the wall, engines screaming as they worked up to maximum rev and gouts of flame bursting from the exhaust ports on the machine's back.

One block of stone, the size of a building, tumbled down towards Lysander, smashing off armour plates as it fell. Lysander leapt off the side of the war machine before it could crush him, covering his head and rolling with the fall. Everything was earthquake and thunder, the heat from the machine's engines and the battering of stone against his body.

Somewhere in the chaos Lysander landed. The noise barely died down as the siege idol ground forwards ahead of him. He had come to rest just past the vault's back wall, where the structure of the fortress had given way to smaller chambers now torn through and shattered by the idol's passage. Among the rubble he could see an eclectic mix of war trophies – captured banners, weapons and armour, scattered and crushed by the sudden destruction. Lysander waved away the worst of the rubble dust choking him and a bright silver gleam caught his eye – the polished chrome casing of an alien weapon, like an oversized rifle with a barrel made up of interlocking crystal shards. He recognised one of the banners on the wall, embroidered with the rose and skulls of an order of the Sisters of Battle, hanging beside a crude rendering of a stylised bestial head probably taken from a defeated ork warlord.

Lysander rummaged through the debris. The Iron Warriors kept captured arms and armour here, and there might well be something he could use. Even if he got out of Kulgarde into Malodrax, he would have a far better chance of surviving whatever the planet had to throw at him if he was armed.

He threw aside another alien firearm, something like a multi-barrelled cannon with barrels consisting of living wormlike creatures stretched out over a black steel hub. A sword he found had been fine once, but the falling masonry had shattered its long, elegant blade – he thought it might have been alien in design, too, perhaps a weapon of the eldar, or a particularly fine example of pre-Imperial craftsmanship.

A warmth rose in both his hearts as his hands closed on a familiar hilt. A chainsword – an Imperial Fists chainsword, taken from one of his squad. He held it up and gave himself a second to look along its length, the golden livery and fist symbol of his Chapter emblazoned on the weapon's casing. It was undamaged, its chainteeth still bright and sharp.

The sound of something huge landing among the debris behind him was all the warning Lysander got. By the time he turned to see his assailant a meaty fist clubbed into him and threw him aside. He kept his grip on the chainsword but felt his arm pinned as Overseer Gortz leapt on top of him.

Gortz's torso had split open and from his back had grown a new limb to replace the arms broken by Lysander moments before. It was sinewy and raw, the skinless muscle oozing blood, but it was strong and its malformed hand was gripping Lysander's sword arm.

Gortz roared as his battered face, too, split open. A second set of jaws, with an array of sharp teeth, was forced out of the front of his skull. He was mutating second by second, the second jaws opening wider than his humanoid mouth could have, revealing a wet red tendril of a tongue.

Lysander groped in the rubble with his free hand, trying to find a chunk of stone. Instead he found something less weighty but just the right size for his hand. He brought it up, smacking it into the side of Gortz's mutating head.

It was a book. The metal fastenings and lock gave it a hard edge, and the thousands of pages were packed densely enough to give it weight. Attached to it was a chain, as if it could be hung from a belt or looped over a shoulder. Lysander changed his grip to the chain and swung it like a flail, battering Gortz's head back two, three times. One of the fittings came away, embedded in the side of the mutant's skull. Hot blood sprayed down over Lysander's face.

The grip on his sword arm loosened. Lysander pulled his hand free and rammed the chainblade into Gortz's upper chest, forcing down the motor's activation stud. The chainteeth growled as they churned through the bone and muscle of Gortz's ribcage. Lysander forced the chainsword down, sawing through sternum and ribs.

Gortz's head hung limp, the second jaws yawing wide and the tongue lolling. Lysander pushed Gortz off him and made sure of the kill with a thrust through that mutant head. He looked down at the book hanging by the chain he held in his other hand.

Being A Description Of Malodrax And Its Foulness, read the title. Beneath that was branded on the leather cover the stylised 'I' of the Inquisition.

A Space Marine chainblade and a volume on this world apparently written by an inquisitor. Twin omens. It wasn't much, but Lysander would take it. And the book itself was hefty enough to serve as a reasonable weapon until he could find a better replacement. Lysander wiped the back of his hand across his face to get the worst of the blood off it, and walked around the drift of fallen debris to see the path the siege engine had taken through the body of the fortress. A crumbling tunnel had been driven through a mass of wreckage and destruction, and Lysander could still hear the rumbling of the siege idol's engines as it continued on its journey.

The Iron Warriors would definitely be down to

investigate the destruction, whether word had reached them of Lysander or not. He ran down the siege engine's path, noting the glimmer of ruddy light up ahead that could be sunlight. A wave of ashen air, tasting of dry earth and smoke, reached him, and he quickened his pace as the sounds of pursuers came from the vault behind him.

His first glimpse of Malodrax was of a grey-brown smudge under a discoloured sky, the siege idol rumbling off towards the broken horizon, two moons staring down through a mask of clouds like mismatched eyes. It was not an inviting landscape, but it was better than what he was leaving behind.

Lysander tightened his grip on his chainblade, and fled into Malodrax.

7

'The natural history of Malodrax is beyond understanding without first abandoning the principles of cause and effect. A creature might devolve into a new form, the fossils of its ancestors far exceeding it in sophistication. Others are born through sheer randomness, from the coalescing of raw warpstuff into a form that matches the definitions of life, from sheer bloody-mindedness, as if to prove that life can exist where there should be only death.'

– Inquisitor Corvin Golrukhan

THE SPHINX THAT guarded the palace of Shalhadar fought well. It flew down on wings of stained glass, the light of Malodrax's sun shimmering in a blinding rainbow of colours, its four front legs each sheathed in gilded claws. Its massive stone-clad chest and impassive face turned aside bolter fire as it descended, holes battered through its gold and lapis headdress. It landed on the bridge that crossed the canal before the gates of the palace and roared, a terrible sound that shattered the pyramid's grand windows and sent the golden gargoyles fleeing from their perches among the city's rooftops.

First Sergeant Kaderic called out the sphinx, taking on the role of Dorn's champion on this world. The sphinx, in turn, singled him out, and Kaderic dived and rolled between its enormous paws as it tried to crush him down into the bridge's jewel-studded surface.

Kaderic drove his chainsword into the sphinx's paw, hacking off a chunk of stony flesh. The sphinx reared back and, honour satisfied, Chaplain Lycaon gave the order to open fire. Squad Gorvetz opened up into the sphinx, blasting chunks from its body. The sphinx rampaged into the strike force, batting one Imperial Fist aside and forcing another down its gullet before the Imperial Fists charged in.

Lysander looked it in the eye. The sphinx returned the look, and even though it was surely dead, it smiled. Its lips, smeared with the blood of Lysander's battle-brother, cracked as they were forced into the unfamiliar expression. Lysander's chest flared with anger and he shouldered his way into the fray to drive his chainblade into the sphinx's side.

The sphinx said nothing. Even as Lycaon vaulted up onto its neck and hacked his crozius into the back of its neck, it fixed its eyes on Lysander in silence. Lysander grabbed a handhold on the side of its face and drove his chainblade into its eye, the teeth grinding through glass and stone. Thick, oily fluid sprayed out, something like blood and something like machine oil. The sphinx fell onto its side and Squad Kaderic fell on it like hunters butchering a kill, hacking the sphinx into gory chunks as the bridge was flooded with its blood.

'What was it?' asked Lycaon, when the sphinx was dismembered and only the jewelled gates lay between the strike force and the palace of Shalhadar.

'I know not,' said Lysander. 'A daemon. The guardian of the gates.'

Lycaon ordered the strike force to make ready to breach the gates of the palace. Space Marines stacked up beside the gates as Techmarine Kho, his Land Speeders hovering at the other end of the bridge to watch for enemies approaching, affixed magnetic breaching charges to the doors.

'It saw you,' said Brother Halaestus. He had walked up behind Lysander who took his place in the stack of Imperial Fists ready to storm through the gate. 'It knew you.'

It wasn't quite anger in Halaestus's face. It was a questioning, an aggression.

'This world knows me,' replied Lysander. 'Its creatures know me. Shalhadar learned of me, no doubt. Few escape from Kulgarde, and fewer still go back.' He turned to the gates, but Halaestus grabbed his arm and turned him round again.

'Did you come back for us alone?' demanded Halaestus. 'Or did you have help?'

'Breach!' yelled Techmarine Kho. The Imperial Fists

backed against the pyramid wall as the charged detonated, blowing the gates off their hinges and locks. They fell in and before they had hit the floor the Imperial Fists were charging into the shadows beyond, fingers on triggers and chainswords in hand.

'Shalhadar!' yelled Lycaon. 'The eye of the Emperor reaches you even here! Even in this foul place you are not beyond His hand!'

Inside the palace, the shadows resolved into the pyramid's interior. Pastel-coloured silken drapes and intricate tapestries of intertwined bodies hung from walls tiled in a mosaicked riot of colour. Geometric tiles picked out infinitely complex designs on the floor, shimmering fractals that baffled the eye and the brain. The high curving ceilings, their petal-shaped panels interlocking high above, were covered in frescoes of dancing daemons draped in human skins, gambolling across heaps of flayed bodies. The place dripped with a lustrous corruption, enough to break and bewitch a weak mind.

Curving staircases swept upwards, leading to upper half-floors and balconies criss-crossing the pyramid's interior. 'Gorvetz!' ordered Lycaon. 'Scout above and cover us! Kaderic, with me!'

'Nothing up ahead,' voxed Kaderic, whose tactical squad was at the head of the strike force. His men swept their bolter sights across side chambers and galleries branching off in every direction. There were podiums for sermonising, surrounded by seats with spikes and restraints in the armrests. Baths of steaming perfumed water. Walls racked with implements for paring and skinning, with gold and ivory handles arrayed like glittering waterfalls of blades. But no enemies. 'We're alone in here.'

'You know better than that, First Sergeant,' replied Lycaon. Overhead armoured boots clattered on mosaic tiles as Squad Gorvetz got into position to cover the rest of the strike force from above. 'Lysander? What do you know of Shalhadar?'

'Lord of this city, absolute tyrant of his people. Disloyal thoughts are a crime.'

'Do you know how to kill him?' asked Lycaon.

'Cut him into pieces and burn them.'

'That is what the people of Malodrax say?'

'No,' replied Lysander. 'But that works on everything.'

The palace shuddered and a ripple of power ran across its every surface, sending sparks shimmering up Lysander's spine. The two squads on the ground floor drew together, every bolter trained on the corners from which an enemy might leap.

'The opening act left something to be desired,' came a voice echoing from all corners of the pyramid. It was drawling and arrogant, with an inhuman resonance that demanded respect in spite of the scorn that dripped from it. 'But that was just a taster, deliberately sour so our expectations were lowered. The death of my sphinx, rather dull. The blood in the streets quite unnecessary. But what follows will be the more delicious for it, will it not?'

'I will not match words with a foul-born daemon!' yelled Lycaon in reply. 'An Imperial Fist has a tongue of steel and a voice of gunfire!'

'Come, will you not allow me at least some drama?' came the reply. 'No agonising with the struggle of inflicting death? No conflict between duty and fear? But no, you are not like those who come to Malodrax as pilgrims to my majesty. You have not arrived in my city to seek something within yourselves, to kneel at the foot of a mighty throne. No, your tales are quite different. Your weakness is not worn on the outside. It is deep inside you. This second act will see that weakness being extracted from your flesh. I think I shall enjoy this production.'

Music began, a sick, pulsating skirl that brought the awful daemonic music on board the *Shield of Valour* to the front of Lysander's memory. Onto a balcony above the strike force somersaulted a lone figure in bright, clashing garb, with slashed sleeves and a hooded red and blue checked cloak, like a fool from a noble's court. The fool bowed and spread his hands, then straightened up and clapped briskly as if to signal the beginning of a stage act.

Chaplain Lycaon shot down the fool, and as far as Lysander could see from the body that fell from the balcony, it was human. The music changed tone to a fanfare and suddenly, everything was movement.

From the tapestries unravelled the shapes of cavorting daemons, their forms indistinct and malleable as if they had been picked out from only one angle in golden thread and in reality they were not all there. Shapes blistered up from the frescoes overhead, the painted daemons now come to life, dripping with colour as if they were composed of an artist's paint that had not dried. They left bright hand- and footprints on the ceiling as they scurried.

Squad Gorvetz hammered fire up into the daemons swarming towards them. Heavy bolters blew slabs of painted plaster down from the ceiling and the squad's heavy plasma gun left smouldering craters where it hit home. Bolter fire joined the heavy weapons, Gorvetz yelling orders to split up into fireteams and catch the daemons in a crossfire.

From the floor leapt fractal dancers, their shapes spiralling and breaking apart as they flipped and twirled. They defied the eye, leaving trailers of swirling colour wherever they went.

'It's a ruse,' said Lysander as the dancers and tapestry daemons closed. 'A performance. He wants to tie us down here. We have to push on through this.'

'First things first,' replied Lycaon, his crozius's power field shimmering into life.

The Space Marines of Squad Kaderic were caught by the assault. Bolter fire blasted a tapestry daemon apart, spraying multicoloured blood where its impossible form was ruptured. Kaderic dived into the fray as he always did, and Lysander lost sight of him in the coil of a fractal dancer that somersaulted around him as he struck about it with his chainblade. Lysander's own blade cut off the limb of a fallen fresco daemon that thudded into the floor beside him – it was a vivid red, its body the hub for a dozen limbs, amber-coloured eyes set into liquid sockets like polished gemstones in a pool of blood.

Lycaon finished off the daemon with his crozius, splitting it in two. It liquefied and the paint used to create it spread across the floor.

'Imperial Fists!' ordered Lycaon. 'We cannot tarry here! Shalhadar fears us and sends his lackeys to slow us down, but we will falter not one step! Onwards, my brothers! Onwards!'

A daemon rushed at Lysander, the threads of its body unravelling and reforming into claws to rend and hack. Lysander caught the claw on his shoulder guard and threw the daemon aside, trusting the blades and bolters of his fellow Imperial Fists to finish it off.

Ahead the pyramid was changing, the walls bowing out and balconies receding to form a vast auditorium centred on a semicircular stage. Background flats fell down onto the stage – a galaxy, a castle, heaps of bodies, distant mountains, all daubed with paint. Sparks fell in a burning rain and great globes of light flared into life above the stage, casting shafts of hard silvery light.

'The stage!' yelled Lysander. 'He exists in the story! He can be brought forth to die if the story is acted out!' Lycaon and Kaderic were fighting their way towards

Lysander, following him in the direction of the stage.

Banks of seating rose from the sloping floor like rows of teeth from a jaw. The ceiling soared up impossibly high, studded with royal boxes and half-formed statues like drowners breaching the marble surface. Darkness ran down the walls, the stage drawing the harsh light to it as if jealous. Lysander vaulted the seating even as the statues broke away from the walls, stone limbs broken at the joints to give them motion, animated by sparks of black fire dripping from their eye sockets.

Lysander smashed one aside. A hard stony hand grabbed him by the throat and wrestled him to the floor. Lysander was on his back before he could get his bearings, the blank stone face with its mouth gaping wide drooling black flame. Marble fingers found Lysander's mouth, gripping his jaw and forcing his own mouth open.

A crescent of burning light arced across Lysander's field of view, scorching a crimson slash onto his retinas. He rolled aside as the weight went off him and saw Chaplain Lycaon's follow-up swing taking the animated statue's head off, his crozius slicing through marble as if it were no stronger than flesh.

Lysander said nothing as Lycaon offered his hand. Lysander took it and was pulled back to his feet.

Dozens of the statues were crawling down the walls. Imperial Fists making it into the theatre were sniping them down as they advanced down the aisles towards the stage. Kaderic was leading them, crying out the name of Dorn and the fallen forefathers of the Imperial Fists.

'And so,' said Prince Shalhadar, 'the protagonist walks from the wings. And every story needs an end.'

Lysander reached the stage and swung himself up onto it. Chaplain Lycaon was beside him. First Sergeant Kaderic got there at the same time.

The light falling on the three Imperial Fists was fierce enough to burn. The rest of Squad Kaderic fighting in the auditorium were rendered shadows on shadows by the contrast.

'You know more about this Shalhadar,' said Lycaon. 'Willing to share anything further, captain?'

Any answer from Lysander was cut short as the scenery was consumed in a blast of multicoloured flame that rushed into the air above the stage and from which strode the form of Prince Shalhadar the Veiled.

The idealised human form, as chiselled by sculptors from one side of the galaxy to the other, was rendered in solid gold. It was achingly beautiful, painful to look at, with a face moulded into an expression of wisdom and sorrow, majesty and sympathy. A mortal sculptor could never match it. The geometry was too perfect, the emotion too vividly written, to be the product of an artist's hand. It was forged in the chill fires of the warp, where the thing that was Shalhadar had conjured its body to enthral and bewitch the humans it desired to serve it.

Shalhadar was three times the height of a man. He

had wings of feathered light. Stained glass was embedded in his golden form, in panels in his abdomen and chest depicting what a mortal mind might make of great powers of the warp – a knot of flesh and limbs, a great burning eye, a host of flying devils. His eyes were glass, deep green and blue, and a light shone through every panel illuminating the air around him as if he swam in a sea of colour.

In his hand he held a mace, its head a globe of filigreed gold containing a white flame like a caged sun. His other was fitted with gilded blades on each finger. He wore a cloth of crimson and blue around his waist, flowing in the warm incense-scented wind that accompanied the prince.

Prince Shalhadar's golden feet touched the boards of the stage as he descended.

Lysander realised that he was standing watching the daemon – not laying about him with bolter and chainsword, not rallying his battle-brothers to join him in killing Shalhadar. He was just standing there and watching him, and he could not move.

He imagined being bathed in pain, a sea of fire around him that would get worse and worse unless he could move. He imagined his mind a wall of diamond through which no influence could reach.

His hand twitched around the hilt of his chainsword.

'A fine entrance,' said Chaplain Lycaon. 'How many have fallen at your feet when they see it, daemon? How many minds did you break?'

Lysander forced his head around. Lycaon was grimacing, fighting to move. Kaderic, too.

Shalhadar leaned down close, his too-perfect, shining face a few centimetres from Lycaon's.

'As you reckon numbers, mortal, they are beyond counting. As the warp reckons them, but a drop in an ocean of obsession. But a whisper in the hurricane.'

Kaderic roared and brought his chainsaw down in a clumsy, swingeing blow, such as would shame a novice handling the weapon for the first time. Shalhadar, without looking, caught the chainsword in his clawed hand and turned, a smile on his gilded lips, towards First Sergeant Kaderic.

'And which role do you play?' said the daemon prince. 'The Fool? The Master? The Misbegotten One? Everyone has a role in the tale. Everyone plays it whether they know it or not.' The daemon cradled Kaderic's face in his claw, and pointed to Lysander with his mace. 'And your captain here has already played out plenty of scenes of his own. Do you know, First Sergeant, Chaplain Lycaon, the role Lysander took on while he languished on Malodrax? Do you know what he has done?'

A shot hammered out and Prince Shalhadar's head snapped to the side. A circular dent had been blasted into his temple. Through the blaze of light hovered the ruined face of Brother Halaestus, armour scored and smoking. Though Lysander could not see the mangled remains of the daemons he had cut his way through to get to the stage, there could be no doubt they lay behind him.

'No!' yelled Shalhadar. 'The story must be told!'

He swung his mace in a great arc that would have crushed Halaestus had he not thrown himself through the scenery flats before it smashed through the stage. Shalhadar grabbed Halaestus around the waist and held him up in the air, about to dash him back down against the stage.

Shalhadar's perfect face was blemished. The enthralling spell was broken. Lysander moved as if through glue, but he moved, and he dived at Shalhadar's back leg. Heavy, cold metal met him as he threw his full weight against Shalhadar. The daemon prince dropped to one knee, letting out a yell of anger that sounded like a great tolling bell.

Lycaon leapt onto the daemon prince, finding a handhold among the gemstones and glass studding Shalhadar's shoulder, so he was face to face with him. He drew back his crozius and slammed it down.

The power field discharged and split Shalhadar's torso from his shoulder down to his abdomen, shattered glass and jewels scattering in a bright rain across the stage. A fractured rainbow of light sprayed out, a multicoloured torrent of power that fountained from Shalhadar's sundered body. Lycaon was thrown off Shalhadar by the force of it, and Lysander just had time to see the Chaplain sprawling across the stage before the sheer madness erupting from Shalhadar overwhelmed his senses.

The question of what Shalhadar the Veiled actually

was could never be answered. It was, like everything born of the warp, immune to logic. The gilded body was a vessel for the real daemon, symbolic of Shalhadar's true nature but not identical to it. The daemon itself was an essence, a mind, a mass of thought, something incorporeal by human reckoning but a force as real as anything could be in the warp. Daemons could take on an infinite variety of shapes in realspace, and Shalhadar had no shape at all.

It was Shalhadar who saturated the theatre of his palace, flooding it with the mass of emotion and knowledge that comprised his true self. Lysander was blinded with colour and deafened by noise, swimming as if in an ocean surrounded by it.

He fought like a swimmer trying to reach the surface, but there was nothing to push against, no sense of direction. It was not a physical struggle that would show him the way.

Lysander turned his focus inwards. It was a technique taught early in a novice's conversion to a Space Marine, because it was in a state of internal contemplation that a novice was receptive to the hypno-doctrination that filled his mind with the Chapter's accumulated battle-lore. His mind fought against the sensory bedlam. Part of his mind, the part left over from the man he might have been had he never become an Imperial Fist, demanded that he curl into a ball and let unconsciousness sweep over him. But that part had been quiet for a long time.

His surroundings resolved into an ocean, burning

light below, moonless dark above. Lysander got his head above the surface. He knew this was not real – that in some sense he was still on the stage in Shalhadar's pyramid. But if he let that reach the forefront of his mind, he would sink and pass out.

The ocean churned. Gilded limbs broke the surface as a hundred Space Marines fought to stay afloat. The eyepieces of their white-painted helmets were shattered and they struggled blindly, thrashing at random to stave off a fate they did not understand.

A great looming presence in the darkness dominated the horizon. A mass of boiling rage, like the smouldering mountain of burning ash from a volcano. Twin cauldrons of fire roared into life, and the ocean of light turned a dark red with their reflection. Shalhadar's eyes narrowed as they fell on Lysander.

Lysander found rocks beneath his hands and feet. He hauled himself up onto a rocky shore, a scattering of islands just breaking the surface. 'Lycaon!' he shouted. 'Chaplain! First Sergeant!'

'Give me an enemy,' said a strained and hoarse voice beside Lysander, 'with a heart I can cut out and a head I can sever. Not this pit of lies.' First Sergeant Kaderic lay on the rocks, his armour scored and battered.

'Stay strong. Stay focused, brother. The daemon lies and evades us, but it is never invulnerable. It is never beyond justice.'

'The First?' said Shalhadar, indicating the Space Marines drowning in the endless ocean.

'My memory of them,' said Lysander. 'The daemon brings it forth to break me. It will not work.'

Shalhadar swarmed overhead, his dark mass lit from within by the flames of his eyes. There was something of that arrogance there, something of the tyrant who broke men's minds so he had a legion of them to worship him. If he had a true form, it was this – the raw desire for power, overwhelming and dark.

Lightning crashed down. Kaderic got to his feet and held his chainsword, still smouldering with daemon blood, up to the sky. 'Will you kill us with deceit, daemon?' he demanded. 'There is no lie that ever pierced a Space Marine's heart! Face us with steel or skulk back to the warp!'

Shalhadar's bellow was a crash of thunder and the blackness fell, roaring down onto Lysander and Kaderic. Lysander drove his chainblade up and felt it cutting through substance. Ropy black limbs swarmed around him and he cut about him, snapping and rending. Somewhere nearby Kaderic was roaring as he did the same thing, spitting curses at the daemon prince that constricted and writhed all around him.

The darkness split and tore. Lysander felt the blood-slicked boards of the stage under his feet. He spat out a mouthful of rancid blood and tore his chainblade free of Shalhadar.

Shalhadar's golden body lay on its side, its torso split open. The rubbery black mass of the prince's body writhed from the statue, its coils wrapped around

Chaplain Lycaon, who stood on the fallen statue. Lycaon brought his crozius arcanum up, the power field crackling around its blade, and brought it down in a bright arc of lightning.

In a burst of light Shalhadar was blasted open, shredded and dissolved in a gale of light and noise. Lysander was thrown onto his back beside Kaderic, who like him was slathered in Shalhadar's black-grey blood.

The glare in Lysander's eyes died down. He clambered back to his feet and helped Kaderic up. What remained of Shalhadar the Veiled was a few scraps of charred gold, in a splintered and burned hole in the stage. Chaplain Lycaon lay beside the wreck, stirring as he grabbed his fallen weapon.

Lysander and Kaderic pulled Lycaon to his feet.

'It is dead,' said Kaderic.

'It is banished,' replied Lycaon. 'Imperial Fists! The beast is defeated. Let us be gone from this place.'

THE WITHDRAWAL FROM Shalhadar's city took a few minutes. While reaching the palace the Imperial Fists had fought through hundreds of daemons sent from Shalhadar's court to stop them, but with the daemon prince abolished the resistance was gone.

Instead, there was a terrible wailing, coming from every doorway and window. In the street, in a gold-plated gutter, lay one of the city's citizens, curled up and mewling. Like many inhabitants he wore leather straps over pallid, pinkish skin, and he was marked with scars from whips and manacles. Whatever rites of passage the people of this city went through, it required a long period of torment and incarceration.

Lysander passed by the creature. It paid no attention to the Imperial Fists marching past.

'These people have lost their god,' said First Sergeant Kaderic beside him. 'This is the desolation that Chaos brings.'

'There will be another one for them,' replied Lysander. 'There is no shortage of would-be gods on this world.'

'Brother Lysander,' came Lycaon's voice over the vox-link. 'Join me at our head.'

Lysander quickened his pace to where Lycaon led the Imperial Fists, moving rapidly down the main thoroughfare towards the gate through which they had entered the city. They would be gone long before news of Shalhadar's death reached the city's forces outside the gates, and would be vanished into Malodrax's badlands before the prince's army had a chance to return and seek revenge.

'The daemon,' said Lycaon when Lysander was alongside him, 'is made of lies as we are made of flesh and bone. It is a being solely of deceit. Whenever it speaks it lies.'

'So have we been taught by the lessons of Dorn,' said Lysander. 'And so we have all seen.'

'Shalhadar's lie was the story,' continued Lycaon. 'A story is a sort of lie. He lived in a world that was not real, where everything obeyed the rules of his story.

Even his destruction was a part of that. Perhaps he saw himself as a tragic hero brought low by the random chance of the galaxy.'

'Or perhaps,' said Lysander, 'this is the end of a first act, and he will return in a thousand years for the finale.'

'Quite,' said Lycaon. 'And he lied to me, as well, right down to the final moment. Daemons have sought to do the same, of course, as has every enemy capable of a man's speech who thought it might do him good. Shalhadar turned to me, just as my crozius came down and he told me that he was surprised it was not you who laid him low.'

'Me?' asked Lysander.

'You said you were famous on this world. Could Shalhadar have heard of you?'

'There is no doubt,' said Lysander. 'He probably knew most of what happens on this planet. He could scarcely have remained a power on Malodrax if not.'

'And his words were intended to place doubt in my mind, that when you first came to Malodrax you somehow played a part in Shalhadar's story that you have not told us, as was his suggestion when we first encountered him?'

'Again, Chaplain, there is no doubt.'

The strike force reached the gates, still in ruins from when they had blown it off its mountings. They were marching now through the detritus of their battle with Shalhadar's daemon court, and the ground was littered with shell casings and scraps of arms and armour. The daemons themselves had dissolved away, leaving no more than bloodstains and scorch marks. Around the gate lay the city's exiles – they had run into the city as soon as the Imperial Fists were clear, but had been stunned into senselessness by the destruction of their god. They lay with eyes open, staring vacantly, as if there could be nothing in their world any more with Shalhadar gone.

'A crude lie, would you not say?' said Lycaon as the strike force marched through the shadow of the gateway. 'No great finesse. No devastating stroke to leave us confused and in doubt. Surely not the finest work a being like Shalhadar has ever wrought.'

'Shalhadar was faced with a superior force that could destroy him,' said Lysander. 'He was desperate. For all the daemon claims to be beyond human weaknesses, he can still know fear. He was afraid, and he clutched at what hope he could.'

A procession was crossing the road behind the strike force, ignoring the Imperial Fists. They were broken and weeping, hundreds of them, citizens of Shalhadar commemorating their dead god with blades and whips. They cut their skin and that of their neighbours, and when one fell from exhaustion or misery he was beaten into the ground by those who walked over him. One threw his head back and screamed, and the others turned on him as if he had begged them to, rending his flesh with their fingers and teeth to drown out their misery with blood.

Smoke coiled up from the gilded towers as others marked Shalhadar's death by setting light to everything around them. Shattered glass and screams of pain mingled with the cries of despair.

'This city will tear itself apart,' said Lysander.

'Good,' said Lycaon. 'Then we have done some righteousness here.'

The Land Speeders buzzed over the wall as the strike force passed through the gateway and out of Shalhadar's city. They had done there what Space Marines did – they descended on a place, left it a beheaded wreck, and never returned.

8

'An inquisitor learns not to speak of his acolytes for either good or ill, for he must accept that they will come and go as the attrition of his work claims their bodies and minds. Yet I cannot allow a man of the calibre of Kalastar Venn to go unsung, he who served me as shield-bearer and master of arms for three decades, who was claimed by nocturnal predators while standing vigil over our camp. Nor can I wash my hands of the fate of my Interrogator, Talaya, who deserved not to suffer betrayal – and yet had I not paid her to the tollkeeper, I would never have glimpsed the battlements of Kulgarde, and I am certain she would have accepted the sacrifice.'

– Inquisitor Corvin Golrukhan

THE STORM THAT raged across the badlands carried handfuls of flinty shards that bit at Lysander's face and back as he struggled through it. Malodrax knew he was there, he was sure of it, and it had thrown down shearing winds to grind him down and leave him a skeleton buried in a drift of rocks. He held up a hand in front of his face as he struggled towards the dark smudge that was all he could make of the landscape around him, and his palm was slashed open. He wore only layers of rags and the heavy hooded cloak he had found to disguise himself in Kulgarde, and they now clung to him in bloody strips.

He could die out here, if Malodrax decided he would. In the sky through the seething darkness a moon shone yellow-white, narrowed like a mocking eye. He could hear laughter on the howls of the wind. The ground was broken under his feet, constantly seeking to trip him up, and if he fell out here, exposed, he could be dead where he lay before the storm relented.

The ground fell away beneath his feet. His next step sent him tumbling into a ravine, head over feet down a slope of broken rock. More cuts opened up on his knees and elbows before he came to rest at the bottom of the gulley, down in the dirt.

Lysander had made it out of Kulgarde with two possessions aside from his rags. One was the book, and the other was the Imperial Fists chainsword. That represented everything he had in the galaxy. He was laid low, battered, bloody, alone and on his knees. He was everything a Space Marine should not be. A Space Marine was towering, noble, the reflection of the Emperor himself, and an Imperial Fist was even more than that – he was the legacy of Dorn, the continuing will of his primarch. On Malodrax Rogal Dorn was cut to pieces, weak, stranded and all but unarmed.

Lysander forced the thoughts out of his mind. A Space Marine did not know fear – the galaxy at large knew that. But more than that, he must never know despair.

The gulley ran in both directions, and Lysander could not see where it ended – it seemed to cut across the landscape, a deep scar dealt by some past catastrophe. He kicked some loose rocks aside and saw the brittle remains of bones there, gathered like trash in the corners. He saw a human jawbone, and the cranium of something that was not human. There was no telling how many ways this place had to kill someone. Lysander had to keep moving. And of the choice of two directions, the best bet was the one that took him further from the fortress of Kulgarde.

In the depths of the warren squatted the mother of the brood. The brood hatched from her belly, bursting from cysts in her skin, and they existed to feed her. From their substance she created more offspring and consumed them in turn, a cycle of life and death she had presided over for ten thousand years. She was born from the black blood of Malodrax, the filth of pure corruption that bubbled up from its depths, the pus of an infection that took root when the planet first felt the touch of the warp. The brood mother was everything that Malodrax was.

The first Lysander saw of her was the shadow she cast on the wall of her cavern. The place was hung with trophies and trinkets – bones, weapons, polished gemstones, hanks of filthy hair, rotted hunter's trophies, fragments of eggshells and ancient fossils. Her shadow was at once bloated and spindly, with a massively swollen torso and abdomen, skinny arms and a long, crooked neck supporting a head that hung low like that of a vulture. The shadow played across her collection, flaring with the guttering of the fire that burned in its pit before her.

'A shelterer from the storm,' said the brood mother. 'A fugitive from the embrace of our world. From her touch you have fled like a whipped child and now you come to me. Do you fancy my embrace to be more tender?'

'There is something I seek,' said Lysander.

'Of course there is,' said the brood mother. She pulled a squirming chunk of flesh from one of the glistening pods on her abdomen, and deftly spitted it on a sharpened stick. It squealed and flopped around, and the brood mother pushed the stick into the dirt, holding the morsel over the fire. Its flesh bubbled and spat. 'You smell of another world. There is a land far away where the people worship a dead god, and where that god's servants police their very thoughts. They fear Chaos such that they bow under a law that crushes them to death. A strange place, I have heard. Are you from that world, traveller?'

'What do you care where I am from?' replied Lysander. 'You are the brood mother. I am not the only one in this cave seeking something.'

The brood mother smiled and her face split open from ear to ear, exposing the sinews of her skull and the grey-brown stumps of her back teeth. 'You know of me? Oh, how flattering. Come closer. The fire does not reach you back there.'

Lysander took a few steps forward, into the glow of the fire. The blood on his hands and face glinted like jewels, where the accelerated clotting agents of a Space Marine had crystallised it into ruby clusters.

'Now that is something I have not seen for a long time,' said the brood mother. 'Something handsome.' She pulled the stick out of the fire and examined the charred specimen skewered on it. 'How long has it been since I had some new blood? My young always taste the same. I cannot remember when they last had a new father. You are right, servant of the corpse-god. There is something I want.' She ran a spindly hand, its fingers like spider's webs, over the greyish, blistered flesh of her torso.

'This,' said Lysander, 'is all I have to give you.' He took from its makeshift sling on his back the Imperial Fists chainsword. It was clotted with blood from killing the overseer in Kulgarde, and its casing was dented and scored with use.

'That little thing?' said the brood mother. 'That is not the weapon I had in mind.'

'I read of you,' continued Lysander levelly. 'You are the crossroads of all knowledge on Malodrax. There is nothing you do not know. I know you were once beautiful, and that you sought out a god of the warp as your consort. I know you tried to betray him, but his guard was not down as you feared, and so he cursed you. If you will turn on your god for some fleeting moment of power, he decreed, then you will always take the lesser of any deal offered to you. Is that not so?'

'What lies are these?' spat the brood mother. Her body quivered with rage.

'The lies of Inquisitor Golrukhan,' said Lysander. 'A collector of legends of Malodrax. He stood before you and bargained your story from you. Did he not?'

The brood mother's face creased as she tried to think of some pithy reply. But there was nothing. 'He was not so handsome,' she said. 'He called me abomination. He called me ugly! I was glad to see the back of him, that limp little whelpling. What did he have to offer me?' She rummaged in the piles of trash behind her, spilling skulls and random scraps of weaponry and armour. She took out an embroidered glove, once burgundy with golden stitching but now spoiled with mould and dirt. 'This is all he had! The last he possessed of some crea-ture named Talaya. That is what I took in return for my story. Would that he had asked anything else! Alas, that a mere man knows my shame! I hope my world killed him in the end.'

'But that is your curse,' said Lysander. 'You have to make a deal.'

'Only for that which is valuable!' retorted the brood mother sharply. 'I can only take something you hold dear! No piece of random trash, hear me! It must be something you value, something you will grieve to have lost, or there will be no deal!'

Lysander held up the chainsword. The light glinted on its teeth, where the edges showed through the dried blood. 'This was the weapon of my battle-brother,' he said. 'He now lies either dead or imprisoned in the dungeons of Kulgarde. This is all I have of him. More than that, it is a weapon of a Space Marine, of my people. It is a symbol of what we are. Without it, I am less a warrior. That is what I offer you.'

'Hmm.' The brood mother peered at the chainsword. Idly, she slid her young off the blackened stick with her teeth and chewed on it. Green-black blood ran down her scrawny neck. 'Sit,' she said, indicating a patch of earth in front of the fire.

Lysander sat down. The brood mother towered over him, her spidery shadows flitting all across the walls and ceiling of her cavern. Up close the smell of her was worse, sickly sweet and full of rot.

'What do you seek?' she asked, a new graveness in her voice as if this were the opening line of a prayer.

'I want to kill Kraegon Thul,' said Lysander.

The brood mother cackled, spilling scraps of bloody meat from her mouth. 'Do you know, you are the second one of your kind to ask that? That ugly little inquisitor man, he said the same thing! To excise the cancer, he put it, to lance the tumour that sickened Malodrax. As if there was but one heart to the corruption, to be cut away! And now you seek the same thing.'

'That inquisitor was doing his duty. I have that same duty, and it drives me as it did him. But I seek revenge as well.'

'No man can speak of revenge,' replied the brood mother, 'if he expects to walk away from it.'

'I would accept death,' replied Lysander, 'if it meant looking into Thul's dead eye before I go.'

The brood mother's head hung low over the fire as she peered more closely at Lysander. 'You did not find this place by hiding from the storm,' she said.

'And you do not give me what I ask from the goodness of your heart,' replied Lysander.

The brood mother steepled her fingers and thought for a long moment, the light of the fire playing across the abomination that was her face. 'You cannot do it alone,' she said. 'But you have no allies on this world. You must make sacrifices and they will not be of your flesh. The question you will ask yourself, servant of the corpse-god, is how far you will go for victory. What will you do to win? No doubt you would reply 'anything', but it is not that simple for one such as you. You have these… these cages in which you imprison yourselves. These principles. These moralities your people force into your minds. You will have to fight those long before you get your hands on Warsmith Thul. Long before.'

'I accept that.'

The brood mother waved a hand. 'Of course you do,'

she said. 'You do now. But you have not seen what you must do. I will not say I can perceive every moment that will come, but I can see the way the path winds. And of course, you will ignore any warnings I might give. You want to be shown the way. Well then! The path winds to the city of Shalhadar the Veiled.' The brood mother's eyes shifted as she focused far away. 'He courted me once. It was a lie. Everything he says is a lie, excepting that which you expect to be a lie, in which case it will be a truth that could destroy you to believe. He almost destroyed me, and I will never forgive him, but still I imagine those dark tendrils around me! Those golden eyes on my body!'

'How do I reach the city?' asked Lysander quickly.

'From this warren, westwards. The third moon should be on the horizon. Follow it. You will see the spires of the city long before you reach it. Shalhadar does not hide his glories. He is proud, a pride which Malodrax has tried to grind down, but the Veiled One has raised his spires high in spite. There is no other world where one such as Shalhadar could thrive so. It hates him, but it needs him, for without an object of its hate it would shrivel away into one more asteroid floating in the void.'

'Will he prove an ally?' asked Lysander.

'Now that, servant of the corpse-god, I cannot tell you. Shalhadar needs to be served and he finds a use for all who walk through the gates of his city. That is all.'

'Then I shall journey to the city of Shalhadar,' said

Lysander. 'Whatever happens there, happens, so long as it brings me closer to Kraegon Thul.'

The brood mother tilted her head, listening. 'The storm blows still,' she said. 'It will not be over for many hours. It would be a rash creature that did not take what shelter he could find. Will you not stay here, until it dies away?'

Lysander stood. 'I cannot tarry here while my brothers are captive,' he said. 'Every hour that goes by gives Thul another chance to have them on an executioner's block.'

The brood mother held out her hands in a pleading gesture. 'Please,' she said.

Lysander turned and walked towards the cave entrance, the flames casting shadows across his back.

'Then you should know,' said the brood mother, 'that I do not eat all my young.'

Shadows leapt, sharp and flickering. From pools of them scuttled insectoid creatures, each waist-high to a Space Marine, with compound eyes that glimmered in the firelight. Their bladed mandibles snickered and their chitin talons rattled on the stone floor as they made for Lysander. Dozens of them were suddenly all around him, whickering blades lashing at his legs and torso. One leapt from the ceiling and onto his shoulder. His hands reached up and felt hard limbs and a pulpy central mass, pulsing and oozing like the brood mother's abdomen. He ripped a leg off the creature and threw it behind him into the fire.

The brood mother shrieked as her young squirmed

and squealed, flesh spitting in the fire. The flames leapt higher as Lysander struck around him, unarmed save for the heavy book he still carried. He slammed the book down, crushing the head of one creature, and yanked another one off the ground by a leg before slamming it into the floor.

'Take his arms!' cried the brood mother. 'Take his legs! But leave the rest for me!'

Lysander stamped on a leg and felt it snap. He swung the book and knocked three or four of the creatures away from him, and broke into a run for the exit.

The cries of the brood mother followed him. Those young he could not outpace he grabbed as they tried to climb up his body, and tore them apart or dashed them to pulp against the walls. The warren wound this way and that and Lysander ran almost blind, striking out with every pace against the brood mother's young that swarmed from every bolthole and side passage.

He emerged into what passed for fresh air on Malodrax, into the roar of the storm. The warren emptied into a valley with the worst of the winds shrieking overhead. One of the brood mother's young clung to Lysander's back, talons digging into his skin. He grabbed a handful of its moist bristly abdomen and tore it off.

It was a fat wingless insect of unsurpassed ugliness. Its body was a wrinkled sack of entrails, and its limbs were cased in dark-grey exoskeleton. Its head was a nest of mandibles with two huge compound eyes that glittered in the faint light reaching down through the hail of stone. It squealed pathetically, as if begging him not to kill it now he had it at his mercy.

Lysander scrambled up the valley slope and held the insect above his head, into the worst of the stone shards. Its compound eyes burst and its body was shredded, hanging in deflated fragments. Lysander threw the remains up and the wind snatched it away.

Down by the horizon was a pale smudge, the moon of which the brood mother had spoken. That way lay Shalhadar's city – if the brood mother had told the truth. Whatever he found there, he would twist it into a way to kill Kraegon Thul, or he would die trying.

It was an oddly comforting thought, full of certainty. Lysander wrapped his rags around him and forged his way forwards into the storm.

ONCE, THERE HAD been empires on Malodrax. They were the empires of its native species, a proud people who had competed to create the mightiest kingdoms, surpass their neighbours, eclipse the achievements of the past and humble the generations of the future. Ambition was their religion, and they worshipped themselves.

Whatever nightmare had befallen them when Malodrax became a world of daemons and heretics, it left on the surface of the planet the faintest scars of what had been there before. Malodrax's new order was jealous, and the storms descended to scour the Malodracian cities from its continents. The stone shards obliterated the faces of the forebears who first raised their castles and palaces over the planet's skylines, and the half-finished statues of the last generation. Cathedrals fell. Billions of homes ceased to exist, as completely as if they had never been there. But Malodrax did not carry out its vandalism completely.

In the broken lands, ruins survived, sheltered among the hills and valleys. The greater substance of even these places was scrubbed away, leaving the stumps of proud cities like rotten teeth sticking up from the upheaved earth. Mosaics were picked clean and streets torn up. But ruins remained, the faintest trace of what Malodrax had once been, stamped down and mutilated by the daemon world's anger.

Space Marines did not dream as other men did. A sleeping man was a vulnerable man, and a Space Marine could never be vulnerable. Instead the lobes of his brain were separated by a membrane, cultured from his primarch's gene-seed and implanted during his conversion into a Space Marine, which allowed one half to fall into torpor while the other was awake. The animal brain stayed alert, ready to snap the Space Marine back to full readiness. What passed for dreams in that half-sleep were impressions of his surroundings, seen through the eyes of that predator.

As Lysander rested, his mind built up those cities of Malodrax from the ruins around him. Arches and towers rose up like the pinnacles of a crown surrounding the city, encompassing an expanse of sculpted stone.

The image broke and shattered, collapsing into the

dark ruins around Lysander. He peered through the darkness, but whatever had woken him from half-sleep, it was nothing that could be seen.

Lysander stood and leaned against a half-fallen wall, pausing to orient himself. This valley was relatively safe from the storm, but still in the swarming darkness it was easy to get turned around and lost. Ahead was a maze of collapsed buildings, uprooted foundations, and the remnants of some great decorative edifice, a palace or a place of worship. Swirls of carved stone resembled clouds or waves, abraded and crumbling from the work of the storms. Half a face loomed out of the dirt, part of a vast statue, and Lysander recognised an echo of the surgeon's features – that surgeon who had stood over him ready to cut him open, the surgeon he had killed. It had been of that species, the native xenos who had made Malodrax their home. Those who had not perished had been corrupted.

He had been woken by the wind, nothing else. That did not mean he would cease to be alert. If a Space Marine's instincts spoke up, it was wise to listen to them.

Lysander's eye found the book that lay in the dirt by his feet. *Being A Description Of Malodrax And Its Foulness.* Lysander had read only a few passages, but they had described the brood mother, her curse, and the means by which he might bargain with her. It had not mentioned quite everything about her, of course.

Lysander turned to the first couple of pages. The whole

book was written by hand, perhaps by the author, perhaps by one of his acolytes. It was signed in a florid hand by one Inquisitor Corvin Golrukhan. Lysander did not recognise the name, but anyone who claimed the title of inquisitor demanded at least respect.

'*I know not the date or time when I came to Malodrax,* Lysander read. *Somewhere beyond its lower orbit, time and space themselves cease to matter. No chronometer on my ship would tell the same tale. So I can say only that it was the first day. From the air, as my shuttle descended, I saw the delta of a river of blood emptying into an ocean of rot, and therein wallowed a titanic being. It was vast of girth, tattered wings spreading from its back, and a mass of tentacles broke the surface around its waist. Its four arms were clawed and its face a single mouth yawing open to reveal endless rows of teeth. And in that moment I imagined I was looking on a god that ruled this world and that with a thought it could swat my shuttle from the sky and send my acolytes and I to drown in the rot. But I did not look upon a god – I looked upon a corpse. As we closed I saw its flesh hanging in rags, exposing grey and dusty bones beneath, and colonies of filthy scavenger-birds swirling around as they picked away the last morsel to be found inside it.*

'*In a past age, this thing had ruled Malodrax, I have no doubt, fed a river of gore by a legion of worshippers who gave it such sacrifices that an ocean was filled with their remains. But that age had passed, and new powers ruled on Malodrax now.*

'How many gods have claimed to rule this world? I cannot say. The thing in the ocean, certainly, and perhaps many more in ages past that have since fallen into dust and been forgotten, leaving only a trunkless statue or idiom of language to suggest they ever existed. Though each one might last an aeon, it falls eventually. Malodrax yearns for chaos and stasis of power, for a mosaic of rulership that ever shifts and is refounded in constant bloodshed. That god I looked upon had thought itself inviolable and eternal, but in truth, only Malodrax itself can claim such a title.'

LYSANDER DID NOT much care for Golrukhan's language. The battle-lore of Rogal Dorn was written simply and directly, without using many words where one might suffice. The inquisitor had a high opinion of himself and had probably been even less sufferable to listen to than to read. But he had been right about the brood mother. He had survived on Malodrax long enough to write down what he saw. And a man did not attain the title of inquisitor without knowing what he was doing.

Lysander regarded the book he held. It was his only possession. The cover was newly bloodstained – he had killed with it, which gave it a kind of sacredness to the Space Marine who had wielded it. And it had taught him enough about the brood mother to get a deal out of her, as ugly a deed as that had been.

'Even here the Emperor's light must shine,' said Lysander. 'Perhaps it is His fate that threw you into my path. And if not, should the night turn colder I will at least have something to burn.'

THE FIRST LYSANDER saw of Shalhadar's city was its condemned, staked out by the roadside. The road sprung abruptly from the wastes, paved in marble blocks carved with sigils that might have been prayers or curses, mortared in with crushed bone and muscle. Hands reached from the dirt at the roadside, perhaps severed and planted there, perhaps still attached to arms and buried bodies – Lysander did not stop to check. Drifts of stone shards were piled up from the storm but they did not sully the roadway. Perhaps the builders had a pact with Malodrax to keep it clear, or it was sorcery.

The condemned hung from their wrists, which were manacled to the tops of tall spiked poles. Dozens of them lined each side, stretching off at regular intervals into the distance where the road wound into obscurity. They seemed dead at first glance, food for the filthy winged lizards that flitted from one body to another, but then one of them would stir or moan. They were emaciated and pallid, skin stretched and torn, knobs of bone poking through their joints. Lysander saw each had a brace around his head that kept it turned to one side – the same side, all looking towards the sudden end of the road. Each tried to turn his head against the brace, driving its spikes deeper into the side of his face.

Lysander looked in the direction the condemned were forbidden to look. There, stretched from one distant peak to the other, was the city. Spires and battlements broke the mottled cloak of Malodrax's sky. Even from here its magnificence was clear. Lysander could make out the pinnacle of a pyramid in the heart of the city, glinting as if covered in gold.

'What was your crime?' asked Lysander of the first condemned. He did not expect an answer, but the question had demanded a voice. The condemned struggled feebly against its manacles and brace. Lysander could not even tell if it was a man or a woman beneath the leather straps padlocked around its body.

Whatever it had done, its punishment was not death. It had been something worse – it had been condemned to live on, but never to look on Shalhadar's city again.

'With sorrow I approached the sight of that city, Golrukhan had written. *In the night, Sergeant Voss had died from the injuries he sustained breaking out of our besieged camp. He had suffered those wounds bravely, fending off the dozens of desert spirits that sought to snatch our souls away. His ensorcelled bolter shells felled countless such abominations, but alas, their chill touch had riven muscle and organ to his very core and those organs failed him just before dawn broke.*

'*Sergeant Voss did not live to see Malodrax's next day touching the spires of the city. There was something obscene, something that churned a holy man's gut, to see such opulence set among such desolation. Whatever horror had fallen on this region in a previous age had left the ground dry and shattered, inimical to all life save the daemon. But that* city sat like a crown in a heap of funeral ashes, bright and mocking, in defiance of the hatred Malodrax had for all who dwelled on its surface. Even then I detected the presence of he who ruled that city, for only a truly powerful and unholy intelligence could keep such a monstrosity intact when the planet was surely intent on levelling its towers.

'Talaya suggested that we skirt around it, avoiding any sentries or outriders. She was a fine strategist, but she did not possess the drive of an inquisitor, as much as she wished one day to rise to that station. She did not understand the devotion to duty that brought us here, that compelled me to seek out the very heart of the enemy that I might fulfil the quest I had set myself.

'My acolytes and I approached the gates. The brothers Grun and Thol, those hardy feral-worlder fellows who owed me a blood debt, flanked me as if I were a visiting dignitary, their muscular frames and the many trophies of their various kills making me look quite the part. I wore not the marks of an inquisitor but instead the xenos-plate armour I had earned in my service to my master, Kellion of the Hereticus, and Talaya carried the smoke-stained and torn banner Sergeant Voss had worn in its case on his back until the moment he died. It resembled another trophy, taken from a regiment of the Imperial Guard, displayed as a measure of calibre of those who had fallen before me. It was a fine ruse, concocted in a hurry but nonetheless effective in earning us a greeting from a daemon courtier at the gates instead of a volley of arrows or a torrent of boiling oil.

'"Who is your god?" the creature demanded. It had about

it the look of one who served the Lord of Unspeakable Pleasures, its body lithe, its movements snake-like and hypnotic, and its features possessed of a terrible beauty.

'"Bokor the Wildsman," I replied, naming a lesser power of the warp that I had encountered while investigating cult murders on the hive world Anathema. I could not say if Bokor still existed, or perhaps was even an alternative name of whatever power this daemon served. But I had lived thus far by taking such risks in the pursuance of my duty.

'"What is your purpose?" demanded the daemon.

'"To seek understanding," I said, and felt a strange pride that in an effort to deceive this daemon, I had in fact spoken the truth.

'"With whom do you seek audience?"

'"The lord and master of this city."

'"Many have sought it," said the daemon. "Many have waited a lifetime for the honour. What places you above such dregs?"

'"But nothing," I replied, "save that which is perceived in me by your lord."

'The daemon bowed and bade me enter. Thus we see the daemon is much like a man in the lowest and most crude of its faculties. It desires to be worshipped and will allow the serpent into its crib if that serpent fawns over it as if it were a god. I knew that from that point onwards it would not be so simple, but for the time being flattery was enough to gain my warband entry.

'Beyond the gate stood a mighty beast, a sphinx that seemed conjured from the treasure vault of a giant. In the

scintillating stained glass of its wings a man might look
upon an infinity of possibilities, a vastness of timestreams
spiralling out into forever. Indeed I could imagine myself as
a young man, untempered by the work of the Inquisition and
with my mind impiously open, staring for a lifetime into the
potential there revealed. But I tore my eyes away and entered
the city, which later I would understand was the City of
Shalhadar. Of the sphinx I will write more anon.'

LYSANDER STOOD BEFORE the gate and knew a little of
what those condemned must have felt to know they
would never return to this city. It was magnificent. It
did not look to have been built so much as wrought by
a jewelsmith in infinite detail and then expanded to its
monumental scale.

The gate was open. Beyond, a festival was in full
swing. Fireworks burst across the skyline in a burning kaleidoscope, sending sprays of multicoloured fire
that overcame the oppressive darkness of the sky. The
towers and spires were hung with pastel silk banners.
And the people were everywhere, thronging the streets,
dancing to an overlapping wall of musical noise. They
danced with such abandon they threw out joints and
tore muscles – where they could dance no more they
lay in the street, convulsing in time with the beat they
felt the strongest.

Lysander tried to make out some pattern in the
appearance of these people, but there was nothing
except for their desire to be seen. Some of them were

in lavish furs and silks, barely able to move in the layers of their finery, while others were all but naked, bodies bound in leather and chains, flaunting open wounds on their bodies as they writhed and convulsed in dance. One group were partially flayed, the muscles of their upper arms, chests and thighs wet and open to the air. Others were painted gold, with fat gemstones implanted in their skin.

The city was open – it was a time of celebration and pilgrims were welcome to join the revelry. Lysander was very aware that he could not pretend to be one of these people, however – he was not a pilgrim, at least not of whatever power ruled this city. He still wore rags and was covered in undecorative scars from the storm. He saw no one who matched his stature – no brute-mutants or hulking xenos with the height and bulk of a Space Marine. He would not go far without being noticed for not belonging.

A parade passed down the street leading to the gate, and turned into a side road between the buttresses of a great gilded fortress. Chariots drawn by lowing pack beasts carried bands of dancers, whirling in circles around a daemon that danced in the centre. Each daemon was unique, as was the way of the daemon, but shared serpentine muscles and a mesmeric quality to their movements, carefully honed by the warp to beguile the minds of the onlookers. Lysander had to force himself to look away. Another carriage was an altar and carried a slab of gold loomed over by a statue of a handsome winged humanoid. Gilded manacles hung from the statue's chest. The only still people in the whole panorama were the altar's attendants, who flanked the altar with their hooded heads bowed as if waiting for the signal for the celebration to end and the sacrifices to begin. The parade was followed up by a gilded dragon of a dozen segments each carried by a band of celebrants, winding through the street as it danced. Some revellers threw themselves into its path and its hinged jaws opened, and they hurled themselves down its gullet between sharp silver fangs. It left a smear of blood in its wake and spread drops of gore with the lashing of its long plumed tail.

A dancer grabbed Lysander's arm, trying to drag him into the fray. Lysander shrugged her aside. He stayed under the eaves of a splendid temple building as he moved down the road, head down, hoping that he would not seem too outlandish a sight compared to the dancers and revellers. But he was the only one wretched, the only one not celebrating.

A man in grotesque makeup, his face painted like a mask of bleeding wounds, loomed down off a passing carriage. 'I can smell the blood in his veins!' he cried. 'Sing with us, brother! Dance! Bleed with us!'

'Dance! Dance!' the crowd cried out, and suddenly dozens of them were around Lysander, grabbing at his arms and legs as if to move him like a marionette. Lysander threw them aside. He could not get bogged down here, but he could not cause a scene of great violence. Instead he shoved and knocked them down, and ducked into an alleyway that led off from the main thoroughfare.

The music followed him, now echoing and muted. The narrow alley was a dumping ground for spoiled finery. Torn silk and tarnished gold covered the ground, crushed into the city's brown detritus. Lysander moved quickly, almost in a run, his wide shoulders grazing the painted walls. A mix of filth and perfume filled the air, a cloying mass that stuck to the back of his throat.

He paused to get his bearings. He had the impression that the city radiated out from the pyramid he had glimpsed at its centre. Perhaps he should head there, or perhaps he should avoid it at every opportunity.

The sound of laughter caught his attention. It was coming from the basement window of an ornate tower that rose just ahead, as if pinning the surrounding districts to the ground. He crept up to the window, kneeled, and looked in through the panels of multicoloured glass.

The room below was lit by candles, guttering in their hundreds on the floor and in niches on the walls. Chained to the far wall was the source of the laughter – a man, naked save for a length of bloodstained fabric tied around his waist. His bare chest had been pared open, skin and muscle peeled away from the ribs which were being removed one by one by a surgeon in a hooded robe of purple and gold. The patient was giggling as if the scalpel were doing no more than tickle. Observing stood several more hooded figures, each one with his robes embroidered in a different pattern of gold and silver. From beyond the window came a murmuring drone, as if they were all reciting a different passage to consecrate the laughing man's vivisection.

The patient looked up at the window. His eyes widened and he tore one arm free, spiked chains stripping flesh from his hand and forearm, spilling entrails down over his thighs. He pointed straight at Lysander and screeched in laughter as if Lysander's face at the window was the most hilarious thing he had ever seen.

The surgeon turned around. His face was stitched closed, his eyes, mouth and nostrils sealed shut with silver thread. He put the scalpel to his eyelids and cut the threads, and his bloodshot eyes opened to see what the madman was pointing at.

The other cultists turned. They, too, were tearing their eyes open, this time with their hands. Muffled cries of outrage reached Lysander as the cultists drained out of the chamber, leaving the sacrificial victim coughing up ropes of bloody phlegm as he shuddered with laughter.

Lysander hurried down the alleyway, away from the cultists' chamber, towards where the alley opened into a larger space shadowed by the overlapping roofs of the buildings surrounding it. Cultists burst out into the alley as Lysander ran, accompanied by a screeching note from a reed instrument blown like a hunter's horn.

Cries and screams came from every direction, from

the buildings around, from the rooftops and the basements. Lysander burst into the square and saw the flagstones were covered in spikes, and celebrants of the festival were writhing there, puncturing and tearing their skin. Other bodies lay dead or unconscious, bled white into red-brown stains around them. More bodies were impaled on spikes that jutted from the walls bounding the square, their faces locked in expressions of exhilaration and ecstasy.

Lysander looked for ways out. Behind him, the stitched cultists were rushing down the alleyway. More were streaming in from other entrances to the square – dancers in leather and steel, performers in featureless masks, celebrants with strips of skin removed forming patterns of scab and open wound. Countless flavours of the city's damned, brought to join in the hunt.

He was a part of the festival. He was the entertainment. He was not an intruder at all – he was one more attraction, a part of festival season, another way to honour the city's lords.

The spikes bit into Lysander's rag-bound feet. He held the heavy book in one hand with the other ready to punch or grab.

More cultists were watching from balconies overlooking the square, shouting encouragement or leaning over fascinated by what was about to unfold.

A scream went up, a signal. The cultists rushed at Lysander in a mass, a multicoloured tide of them streaming at a sprint. Their eyes were rolled back as if in the grip of a religious revelation. Some fell, trampled into the spikes.

Then, suddenly, they were within arm's reach.

A Space Marine was not like a normal soldier. A soldier was a man, and a man was safest the further away from the fighting he was. He knew not to rush into the fray, and to cling to what safety there was on a battlefield, out of sight or in cover. But a Space Marine knew that he was safest in the midst of the battle, where an enemy had to take him on face to face, because that was the way a Space Marine was created to fight.

Lysander dived into the mass of cultists. He hit them like a missile, scattering bodies. He drove the heel of a hand into a jawbone, felt a neck snapping back, and brought the book around like a club into the press of bodies.

The gap he had opened closed. Scarred or silk-wrapped bodies crowded around him, constricting him. He ducked down, felt them close over him, and erupted out, throwing bodies over his shoulders. He struck out again and again, jarring impacts running along his arms as he pounded at the cultists swirling around him.

He threw one to the ground, into the spikes. He grabbed another by the hair, hauled him off his feet and swung him into the crowd, scattering more bodies. The training of a thousand sparring circle sessions took control of his muscles and he did not need to think to strike out with an elbow or a heel, to crack open a cultist's face with a headbutt or shatter a knee with a downwards stamp.

But there were so many of them. They were still trying to force their way into the square. Some were leaping down into the crowd from the balconies, whooping with excitement to join the adventure.

One leapt onto Lysander's back. Then another was there, too, arms wrapped around his neck, trying to weigh him down. They piled on top of him, clambering over one another and trampling the fallen into the spiked flagstones. Lysander threw one aside but there were so many on top of him now. His knees buckled under them. Hands and fingers were clawing at his eyes and mouth. He gritted his teeth and pushed against the weight but it was like trying to shove a mountain aside.

He was down to one knee. Spikes punctured the skin of his knee and shin. He slumped down, spikes pushing through the hand he put down to hold himself up. His face was pushed further and further down by the weight, the spikes spearing up towards his eye.

He reared up, heaving a great drift of bodies off him. He was roaring as he did so, the effort threatening to tear his enhanced muscles off the bone. He gulped down a breath before the human ocean closed over him again and, suddenly, that air was crushed out of him, and he could not breathe.

More were dying around him, their ribcages crushed or their skulls collapsed. He drove a hand upwards, out of the mass, shattering jaws and spines, but there was no room to draw it back in again. He was trapped. There was no way out. The light was cut off completely as the bodies heaped one on top of the other, as if to die in that crush was a religious observance, an honour these people were fighting for.

'Enough!' cried a voice from far above. The sound barely made it down through the groaning of the dying and the snapping of bones.

The pressure suddenly relented. Lysander gasped down a breath and almost choked on it, for it was laden with a heavy, spiced scent that made his head reel. The struggling around him lessened and he was able to force a space around himself. He lifted one foot and let bodies roll in under him, pushing off them to drive himself upwards and out of the heap.

The scent, like incense, was powerful enough to burn his throat. Lysander could feel his third lung struggling to filter out the toxins flooding the square. When he could see up into the square above, his vision was clouded by a clinging red-brown fug.

The cultists, those who lived, had distant eyes with their pupils wide black pools, their jaws hanging open and their bodies limp. They flopped into inaction where they had been clambering over one another to get to Lysander. They were draped over the balcony rails, and even as he watched some were slipping into unconsciousness and toppling down onto the mass of bodies that choked the square. A low, sighing moan was the only sound they made now as if falling as one into a deep sleep.

The buildings that bounded the square reached up into the distant skyline of the city. On one rooftop, clambering down by means of a set of spiderlike mechanical arms, was a humanoid shape. The arms were mounted on its back, into a rig that included two exhaust pipes from which was pouring the narcotic fog flooding the square.

As it descended Lysander made out its details. It wore armour of steel scales, clinging to its form – a woman's form, Lysander realised. She carried a double-headed halberd, each blade wrought into the shape of a dragon's head, and her helm similarly bore a lizardlike mask with a mass of silver teeth.

Lysander coughed and wiped a hand across his eyes to get rid of the residue. He pulled himself out of the mass of lolling bodies, and wrenched the book free. It was still the only weapon to hand.

'I think,' said the newcomer, 'you have taken a wrong turn.'

'What do you want?' said Lysander. His hearts were still shuddering in his chest and his warrior's instinct had not let go. He was still poised for danger.

'Just curious,' said the stranger. She descended on her mechanical legs, and landed deftly amid the bodies. Her mechanical limbs snickered up onto her back like those of a dead spider. She unlocked a catch on the side of her mask and it slid open, its panels folding into the scaled armour around her shoulders. Her face was long, pale and handsome with sharp eyes and nose, thin lips, and short black hair swept back from her face. It was altogether far too human for this city. 'I am the herald of Lord Shalhadar the Veiled,' she said. 'He would greatly appreciate knowing more about the stranger in his city. It is fortuitous that you come to us in the festival season or you would have been stopped at the gates, but now you are in you have my lord's attention.' She spread her arms to indicate the unconscious, broken and dead cultists piled up in the square. 'And some would say that you owe him.'

'I seek audience with Shalhadar,' said Lysander.

'So do millions in this city,' replied the herald. 'But they have not demonstrated a capacity for violence such as you, and so perhaps you will get your wish.'

'Are you daemon?'

'Not yet,' she replied with a half-smile. 'I am Talaya, Veiled One's herald. My lord dispatches me to watch over his city and his people, and to inform him of that which I decide he would wish to know. He knew you were here before you passed through the gate. I was sent to watch, and my lord's interest was proven sound.'

'And now you will take me to your lord,' said Lysander, 'to hand me over and be rewarded. Is that not so?'

'It is not quite that simple,' replied Talaya. She walked across the bodies towards Lysander, looking him up and down. 'But I will take you to the palace, which is further than you would make it on your own. Everything after that is up to you.'

'Then I see no use in dallying here.'

'Of course.' Talaya picked at Lysander's cloak, which still clung to him, sodden with blood. 'But you're not going anywhere looking like that.'

9

'I wonder when it was that I became a heretic. I had always been taught that it was like flipping a switch. One moment passes to another and suddenly one is corrupted and irredeemable, a single definite thought or deed shunting one onto the path of the unrighteous. But when it happened to me, it took the better part of a century. I cannot say when my soul's purity left me, or what the cause was. I became a heretic without realising. Perhaps that it why it is so insidious, and why only one with such willpower as I can be permitted to even skirt the shore of that dark ocean.'

– Inquisitor Corvin Golrukhan

THE IMPERIAL FISTS honoured their dead when they were safely beyond Shalhadar's city, and when they were certain the city's forces would not force them to battle. They found a depression in the broken ground, like a sunken amphitheatre, perhaps a shell crater from an ancient war or the sinkhole from a collapsed warren of tunnels beneath the ground. One Imperial Fist from each squad – Kaderic, Gorvetz and Lycaon's own squad – stood as lookouts. The rest gathered in the centre of the depression, where were laid out the three who had died.

Brother Fornis was of Lycaon's squad. His helmet had been removed and his face was calm, as if in the kind of sleep that was a rare luxury for a Space Marine. A single sharp-edged cut, like a slim dark triangle, in the breastplate of his armour was the only sign of injury – but the daemon's blade had cut through one heart and his spine, and his system had broken down even as he fought on from the ground.

'Let us commend Brother Fornis to the legacy of Rogal Dorn,' said Lycaon over the body. As a Chaplain he had given these rites hundreds of times before, standing over the body of a fallen Imperial Fist. 'There is no death so final that it can rob us of our place in the eternal war against the enemy. There is no fate so grave that it erases our duty. Brother Fornis was among the finest shots in the First Company, and his mind was as sharp as that of any soldier. He did his duty and honoured his primarch and his Emperor. Nothing more need be said of a member of the Adeptus Astartes. He has left this battlefield, but there will be another.'

Two more dead were from Squad Gorvetz. Brother Metzian was the Imperial Fist devoured by the sphinx at the palace gates. Only the upper half of his body had been recovered and lay there on the ground truncated at the waist in a mass of gem-like hardened blood. Metzian's helmet stayed on, for it was split down the middle and his face beneath it was a ruin. Brother Kalanar, lying beside him, had died in the palace as Gorvetz was besieged on the upper levels by a host of daemons. Daemon claws had ripped into his back and gutted him. From the front, scatters of red wounds on his face and rents in his breastplate told a muted tale of what had happened to him. Beside Kalanar lay his plasma cannon, its casing still discoloured with the intense heat of its firing.

'Kalanar and Metzian were as true-born brothers,' said Sergeant Gorvetz. 'Though we all are brothers, yet as we trained and fought I saw in them a shared purpose beyond our duty as soldiers. When the enemy pressed in on us, the brothers of my squad could turn to Metzian and Kalanar and know that in them lay strength of purpose enough for all of us. Kalanar knew joy of battle when he brought the righteous fire. Metzian was a contemplator, a student of battle and its extremes. There were never two sons of Dorn less alike, and yet there were never two who so embodied our strength. They are gone from this battlefield, but there will be another.'

Techmarine Kho stepped forward and knelt by the bodies. One of the mechanical arms mounted onto his backpack cycled to a fine blade tip and reached down to open up an incision in Fornis's throat. In the absence of an apothecary in the strike force, the task of harvesting the gene-seed of the fallen rested with Kho. Brother

Gethor, who piloted one of Kho's Land Speeders, stood behind Kho holding the sample jars which would hold the gene-seed for transport back to the *Phalanx* star fortress and the Chapter.

Lysander watched with the other Imperial Fists as the solemn business was concluded. He found Brother Halaestus's eyes in the gathering, but he could read nothing in that mutilated face.

When the gene-seed was removed, the faces of the dead were covered and they were loaded onto the Land Speeders so they could be brought back to the Chapter and their bodies interred. The gene-seed was the priority – if the Land Speeders were lost then at least the gene-seed, on which the Chapter's future rested, would survive.

'Choose your best!' demanded Chaplain Lycaon when the dead were stowed away.

The funeral games, in a major campaign or when there was more time to observe them, might see every manner of martial competition – marksmanship, athletics, a dozen forms of duelling, and more. Here, when they had to be concluded in less than an hour before the strike force moved on again, there was only time for one such competition. And yet it was ill luck not to observe it, for the dead Imperial Fists had themselves observed many times the funeral rites of their own fallen brothers.

From Squad Gorvetz, Brother Antinas stepped forward, handing his heavy flamer to the squadmate beside him. He stripped off the shoulder guards, breast-plate, armguards and gauntlets of his armour, leaving him unarmoured from the waist up. Antinas's cropped red hair contrasted with his pale skin, the surgical scars of his many augmentations still looking pink and raw. Of Lycaon's veterans Brother Givenar stepped up. He was the largest Imperial Fist there, and the knotted muscles of his arms and chest were covered in incised kill-markings in the style of some of the Chapter's old-est veterans. Each campaign he had fought was picked out there in scar tissue.

Sergeant Kaderic represented his squad. He had kneeled before the Chaplains of the Imperial Fists and sworn never to back down from an honourable combat, echoing the oaths taken by the first champions of Rogal Dorn and those still taken by the rare individu-als chosen to champion the Emperor on the battlefield. Such an oath was a bold statement even for a Space Marine, and the Chaplains told parables of those whose oaths had been learned and twisted by the heretical and corrupt, compelling brave champions of the Imperial Fists to fight impossible odds. To take the oath meant that the principles of courage and honour were more important than petty concerns like survival.

The final competitor was Brother Gethor, his gene-seed duties done, representing Techmarine Kho, Halaestus, and Lysander – those members of the strike force who were not members of one of its three squads. Gethor was barely eighteen months out of novicehood, training under Kho to be elevated one day to the Chapter armoury and the training with the Priesthood of Mars to become a full Space Marine. He showed no trepidation even as he stood alongside three competitors far more experienced than him.

Lysander found himself standing beside Chaplain Lycaon as the first competitors lined up, the spectating Imperial Fists forming an ad-hoc fighting ring.

'You fear for Halaestus,' said Lycaon, quietly enough that only Lysander would hear.

'Fear is a word I will never use,' said Lysander, 'of myself or of another brother.'

'But,' said Lycaon, letting the word hang.

Kaderic and Givenar were drawn to face one another. Kaderic scraped a handful of dirt from the ground and rubbed his hands dry with it. Givenar kneeled and murmured a prayer, fists held in front of him as if he were addressing them, imploring them to serve him as his wargear did in battle.

'I cannot fathom what Halaestus has lost,' said Lysander. 'It is beyond my capacity to understand. It is rare that a Space Marine suffers so.'

'Is he the same one you led as a squadmate?' asked Lycaon.

Lysander paused before he answered. 'No,' he said.

'You must watch him.'

Lysander looked at the Chaplain and realised in that moment that he did not know the man, not as he had known Halaestus and the other members of his squad.

Perhaps that was what Chaplainhood meant – to stand apart from the battle-brothers of his Chapter, to make decisions that one too close to the men of the Chapter could not. 'Of course,' said Lysander. 'I will stay close to him. I have known him a long time, and he will trust me.'

Lysander watched the bout begin, Kaderic charging into Givenar, lunging a shoulder into Givenar's midriff and bundling him to the ground.

'These are not your men, Lysander,' said Lycaon.

Lysander did not reply. Though he had known it was true, he had not heard it said out loud.

'Captain Venharts was not greatly loved,' continued Lycaon, 'for he was crude and forthright of word. But the First respected him, and they knew him for he served as their captain for more than thirty years. When he was lost they mourned him keenly. You are not Venharts, for good or for ill, and they do not look to you as they did to him. Does that dismay you, Lysander?'

Lysander had been tested by the Chaplains of the Imperial Fists a thousand years before, as the Chapter reckoned it, through novicehood and at every stage of his rise to a captain's rank. He knew when he was being tested again, and Lycaon knew he knew. 'Dismay? No, that is too strong a word. I understand what they feel. They are not my men, but I am not yet their captain, either. The First Company I knew was lost with the *Shield of Valour*. That will change, for the bonds that hold us together are forged in battle. If there is anything Malodrax will give us, it is battle.'

Givenar was better on the ground than Kaderic was on his feet. The two rolled over, Givenar with a forearm across Kaderic's throat, trying to choke and submit. But Kaderic was stronger and he forced a knee underneath Givenar's body. He levered Givenar off him, throwing him to the ground, leaping to his feet and wrapping an arm around Givenar's neck from behind.

The brothers of Kaderic's squad cheered. Kaderic bared his teeth at them in a savage smile. Givenar tapped his hand against Kaderic's shoulder – the choke was in, the blood cut off to the brain, and Givenar had to either submit or let himself fall unconscious. Kaderic let Givenar go and stood, beat his chest, and accepted the offered hands of his squadmates.

'What happened to the Vorel?' asked Lysander.

'You do not know?' asked Lycaon. 'It is recorded in the Chapter archives, I am certain.'

'There was shame enough in speaking to the Chapter of how the First was lost,' said Lysander. 'If the Vorel prospered without our intervention, if Imperial subjects suffered at their hands, it would not be conducive to rebuilding my place in the Chapter.'

'The Vorel predated on the frontier worlds for a century and a half,' said Lycaon. 'The declaration of *Xenos Horrificus* was well deserved. A Crusade was called against them and the Guard and Navy shattered their empire. Some still surface as mercenaries, but they are dying out.'

'I see,' said Lysander.

'The blood of the Vorel's crimes stains the hands of the Iron Warriors.'

'I need no more reasons to kill Thul,' said Lysander. 'But for that, too, he will pay.'

THE SECOND BOUT'S competitors were lining up. Gethor and Antinas looked as unalike as two Space Marines from the same Chapter could. Gethor had yet to lose the handsomeness that some novices brought with them, and which was inevitably worn away under scars and years. Antinas was as ugly as sin, scorched and scarred all over, his kill-markings covering his back, chest and upper arms in dark-brown High Gothic lettering. His hands were huge and gnarled and he clenched and unclenched them as the two circled, ready to strike.

'We will march on Kulgarde next,' said Lycaon. 'The ground is rough and broken. Kho tells me that to the north is more cover, where we can travel unobserved should news of our arrival have reached the Iron Warriors. Do you concur with this course?'

'It will slow us down,' said Lysander, glad the conversation had turned to matters of battle. 'But we must assume word has reached Kulgarde that Shalhadar is dead and the Imperial Fists killed him. Have you considered my suggestions for breaching the fortress?'

'I have,' said Lycaon, 'and I will decide on them closer to the time. They are unorthodox.'

'Any plan has to be if it is to succeed,' said Lysander. 'We cannot besiege Kulgarde with the force we have. A million Imperial Guard might not reduce its defences. Perhaps with a Titan Legion we could march on the walls directly, but we lack such a luxury.'

'So I understand,' said Lycaon. 'But I would see for myself what we are facing before deciding how Kulgarde will fall.'

Antinas was stronger by far. He grabbed the younger competitor by the thigh and flipped him onto his back, throwing his head back and yelling at the sky. His squadmates echoed him. Gethor scrabbled to his feet and ducked back, crouching. Antinas beat his chest and advanced.

'We must kill Kraegon Thul,' said Lysander.

'I will not return to the *Phalanx* if he lives,' replied Lycaon. 'And a lifetime of shame will accompany any of us who does.'

Antinas darted forwards, too quickly for a man of his size. He knocked Gethor's guard aside and headbutted Gethor, catching him on the eye socket. Gethor reeled, dropped onto his back, rolled away and staggered upright again just out of Antinas's range. Antinas pressed on, swinging at Gethor with blows hard enough to knock the younger man out. Gethor kept moving, swaying from side to side, desperation on his face as each swing came closer to leaving him in the dirt.

Antinas lunged, driving the heel of a hand forwards, hard enough to shatter a jawbone. Gethor dropped onto his back, locked his feet around Antinas's leg and tripped the bigger man up. Antinas landed heavily and

Gethor was on him, locking one arm behind his back, forcing a knee into his spine and wrenching his head back.

'Your neck is broken,' gasped Gethor.

'So it is,' said Antinas, breathing heavily.

Gethor stood unsteadily, backing off as if uncertain how Antinas would react. The onlookers were quiet, for they were not used to seeing Antinas losing either. Gethor had got him in a simple neck lock that, had Gethor's intentions been lethal, would have let him twist Antinas's head around and back so the vertebrae of the neck separated. It was a good way to kill some-one. Even a Space Marine needed his brain attached to the rest of his body.

Antinas laughed. He jumped to his feet and grabbed Gethor in a bear hug. He hoisted him up off the ground and onto his shoulder, parading him like a conqueror's trophy.

'See!' cried Antinas. 'That's how you kick an old dog!' he pointed at the Land Speeders where the bodies of the fallen were stowed. 'Despair not, brothers!' he called to them. 'You leave your Chapter in good hands!'

The Imperial Fists cheered. They patted Gethor on the back as Antinas carried him around.

The final bout saw Gethor facing Kaderic. It was quick. Kaderic forced Gethor into a test of strength, and Kaderic had more. He wrapped his arms around Gethor's waist, lifted him up and threw him down. Gethor struggled with skill and determination on the ground but Kaderic had the better of him from the moment the bout had started. When they were done and the winner was certain, with Gethor's arm locked behind him in such a way that Kaderic could have broken it at will, the two dusted themselves off and shook hands. Kaderic, as champion, dedicated his victory to the fallen and thanked them for looking on, as was the right and proper form.

'Brothers!' ordered Lycaon. 'Our fallen are honoured. Kho, take the point. I will ride with you. March out!'

ONCE THERE HAD been so much life in those broken lands that it had bubbled up from the ground, reaching up towards the skies in a soaring canopy. That jungle had been dead for an aeon but it had been stubborn enough to leave its mark, and while the leaves had withered in a past age the skeletons of the trees remained. The petrified forest stretched across a great swathe adjoining the north of the rocky broken desert. It was dense and pathless, and the sun's discoloured light struggled to make it through the jumble of stone branches overhead.

Roosts of hardy, leathery creatures clung to the branches in their thousands, scouring the forest for the tough life forms that found a way to survive there. What life there was served only to accentuate the death that had fallen on the jungle in a distant catastrophe, one of the many that had punctuated Malodrax's history.

Kho's Land Speeders flew at canopy level, weaving

between the splintered boughs, relaying their position to the sergeants of the squads marching through the petrified jungle below. They made slow progress by their standards, for underfoot the ground was tangled with stony roots and the terrain rose and fell as if something had heaved it up from beneath. Deep caves yawed in hillsides and choked valleys dropped down to pitch-darkness. Raptors circled overhead, used to treating anything that walked into the jungle as a meal in waiting.

'I do not like the smell of this place,' said Lysander as he picked his way through the roots alongside Kaderic.

'This whole planet is hardly pleasing to the nose,' replied Kaderic. The bruise on the side of his face, inflicted by Gethor in the wrestling bout, had already turned a purple-black and begun receding.

'It smells of ash,' said Lysander. 'As if it were burned yesterday, not thousands of years ago.'

'Perhaps it was,' said Kaderic. 'They say a world held by daemons may not even obey the rules of time. Would that we had a battlefleet and the Exterminatus to be deployed. All of Malodrax would stink of ash then.' Kaderic paused and looked at Lysander. 'Has it changed?'

A thousand years had passed in real space since Lysander had come to Malodrax. He had no way of knowing how much time had passed down there since he had travelled to the *Phalanx* and returned with the strike force. 'It looks the same,' said Lysander. 'But I cannot be certain. This world likes to deceive, I think.'

Movement caught Lysander's attention. It was above them, among the branches of the stone trees. It scurried out of his sight a split second before he could focus on it, but he had an impression of claws and lizardlike hide – and worse, of familiarity.

'What was it?' said Kaderic.

'Hold our position,' said Lysander.

'Hold!' ordered Kaderic over the vox. 'Captain, we may have enemies down here. We are drawing in and investigating.'

Lysander's bolter was in his hands. He hopped up onto the stump of a shattered tree and peered through the stone trunks in the direction the creature had disappeared.

'Antinas, Kollus, go with the captain,' said Kaderic to the two closest Imperial Fists. 'Lysander, could it be an animal?'

'Perhaps,' said Lysander. Antinas and Kollus were alongside him as he moved carefully through the jungle towards a rootbound gulley ahead. Antinas's flamer was held in front of him, the flame flickering in its nozzle. Kollus trained his bolter across the jungle.

'Watch overhead,' said Lysander. 'It could be above us.'

Kollus saw it next. He spun on the spot and loosed off a short burst, throwing shards from the tree trunks.

'Did you hit it?' said Lysander.

'No,' said Kollus.

Lysander took off between the trees. He had followed the movement, too, a scaly dash of motion down between the fork of a tree's branches. He leapt the gulley, hitting the far edge chest-first and scrambling back to his feet.

It was ahead of him. It was almost the height of a man, squatting down on its haunches. Its body was fleshy and sagging, its belly pale and its hide scaly. Its silhouette was lumpy and malformed and its mouth was half insect and half reptile. It bared the nest of mandibles it had in place of teeth and hissed at him.

Lysander had seen something very like it before – this one was more mature, adapted to survive here on its own, but the resemblance was unmistakeable.

The creature darted at him. Lysander lunged right at it, spearing his chainsword forwards. It was used to forcing other predators to back down – perhaps here it was the top of the food chain. Lysander's chainblade punched right through it, spraying green-black gore as its teeth chewed out through its back. The thing was spitted on the chainblade as neatly as a carcass turned over a fire.

Antinas reached him a moment later. 'What is it?' he said.

'One of the brood,' replied Lysander. He flicked his chainblade and the creature slid off the blade, a gory ruin bored right through it.

'More of them,' voxed Kollus. Lysander turned to see Kollus on the far side of the gulley. Movement was flickering around him as the brood-creatures scampered among the trees or between the roots at ground level.

As if brought out by the smell of their fellow creature's blood, they were suddenly infesting the jungle all around. Kollus snapped a couple of volleys, catching one of the creatures and bursting it in a shower of gore. 'They're just animals, captain. Are they of any concern?'

'They are,' replied Lysander. 'It is not them that concern me. It is what might accompany them.' He switched to the command vox-channel. 'Chaplain Lycaon, we're holding position. We have been found.'

BENEATH THE GROUND they had followed the Imperial Fists, a great host of them. The honeycomb of tunnels beneath the petrified forest had let them follow their footsteps – literally, for they were adapted in the darkness to sense the footfalls from the ground above, and thirty heavy armoured Space Marines did not move quietly.

They were members of a species that had lurked there for thousands of years, hunting in the darkness and emerging above ground when the pickings below were lean. They had evolved rapidly as Malodrax changed, their slovenly genetics easily slipping into new forms to let them survive extremes of heat, cold or seismic activity. The result was their sagging, bloated forms, the mishmash of lizard, insect and vermin that made up their features, and a crude but effective intellect. They were intelligent scavengers, predators of opportunity, and prey that could demonstrate an extreme of cowardly cunning.

That day several of them, a scouting caste of unusual perceptiveness, had emerged into the wan sunlight to follow more closely the new arrivals in the petrified forest. Their generations passed by rapidly for their lives were short, and so the image of those enormous figures with their golden armour and the sigil of the clenched fist was by then a legend passed down by their forebears.

One day those warriors from another world would return, they had been told, and those warriors would have to die. Because the mother had told them so.

THE STRIKE FORCE drew in tight, knocking down trees into makeshift barricades. The Land Speeders were landed in the centre, ready to hover up around canopy level and spray the surrounding forest with heavy bolter and assault cannon fire. The Imperial Fists manned their defences as the darkness drew in, making of their surroundings a fortress according to the principles of siege warfare.

The last two hours they had been followed. Hundreds of the predators had scurried through the trees watching them, corralling them, and the Land Speeders reported far greater concentrations following the strike force as if herding them towards a location where they could be trapped and killed.

It was the Imperial Fists way to take a stand at a time and place of their choosing. If an enemy desired a battle they would have it, but on Imperial Fists terms. And so

Chaplain Lycaon had given the order that the Imperial Fists would dig in and face the enemy there, on a low rise that served as the most defensible position for miles around.

'They are more organised than they appear,' said Lycaon as he watched Squad Kaderic at the barricades. Kaderic's men were the front line, with Gorvetz's Devastator squad in the centre of the camp and Lycaon's command squad ready to charge in where needed. 'Malodrax does love its little games. It gives our fellow travellers the faces of animals so we will think them animals, but they are born soldiers. They have by their very nature the instinct of a soldier.' He pointed to a rush of movement to the south, where a multitude of scurrying bodies glinted in the paltry moonlight. 'They send their weakest forward, to test our guns. They learn there of our effective range and of the weight of our firepower. A classic tactic when one has numbers to spare.' Lycaon switched to the vox. 'Kaderic, let them get to half-range, then shoot them down.'

The creatures were permitted well within bolter range before Kaderic gave the order to fire. Standing beside Lycaon, Lysander could see the attackers were far larger than the scouting creatures the strike force had first encountered – they were the size of a man, hunched over as they ran rapidly on all fours through the broken ground and tangles of tree stumps. A volley of fire sliced through the first dozen or so and the others fell over their dead or turned aside in panic, making for all the better targets.

'Single shots!' ordered Kaderic. 'Woe to the man who thinks these things are worth more than a bolter shell each!'

It was a swift and bloody business. The attack was cut down in a few moments, and a handful of surviving creatures limped off into the darkness.

'I suggest,' said Lysander, 'we weather what they throw at us and break out after dawn, when they are drained and exhausted.'

'You would not fight them here to the end?'

'No, Chaplain. Every moment we delay gives Kulgarde more time to learn of our path and prepare for our arrival.'

'Could these things answer to Kulgarde?' asked Lycaon.

'I can only say I hope not.'

From the forest to the north loped an alpha, just beyond bolter range. It was upright, taller than a Space Marine, its filthy, sagging body giving way to sinews around its shoulders powering its forelimbs, clad in chitin as if it had been fitted with a suit of armour. It shrieked and howled at the sky, and the forests around it seemed to seethe with movement. The weak light found wet mandibles and glossy scales everywhere in the shadows. The full part of the predators' power was drawn up around the Space Marines' encampment.

'What sport this will be!' voxed Kaderic from the barricades. 'I would take my blade to them, Chaplain, if I could!'

'Not unless they breach our line, First Sergeant,' replied Lycaon.

'Then I pray one of them does,' said Kaderic. 'Almost as much as I pray they all fall to our guns first.'

The alpha shrieked again, and this time the sound was echoed by the all the predators as one. The alpha dived out of cover and scampered across the no-man's-land before the barricades, followed by the entire host of creatures.

Thousands of them charged as one. Lysander saw in that moment the great variety of their shapes – some bulky and apelike, others slithering like snakes or loping like attack dogs. They varied from rodent-sized to two or three times the size of a man, all armed with every natural weapon evolution could come up with – claws, clubbing tails, mandibles like mouthfuls of blades.

Kaderic gave the order. A volley of bolter fire hammered into the horde. Countless fell. Bolter fire exploded among them, blasting off limbs and ripping bodies open. Lycaon gestured to the men of his squad and they joined Kaderic's men at the barricades, lending their own bolter fire.

Gorvetz concentrated on the biggest. The plasma cannon, once held by the fallen Brother Kalanar, was now in Gorvetz's own hands, blasting fat bolts of white-hot plasma that spitted right through the largest of the predators. Kho took *Dorn's Dagger* a few metres above the ground and rattled off cannon fire into the thickest mass of the enemy.

Lysander felt almost detached, as if he was watching

from far away. It was almost mesmerising to watch the tide of the enemy surge closer, and yet come no closer, because as soon as they reached bolter range they fell. Those behind them surged into the gap, were cut down, and were themselves replaced. It had an inevitability about it, as if he was watching the tides or the movement of the stars.

Lycaon took aim and stuttered off a volley from his own bolter. His crozius was slung on his back, as if he knew he would not have to use it here. His shots threw a couple more dead down into the mass, which was building up like a rampart of shredded corpses in a ring around the encampment. 'There is no battle here,' said Lycaon, with scorn in his voice as if he blamed the enemy for being too weak to be a worthy fight.

Lysander knew Malodrax better than the other Imperial Fists there. He may not have been an expert – not knowledgeable enough to write a book about the place as Inquisitor Golrukhan had done – but he had witnessed the cruel will of the planet and Lycaon's comment stirred something in his memory.

Through the carnage the alpha lurched, shot through with a dozen bolt-rounds. It flopped to the ground in front of the corpse rampart, dragging itself along on shattered arms. A heavy bolter stuttered fire at it from Squad Gorvetz and it reared up as if in defiance, but instead of a letting out a final howl it fell back down silent and dead.

The alpha's death was the signal. The ground

shuddered and pitched to one side. Lysander fell to one knee, and saw Halaestus tumbling off his feet by the barricades. A sound like thunder rumbled up from beneath. Then the ground dropped away entirely, an avalanche of pulverised earth accompanying Lysander down into a deep pit beneath the encampment.

Everything was darkness and noise. An awful stench, again with that note of familiarity, hit Lysander in the face – rot, ashes and long-dried blood.

He came to rest buried, and pushed around to make enough room to dig himself out. For a moment he was back in the heap of bodies in Shalhadar's city the last time he had been on this damned planet, struggling to breathe.

He made enough room around himself to claw at the earth in front of his face. Half a minute later he had broken out of it and was unearthing himself. There was just enough moonlight struggling down from above to see by.

He was in the centre of a great crossroads of warrens, with tunnels leading off in all directions. Shed skins, effluent and trash were gathered around what part of the floor wasn't buried by earth from the collapsed ceiling. Lysander hawked out a mouthful of spit and soil.

He still had his chainsword with him, but his bolter was buried somewhere. He aimed a mental curse at himself for being disarmed in the presence of the enemy. He would have to practice penance on the *Phalanx* for his sin, if he ever saw the corridors of that space station again.

He could see no other Imperial Fists but he could hear them, calling out to one another from elsewhere in the warren. Lysander forced himself all the way out of the drift of earth and tried to get his bearings. He could have tumbled down a sloping tunnel and come to rest a long way from the site of the Imperial Fists encampment.

He tried the vox. 'Lysander here,' he voxed on the command channel.

'This is Lycaon,' came the reply.

'It was a trap,' said Lysander. 'They herded us into position and collapsed the tunnels underneath us.'

'Dorn spoke no good of those who state the obvious, captain,' came the reply. 'What is your location?'

'I don't know, Chaplain. I'm on my own. I can hear others.'

'We are regrouping just south of the encampment site, where several tunnels converge. Find others and make your way to us.'

'Yes, Chaplain.'

A voice in Lysander's memory, perhaps from that man he had once been before he became a Space Marine, reminded him that he knew what the predators were, where they had come from, and what they wanted. It reminded him he had not told Chaplain Lycaon of this. Had he wanted to disbelieve it? Or was he ashamed?

The stench rose. Lysander felt himself choking on it. Through the darkness loomed a shape that also had that terrible familiarity to it, a sagging mass of a torso, spindly neck and vulture head.

'Ah, there you are,' said the brood mother with a chuckle.

The daemon's face was smeared with blood and she dragged behind her the corpse of an Imperial Fist, his torso ripped open. His helmet had been torn off and his bloodspattered face was wide-eyed with shock and pain. Brother Kollus of Squad Kaderic.

'Did you think you could come back to Malodrax and hide from me?' the brood mother continued. Lysander saw she was bigger than the first time he had seen her, gorged on her young. Their foetal corpses dangled from her midriff, neglected and rotting. She was gnarled and armoured with scar tissue, and her red eyes gleamed. 'I can smell you, traveller. I will never forget your tender scent. I would follow you through the blood ocean, across the Mountains of Glass, through the gates of Kulgarde itself!'

Lysander took his chainsword in a two-handed grip. The brood mother stalked closer, swinging Kollus's body playfully. Behind her, Lysander saw another Imperial Fist clambering in through a side tunnel, but he could not make out who it was.

Time, he thought. He needed more time.

'What are you on this world?' said Lysander, squaring his feet and looking the daemon in its decaying face. 'Vermin? The lowest of the low? Feeding on the filth that the higher creatures leave behind?'

'You seek to anger me. I know no anger. I know no fear or joy or hatred. I know only passion, Imperial Fist. I know only the raw emotion of the warp. That you

214

could feel it yourself! That you could revel in it!' She was within a few paces of Lysander now, blotting out the moonlight from above. She leaned in close. 'Stay with me,' she said.

A volley of bolter shots thudded into her side. The brood mother shrieked and lashed out with Kollus's body in the direction the shots had come from, knocking aside the Imperial Fist who had jumped up from the cover of a fallen rock to take aim. She turned from Lysander and bore down on her attacker.

In her other hand she held a weapon – a chainsword. The chainsword Lysander had given her in exchange for the way to the city of Shalhadar.

The Imperial Fist rolled onto his back just as the brood mother raised the chainsword to bring it down and cut him in half.

It was Halaestus, his ruined face defiant.

The brood mother reeled back. 'Oh, what hideousness!' she shrieked. 'Such ugliness!' Her face was contorted with shock, and Lysander saw in her expression what he himself felt to look upon her.

Lysander charged at the brood mother. He slashed at her and sliced through her arm with his chainsword before he slammed shoulder-first into her midriff. She toppled backwards, the atrophied remnants of her dozens of young looking up at him with the wide blank eyes of their dried-out skulls. He thudded on top of her and felt his hand sinking into her pocked flesh as he tried to push himself upright.

The brood mother brought her chainsword – the chainsword Lysander had given her – up towards him. Lysander caught it against his own chainblade and the two screeched as their teeth ground against one another. Lysander was face to face with the daemon, and the stench of her was almost enough to knock him out.

'Stay,' she gasped.

Lysander drew back his fist and plunged it into her face. Bone and teeth splintered. Foul-smelling gore spattered across his face.

The brood mother was shrieking, half in pain, half in an awful cacophony of excitement, a gruesome ecstasy at Lysander's touch. Lysander drove his fist down again and again and the brood mother reared up under him, throwing him off onto his back in the dirt. She clutched at her shattered face, sweeping around her at random with the chainblade.

Brother Halaestus shot her through the throat with his bolter. Her head toppled to the side on its broken stalk. Halaestus punched three more shots through her throat and upper chest.

Insensible, blind, the brood mother flopped onto her front and writhed through the dirt, mewling and spluttering as she groped through the filth.

Lysander clambered out of the refuse pit and took one of the side tunnels, gauging his direction and striking out for what he thought was the site of the encampment. He could hear bolter fire up ahead, and by the time he reached the knot of Imperial Fists fighting alongside Lycaon the brood mother's offspring lay in heaps around them, shot down or cut to pieces.

'Captain Lysander!' said Lycaon. 'You are late to the fight, alas.'

'The daemon who leads them is laid low,' replied Lysander. 'Just behind me.'

'Dead?'

'As good as. A good dose of flame will see to it.'

The Imperial Fists regrouped and forged through the tunnels to the brood mother. She writhed and squealed pathetically, like a whipped animal. Sergeant Gorvetz ordered Brother Antinas forwards, as he had at the war engine, and the result was the same. Antinas drenched the brood mother in burning fuel and the flames of her pyre reached up through the fallen ceiling and into the sky. She shrieked in the flame and clawed at the air above her, her flesh boiling away and only a deformed skeleton left to tumble into the mass of burning debris.

Lysander found Sergeant Gorvetz as the Imperial Fists watched the brood mother die. 'She killed Brother Kollus,' said Lysander.

Gorvetz watched the fire leaping high for a moment, even as the last remnants of the brood mother's shape crumbled away. 'This thing killed him,' he said. There was no emotion in his voice.

'I could not stop her.'

'Her?' Gorvetz rounded on Lysander. 'Her? You know of this creature?'

'She was spoken of,' said Lysander. 'A daemon, called the brood mother.'

'Filth upon the day we came here,' spat Gorvetz. 'This is no place to leave a good brother behind.'

The fire was dying down, the fast-burning fuel feeding a hot but short-lived flame. Lycaon walked through the burning detritus closer to the ashes and scorched bones that remained of the brood mother. He poked around in the debris, bent down, and came up clutching the scorched length of a chainsword. Golden paint still clung to it, and to the clenched fist symbol of the Chapter.

'Brother Lysander,' said Lycaon. 'You left your weapon in your foe.'

'It's not his,' came a voice from across the chamber. Brother Halaestus walked forwards, the dying fire flickering its orange glow across the patchwork face that had so horrified the brood mother. 'It's mine.'

ON THE WAY out of the warrens the moon sank in the sky, as if it were drowning the petrified forest in spite. The few surviving young of the brood mother scurried away from the remains of the battlefield, where they had been scavenging on the carrion of their dead around the crater where the Imperial Fists barricades had been. Kho's pair of Land Speeders patrolled overhead, taking pot shots at the larger creatures that did not flee at the first sound of booted feet on the ashen ground.

'Where did she find it?' said Halaestus. He had walked

up behind Lysander, waiting until they were out of earshot of the rest of the strike force. The other Imperial Fists were securing the immediate perimeter, making ready to move out.

Lysander tried to read Halaestus's expression. He had always been steadfast, rarely emotive, a reliable and trustworthy soldier. Now there was even less to see of the man he knew, the new sections of his face artificial and dead.

'Brother?' asked Lysander.

'You know full well. My chainsword. How did the brood mother get it?'

'The Iron Warriors took our gear at Kulgarde,' said Lysander.

'And how did my blade make it into the daemon's hands?'

'How do I know?' snapped Lysander, a little too sharply. 'Thul bartered it with her. One of the fortress's scum stole it and pawned it away.'

'To a creature that followed us and ambushed us? Two connections between you and the brood mother, Lysander. She has a weapon from one of your squadmates in her hand, and she sought out an army that includes you.'

'Do you intend to accuse me, brother?' said Lysander, forcing his voice level. 'Of what?'

'Accuse you? No, captain. Just state facts. Brothers are dead and your footprints are all over the world that claimed them. Just facts.'

Lysander grabbed Halaestus by the back of the neck and pushed his face close. 'You have lost everything that makes a Space Marine into an Imperial Fist. Your thoughts are not your own. Stay them, Brother Halaestus.'

'You think I have lost my mind?' retorted Halaestus. 'What did you do on Malodrax, Lysander? Answer us. What did you do?'

Lysander let Halaestus go. Now the anger in Halaestus was clear, and a mania simmered behind his eyes that did not belong in a level-headed, disciplined Imperial Fist. 'You are not yourself, brother,' he said. 'Back on the *Phalanx*, that will change. Until then I ask that you trust me.'

Lysander walked back towards the bulk of the strike force, now approaching a long rise in the ground that formed a blasted ridge covered in the stone trunks of fallen trees.

'I have not forgotten you saved my life,' said Halaestus after him. 'But there is only so much that buys. If you betrayed what you are, you will never fully leave this planet. You know that, Lysander! You know I speak truth!'

10

'My own brand of heresy is a common one. I am humble enough to admit that. What if knowledge was a weapon, I came to ask? Knowledge of the enemy, so warned against by the Imperial Creed, which could be a keener blade than ignorance? Instead of obeying the Creed I hoarded such knowledge and most sinfully of all, when I learned I was not alone, I sought the company of others who shared in my heresy. Thus was the name of Malodrax first passed to me, a world of daemons where countless secrets were waiting to become our mortal sins.'

– Inquisitor Corvin Golrukhan

LYSANDER'S FIRST SIGHT of the sphinx was as it circled the pinnacle of Shalhadar's pyramid, light shimmering through it as it came down to land. A canal surrounded the pyramid, stocked with iridescent fish that burst like fireworks when they leapt from the water. The only bridge to the palace led to the main gates, and it was in front of these gates that the sphinx came to land with a grace that should not have been possible for something of its enormous size.

'Keeper of the gate!' called out Talaya the herald of Shalhadar, from the other end of the bridge where she stood with Lysander. 'Someone thinks himself good enough to stand before the Veiled One in audience!'

'Wonderful,' purred the sphinx, its voice a kingly rumble from deep in its barrel chest. 'I was getting hungry.' It padded a few steps along the bridge and brought its massive feline head low, peering at Lysander. 'And is this it?'

Talaya had brought Lysander to a tower of many chambers, most of them dark, smoky dens where citizens lounged in the grip of visions and nightmares brought about by braziers of smouldering narcotics. Among them were stands of antiques, including sets of armour, from which Lysander had been bade select a suit that fitted him. Most were made for men of normal size but Lysander had found a set of oversized full plate, lacquered red and scalloped like the shell of a sea creature. He had not taken the helmet, which was fashioned into an expressionless human face with an extra eye in the forehead, and instead went bare-headed. He had found a sword, too, a fine two-hander which a Space Marine could wield in one, carried in a scabbard of gold and emerald at his waist. He still carried Inquisitor Golrukhan's book, held by a strap to one armoured thigh.

'And why,' rumbled the sphinx, 'would my lord the

Veiled One stoop to share a realm with such a ragged peasant?'

'I have brought you this far,' said Talaya to Lysander. 'The rest is up to you.'

Lysander walked onto the bridge, within a few steps of the sphinx. Its stained-glass wings surrounded it in a halo of colour, shimmering across the stone and gilt of its body. Its face had more of a cat about it than a human, its eyes bright and expressive considering it seemed to have been forged rather than born. A deep purr shuddered the surface of the bridge as its enormous chest rose and fell.

'The Veiled One will see me,' said Lysander.

'Will he now?' replied the sphinx. 'How very certain you sound.'

'I will pay what must be paid.'

The sphinx smiled, showing its teeth. 'I doubt that greatly, strange little thing. I doubt there is anything you have that I could want.'

'You do not want anything, save to serve your master. And you will serve him by letting me through.'

'Do you really want to go through the whole charade? You know I must kill you if you are found wanting. Not that I would wish for anything else, of course, but there are rules that must be followed. One of them is that you must know the consequences of standing before me. Throw yourself on your belly and beg me for mercy, with tears in your eyes, and you may withdraw.'

'Your role as gatekeeper is to weed out the unworthy,'

said Lysander, 'for only the worthy can pay. You are a creature formed from the will of the Prince of Pleasure, the Lord of Unspeakable Excess. Your currency is sensation. That is how I will pay you.'

'Not just any sensation,' said the sphinx. 'Something new. Something I have never felt before. And I am as old as this world! Your race was not yet dribbled from the guts of rotten Terra when I was already ancient. I have seen the infinite thoughtscapes of the warp and the foulest debasements of the noblest men. What can you show me that I have not yet felt?'

'You can read minds,' said Lysander. It was not phrased as a question.

'I can consume them whole,' replied the sphinx. 'That came to bore me many aeons ago.'

'Read mine,' said Lysander.

The sphinx crouched down, folding its arms. 'And what a tiny, closed mind you have. Pray, what is in here that might interest me?'

Lysander felt the daemon's touch. It was like a slimy, unclean thing that slithered around the inside of his skull, extruding feelers into his mind. His skin shuddered and his stomachs tightened up, and every instinct he had told him to draw his sword and set about the sphinx with a view to putting out its eyes. But he held his hand still, took in a breath to steady himself, and threw his mind back to Gravenhand Ridge.

There were many choices for Lysander to bring forward. He chose Gravenhand Ridge because it was so

MALODRAX

Contents

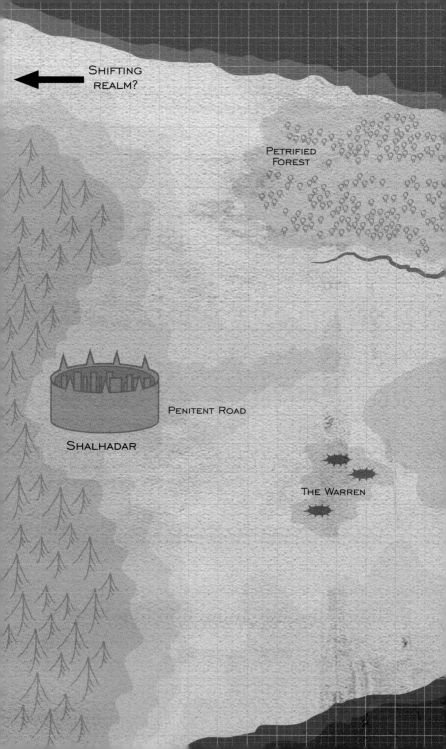

SHIFTING
REALM?

PETRIFIED
FOREST

PENITENT ROAD

SHALHADAR

THE WARREN

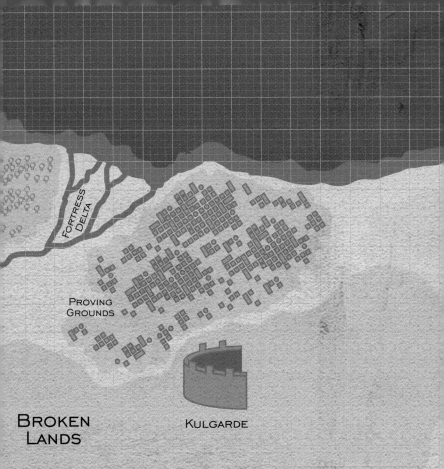

FORTRESS
DELTA

PROVING
GROUNDS

KULGARDE

BROKEN
LANDS

HINTERLANDS OF KULGARDE & THE CITY OF SHALHADAR

Corun Golrukhan

BLOOD OCEAN

KRAEGON THUL

raw, so crude. A madman named Gladian Scraw had risen to power on a promise to restore his home world's aristocracy to supremacy. It was a story repeated on countless worlds with disaffected social classes, vulnerable to men like Scraw who offered them a dream for a future that could not possibly be. There were so many planets like that in the Imperium that the name of the particular world didn't matter.

Lysander picked out a memory of the first time he saw Scraw's stronghold, defended on one side by the stormy cliffs of the ocean and on the other by the steep scree of Gravenhand Ridge. He had seen it from the air, through the viewfinder of a drop pod as it plummeted towards the ancient castle where Scraw was based.

The castle doubled as an execution ground. Its wings enclosed a courtyard where Scraw's inner guard herded the planet's dissidents into ranks to be shot down with volleys of autogun fire. So voluminous were the deaths that a whole social class had grown up to process and murder those that Scraw feared, hated, or merely disliked. At the moment the Imperial Fists drop pods broke through the clouds Scraw was sitting on a balcony overlooking the execution ground, imbibing his regular dose of narcotic and juvenat drugs from a crystal glass as the day's first executions greeted the dawning sun.

Scraw was a noble-faced man, carefully sculpted by the planet's most exclusive skinscapers to resemble the aristocratic ideal. His finely curved eyebrows raised as the drop pods appeared in the sky, hurtling towards his castle, retro thrusters burning to decelerate them as they arrowed in towards the courtyard.

Scraw had sold whatever soul he had to the powers of the warp in return for lordship over his world. From a spectral gateway he summoned marched a host of burning daemons, like suits of ornate armour filled with fire, answering the contract that Scraw had signed. When the Imperial Fists landed among the corpses of the day's first dead, they were met by a legion of daemons of the Blood God.

Lysander remembered the smell – blood old and fresh, the familiar stink of the newly dead. The sulphur and flame of the daemons. He remembered Scraw screaming from his balcony, demanding that his daemonic allies slaughter the intruders where they stood.

But he remembered most clearly the fury of the slaughter. The Imperial Fists met the enemy with a wrath that equalled the daemons' own. The daemons were used to mortal men cowering before them, either fleeing or fawning. The Imperial Fists did neither.

The blades through flesh. The flame washing over golden armour. Lysander brought every moment back to the front of his memory.

The Imperial Fists were led that day by Chaplain Chrysonerus, whose purity of spirit made him the ideal commander to lead his brothers in the face of the daemon. Lysander brought forth the image of Chrysonerus hacking daemons to pieces with his crozius, the power mace in the shape of a gilded winged skull that flashed in his hand as if he were battling with a shard of lightning.

And most of all, he remembered their victory. He remembered Chrysonerus wading through the burning remains of the daemon legion, storming into the castle and throwing Scraw down to the courtyard. He remembered Chrysonerus dragging a sobbing Scraw towards the spectral gateway, which still stood open onto the black flames of the daemons' home world in the warp.

'See, Gladian Scraw,' Chaplain Chrysonerus said. 'To you what lies beyond is an unknowable realm, where powers greater than any of us hold sway. To you it is a place of awe. To us, to the pure-hearted servants of the Emperor, it is one more nest of enemies to be purged. Brothers! Imperial Fists and Sons of Dorn! Will you follow me?'

Gladian Scraw screamed as the Imperial Fists cheered and followed Chrysonerus into the gateway. Lysander was among them as they marched through the gateway to the Garden of Vharlan Ghesh, ruled over by a daemon prince sworn to the Blood God, a realm of bloody madness where his legions battled endlessly for the delight of their master.

Lysander did not dwell on how Gladian Scraw died, doubled up with madness to look on the insanity of this realm. He did not even focus on the revenge the Imperial Fists took on Vharlan Ghesh, or the many battles fought there against the daemons of the Blood

God. He focused instead on that moment when Chaplain Chrysonerus had called on his battle-brothers to charge into hell, and they had followed him.

That was how much the Imperial Fists, the human race, hated daemonkind. That was how deep their disgust and their desire for revenge went. If they could, every Space Marine in the Imperium would storm into the warp and butcher every single daemon, every wayward thought the Chaos Gods gave form, and would march to the foot of those very gods' thrones.

Lysander's mind had a whole gallery of these memories. The memories of hate, the force of a human's anger focused through the discipline of a Space Marine and directed at the daemon. It was a pure hate, a disgust at the unnatural origin of the daemon and a rage at everything it stood for.

Rogal Dorn had written that there was no star in the galaxy that burned as bright as an honest human's hatred, and no hatred as hot as that directed at the daemon.

The sphinx recoiled. Its front paw hovered over Lysander, its eyes focused far away.

'Do you see?' said Lysander. 'Do you understand now what we are? For everything you are, for each one of us you kill, for every one you corrupt and force to his knees, there are a billion more directing every moment of their hatred at you. And what you feel now is something you have never felt, and that is my payment to you.'

'And what is it?' asked the sphinx. 'What is this ice that flows through me? This dark claw that clutches my mind?'

'It is fear,' said Lysander. 'My kind were created to feel no fear, but we understand it. We were all once men who felt fear as does anyone else, and we must know it because it is a weapon we wield.'

'I have never felt this before,' said the sphinx. There was a note of wonderment in its voice. 'This fear. I have heard the word, I have seen it in the eyes of those thrown onto the altars of the Pleasure God, but I have never felt it until now! This is a sensation I feel for the first time. And so the toll is paid.'

The sphinx stood aside. Behind it rose the great golden gates of the pyramid. The sphinx settled down on its haunches, taking up its place watching over the bridge. Lysander walked past it and the gates began to open.

He glanced behind him. Talaya had watched the exchange with a curious smile on her face. As Lysander approached the palace gates she turned away and walked back into the sprawl of the city.

THE SHEER LAVISHNESS of the palace was designed to dull the senses and overwhelm an inquisitive mind. It was a kind of camouflage, Lysander realised, just like scrim nets stretched across an Imperial Guard camp or the baffling burst of signals emitted by a strike cruiser to mask its communications.

The inside of the pyramid was divided into countless chambers, curved and irregular in shape, by walls plated in gold and silver or lacquered in deep blue and vivid violets. Scaffolds were set up everywhere and a small army of the city's people were swarming over them, painting in sketched-out frescoes on the ceiling or laying mosaics on the floor. Lysander could make out the vaguest hints of twisted bodies in the paintings, inhuman shapes and features melting into one another. A sense of uncleanness crawled over him and he looked away. The floor was no better, for while the designs were abstract they were mesmerizingly complex. They seemed to want to draw his eyes right out of his head.

'You!' cried out a voice. Lysander looked up from the floor to see one of the painters advancing towards him. It was a man, his age impossible to guess given the artistic mutilations covering his face. His nose had been cut off, leaving a pair of nostril slits, as had his ears. His eye sockets had been pared back to reveal the whole of his eyeballs, unblinking and rimmed with exposed muscle. He wore paint-spattered robes and carried reams of parchment and canvas covered in paintings and sketches. 'Take up a brush or a trowel, newcomer! Beautify this place! Scrub away its ugliness!' He looked Lysander up and down, appraising his crimson armour and sword. 'Eyes of the warp, you are ugly enough yourself. Just by standing there you put us back months! Make yourself useful!'

'I seek Shalhadar the Veiled,' said Lysander.

The artist dropped the mass of painting he was carrying. 'No one sees the Veiled One,' he said.

'He will see me.'

'We are not there yet!' cried the artist. The painters and mosaicists looked up at his outburst. 'The story hasn't reached his entrance! He is in the wings, ugly one!'

Lysander grabbed the artist by the shoulder, gripped hard and lifted the man off the ground. The artist's mutilated eyes rolled in fear. 'Where is he?' demanded Lysander.

'In the… in the wings…' gasped the artist.

Lysander threw the artist aside. 'Out!' he yelled. 'Everyone out!' He drew his sword and held it high.

The people of Shalhadar's city clambered down from the scaffolds and ran for the gates. Their half-painted frescoes glared down with thousands of eyes set in daemonic faces. Those working on the mosaics fled too, leaving scars in the unfinished floors. Among the artisans Lysander saw the many varieties of the city's heresy – some had decorative scars and mutilations like the lead artist, and others were robed and stitched like the cultists from the alleyway. There were new ones, too, like those with patches of iridescent scales sewn onto their skin or with their flesh blistered up with wriggling egg sacs. The latter reminded Lysander of the brood mother, and he steadied his hand against the instinct to cut them down.

With his sword in hand, Lysander walked further into the palace. It was impossible to tell how far the palace extended, for the dimensions within the pyramid made little sense given its apparent size when seen from the outside. With the artists gone sounds echoed from deeper in the palace – footsteps perhaps, skin on skin, the whispered voices of daemons. Shadows coalesced on the edges of his vision, the movement banished when he tried to focus on it.

Ahead a vast domed space opened up. It resembled, of all things, an opera house, with an enormous pipe organ dominating one wall, reaching high up to the arching ribs of the ceiling. A round stage stood in the centre of the hall, surrounded by circles of seating.

As Lysander entered, the light from thousands of candles hanging in holders from the ceiling went dim, save for a shaft of light falling on the stage. A single figure walked into the light. Lysander couldn't see where he had entered from. He wore a long white robe and his face was heavily made up in white, with black lips and eyes daubed on as if his features were twisted in mourning.

'Many thanks, traveller, for your attendance at our sorrowful show!' said the actor in a wailing voice. 'You could have been anywhere in the infinite galaxies this night! Enveloped in the bosom of fleshy luxury. Riding the waves of the endless ocean of the mind. On some distant world of beauty, grasping its ethereal wonder before it is spoiled by the cruelty of the mundane. But no! You are here, with us, to witness the Tragedy of the Cadaverous Lord!'

Lysander realised he was being addressed, though the actor did not look at him directly and spoke to the whole opera house as if every row were packed with spectators. The actor bowed gravely and was spirited away again, vanished into a hidden trapdoor or by an optical illusion. Lysander chose not to sit.

The lighting shifted to the warmth of a morning sun. Dozens of extras walked across the stage now, in archaic Imperial dress such as that still favoured by some of the Imperium's oldest aristocracies. They wore ruffs and long trains, enhanced with decorative bionics. Their bionics were non-functional, and where they met the skin the actors' makeup could not conceal the torn skin and weeping wounds.

They began a song of longing and misery, echoed by strains of music from the pipe organ and from concealed musicians whose sound boomed from every direction. The actors hit harmonies too complex for their apparent numbers. They sang of how the soul of mankind had withered away, leaving the people empty and barren.

'Where has gone the oversoul that conquered Terra/Where has gone the lust to enslave stars?'

A great and benevolent power saw the suffering of the human race. It was depicted by a voice booming from off-stage, presumably belonging to a man of the city selected for his deep, reverberating baritone. Lysander could not be sure if it was a god or some kind of collective will of humanity.

He could not see where the tale would lead yet, but it brought about such an unease in him that he felt a flicker of a very human weakness. His bile rose and he had a stale, acid taste in his mouth, though he could not place just what in the opera and its performance was affecting him.

He could walk onto stage and throw the actors off. He wouldn't even have to bloody his blade. Bare fists would be more than enough. But he reeled in his hatred again, that only minutes before he had been baring raw and bleeding for the sphinx at the gates. He did not remind himself what he had done to get this far, because it brought about a deepening of his unease.

The god called forth its servants, all garbed like angels from the margins of prayer books. They had wings of wooden frames and feathers, and golden halos riveted to their temples. They danced and sang of the infinite wisdom and kindness of their master, who still went unseen and unnamed. One among them was different – he wore a mask of gold, and his feathers were golden, too, laced with red ribbons and gemstones. According to the lyrics he was most favoured of the god's servants and was sent down to humanity to give them back the joy and life they had lost.

But this servant, over the course of the next hour or so, fell from grace. He first deprecated the temples built to him, and said he should not be treated as a god, but eventually he came to accept them and then to desire them. He lounged among throngs of concubines brought to beautify his court. He gave the people a purpose, but it was to serve him, to glorify him and grant him his every desire. He was corrupted through and through until even the people could not pretend he was anything else.

The actor playing this false god did not remove his golden mask throughout the performance, until a climactic scene where the people finally rose up and demanded he prove to them that he was a god deserving of their adoration. The false god rose from his throne of heaped-up bodies and threw back his hood, taking his mask in his hands as the music swelled and he sang of his power and perfection, and damned those who doubted him. He would show them the face of their god, and they would be struck into blind, mindless servitude to look on it as punishment for rising up.

The false god took off his mask. Beneath was a rotted, skeletal face, the skin peeled away and the muscle turned to a maggoty pulp. The eyes were sunken in their sockets and the teeth grinned from pared-back lips.

A terrible atonal music of horror took over. Actors in Imperial garb rushed across the stage screaming, contorting. They trampled and threw one another from the stage. Such was the violence that Lysander was certain the blood was real. Some were dragged off stage insensible, perhaps even dead.

When it was done and the stage was empty, when even the false god had left for the wings, a few survivors straggled into the light. They sang they would follow the greater power, the one who had been usurped and betrayed by his corrupted servant, for they had seen how the false god's corruption had manifested itself in the face of a corpse. They vowed to worship only the true power, to follow his path and reach his city. They took the symbols of the Young Prince, the Sigil of Pleasure, and the Hand Unchained, to deny the false god's ancient dogmas of obedience, denial and suffering. And so the tragedy ended on a note of hope, a counterpoint to the horror of the climax.

The clown-like narrator shambled back onto the stage, newly spattered with blood. 'You who could have been anywhere, nestled in a velvet pit of pleasure or kneeling before the altar of the awesome, you chose instead to grant us the honour of your attention. And our gift to you is the Tragedy of the Cadaverous Lord! Thus the one called Emperor enslaved the souls of his people. But what of our brave band who saw the fall from grace, who espied that corpse-face on the mask of gold? In this city, wonder of wonders, they gather! Before the Veiled One, Lord of Lords, they kneel! And that is the greatest honour you could give us. To stand among us, to marvel at the beauty of Shalhadar, and to cast back the darkness of the Corpse-God from this holy place.' The narrator bowed low, and with a final soaring note from the hidden musicians the light fell dead and the opera house was full of darkness.

Lysander steadied his breathing. The performance was finished, but he had not finished his business here.

Someone was clapping a few seats away. Lysander looked closer and saw the actor who had played the Cadaverous Lord, still in full costume with corpse mask, applauding the play. A spotlight came up on him and up close Lysander could see the mask was not just a facsimile – it was rotting flesh, wriggling with maggots and shedding flakes of desiccated skin as the actor clapped.

'Such economy of expression!' the Cadaverous Lord said. 'Such purity of vision! A truly great work cuts to the heart of its subject. The cruelty of a regime that shackles the mind, the very function of its creativity, and yet a regime that is borne also of the misguided will of those same minds, must have posed an irresistible opportunity to the author. And a challenge, for who could encompass such grand tragedy? Indeed, it is impossible. The work we have seen does not attempt to do it, but to hint at it, so the mind of the audience fills in for the truly appalling fate of the human race. Do you not think so? Tell me, you cannot have watched this unmoved.'

Lysander looked into the mask's eyes, but there was nothing living there, just the dried-out whites like crumpled paper sitting deep in the sockets. 'You are Shalhadar the Veiled,' said Lysander.

'And why,' replied the Cadaverous Lord, somehow managing to place a quizzical expression on his decaying face, 'would you say that?'

'Because this was meant for me.'

'This, my friend, is an ancient work of the greatest cultural resonance. One of the classics.'

'Everywhere I have gone on this planet,' said Lysander, ignoring the Cadaverous Lord's words, 'I have been tested. A daemon tested me to let it relive the glory of the time it spent before slavery. Another challenged me to best it in a trade, to get what I wanted without giving up what I could not afford to lose. And the creature you keep outside tested me, too, to pay its toll. That is what this world does. Every planet touched by the warp has its own way of inflicting suffering. I have walked on them and seen it. Malodrax likes to make us dance, to complete tests as if we were schoolchildren, before we can get a glimpse of what we seek. I will play its game, daemon prince, for now, which is just as well for you because that performance was another test.'

'What a curious interpretation,' said the Cadaverous Lord, his voice conversational as if he and Lysander really were two enthusiasts of the arts discussing the latest performance. 'So the creator of this work has set us a challenge. Thus we are not passive, as witnesses, but active, as participants, striving against the author's will! Truly he is a master. But if this is true, my new friend, what is he testing in us?'

'Not in us,' said Lysander. 'In me. I am a Space Marine

and a servant of the Emperor, as you became aware from the moment I came within sight of your city. A Space Marine witnessing the blasphemy of your play should feel disgust and anger, and more than that – he should feel hatred. Hatred enough to storm onto the stage and butcher the actors, and tear your city apart searching for the playwright. If I had done that, you would have no use for me, because to merely be in your presence would cause me such revulsion that I would strike out against you. This is my duty, reinforced by the hatred a Space Marine must feel.'

'Just as well you passed, then,' said the Cadaverous Lord.

'There is a deeper hatred in me than your heresy inflamed. Even seeing you dressed as my Emperor, pantomiming him as a betrayer and a tyrant, was not enough to eclipse it. That was what I was being tested for. A hatred deep enough for you to use to your ben-efit. That is what you need from me, Shalhadar the Veiled. That is what I have shown you.'

'So,' said the Cadaverous Lord, 'you would not call yourself a fan?'

'It seems I overestimated Shalhadar,' said Lysander. He stood and turned for the exit from the opera house. 'I understood he needed useful men he could exploit, by offering them what they desired in return for their service. Evidently he has no use for a Space Marine after all.'

'I did not say that,' said the Cadaverous Lord.

Lysander stopped in mid-stride. 'What does it matter what you said? You are just an actor.'

'As are we all,' said the Cadaverous Lord. He removed the mask of rotting flesh. Inside there was no face, just a deep, swirling darkness like the depths of an ocean or a starless tract of space. 'The greatest vice to which I will admit is curiosity. After so many tens of thousands of years of existence, it is rare that my attention is grabbed. But you have grabbed it. A Space Marine on Malodrax is hardly new, for the Iron Warriors have infested it since your Age of Heresy. But one who claims loyalty to the corpse-god is something else, especially one who walks willingly into my city.'

'And what do I get for satisfying your curiosity?' said Lysander.

'You get what everyone desires on Malodrax,' said the Cadaverous Lord. 'You get to pull some strings instead of just being the puppet. So tell me, Lysander of the Imperial Fists. Just what is it that you hate more than the blasphemy of my court?'

'I hate Kraegon Thul,' said Lysander.

'I see.' The Cadaverous Lord seemed to ponder this for a moment, the void of his face churning. 'And what do you intend to do about it?'

'Kill him. And rescue my battle-brothers he holds captive in Kulgarde.'

'And you have come to my city to ask for my help.'

'Your help? You have never helped anyone or anything. It is not in the nature of the daemon. No, I am here because the creatures of the warp are jealous. You want to rule the whole of Malodrax. Your kind hunger for power and domination. One look at this city shows me that. You crave worship. This place is one huge church you built to yourself. Kraegon Thul stops you from building that church across half of Malodrax. You hate him just like I do, and through me you can wipe him off the face of this world. You will betray me, I do not doubt. You will make of me an offering to your god, if you can, once I am no longer useful to you. If, of course, I do not destroy you first.'

'You are not the first to have tried,' said the Cadaverous Lord.

'I have no doubt,' replied Lysander. 'Kulgarde was built for a reason. I dare not guess how many have been lost trying to breach it. But remember, Veiled One – none of them were Imperial Fists.'

'I left most of the decisions to Agent Sildyne, who while serving as my favoured assassin and spy had shown exceptional skill at reading the customs and perils of urban environments. At his suggestion my warband took over the home of a musician, evidently one of a class of performers and artists constantly competing for the attention of Shalhadar and the chance to enter his court. In spite of my losses myself, Sildyne, Grun and Thol, Talaya, the pilot Maskelin and Archivist Grunvelder still represented more than enough of a fighting force to despatch the occupant without any trouble. Thol and Grun squabbled over his

scalp, but I talked them down from settling matters with a knife fight.

'From this base I set about exploring and cataloguing the nature of this city. It was an impossible task, for like all things touched by Chaos it did not obey the rules that a saner place might cleave to. For instance, there was no economy to speak of, not as we understand it. How was the city's population fed? How did it maintain a population at all given the sacrifices and random blossomings of bloodshed that took place hourly? Who kept the gleaming spires and gilded streets clean of filth, so it met every day's dawn with a blaze of reflected gold and silver? Archivist Grunvelder was most perturbed by the lack of answers to these questions, and by now I was most aware of the decline of his mental faculties. But Sildyne understood. The wily assassin knew that only life and death are constant, for to him they were the defining features of every level of existence.

'The function of the city, if not the intricate details of its various interactions, became apparent to me. Though I ventured out little, leaving Sildyne and the feral worlder brothers to roam abroad for information and supplies, my perceptiveness is such that I beheld the most important truths. The pyramid was at the centre of the city, both physically and in the hearts and minds of its people. They lived, and the city existed, to fuel the need of the palace for beauty and talent, even though such beauty was often abhorrent to a sane mind. From the deprevations and devotional displays of the population were made apparent the most devoted and capable of celebrants, who might then be granted entry to the palace. Artists, musicians, actors, singers and dancers were in great demand, as were playwrights and those who were merely beautiful (by whatever strange standards of beauty applied there). The most depraved seekers of new sensations could also be plucked from their opiate-drenched dens to continue their debauchery at court. The means by which the power in the palace, this Veiled One, discovered the most talented citizens was obscure to me. I imagine he had agents in the city observing, much as Sildyne and the feral worlders served me.

'I concluded that entry to the pyramid, or at least the placing of an agent within, was of the greatest importance. Sildyne observed a beast guarding the pyramid's gates that, going by his description, resembled the centauroid half-feline beasts common from the myth-cycles of primitive worlds. Legend among the people, picked up by Thol who had proven able at sharing in a friendly drink with the locals while keeping his ears open, suggested the sphinx was the gatekeeper and decided who was permitted entrance. It is unlikely our strength could despatch such a beast. I determined that subterfuge, not force, was the key that would unlock the palace of the Veiled One to this agent of the Emperor's Inquisition.'

11

'That lies are the very substance of Chaos is a truth that need not be taught to anyone with the capacity to read and understand these words. Yet in our arrogance we assume that we alone are lied to, and that every movement and utterance of the daemon is intended solely to deceive us. Indeed not, for it is my belief that the greater part of daemonkind concern themselves not with humanity, but with other creatures of the warp. Among themselves they make war, forge pacts, make bargains, bind one another into servitude, and destroy. And among themselves, they lie.'

– Inquisitor Corvin Golrukhan

THE AMBASSADOR'S ENTRANCE had its own grandeur. It was at odds, deliberately so, with the aesthetic of Shalhadar's city, but was no less crafted for all that. It entered through one of the city's main gates and was preceded by a host of mutant slaves, chained together with links fixed to their iron collars, their feet shackled so they

could only shamble at walking pace. The procession
had to be seen, just like the city's own revellers and
works of art.

The mutants wore their status on their skin, not just
their many deformities, but the scars and brands that
covered them. They were the image of servitude, of
subhumanity – living, sentient beings crushed down
to something far less than that by the will of another.
Some were xenos – some could have been, if they were
not hugely mutated humans. Among them were the
lipless, gangly creatures that survived from Malodrax's
native species, and a few other more exotic things
beside – a couple of greenskinned orks, their flesh covered in scar tissue as deep as the bark of a storm-lashed
tree. A quadruped with dextrous mandibles, harnessed
like a beast of burden. An avian with the feathers fring-
ing its arms and torso ripped out, leaving a few wisps of
plumage hanging from its torn and pinkish skin. They
all walked in time, as if to the beat of a silent drum.

They hauled spiked chains attached to a war altar
that slid along the ground on rollers. The altar was set
on a slab of gleaming obsidian, and was crowned with
smokestacks belching out columns of grey-black fumes.
A pit of bubbling molten steel sent out waves of heat
haze, and set into it was a slab of stone. A blade was laid
out on the stone, a broadsword of exceptional ornate-
ness and size. Standing over the altar, like the smith
about to start work, was the ambassador himself – an
Iron Warrior, in the brutalist armour of his Legion, dark

gunmetal with black and yellow warning flashes at the joints.

Behind the altar was another mass of mutants, pushing it from behind. These were brute-mutants, swollen masses of muscle grinding beneath the scars on their backs and shoulders. Some of them were implanted with banner poles grafted onto their spines, flying standards depicting the iron mask symbol of the Legion. They left footprints in blood and filth on the gilded flagstones.

Thousands had emerged from their homes to watch the ambassador's arrival. The ugliness of the spectacle was a rare experience in Shalhadar's city. The stench of sweat and misery was even rarer. Nobles and aesthetes held nosegays to their faces. Others just gawped, and shuddered when the visor-slit of the ambassador's helm fell upon them.

Lysander watched from a high balcony, adjoining the tower floor assigned for his use. He could smell the greasy smoke from the forge-altar from his vantage point. He felt a spark of fire leaping in his chest as he recognised the ambassador's armour – it was the one Kraegon Thul had named Captain Hexal, the leader of the raiding party that had boarded the *Shield of Valour*.

Captain Hexal's hands were soaked in the blood of Brother Drevyn.

The sound of metallic clacking came from below the balcony. Talaya, the herald of Shalhadar, climbed up the wall, her steel talons digging into the stone. She stopped level with Lysander and cast a bored glance down at the ambassador's parade.

'You know him?' she asked.

'In passing,' replied Lysander.

'He is here to demand tribute,' continued Talaya. 'Kulgarde loves to remind us that we are not the only power on Malodrax. In a few moons we might send our own demands. These things ebb and flow.' A cruel smile came across Talaya's face. 'You could kill him,' she said.

'I was just thinking that myself,' said Lysander. 'A soldier always does. It is a reflex.' He leaned against the balcony rail, looking down at the crowds in the street. 'The drop is potentially fatal but the crowds will break my fall. If I am still mobile after the landing I can make it to the altar before the mutants in front of it react. Their collective reflexes will be slow. They are not a factor. Once on the altar, I can vault the anvil and be face to face with Hexal in three or four seconds.'

'Could you take him, if you got that far?'

Lysander drew his blade. It was exceptionally fine, the edge so keen it glowed, the blade shimmering with the patterns of countless foldings. 'This is a good sword,' he said, 'but it would still be an unpowered weapon against power armour. Hexal's armour is of an ancient mark. The weak points are the joints at the waist and between the arms. But that is only speaking relatively. Those points are still sounder than any mundane armour. Moreover, the first blow must be fatal or debilitating, otherwise Hexal will have the time to draw a weapon and fight back, as will the brute-mutants to the rear.'

'What are your chances?' asked Talaya.

'Of killing him? One in four. Of killing him and making it out of the street alive? A few per cent. Perhaps fewer than one if Hexal has a weapon to hand.'

'But there is a chance,' said Talaya, leaning a little closer, the mechanical arms mounted on her back hissing and spraying a fine mist of steam. 'You could kill him now. It is why you are here.'

'I could,' said Lysander. 'And a duty to the human race would be done. But even if everything went right, even if I killed Hexal and escaped in the bedlam, Kraegon Thul would still be alive and Kulgarde would still stand.'

'Then Hexal will survive,' said Talaya. 'For now.'

Lysander leaned back from the rail. 'So what is the next stage?'

Talaya pretended to think about this. There was something unwholesome about the sly, flirtatious smile on her face. 'That depends on what Hexal demands,' she said. 'Whatever it is, the Veiled One has a way to exploit it. He will state Kulgarde's demands in the stadium.'

'Then I will hear them,' said Lysander.

Below, a couple of brute-mutants were knocking aside spectators who got too close to the procession. The altar ground further into Shalhadar's city, leaving a trail of broken mutant stragglers as it went.

* * *

'It is time I write of what happened to Talaya.

'Some of my work I wrote down as it happened, always assuming that I would survive to leave Malodrax and dictate this memoir of my deeds there in the comfort of my spacecraft as I returned to my conclave's fortress. It has become apparent, however, that such a luxury may not be afforded me. Therefore I write of these events while I have yet to depart Malodrax, two days' march outside Shalhadar's city. Archivist Grunvelder is no longer with me – indeed, only Maskelin and Thol remain in my band – so I must write by hand in this blank volume I recovered from Grunvelder's effects.

'It was apparent to me that only by receiving an audience with Shalhadar could I acquire the understanding essential for the cleansing of Malodrax. It was always my intention that once I returned to my conclave, they would use the knowledge with which I presented them to return and sear this world of the filth encrusting it. I could hardly return to those ancient and powerful Inquisitorial heretics with nothing to show for this expedition, against which so many had argued. So I determined that I would do whatever it took to get the attention of Shalhadar, who thus far had more than earned his sobriquet of the Veiled One. Indeed, the name was coined for him purely because he bestowed a personal appearance so rarely.

'How many thousands of the city's inhabitants went through a lifetime of devotion, only to die never having laid eyes on Shalhadar? But those people were not inquisitors. Through the investigations of the city I had come to learn of *the great spectacles held in the stadium, a vast structure built into an impact crater adjoining the city and around which a great curve of wall had been erected, bulging beyond the roughly circular shape of the city like an enormous cancerous growth. Therein the spectacles were held not just to entertain the people, but to exalt the greatness of Shalhadar and, perhaps, to acquire entry to his court with a particularly grand display of skill or devotion.*

'The expedition to the stadium required a display of pageantry. Grun and Thol did not greatly appreciate their garb of heavy robes and various cultish accoutrements, but I permitted them to retain their lucky scalps and jawbone clubs under the folds. Maskelin, who in his youth had been an enthusiastic musician earning coins in the slums of Devlan, went ahead of us playing a set of pipes to herald our approach. As the member of the warband with the greatest personal gravity and natural authority, I garbed myself as a high priest of some obscure splinter warp religion with Talaya as my bearer of sacrificial implements.

'Grunvelder has been plagued by visions, and when I ordered him to spend several hours writing out scripture to cleanse his soul, the result was reams of pages scrawled in a dark tongue I did not know. I left him back at the tower we used as our base. By then we were all aware of what would be his fate, not least Grunvelder himself, though none spoke of it aloud.

'The stadium rose ahead of us, a magnificent crown of carved ivory. The donor creature was an immense leviathan, perhaps hauled out of the blood ocean I had seen when first

landing on Malodrax, its vast and misshapen skull mounted above the main gates. The gates of whalebone were etched with intricate scenes of sacrifice and mutilation, all carved with the bloodied fingerbone stubs of a caste of worshippers who gouged the carvings into the stadium's ivory. These souls gave their lives to the art, wearing their hands away until the few who reached a great age had worn their arms away to the elbow. I wondered how many of them ever knew what it felt to have the Veiled One's eye on them, or if they had all slaved, suffered and died without earning their lord's attention.

'But those hapless, forgotten souls were not inquisitors.

'Sildyne had preceded us to the stadium, and had concealed himself among the rafters. By our secure vox-link he informed me that the spectacle for that day was to be the construction of a living monument to Shalhadar. This suited my purpose well, for the Veiled One had been known to attend such acts of mass devotion in person. At the very least those who watched the city for their lord's benefit were sure to be in attendance.

'What can I say of what we saw there? A bald and workmanlike description will have to suffice. I cannot count the numbers who crowded the stadium's galleries, and while among them was a multitude of strange sights, they were not the true spectacle. No, that took place on the sand of the arena.

'Ten thousand men and women entered through the archways at stadium level. They had shed their various devotional fashions and wore silks of purple and light blue, which *were among the colours of Shalhadar's patron powers among the warp. Their feet were bare upon the sand. Many among them wept with joy. A great cheer went up when they made their entry, and yet there were angry mutterings beneath the sound for the crowds watching all wished they had the honour of serving in the spectacle.*

'Sildyne joined us, making his way like a ghost through the throng, and whispered in my ear that a covering of silk in the stands opposite housed a great dignitary searching for useful subjects to beautify or scandalise the court of Shalhadar. Thus I was assured my journey, and the risk it entailed, were not for nothing.

'The spectacle itself was as grand and awe-inspiring as it was appalling. The supplicants clambered together into a great living statue, an approximation of the icon I have seen scrawled in forbidden texts and carved into the skin of madmen – the sigil of the Lord of Pleasure, the warp power whose will Shalhadar served. Hundreds upon hundreds heaped themselves up to form its base, the shape growing higher, like an organic thing spreading branches, until I recognised with a note of horror in my soul what I was watching.

'Those at the base were crushed. Their blood stained the sand pink. Beneath the cheers and chanting of the crowds I could hear the weak screams of the trapped, and the sigh of bones snapping by the dozen. Some fell, dashed to death on the sand. Some faces I could see, eyes and tongues bulging as their midriffs were compressed beyond the point of survival. The living statue did not keep its shape for long, but in the moments it did I felt the eyes of the warp on me, its raw

malice bathing that stadium and its cold fingers probing for my soul.

'In the warp, the Lord of Unspeakable Pleasures was looking on. I knew he must see me there, and know I did not belong. I saw then how quickly my work in the city must be done.

'The sculpture dissolved as if in a rain of acid, its points and edges blurring as the bodies keeping its shape died. Those in the outermost layers, relatively low down, tumbled to the sand alive. Bodies fell after them crushed or suffocated. I did not watch, save to make sure that their sacrifice did not bring forth some monster from the warp. It is more awful to me that it did not. They went to their deaths willingly, not to bring about a great revelation or the birth of some patron beast, but solely to create a monument that lasted seconds for the benefit of a daemon prince not even in attendance.

'I travelled through the crowds, taking on the air of someone who does not expect to be stopped while going about his vital and sacred business. Thus the crowds parted for me tolerably quickly, with the feral worlder brothers shunting the stragglers out of my way. When I came within sight of the pavilion's inhabitant I called forth Talaya and asked her if, in the many works of mine I had ordered her to read, I had before recorded its like. She said I had not, which came as some relief, for it meant that the creature did not know me, either, and would not have encountered me in a guise other than the one I was wearing.

'A court of daemons lounged there amid sumptuous furnishings and clouds of opiate incense. Various beautiful

citizens lay alongside them, each one with a mark of owner-
ship on them, a disfigurement that was only visible from one
angle. Thus a beautiful woman might have one eye burned
out, and so appear hideous if she did not lie on one side as
she did among the daemons. The skin of a youth's back was
scorched and pared away, so he lay on his back. Thus the
possessions of this particular daemon were both marked as
his property, and rendered useless for anything other than the
very specific need he had of them to lie just so. The daemons
were like those of the court I had glimpsed before in the city,
lithe and athletic of limb, with pallid mauve skin and a her-
maphroditic allure that, thankfully, my studies had prepared
me well to resist. I saw in them the ugliness of their true
nature. Nothing is so foul as that veneer of beauty stretched
over corruption incarnate.

'The champion was something like them, sporting six arms
and a rack of antlers like those of a fine stag. He went barely
clothed, showing off the details of his anatomy which, while
humanoid, were inhuman enough to turn the stomach. He
dripped with jewels, gold and silver, and his eyes were ovals
of inky black.

'"So one among us has fought off the tedium," it said as I
approached its pavilion. "I feared I would waste away from
boredom. These insects truly believe they create something
wonderful with their fumblings." He waved a hand at the
arena, where hundreds of cultists of some funerary church
were hauling away the bodies across the bloodstained sand.
"What magic could be wrought that would instil some
imagination into them? Always they throw themselves upon

our altars and expect us to act as if a million have not done so before."

'My heresy had equipped me well with the means to converse with creatures abhorrent to the soul. "It held my interest," I said, "for among the worshipful of my world the form is to take the life of another, not give one's own. The sentiment is novel to me, if crudely articulated."

'"Oh, to witness something new!" the champion sighed. It breathed deep of the heavy air and exhaled a stream of smoke from gills that opened in its neck. My own respiratory implants kept the opiate from affecting my faculties, though the odour of it was hard to stomach. Talaya, standing by my side, had similar enhancements, though the feral worlder brothers did not and had thankfully remained outside the silken enclosure. "Do you bring with you some diversion that can illuminate these tedious hours? I wonder that my lord does not despair of it. All he wants is something original, something that has not been seen before, and yet all he gets is…" He waved one of his six hands at the arena again by way of illustration.

'"The city needs new blood," I said. "Literally, and figuratively."

'"And you have come to me," replied the daemon, examining the back of a hand, "because you are that new blood?"

'"A hundred thousand men fought on the cliffs above the Sea of Suffering, until but ten stood by the edge and the rocks foamed red. Those ten roamed the galaxy for a thousand years, and each brought back the skulls of a nation to the throne of our god."'

'These were the ramblings from the mind-journey of a madman whose memoirs were written on the walls of a cell. That cell was in the depths of my coven's Inquisitorial fortress, and I had studied them at leisure while recovering from a troublesome xenos lung-rot. I was thus armed with a whole catalogue of such blasphemies.

'"A little crude," said the herald.

'"That is the way the Blood God prefers his sacrifices," I said. "I call no one warp power my lord above others, and while I understand that such apostasy is obscene to those with little imagination, I thought the city of Shalhadar would be more open-minded. I am something of a freelancer in my trade. I have travelled the breadth of the galaxy and seen every flavour of worship that can be crammed into a human mind. I would not seek to win the graces of the Lord of Pleasures with a heap of a million skulls. Here there must be art to our devotions."

'"I see," said the herald. "A wandering priest, a missionary of the obscene."

'"I learned my trade in the Missionaria Galaxia of the Corpse-God," I ventured. This gambit was a risk, but there was no stepping back from the brink ahead of me. "But among the stars we see the truth, and the truth resides among the powers of the warp."

'"Would that the choice was solely mine," said the herald with a smile on his face. It reminded me faintly of a fish, as the mouth spread a little too wide and the eyes flickered black. "But by now you will have learned the balance that holds this world. There can be no true Chaos without some rule, no bedlam without a spark of sanity. There will be a payment for everything on Malodrax, and for me to put you in my lord's good graces comes with its own price."

'"As it must be," I replied. "Name it."

'"Something you love," was the reply.

'I had no way of telling if this was some curse or ban to be obeyed, or simply the herald's wanton tastes finding expression. In truth, it did not matter. If I was to stand face to face with Shalhadar the Veiled One, the toll would be paid.

'Of every million men, perhaps one might be suitable for the employ of the Inquisition. He must be prepared to do anything, starting with killing and dying and becoming ever more onerous, for reasons he does not understand and at the behest of an inquisitor he might never meet. He must murder those who do not deserve it. He must guard those he hates. And he must do all this in the necessary ignorance in which the lower echelons of the inquisitor's network are submerged.

'Of every million such men, perhaps one might have the qualities to serve as an acolyte in the direct employ of an inquisitor, privy to the dealings of his conclave and bearing the keys to his master's armoury. He must take upon himself a measure of responsibility that might encompass whole worlds, entire civilisations, which might be saved or extinguished by his endeavours. He must sometimes stand by while atrocities are committed, and participate in the committing, and comprehend the great dangers and evils that might ensue if they tried to stay on the path of good. He must see the worst the universe has to hurl at him and in response, shed the shackles of morality instead of his sanity.

'Of every million such men, one might rise to the rank of inquisitor, and bear the ultimate authority that can exist in the Imperium short of the Emperor Himself arisen. He must kill worlds, because letting them live threatens a greater catastrophe that might come to pass in thousands of years. He must have already handed his life to the Emperor's service, and consider himself dead. He must make the survival of the human race his responsibility, and encompass the enormity of that task with intellect, willpower and hatred.

'How many men could have turned in that moment to Talaya, who stood by my side? Only an inquisitor, I think. Only an inquisitor could have pushed her forward, to the foot of the herald's silken throne. To register the glimmer of understanding in her face? To see the smile of agreement on the herald's, and not drive a blade into his throat, a stake into his heart, a bullet through his brain? To let him take her in his spindly arms and pass her, just starting to struggle, into the embrace of his daemon handmaidens? Only an inquisitor.

'"Corvin!" she cried as the daemons hauled her to the back of the pavilion. "Corvin, no! Please! For the love of the Throne, Corvin, what about… What about everything?" Her voice trailed away as she was dragged out of sight, and her words were muffled.

'I did not glance back at my other companions. They had earned my trust and would not try to stop me.

'A voice inside me was crying out, but I had silenced it so long ago I could no longer give it a name.

'"Then attend upon me on the palace bridge after sundown," said the herald. "I feel this is the dawn of a much-awaited age."

'I bowed and, with a gesture, bade my acolytes accompany me as I left. In the arena below the bodies had been shifted with well-practised efficiency, and only the blood remained.'

12

'My coven embraced knowledge of the enemy as a weapon, a heresy of thought that invited corruption, and yet which was the only means, we believed, by which the true enemy could be fought.

'This is the greatest strength of the inquisitor. There are men, yet, who would condemn worlds and species to extinction – but how many of them would also condemn themselves? Not to death, for everywhere we find men eager to die. No, condemnation to a spiritual oblivion, to the awful fates of corruption and enslavement to the dark power beside which death seems the Emperor's own blessing. Not even all inquisitors can truly make such a sacrifice. It is what sets me, and men like me, apart from the greater part of humanity, and what enfranchises us to determine how humanity shall be manipulated, spent, culled and eventually saved.'

– Inquisitor Corvin Golrukhan

THE PETRIFIED FOREST gave way, after a solid two days of marching, to the shattered delta of a land that was once pierced by a mighty river. A vast and terrible event had fallen on that land, and splintered it into a thousand islands through which the river now rushed, forming a land of rapids and swirling lakes. To the east lay the hinterland of Kulgarde, which spread across the broken land to the south – the delta was unclaimed, and had been ever since the destruction of the kingdom that once stood there. A few towers and fragments of palaces still stood, now isolated and half eroded by the hungry waters. They had been brutal buildings, the towers and walls built for siege, the palaces monuments to war. Here and there the remains of enormous armoured figures lay fallen or worn away, a helmeted head, a mailed fist gripping the black stone hilt of a broken sword.

Brother Kollus's gene-seed was taken by Techmarine Kho in a truncated ceremony once the strike force was clear of the forest, and his remains loaded onto *Dorn's Dagger*. With the prayers said and with no time now for funeral games, Lycaon ordered the strike force on across the delta.

'If we lose another,' said First Sergeant Kaderic as he and Lysander forded a rushing branch of the river, 'we will have to stow them on the *Talon Blade*. Should the *Blade* be full we will be leaving bodies behind on this world and taking just their wargear back to the *Phalanx*.'

'An ill omen,' said Lysander.

'A great shame,' replied Kaderic. 'I would sooner go back missing an arm or an eye than missing the bodies of all who marched with me.'

'Do you believe we should not have come to Malodrax?' asked Lysander.

Kaderic, who was pulling himself onto the slippery granite rocks of the next island, paused to look at him. 'Why do you say that?' he asked. 'I am loath to leave my brothers behind on this world, but that does not mean I would not make war here. Kulgarde must fall and Kraegon Thul must die. That any Imperial Fist would say otherwise is out of the question. You know this, Lysander.'

'Of course, First Sergeant,' said Lysander. 'But I have seen what doubt in one's duties can do.'

'Among Imperial Fists?'

'No. Among others.'

Kaderic did not pursue the question further, for Lycaon gave the order for the strike force to draw in and make camp until the sun was up. Though a Space Marine did not strictly need to sleep, his effectiveness in combat dropped off after a certain span of hours, and though their histories were full of heroics lasting for days on end, a Space Marine commander did not let the battle-brothers under his command lose their edge through fatigue. Already the strike force had done in a few days what an Imperial Guard regiment might do in months, mostly on foot and fighting along the way.

The strike force drew into the shelter and cover of a section of city wall that sagged down into the waters, its enormous black stone blocks gradually being broken up and washed away where the waters slowly eroded its island of dressed parade ground. Three of Gorvetz's squad took the early watch as the sun dissolved away into ruddy darkness overhead.

'This is the kind of ground that spurred me to take us on foot,' said Chaplain Lycaon as Lysander observed his wargear rites in the wall's shadow.

Lysander was anointing the major components of his bolter with machine oil, scraping away dried blood and grime. His chainsword would receive the same treatment, then he could rest in half-sleep until his watch came. 'What I saw of this world suggested that even the Land Raiders of our Chapter would find it heavy going,' he said. 'And over such ground men on foot are swifter than tracks.'

'It was not universally agreed upon,' said Lycaon. He sat beside Lysander, placing his own weapon on the stone. 'Neither was coming to Malodrax at all. Does that shock you, captain?'

'I will abide by the orders of my Chapter command,' said Lysander.

'You must speak freely, Lysander.'

'Then I will say that if the Chapter had not sent what men it could spare to Malodrax, I would have come here alone to do my duty.'

'You would have abandoned your duties to your Chapter to do so?'

'I would have, Chaplain. To see Kraegon Thul dead, I would give up the companionship of my battle-brothers and put myself beyond the aegis of my Chapter.'

Lycaon nodded in thought. 'Seeing Thul dead is your duty, or your revenge?'

'In honesty?' Lysander finished cleaning the action of his bolter and slid the breech closed. 'I do not know.'

'Then it is good we came with you. I must see to my own wargear rites, captain. Do not neglect your rest. The world hunts us and the night will not go without need for good watchmen.'

Lycaon left and Lysander finished cleaning his bolter in the shadow of the fallen civilisation's crumbling palace wall. When he was done he cleaned the teeth of his chainblade, for there had been much killing so far, and it had to be ready again for more.

LYSANDER'S WATCH SAW him posted up on the wall, where climbing to the top was made easier by a mound of fallen masonry. The sounds of the waters had become a constant background, barely perceived now. The moons and stars changed by the hour, and as Lysander began his watch three watery moons glowed in the sky through breaks in the clouds. One grew brighter as the other two waned, as if the brighter one was a vampire draining the light from the others.

The closest Imperial Fist was watching from the elevated stretch of smooth stone where the two Land Speeders were parked. Lysander was out of sight of another Imperial Fist for the first time since landing on Malodrax, and might not be again before Kulgarde came into view.

He snapped open a compartment on the waist of his armour, where spare ammunition or grenades were usually kept. Instead, he slid out the copy of *Being A Description Of Malodrax And Its Foulness.* Even a Space Marine's eyesight was unlikely to spot the volume in his hands unless they were looking out for it. Lysander flicked through its dog-eared pages.

He could not find a reference to the delta and its fallen kingdom. That was no great surprise. Inquisitor Golrukhan had not been given the luxury of enough time to catalogue everything between Kulgarde and Shalhadar's city. Nevertheless Lysander had suggested this route, skirting most of Kulgarde's proving grounds to the north, and he would have been far more confident about the strike force's likely progress had he known more.

His eye caught Talaya's name again. Lysander was unsure what to feel when he saw it. He had not known Talaya, not as Golrukhan had written about her, but Golrukhan's words suggested a world of the mind beyond what a Space Marine experienced. A world where one person might feel for another something that could spur them on to astonishing deeds and awful mistakes. How much did a man leave behind when he ascended to the ranks of the Space Marines? If Lysander really knew what happened in the minds of those unaugmented men and women, who had not been sleep-taught Rogal Dorn's battle-genius and been transformed into something else, would he miss it? So often the power of those emotions was tied up with all manner of the foulest corruption. The powers of the warp enjoyed nothing more, it seemed, than to take the emotions of joy and weave them into hatred. But to go without the emotion of such connections meant to remain ignorant of so much. Was a Space Marine something less than a man, as well as more?

A Space Marine was not without emotion. Some in the Imperium thought of them as automatons, mind-lessly executing the will of the God-Emperor, and perhaps some were. But inside Lysander was a well of emotion that he could draw from just as he drew from his training, or the doctrines of Dorn's battle-lore. There was a well of hate and anger inside him. A Space Marine's discipline could keep it bound until it was needed. He could have faith in that, he told himself, as he had done many times since he had stumbled from Kulgarde into the wastes of Malodrax. He had faith in the hatred.

Lysander closed the volume again. There was nothing in it that would help him now, and anything that did not bring Kraegon Thul closer to death was not relevant.

The vampire moon had killed its siblings, and was splitting into pieces, sharp black cracks running across its surface. A chill wind blew off the water, and on it was a voice.

Lysander could not make out the words. He drew up his bolter, his muscle memory reminding his limbs of the motions needed to bring it to his shoulder or to draw his chainblade. He could see nothing save a gathering of mist down the wall, at the base of what had once been a watchtower ringed with visions slits.

Lysander looked closer. In the swirling of the mist was the suggestion of a more solid shape. It came closer and Lysander brought up his bolter. The shape was humanoid, walking slowly along the wall as Lysander watched down his gunsights.

It was one of the xenos whose existence had been suggested by the features of Kulgarde's surgeon and the monumental sculptures of their fallen cities. It had the same long-limbed shape, and the same flat face and large liquid eyes. Its features became more distinct and Lysander could see the embroidered finery it wore, trailing long tails of ruffled silk, dripping with jewellery. It did not belong among the brutalist architecture here.

It came as no surprise that Malodrax had its ghosts. Lysander had seen enough remnants of the planet's many past falls to wonder when they would appear.

From behind Lysander came another shape, accompanied by a blast of chill that made him spin around. It had passed through him before he had got his finger onto the trigger or his chainblade in his hand, and advanced on the xenos ghost with such an attitude of menace Lysander knew what it must be before it was fully formed.

The new ghost's back formed into a mass of knotted muscle supporting a hunched and elongated head with a pair of ribbed horns. It held a jagged, brutal sword in one hand and pointed a talon at the xenos with another. Save for the basic humanoid layout of its limbs it could not have been more different. The alien ghost fell to its knees, even its inhuman features unable to obscure the raw fear.

The second ghost was a daemon of the Blood God. Lysander had encountered them before – footsoldiers of the warp, one moment drilling in their thousands, perfectly in step, the next running random and wanton as they dispensed butchery on the world of real space. Each was different, for such was the way of the warp, but each had the same air of brutality and the lust for violence. Men of the Imperium, where they could speak of such things at all, called them bloodletters.

The xenos was begging on its knees. The ghost of the bloodletter slashed its spectral blade through the alien and cut it in two at the waist.

'Brother,' voxed Lysander. 'Are you seeing this?'

'Aye,' came the reply from Brother Kallis of Squad Kaderic, the closest of Lysander's fellow watchmen. 'No surprise this place is haunted.'

'We are watching the past,' said Lysander. 'This is how this place came to be.'

More and more apparitions glimmered into life along the walls and among the fallen battlements. Bloodletters were charging at the alien ghosts, cutting them into pieces without mercy. It was a work of crude butchery, and Lysander wondered how long it had taken for the servants of the Blood God to reduce this corner of Malodrax's native civilisation to nothing. Perhaps it had taken place over a single night – a few hours of concentrated murder, at once a military conquest and an act of worship. The ghosts of cultists were swarming across the delta's ruins now, wearing masks of flayed skin and crude spikes hammered through their bodies.

Brother Kallis was hailing the rest of the strike force, waking them from their half-sleep. Many had already snapped into full awareness as the ghosts danced among them. Some cultists turned on one another as the last of the xenos were cut down, or threw themselves onto the blades of the bloodletters as offerings to their god.

'This must have happened an aeon ago,' voxed Lysander over the command vox-channel. 'We are looking at the birth of a daemon world.'

'Are we subject to a moral threat?' came Captain Lycaon's reply. In the parade ground below Lycaon was on his feet, crozius in hand.

'I know not,' said Lysander. 'But this history is not complete.'

Spectral walls rose in the moonlight, the ghosts of the long-fallen battlements and watchtowers. These were fortress-temples to the Blood God, whose warlike worshippers saw everything in terms of raw strength and conquest. They rose up in oppressive banks of masonry, enormous battlements enclosing parade grounds and execution squares, and barracks and training grounds where the ghosts of summoned bloodletters duelled with would-be champions of the Blood God.

There was no telling how many thousands of years might be encompassed in those moments, as the bloodstained empire rose. Heads and flayed hides were mounted on the spiked battlements. Armies marched out to war, and marched back in through the fortress gates laden with captured banners and cartfuls of skulls for the altar of their god.

Lysander knew what the next ghosts would be. They appeared on the horizon, the spectral hulks of enormous war machines. The siege engines reached the outermost walls, and in silence began to tear them down. Some were heavy with cannons that blasted silver explosions across the fortifications. Others were equipped with simple rams, driving straight into the walls and sending great hunks of stone tumbling. Some chunks of fallen masonry still lay where their ghostly counterparts had landed, now half submerged in rushing waters or eroded into shapelessness.

Siege towers disgorged squads of ghostly Iron Warriors onto the walls. Lysander recognised the marks of their armour, the same as those worn by the traitors who had taken him and his battle-brothers into Kulgarde. Where the bloodletters had conquered with brutality and frenzy, the Iron Warriors treated warfare as a grim, methodical business, moving with efficiency and precision as they mowed down scores of cultists with bolter volleys or launched lightning close combat assaults with chainblade and lightning claw. Siege engines pulled down the watchtowers and demolition charges brought down the walls. Iron Warriors squads despoiled the temples and choked the parade grounds with oceans of silvery blood.

It was not the scale of the bloodshed that was awful. Any Space Marine had seen death inflicted on such grand scales before. It was the manner of it that wrenched at Lysander's gut, because it was so familiar. They fought like Imperial Fists, with expertise born of a lifetime training to fight and break the siege. Rogal Dorn had been a siege warrior, a builder and breaker of the mightiest fortresses, but so had the Iron Warriors primarch, Perturabo. Lysander realised in that moment just how close a mirror the Iron Warriors were of the Imperial Fists, created to fight the same wars in the Emperor's name, diverged onto two different paths in the fires of civil war.

Lysander had never hated them more. The thought was a foul taste in his mouth. That the Imperial Fists and the Iron Warriors could be so close, separated by chance alone, by fate…

'No,' said Lysander aloud. 'We are nothing alike. Keep your lies to yourself, Malodrax. They will find no purchase here.'

As if in response, the broken moon above shattered into a thousand tears of burning light, raining down like a host of shooting stars. In their sudden fractured glare the ghosts waned, the sight of Iron Warriors slaughtering the defeated cultists growing dim and the sound of the rushing waters rising. A slab of wind-worn stone fell into the river from a short distance along the wall, and it seemed to break the spell that had conjured the ghosts of the delta's past.

The light died down. There were no new moons in the sky, only the starless dark. The last of the ghosts dissolved away.

'Whatever its meaning,' voxed Lycaon, 'let us hope it is over but not assume it.'

'Everything on Malodrax is a test,' voxed Lysander in reply. The other Imperial Fists on watch were voxing in the all-clear as the rest of the strike force peered suspiciously into the night from the parade ground's perimeter. 'This was no exception.'

'If this world means to scare us away,' voxed First Sergeant Kaderic, 'then it chose the wrong audience for its light show.'

'Back to your posts,' said Chaplain Lycaon. 'Next watch, take your positions. The rest of you, we have little time before we must move again. Make the most of it, for tomorrow may see a battle and I would have you fresh for the fight.'

The shifting night turned again as Lysander found a sheltered spot below the wall, and let his mind drift down into half-sleep.

THE STRIKE FORCE reached the edge of the delta towards the end of the next day. Its edge, a carved gorge through which a branch of the original river ran dark and fast, gave way to rocky desert. This was the northernmost extent of the broken hinterland of Kulgarde, and in the distance rose flinty ridges of uprooted stone in a mountain range birthed by some enormous violent force. Far to the south this became the broken land where the strike force had first landed, and across which Lysander had hiked on his way to Shalhadar's city. Here, it was a land of fortresses.

The fortifications crossed the desert in an infinitely complex puzzle, walls intersecting in a labyrinth. The buildings clustered on the pale rock like eruptions of a skin disease on Malodrax's surface, too many to ever count, thousands of years' worth of construction encrusting everything.

Even the strike force veterans, who had seen some of the stranger sights the galaxy had to offer, paused to take it in. Watchtowers sagged and crumbled, as if half dissolved away by acid. Battlements lay on top of each other as if the fortifications had been haphazardly dropped from above, crushing and warping everything underneath. Enormous craters were bite marks taken out of the landscape, revealing torn strata of past construction. Massive scars several layers deep ran across the fortresses as if gouged by huge claws.

The closest construction shivered with movement. At first it seemed to be heat haze or a mirage caused by the trapped heat that glowered beneath the overcast sky, but as the strike force approached it became clear that a multitude of creatures covered the huge blocks of stone, swarming everywhere like termites. They were daemons, surrounded by a fug of bituminous chemical stink boiling in the heat, oozed out from Malodrax's pores to serve its masters.

Each had a knot of pale flesh for a torso, with a lolling, drooling mouth on the underside, and four limbs that each ended in the same combination of hand and foot. They moved on all fours but could also use these limbs to lift the blocks of stone that had fallen from the walls of the fortification they were working on. They were stronger than they looked and could wedge themselves under huge blocks of masonry, forcing their limbs straight and levering the blocks off the ground. In groups they were moving the stones back into place, rebuilding the walls and crenulations.

'These are the proving grounds,' said Lysander to Chaplain Lycaon as they watched the builder-daemons working. 'Kulgarde bloods its siege engines here. They are tested against the fortifications, and the walls are rebuilt every day by the daemons.'

'Very much like the Iron Warriors,' said Lycaon, his eye roaming across the criss-crossing walls. An Imperial Fist automatically sized up every fortress he came across for its strongest and weakest points, the methods of entry, the most dangerous firing zones – it was as much the legacy of Rogal Dorn's genetic pattern in their gene-seed as a matter of training. 'They have an efficiency about them that makes their corruption all the darker. It lies deep indeed to leave the surface undisturbed. Discipline without, but in their hearts there is a deviance I am glad I cannot imagine.'

'The route through the petrified forest spared us this ground,' continued Lysander, 'but we cannot avoid it any longer if we are to reach sight of Kulgarde. And the plan of attack requires us to head into it.'

'The plan of attack has yet to be decided,' said Lycaon.

Brother Halaestus broke off from the strike force's order of march, clambering up onto one of the blocks of fallen masonry. He drew his blade and sliced a limb off the nearest daemon. It let out a rumbling sigh and slumped to the ground before Halaestus drove the monomolecular blade down through its body. Halaestus kicked the dead creature aside, took out his pistol and loosed half a dozen shots through the daemons scuttling around the block, tearing out chunks of vermillion flesh and spattering the stonework with their blood.

'Halaestus!' called out First Sergeant Kaderic. 'We have not the time to waste ammunition on these things. Stand down!'

'Would that I had a universe of bullets,' said Halaestus, his eyes looking right through Kaderic as he spoke. 'I would fire them all at Malodrax.'

The *Dorn's Dagger* descended shortly ahead and came down on its landing jets. Techmarine Kho leaned from the cockpit. 'I cannot cover you well from the air,' he said, 'if you will be so often out of sight moving through these ruins. And any enemies will likely be adapted to hiding from eyes above. I can continue to support from the air but I will not be your eyes as you would wish, Chaplain.'

'Then your task is to scout out Kulgarde's war engines,' said Lycaon. 'I must know if we are closing in on one, or if one approaches us. They cannot be predicted and if one's course takes it towards us we must know. Stay out of sight as much as possible, for the Iron Warriors will have eyes out here. And take the greatest care, Techmarine. We will need you soon.'

'Of course, my Chaplain,' said Kho. The engines of the *Dorn's Dagger* burned again, tinting the heavy air with the smell of burned fuel as they punched the Land Speeder back up above the fortifications.

'Move out!' ordered Lycaon, and the strike force marched on into Kulgarde's proving grounds.

13

*'"Behold!" cried one, and the other hundreds of suppli-
cants were thrown to the ground as if by a great hand
slamming down on the cathedral floor. From the skin
of their naked backs burst spined growths, like thorny
vines that spiralled out into razor-sharp thickets. Leaves
sprouted, and fat strange-coloured flowers. Odd creatures
gambolled through the forest thus created. The priests
of the Chaos gods looked on, but their gods looked not.
A thousand men dead in that cathedral and the powers
they worshipped cared nothing, for that is the greatest
evil of Malodrax. A life might be spent in devotion, but
the indifference of the warp means it is a life devoid of
meaning.'*

– Inquisitor Corvin Golrukhan

CAPTAIN HEXAL HELD court in the city's arena. His palace
was a pavilion of flayed skins set up on the arena floor,
around which crowds flocked to be bludgeoned back
by the ring of mutants guarding it. The skins chosen for
his pavilion were those covered in tattoos, so the whole

foul creation was as obscenely decorative as Shalhadar's own palace.

Lysander watched from the stands. The arena itself, a spectacular creation of carved bone, did not interest him. It was no surprise there was somewhere in the city for combats and death spectacles to be waged in honour of Shalhadar. His soldier's mind worked on its own, telling him he would be unlikely to make it through the cordon of mutants with enough speed to get to grips with Hexal before he could prepare or escape. What truly concerned him was what Hexal might want.

The sound of Talaya's mechanical limbs conveying her across the bone and stonework had already become familiar. Lysander did not have to turn around to know she was drifting regally towards him.

'Lord Shalhadar has decided to receive Ambassador Hexal,' she said.

'Who is to hear his demands?' asked Lysander.

'I am.'

Lysander looked around at her. 'And who will go with you?'

'That is a matter for my own discretion. It would hardly become the herald of this city's lord to enter the presence of a hostile power alone.'

It occurred to Lysander to wonder how Talaya would fare if she faced Hexal one on one. She was quick. He knew that, and her limbs gave her greater range. There was no telling what concoctions the generator mounted on her back could pump out – perhaps something potent enough to knock out the Iron Warrior. But if Hexal got within reach of her mechanical talons, he had the strength to tear her apart – Lysander was sure.

And what would happen if Lysander fought her? He had no idea.

Talaya gave him one of her hateful little smiles and clacked off down the seating rows towards the arena floor. Lysander stood and followed her.

The crowd parted for Talaya – Shalhadar's city knew her well and they were afraid of her. They were afraid of Lysander, too, but then he was twice the height of many of them and clad in spectacular crimson armour, so that was no surprise. Many kneeled when Talaya went past - others tried to scramble away. Lysander, however, followed in her wake.

The mutants barred her way. One of the diminutive creatures that Lysander recognised from Kulgarde's medical wing hurried from the pavilion and chattered away in the ear of the biggest and ugliest of the mutants. It bowed and stood aside, letting Talaya through and Lysander after her. The smell of the uncured skin hit him and he realised it had been flayed from its donor creatures only recently, without being tanned or pre-served. The orderly held a flap aside and Talaya entered, her limbs letting her down onto the arena floor so her head did not brush against the raw skin.

Inside, the pavilion was dark and noisome. The uncured skin hung with scraps of fibrous muscle and organ, and dripped blood on to the sand underfoot.

The stink of it was awful. The effect was rather like walking into the inside of a huge living organ. More of Kulgarde's mutants stood as an honour guard, this time armed and armoured like a parody of a standing army, holding the banners of Kraegon Thul's warband. Thul's heraldry was the stylised mechanical hand of his Legion, an open book, a tower with a crack down the centre and a pair of severed hands hanging from a hook, each depicted on the various banners.

On a throne constructed from steel blocks sat Captain Hexal of the Iron Warriors. His chainsword leaned against the throne beside him and a diminutive mutant held his bolter. Hexal wore his helmet, showing only the brutal, inhuman, mechanical face worn by his Legion.

'Lord Hexal,' began Talaya grandly, 'my Lord Shalhadar the Veiled One, Sovereign of this city and claimant to all of Malodrax, gives you leave to enter his city.'

'My Legion does not indulge in your pleasantries,' replied Hexal. Talaya did not flinch at his bluntness. 'I am here to make demands, as befits one who speaks for Warsmith Kraegon Thul, true lord of Malodrax.'

'Then in the name of the Veiled One, I may hear them,' said Talaya.

Lysander had stayed near the back of the pavilion, wary that Captain Hexal might recognise in this crimson-armoured warrior something of the bearing of an Imperial Fist. Seeing Hexal again this close gave him an empty, dead feeling, and he recognised it now as the knowledge that his duty was not being done. Hexal had taken the lives of his brothers and stood for a Legion whose very existence was an insult to every Imperial Fist – and yet Lysander was standing back and letting Hexal speak. Lysander forced the feeling down, with its mingled threads of anger and shame. Hexal was going to die. Lysander would be the one to kill him. He was letting Hexal live for the time being, because if he tried to take him on now Lysander would die in the attempt and Kraegon Thul, the true enemy, would live on.

'Ten thousand sacrifices,' Captain Hexal was saying. 'Dominion over the Kalinik Reach and the passes through the Vorn Mountains. The mutants of this city as slaves for our forges. The fealty of Shalhadar the Veiled One, expressed in obeisance to the throne of Warsmith Thul.'

'I see,' replied Talaya. 'I shall convey your suggestions to the Veiled One. Now I believe this is a fine opportunity to communicate the demands Shalhadar has of your Warsmith.'

At this Hexal held out his hand and the mutant cowering beside his throne handed him his bolter. The mutants standing at guard closed in around Talaya. Talaya's face changed, from unflustered and diplomatic to a violent scowl. Noxious fog billowed around her, filling the pavilion with a toxic darkness. Lysander heard the bellowing of mutants and the sound of metal talon through flesh. Bodies pressed around him and he drew his blade, hacking at the mutant hands trying to drag him down.

He turned and cut a long slit through the skin of the pavilion's side and forced his way out. A billow of poisonous fog followed him. Outside the people were panicking, shoved back and clubbed to the ground by the cordon of mutants. They were already fleeing across the stadium's seats, or crying out as they were trampled beneath the feet of their neighbours.

One mutant rounded on Lysander. It was huge, half again as tall as a Space Marine, larger than any Lysander had spotted in the depths beneath Kulgarde. Lysander ducked under its swinging paw and cut up at its bull neck. The sword sliced through skin and sinew, lodging in the spine – Lysander twisted it and the vertebrae parted, sending the mutant tumbling to the ground with its partially severed head flopping over one shoulder. He reminded himself this was a mundane blade, not a chainsword.

Talaya emerged through the torn pavilion behind him, clambering on her talons up the side of the tent. Her double-headed halberd was in her hands and her armour's mask had slid up over her face. She spun the halberd in her hands, the sweep of the weapon passing over Lysander's head and slicing off the arm of a mutant lumbering towards her. Before the arm had hit the arena floor the blade had carved down and split the mutant's head in two.

Talaya dropped down onto the sand of the arena. Still

her feet did not touch the ground – instead her clacking mechanical legs carried her.

'That went well,' she said.

Lysander was not sure if Talaya was being sarcastic and did not pause to ask her. He forged into the gap in the mutant line and was among the fleeing people in a handful of seconds. Mutants tried to pursue but were caught up in the cultists scrambling to get out of their way. One mutant, with the body of a giant and a multi-legged, spiderlike growth taking up everything above its shoulders, picked up a cultist and threw it aside, its compound eyes swivelling to focus on Lysander. He ran on, reaching the edge of the arena seating, before clambering onto the first row and turning. The mutant was almost on him, a trail of trampled bodies behind it.

Lysander leapt at the mutant. Its segmented upper limbs unfolded to catch him. Lysander rammed an armoured foot down into the centre of where its head should have been – bristly, gnarled flesh crunched where he hit. He grabbed a leg with his free hand and grappled himself upright, the mutant's huge human-oid hand reaching up to grab him and throw him off. Lysander cut off a handful of spider's legs and crushed one of the compound eyes with a stamp – it broke like glass, the individual facets raining down. The mutant reeled and Lysander was finally able to reverse his grip on the sword and drive it down.

He did not take a chance this time. A chainblade

would have made a gory mess but he had to make sure this normal blade hit something vital at first blow. He drove the hilt down hard, feeling the tip punching through insect organs, collarbone and heart. He pulled the blade out half its length and plunged it down again. This time he could hear the juddering heartbeat vibrating up the blade, hammering haphazardly as the muscle of the heart was torn open.

The mutant lurched to one side, then the other, and toppled over. Lysander jumped off onto the front row as it crashed to the sand.

The arena was in bedlam. The mutants were rampaging through the crowd, clubbing and butchering at random. The sand was wet with blood. Fleeing citizens were streaming to the arena exits or swarming over the seating.

It was, Lysander realised, its own form of worship. Just like cultists hurling themselves to their deaths or the dark rituals held hidden from the city's eyes, this was an act of devotion. The citizens had come here in no small part hoping that violence would break out, so they might die as martyrs to Shalhadar and his city, or that their deaths would illustrate the treachery of Kraegon Thul and demonstrate Shalhadar's right to rule Malodrax.

Talaya was already on the stadium roof, watching the carnage from a safe vantage point. She had killed her way to safety even more quickly than Lysander, and her halberd blades were slick with mutant blood. Her

armoured mask slid down and Lysander was sure she
was smiling, not the sly smirk she used with him but an
expression of true joy. To her, this slaughter was beautiful. The death of the city's people pleased the Veiled
One, and so it pleased his herald, too.

THE PALACE WAS hung with the colours of mourning.
White was the chosen colour, with accents of red,
representing desolation and bloodshed. Mourning banners hung over the frescoes and tapestries, and a singer
wailed a funeral dirge from the upper balconies.

Shalhadar wore the veil of a broken old man, the last
of his line, surrounded by the keepsakes and heirlooms
of the family he had lost. It was an obvious role to
take but the one the palace entertainers and artisans
expected of him. His face was long and wrinkled, the
features almost lost in the weight of its age, his shoulders hunched, his clothes long-faded velvet finery.
His eyes should have been watery but instead they
were hard and black, the one feature that reminded
an onlooker that the old man was not truly what he
believed him to be.

'Come,' said Shalhadar. 'Sit. Mourn with me.'

Lysander had entered the palace to find Talaya waiting
for him. He paused only to clean his blade at the palace
threshold before following her to the inner rooms of
the palace, the layout of which he was sure had changed
since he had witnessed the blasphemous opera here.
Lysander obeyed Shalhadar's command and sat on an

upholstered bench covered in torn diary pages, while Talaya settled on her mechanical haunches beside a broken clock and a pile of mouldering dolls and toys. Lysander wondered where the trappings of this veil had come from. Was there a storeroom with all these symbolic knick-knacks waiting for an appropriate occasion? Were they illusions conjured by Shalhadar's will?

'No doubt,' said Shalhadar, 'sorrow fills your hearts at the offence done to this city by Ambassador Hexal. Alas, he escaped the city by force while the wounded were yet crying out for succour. And so our thoughts must turn not only to the suffering of our people, the woes of our city, but to the restitution of balance. I speak not of the healing of our scars, of the interring of the dead. I speak of revenge.'

The old man's fist balled up and the veins stood out on the back of his hand, a gesture of defiance all the more powerful for the ancient body's weakness.

Shalhadar looked Lysander in the eye, and there was no trace of true sorrow there. 'Good?' he asked.

It was Talaya who answered. 'Convincing enough for the citizens,' she said. 'But then they live in the story. We who live outside it know the truth.'

'And what is the truth?' asked Shalhadar. He held up a hand before Talaya could answer. 'Lysander?'

Lysander still felt an internal shudder to hear his name spoken by the daemon prince. 'It is a cycle,' he said. 'No power on Malodrax can permit any other to exist without trying to impose its superiority. This turn of the wheel, it was Kraegon Thul who sought to remind you. Next it will be you who sends an envoy to antagonise the Warsmith, or whatever other power might have risen on Malodrax. It is its own sort of performance. Hexal probably thinks he is truly striking a blow against your city but Kraegon Thul knows the game he plays.'

'And are the Iron Warriors content to play the game, do you think? Your kind know them well. The Imperial Fists have history with Perturabo's brood. Is he a creature of Malodrax, content to perform his role until his story ends?'

'No,' replied Lysander. 'He plays it as long as is necessary. He has a plan in place to win all of Malodrax. He will turn the whole planet into a forge for his war machines, or just mine it dry and move on. This world alone cannot satisfy Thul's ambitions. I doubt anything truly would.'

Shalhadar smiled, all pretence of sorrow gone. 'Then we had better kill him,' he said.

'Plenty have tried,' said Talaya. 'Simply walking up to Kulgarde's door would do nothing, even with the whole population of this city armed behind us. And Thul himself will not be easy to kill. In all honesty, I do not think there is a being on Malodrax that has a meaningful chance of slaying him face to face. Not to mention those he keeps close to him.'

'The alien,' said Lysander.

'Ah,' said Talaya. 'You have met.'

'He watched over my vivisection,' said Lysander. 'I am sure Thul sent him to make sure I suffered before I died.'

'You speak of Karnak,' said Talaya. 'The warp alone knows his species, but he has served as advisor and castellan to Thul since the Iron Warriors laid the first blocks of Kulgarde. You are the first I have met to have seen him in the flesh and lived. Every one of the scum and vermin in that fortress answers to Karnak, and he answers to the Iron Warriors. Then, of course, there are the other Iron Warriors, Hexal and his ilk, to get through. Imperial Fist, as deep as your hate might run, I think even you would see ill sport in getting a foot past Kulgarde's threshold.'

'And that, dear child,' said Shalhadar, 'is why you will remain ever a mortal vessel, and never ascend to the glories of daemonhood. You have no imagination! Lysander, you say, has no chance of entering Kulgarde. But did not Thul's underling, Hexal, enter my city? Did he not set up camp in my stadium, as bold as a painted whore? Thus have the enemy shown us how we might put our living weapon here into the presence of Kraegon Thul.'

'Will not Kulgarde be closed to an envoy of ours?' asked Talaya. 'We could hardly dance in and start reading off demands. Kulgarde is in the ascendance, they have no obligation to receive us.'

'But they do have a desire to humiliate us,' said Lysander. 'Hexal demanded you kneel before Thul's throne. We might deign to give him the next best thing, an envoy sent to grovel and beg for mercy. Would Thul not be eager to let such an envoy through the gates, if only for the chance to execute him as he kneels?'

Shalhadar gave Lysander an evil, toothless grin, the daemon's malice bleeding through the old man's body. 'And who would be the damned soul to be sent as such an envoy?' he asked.

'That would be me,' replied Lysander.

'I feel I must write of Talaya.

'Of her qualities I have already spoken. She was a fine Inquisitorial agent in her own way. Her ambition was to carry the Inquisitorial Seal herself, and though she would never have reached those heights she served the Holy Ordos as faithfully as any of us. She was a fine shot, an outstanding swordswoman, a fearsome interrogator and a possessor of a fine analytical mind. In spirit she was pure and as close to incorruptible as any of her rank.

'In those days when I first glimpsed the court of Shalhadar, granted access for a few hours to the library of his palace, I came to think about all the other qualities she had. The above are true and wondrous, but could apply to hundreds of acolytes that have served me or other inquisitors of my conclave. And yet it was only to Talaya that the human thoughts, those that still exist unguarded in the mind of an inquisitor, turned in my mind during that time.

'I cannot say what she truly meant to me. I will not trot out the words of the great poets and playwrights, of which every civilised world seems to have two or three. I will say only that she occupied my mind, that part of it I permit to wander, while I laboured there in the darkness of Shalhadar's library.

'This was the prize for which I had given up Talaya. A lower floor of the palace housed Shalhadar's library, and there I was taken by the herald from the arena. My task there was to seek out the sacred writings that would give Shalhadar dominion over the whole of Malodrax, and which it was certain lay somewhere in the stacks there. It was an ancient, rarely walked part of the palace, and while I was aware of obscene finery just outside my sphere I was immersed entirely in its decrepitude and darkness. I delved into the volumes held there, ancient decaying tomes each one full of fouler lies than the last. Transcriptions of madmen's raving I found there, and collections of observations from dream-journeys into the warp.

'I guarded my mind with prayers. I put a drop of holy water, consecrated at the foot of the Golden Throne, on my forehead to ward off the tendrils of profane knowledge that might try to find root there. My acolytes were not permitted to join me, and I would not have let them into the library in any case, so I laboured alone. For this I was grateful, because it meant I could be alone with my Emperor and bore the responsibility only for His work rather than the souls of my acolytes.

'Each tome was connected to those beside it by a tenuous link of subject or concept that rendered them almost, but not quite, entirely random, thus creating a maddeningly vague sense of direction which would drag me astray as often as it would lead me onwards. As I forged on, seeking the bound collections of unholy pacts and contracts where I felt sure my quarry would lie, I became aware of another task being performed.

'Day after day I stayed there, working. Agent Sildyne passed on messages to me by means of an arrangement of dead drops, through which I learned that he, Grun and Thol, and Maskelin had set up in an abandoned tower having left our previous lodgings. Archivist Grunvelder had by that time disappeared, for which I was both sorrowful and relieved. According to Sildyne, Grunvelder had run off into the city's night, crying out about worms eating his brain. I prayed that he died soon after, one more corpse in the city's gutters. I fear there can have been no less grim fate for him.

'And yet through this, thoughts came unbidden, telling me that I was not merely there to perform a task for Shalhadar that might ingratiate me into his court. Often it was Talaya who voiced such thoughts, for it was she I saw often when I closed my eyes or when a gust of wind blew out my candle and all was darkness. Thus I associated such doubt with her, and she became to me an advisor always voicing caution.

'I had suffered much, I think. There is no mind so holy that it can remain free of the mental sludge that comes with contacting such corruption as I found in those books, just as there is no saint's garment so holy that it will not be besmirched by filth if it is cast down. I burned away the grime with prayer and contemplation, but while the flame of the soul can cleanse it must also burn, and in agony I lay haunted by angry nightmares born of the knowledge I purged

293

from myself. My body, always kept in the peak of human condition, atrophied and became pale, like that of a thing that had lived its whole life in a cave. I do not know how long I was there, but to put the stretch of time in months would be conservative.

'It was this degeneration that first gave me the clue as to the truth. It was in a thought of Talaya that I was reminded that everything on Malodrax is a test. The planet, so jealous of all those who walk on its surface, puts all its inhabitants to a trial so they might prove their worth to the powers of the warp. Was my labour there a test as well?

'Of course it was. I cursed myself for a fool. Corvin, you wretched old heretic, you blind and ignorant student of stupidity! Thus I cried to myself as I recoiled from the hateful tome I was reading through at that moment.

'A trial this was, and my first task was to discover what faculty of mine was being tried. Was I being put through an ordeal of the will, exposed to volumes of corruptive horrors to see if my mind broke? No, I said. That was too crude, too obvious, for Malodrax. Perhaps Shalhadar was doing that to me for his amusement, but the powers of the warp would never be satisfied with tormenting an inquisitor thus.

'Was this a physical test? My body was suffering. Was this a trial to exploit the inquisitor's belief in the mind as the ultimate weapon, challenging my mental faculties in the hope I would neglect my body and cause me to waste away or starve? Such would tickle the humour of the daemonic and perverse. But no, I did not think this was the cruellest fate to which I could be condemned. A physical trial concocted by the powers of the warp would have to compete in malice with the trials by ordeal used by many of my fellow inquisitors, and wasting away in this pit of corruption, while not the end I would choose, could not compare to the Test of Flame or of the Sliding Blades.

'It was as I perused a map, purported to describe a realm of the warp, that the answer came to me. This map was etched on sheets of paper-thin stone, the acidic wash bringing out fanciful mountain ranges and oceans of thought. The names of warp denizens were labelled alongside their supposed lairs, where the cartographer had encountered them and bargained his soul away for secrets of the warp. His sacrifice had bought only lies, for this map was no less a fiction than the transcribed insanity of the broken-minded cultists filling the shelves around me. The futility of his endeavour inspired me as to the truth.

'What was I doing there? Labouring at an obscene task, to validate the rule of a daemon lord over a realm of madness and death. Giving up the lives of my acolytes, one through willing payment, one through negligence, for the right to pursue that task. Abandoning the oaths I had made to the Holy Ordos of the Inquisition, casting away finally those few vestiges of honour I had clutched to my heart when I pursued my path of heresy. And for what?

'To gain the favour of Shalhadar the Veiled, the very image of the enemy I had dedicated my life to destroying.

'No! I shouted it out loud. The price is too high! To walk in the court of Shalhadar, to get close enough to kill him – as great a prize as that is, I will not become what Malodrax *desires to win it! This world will not take me. This world will not turn me into one who walks it as a supplicant to the Dark Powers.*

'The test was to see how far I would go to walk the path I had set myself on Malodrax, and had I walked it to the end, I would have failed that test. I would have become a slave to Shalhadar, and served him perhaps like the foul multi-armed creature to whom I had given Talaya. I would have walked into damnation willingly, the kind of victory most beloved of the Dark Powers.

'Most men could not have walked back from that brink. Having given up Talaya, they would have seen no meaning in the righteous life and would have sought the oblivion of damnation. But I was not most men. I am an inquisitor, and there is no brink from which I cannot turn.

'I cast down the madman's map, and it shattered on the floor. I knew I had to leave that place and abandon the dream of breaching the court of Shalhadar to which I had been devoted since I arrived at the city. I forged through the library stacks, suddenly aware of how deeply I had travelled into the levels beneath Shalhadar's palace and how they seemed to grow around me, spreading into new configurations of the labyrinth to addle my senses. I had anticipated such traps, however, and had placed certain volumes at key intersections that I could recognise and suggest to me the correct route. I reached the entrance to the library floors, a great arch leading downwards from the grand entrance hall of the palace.

'This hall was a soaring monument to Shalhadar. It

was dominated by a huge golden statue of a perfectly proportioned human figure, its gender uncertain and its face obscured with a featureless mask. Daemons scrabbled across it, ornamenting it with brilliant lacquers and gemstones. They turned their malformed faces towards me as I burst from the archway, no doubt appearing more like a bedraggled madman from the streets than an inquisitor of the Holy Ordos. That impression was hopefully vanquished when I drew from my robe the Inquisitorial Seal, the badge of my office, into which I had wrought a powerful hexagrammic ward. I held up the seal and the daemons recoiled, the light suddenly blazing from my hand too much for them to bear.

'Thus it was that I made my escape. I had not forgotten the sphinx that guarded the bridge. Before it could turn on me I had leapt from the bridge and into the canal surrounding the palace, and thanks to the Emperor, it did not pursue me. Perhaps to it I was no more than a morsel, a stray creature to be devoured if pursuing me proved no burden, and it was unwilling to follow me into the canal. Whatever the reason, a current caught me and dragged me out of sight of the palace, down into the tunnels and sewers underneath the city.

'I had never sought to understand what lay beneath Shalhadar's city. What lay on the surface was gruesome enough. I saw then the remains of an alien metropolis, with great towers of homes arranged around circular meeting-grounds ringed by statues. They were crushed and mangled by the settling down of the city above, mutilated by the torrents of filth mingling with the underground rivers rushing through the underworld.

'In this darkness I began to rebuild the plan I had for Malodrax. Entering Shalhadar's court was a chimera, a fiction,
one that would lead me to damnation. I had to abandon that
path. Dragging myself from that black river of corruption, I
walked the first steps on my new path.'

EVERY CITY HAD its slums. In Shalhadar's city they were
jerry-built shacks and hovels crammed into the looted
shell of ancient palaces – from the outside they were
pristine, save for the heaps of living refuse who gathered in their doorways and alleys. Like beautiful bodies
hosting a vile disease, the poverty of Shalhadar's people
was concealed by the mask of opulence the whole city
wore.

The hovels formed vast narcotics dens, suffused in a
dizzying fog of opiates and heaving to the music of the
moaning half-dead. Some were all but comatose, stirring in feverish dreams. Others shivered and twitched,
or occasionally shrieked out loud. In a city where seeking new sensations was a form of worship, these places
were churches to excess and novelty.

Lysander felt a distaste that went beyond the stink of
the slum as he walked in through the archway. Before
him lay a cultist, naked save for a stained loincloth,
his skin ragged and peeling away to reveal the pitted
bones underneath. A medical device was hooked up to
a needle stuck directly into his spine – whichever drug
it contained, it had caused his body to atrophy while
his mind travelled in strange places. Lysander stepped

over the body as he pushed a curtain of rags aside and forged further into the slum.

The bodies were everywhere. They were curled up in the corners or stretched out across the floor. One cultist, a leather mask stitched on his face, was babbling about serpents that swallowed stars and worlds drowning in oceans of tears. His hands were raw and bleeding, and the bloody talons of his fingers were scratching deep red furrows in his midriff. Another was a woman who convulsed on the floor, dried foam crusted around her mouth. Some of the bodies were completely still and, for all Lysander knew, dead – certainly the smell of death hung about the place, mingling with the dizzying fog.

'I seek Valienne,' said Lysander out loud, addressing no one inhabitant in particular. 'The last anyone heard, she was here. The Veiled One commands I be shown to her.'

One of the slum-dwellers crawled out from the bundles of torn-down curtains and tapestries he was using as bedding. He put a hand on the greave of Lysander's armour. 'The Red Knight!' the cultist gasped. His throat was raw and his voice rasping. It was impossible to tell his age from his hollow eyes, and miniature braziers mounted on his shoulder surrounded his head in a permanent haze of smoke. 'I saw you! You rode the tides of the warp! Your mount was hatred and your sword was despair! I followed in your wake as I soared!'

Lysander pushed the drugged cultist aside. Ahead, the

shanties surrounded an open space, roughly circular, where an altar was set up consisting of a great stone basin. From the ceiling hung countless trinkets and offerings, jangling in the smoky air – bones, needles, pieces of jewellery, severed fingers and ears, bullet casings. The basin was half filled with blood, congealed and rank, and rivulets of it spilled down the sides. The smell was awful.

Here were gathered the celebrants of Shalhadar, those who still sought to worship their lord even though their fortunes had waned until they were forced to live side by side with the human refuse of that place. They wore patched and crudely embroidered robes, covered in images of open eyes and hands, and scurried like insects as Lysander approached. There were signs of disease on their faces. Lysander pointed at one, whose gnarled staff of wood suggested he was the leader of this group.

'Where is Valienne?' demanded Lysander.

The man stared back dumbly. Lysander guessed he was among the oldest residents here, his wrinkled and sunken face disfigured by boils covering one cheek and half his jawline.

'The Chronicler of the Sun and Stars,' Lysander continued. 'The Light in the Darkness.'

One of the cultists pointed a shaking finger upwards, towards the higher levels of the buildings where the hovels formed precarious layers of salvaged materials. Lysander left them to their worship and found a rickety ladder leading up. It barely held his weight, the same being true of the floor he now walked on. Up here worshippers lay in hammocks slung from the building's rafters like roosting bats. Someone had scrawled thousands of lines of text on the walls and floor, a stream of syllables that Lysander was wary of reading in case he found meanings there that might bewitch his senses and leave him vulnerable. Even here there was power, born of despair and desperation, that the Dark Gods could turn into conduits for their corruptive influence. Lysander would not be caught with his guard down here.

The few that noticed him turned away in fear. In his crimson armour and with a Space Marine's stature, he must have looked to them like an avenging herald of Chaos sent straight from the warp to pronounce their punishment. No doubt many of them were certain their time had come, and he heard them whimpering their last prayers for forgiveness or pity as he passed.

A section of the upper floors was curtained off with lengths of chain, locks of hair and fragments of broken gold woven into them. Lysander pushed the chains aside and looked into a chamber lit by candles and full of torn or screwed-up sheaves of paper, forming deep drifts in the corners. In the middle of this nest was a figure hunched over, scribbling away with a pen on another sheet that was already illegible with spilt ink. Greyish hair hung down over narrow shoulders.

'You are Valienne,' said Lysander.

The figure turned around. It was a woman, under the grime and the inky finger marks on her face. Her large, greyish eyes widened at the sight of Lysander standing over her.

'That is one of my names,' she said. 'I am the concept sculptress. I am she who weaves new worlds from nothing.'

'News has reached the court of your work. The *Chant of the Changing Ones*.'

Valienne gasped. 'He has read it?'

'He desires it to be performed.'

Valienne put her hands to her heart as if she feared she would die. Her breathing quickened. 'Then... then the lords of the warp have heard me!' A light went on behind her eyes as an idea hit her. 'And you!' she exclaimed. She stood up and looked Lysander up and down. 'You shall be my Executioner!'

'Bring the finished work,' said Lysander, 'and come with me.'

VALIENNE'S PLAY WAS about death. She had spent her whole life writing it, revising and perfecting it, each character the personification of a way in which life could be ended. There were roles for Pestilence, Vengeance, Madness and Fate, and the dialogue was an impenetrable web of metaphor. Its staging called for countless deaths on stage, illustrations of how death could be both random and carefully plotted by powers beyond the comprehension of those involved. It was a work of cruelty, of infinite bleakness.

To Valienne, this was a work of joy. By illustrating the meaninglessness of life and the supremacy of death, she sought to make the acts of worship by Shalhadar's citizens shine brighter in that darkness. This was the explanation she gave to the courtiers who received her into Shalhadar's palace, who directed her into some lesser-travelled wing where she would not lower the tone of opulence and beauty.

The manuscript of the *Chant of the Changing Ones* was taken to Shalhadar himself, whose courtiers had already begun to assemble a cast and crew for the play's production. The palace chambers were full of costumers and artisans. Crafters of flesh pared skin and muscle to make new faces and shapes for those hoping to serve in the chorus. Bizarre mutants, with brightly patterned skin or malformed limbs, auditioned as freak show exhibits. Psykers performed tricks of telekinesis and pyromancy, hoping to make the grade for the performance.

Lysander had watched it unfold from an upper balcony of the palace. It had been extraordinary the speed with which it had kicked into gear, as if the whole city had been primed to gather its resources of performers and madmen for just this occasion. Talaya was walking through the midst of it, ignoring the cultists and hopefuls who clamoured for her attention. She waved aside acrobats whose long, multi-jointed limbs were stripped of skin and flicked a grovelling supplicant away with a kick of a mechanical leg. She switched without breaking a step into climbing up the wall below Lysander, reaching the balcony in a few strides.

'How much it must pain you,' she said.

Lysander looked at her, but gave no reply.

'How can you keep it all bottled up inside you, Lysander?' continued Talaya. 'Everything you see on Malodrax offends you to its core. These people and their acts of worship. This palace. This city. Me. You must want to drive that blade right through my heart, Imperial Fist. But you cannot, because playing along with this world is the only way to kill Thul. What delicious suffering I can taste on you! It twists up inside you and bleeds, does it not? It bleeds that hatred into the rest of you and rots you away. I would be there when you give vent to that hatred, Lysander. It will be something to be seen.'

'Are we done here?' said Lysander.

'The Veiled One has given the order,' said Talaya. 'On the next dawn we will move out.'

'Good,' said Lysander. 'I will be glad of it.'

'But you are not done yet!' Talaya gestured down at the crowds below. 'You still have to undergo your transformation. After all, you are to be our Executioner.'

14

'*My conclave was created to seek out knowledge and use it, not destroy it out of hand through some hysterical fear of corruption. It was some way into my Inquisitorial career when I found them, having heard of them from a fellow inquisitor in the form of a cautionary tale of how far those in the Holy Ordos might fall. They did not welcome me with open arms, for anyone who sought them out must by definition come under the gravest suspicions. That is how I knew I was on the only road I could walk.*'

– Inquisitor Corvin Golrukhan

'HOLD!' ORDERED CHAPLAIN Lycaon, and the strike force dropped into cover behind him. In the cavernous fortress ruins there was plenty of cover but limited visibility, with every approach obscured by the walls and battlements rising all around. Techmarine Kho's Land Speeder droned along just above head height, playing its guns across the surrounding ruins.

'We have a sighting up ahead,' voxed Sergeant Gorvetz.

'Is there anyone to spot us?' asked Lycaon.

'I cannot tell,' replied Gorvetz. 'I do not think we were seen.'

'Lysander,' ordered Lycaon. 'Join Gorvetz and scout ahead. Let me know if we have a viable target.'

Lysander headed through the rubble field left from a collapsed wall, picking his way from cover to cover as he passed the rest of the strike force and headed towards Gorvetz's position. The Devastator squad had the point for that segment of the march, and had spread out through the hollow floors of a multi-levelled pale stone building. The late sun was slanting through breaks in the clouds, fractured by the ruins into beams that passed slowly across the dusty wreckage. Lysander spotted Gorvetz's Imperial Fists ahead, crouching at the far end of the building, their heavy weapons shouldered, watching ahead through magnoculars and viewfinders.

The horizon was a broken mass of ruins. Sergeant Gorvetz was scanning it through his magnoculars as Lysander crouched down behind him.

'Where is it?' asked Lysander.

Gorvetz was not a man of many words, and simply pointed into the distance. Lysander looked in that direction, trying to filter some meaning from the tumbledown towers and battlements.

Then, he saw the movement. His vision adjusted to the distance and he made out the shifting clouds around its upper reaches – birds, flying vermin, clustering around the corruption.

It was a war engine. This one was in the shape of a siege tower, its upper floors fronted with a drawbridge forming the lower jaw of an enormous daemonic face. Huge gun emplacements bulged from the tower's sides, their massive-bore cannon traversing menacingly across the surrounding landscape, fed by ammunition hoppers so large they gave the siege tower a top-heavy, hunchbacked shape. Banners, tattered and fire-stained, hung from its timbers, bearing the iron face mask symbol of the Iron Warriors.

'I take it,' said Gorvetz, 'that's what we were looking for.'

'It is,' said Lysander. 'Are there any sentries on its battlements?'

'None that we've seen.'

'Then it's probably wild,' said Lysander.

'Bloody waste if you ask me,' said Gorvetz. 'Make a war machine and just turn it loose.'

'Kraegon Thul is not a fool,' said Lysander. 'The wild war engines are left to test the others. They are sent out here to prove themselves before Thul will export them to whatever warzone demands them next. If they can survive beasts like this, they are fit to fight in the colours of the Iron Warriors. That machine has no doubt accounted for plenty others of its kind.'

'Good,' said Gorvetz. 'I was worried this would be easy.' He said it without a smile, and Lysander could not be certain there was any humour in the Devastator veteran at all.

'The target is good,' voxed Lysander to Lycaon.

'Then we must move quickly,' said Lycaon, 'before our position becomes known. We make the approach. Imperial Fists, to battle order!'

UP CLOSE, THE stench of the machine's corruption suffused the ruins and it was clear what had attracted the clouds of winged vermin that followed in its wake. It was the stench of carrion, of the battlefield dead. It was a smell that Lysander had become very familiar with, and it brought his mind back to the hundred battles he had fought in the colours of the Imperial Fists.

Had that been the same man? He answered to the name Lysander, he wore the golden armour and the symbol of the clenched fist, but would that man recognise the thoughts in his head, the recent memories? What would that Lysander have said of a man who had recited a list of sins the current Lysander had committed – trafficking with daemons, permitting witches and mutants to live, shirking one duty to fulfil another to his battle-brothers?

Lysander threw out thoughts like that. He had no room in his mind for anything save the thoughts of a soldier now. Squads Kaderic and Lycaon were moving parallel to the siege tower, keeping the ruins between them and any sensors the siege tower must have. It had to be autonomous, controlled by a corrupt machine or daemon, to roam unscrewed through the ruins, and it would be watching for prey just as it had been the day it rolled out of Kulgarde's forges. The closer Lysander got the fouler the glimpses he had of the machine. Its upper reaches were covered in corpses, mounted on spikes jutting from the blackened timbers. They were old and new, many of obvious mutants, others of ragged creatures dressed in all-covering pale robes who might have been nomads or wandered eking out lives in the region. Hoppers mounted on the engine's sides seemed to be there for the sole purpose of holding more bodies, many rotted away to skeletons, a few fresh and bloody.

'We are closing,' came First Sergeant Kaderic's vox. 'All squads, be ready for contact.'

Ahead, a body lay among a host of fallen rubble. The body was of one of the nomads – so far the strike force had not seen any alive but had come across a couple of bodies on their way through the ruins. This one looked to have been trapped by the rockfall, one leg crushed beneath a block of stone, and to have perished where he lay. With a clack of metal on metal a spidery creature, somewhat larger than a man, scuttled over the fallen wall and over the body. Without a word the Imperial Fists shifted into cover, each man putting something between himself and the creature.

It was a form of servitor, a mechanical creature controlled by a biological, human core component. The Imperium created them from condemned prisoners, or those pious folk who left their bodies to be used to continue the Imperium's work. Presumably this one had been made in Kulgarde – its body resembled that of a ten-legged spider, its body made up of a human torso with the head hanging upside-down to form its face, a single wide lens mounted in the mouth. A forelimb snickered out and sliced the trapped leg off the corpse, before the servitor threw the corpse over its back and carried it over the ruins towards the rumbling of the siege engine's wheels.

'It collects them,' voxed Brother Givenar of Squad Kaderic, the huge Imperial Fist who had wrestled at the funeral games outside Shalhadar's city.

'Not for much longer,' said Kaderic. 'We're coming up to the crossroads. Break cover on my word.'

The sound of the siege engine was so loud Lysander could hear nothing else save for the vox, transmitted directly to his middle ear.

'In position,' came the vox from Sergeant Gorvetz.

'Go!' ordered Lycaon.

The Imperial Fists broke from cover and burst into the crossroads ahead. Soaring walls formed a sheer-sided chasm in one direction – in the other wound a labyrinth of collapsed buildings, countless layers of floors tumbling down over one another. Through this labyrinth the siege tower approached, crunching through the ruins, heralded by a cloud of rubble dust.

Lysander jammed his helmet over his head as the dust cloud rolled over him. Amidst the sound of the siege tower's engines was the screech of metal on metal as the gun emplacement swivelled to aim at the Imperial Fists that had suddenly appeared in its path.

Bolter fire stuttered up at the engine, pinging off the armour plating that covered its front. Corpses were shot off the spikes covering its upper levels. The huge daemonic face grimaced down at the Imperial Fists as the tower's guns opened up.

Great rents were opened up in the chasm walls as the guns thundered. Shattered stone rained, red-hot and razor-sharp. Spent cannon shells the size of men fell as Lysander sprinted to one side to avoid them. The percussion of the shots was like a hammer against Lysander's armour – Imperial Fists were thrown off their feet.

'We have its attention,' voxed Lycaon.

Another volley from the siege tower's guns threw an avalanche of shattered rubble into the crossroads. Lysander saw a sprawling golden-armoured figure vanish under the torrent. He hauled chunks of rock away until he exposed the battered shoulder guard of another Imperial Fist – Brother Givenar. He pulled on the guard until Givenar came loose. Givenar roared and leapt to his feet, throwing rubble in every direction, furious he had not been strong enough to free himself.

'Is that it?' yelled Givenar up at the siege engine. 'I'll tear you apart by myself!'

One of the guns was angling down at them. Lysander grabbed Givenar again and dragged him into the relative cover of a section of fallen battlement as the gun roared. The blast picked up Lysander and threw him against a stretch of wall, and he blacked out for a split second in the storm that slammed into him.

He came to on the ground, billows of dust roiling around him. It was Givenar who hauled Lysander to his feet this time, and the pain that ran through Lysander's limbs was a reminder that they were all basically intact. Lucky, he thought. We have been lucky so far.

'Get in closer!' shouted Lysander over the din. He and Givenar forged their way through the debris towards the roaring of the siege tower's engines. The dust was blown away by a blast of exhaust and the wheels of the siege engine loomed through the half-light. They were three storeys high, of dense black wood and studded with iron spikes. The structure's lower floors were stained black with old blood, the splits and gaps packed with the long-dried bodies of forge labourers and the sacrifices made to awaken its machine-spirit. More spent shells clattered down against the wheels, crushed flat under them as the siege engine rolled on through the ruins.

Rogal Dorn had written more on the art of the siege than had anyone else in the history of the Imperium. It was his genius, the purpose for which the Emperor had created him at the dawn of the Great Crusade. Every Imperial Fist knew the core tenets of Dorn's siege-lore – the reduction of fortifications, the murderous geometry of firing zones, the million and one ways in which a set location could be made lethal to any who approached and the equal number of ways to kill an enemy while he skulked behind his walls. Among those principles was one which spoke of the purpose of siege engines, from the primitive rams and ladders of feral peoples to the Imperium's own Titan Legions. The guns on a siege tower such as this were designed to clear enemy walls of opposition, to open up breaches in their fortifications, and to pound the enemy's fortress from a distance to soften them up for the approach. They were not designed to kill enemies swarming around the base of the fortress, since such an enemy should be within his walls sheltering from the bombardment as the siege tower rolled forwards.

The Imperial Fists stayed close, moving with the siege engine. Its guns thundered, but they could not target enemies on foot at so close a range – even if they had the flexibility of elevation, they would have blasted the tower's own wheels off. Thus the theory went, and as Lysander and the rest of the strike force struggled through the rubble to the base of the tower that theory was put to the test.

The theory had not taken the servitors into account. The Imperial Fists, however, were ready for them. Like spiders bursting from their egg sacs, the servitors tore free of the metal blisters covering the middle floors and scurried down the tower's sides towards the ground. The blisters gave the tower a scabbed and diseased appearance which was not lessened by the knowledge they contained the host of spider-servitors.

The servitors dropped down among the Imperial Fists and, scattered by the storm of gunfire and falling rubble, the Imperial Fists had to face them in ones and twos. One dropped right on top of Brother Givenar, its legs clacking as an industrial pincer tried to slice into his armour. Givenar threw the servitor to the ground in a perfect wrestler's move and stamped down on the human torso at its centre. Ribs splintered and transparent greyish blood spattered up over his greaves.

Lysander found himself facing another configuration, this one with three upright human bodies fused together at the spine, each with its mouth wired open and a gun barrel jutting from between its teeth. It moved on a cluster of jointed legs, chunky and industrial, and its abdomens were fused to the centre of the cluster with a joint that permitted them to rotate. As it closed with Lysander it spun and Lysander realised a split second before it opened fire that this servitor was designed to spray bullets randomly in all directions, lethally imperilling anyone nearby.

Lysander dived into a roll as the servitor's guns opened up as one. A spiral of gunfire ripped over his head, filling the air with a buzzing mass of hot shrapnel. Any other soldier would have fled from the servitor, trying to put distance between himself and the stuttering waves of gunfire. A Space Marine knew better. He knew that an enemy with a gun was most dangerous from a distance, because he had time and space to aim and close the gap with a well-placed shot. A Space Marine, on the other hand, was deadliest up close.

Lysander slammed into the servitor and rammed

the barrel of his bolter up into its closest ribcage. He squeezed the trigger and hammered half a magazine into its central mass. Desiccated flesh flew as the explosive bolter shells ripped through the servitor from the inside. Lysander kicked over what remained of the servitor to see Brother Givenar reeling, clutching the bloody side of his face.

'Brother!' shouted Lysander.

'Damn thing took my ear off!' replied Givenar, more angry than hurt.

'We have a shot!' came the vox from Sergeant Gorvetz.

'Take it!' was Chaplain Lycaon's reply.

Gorvetz's Devastator squad had used the chaos to get into position overlooking the intersection. Now, as one, they opened fire from an upper floor, directly into the side of the siege engine. Gorvetz had chosen a spot where an ammunition hopper met the armour plating, where the armour seemed thinner than on the rest of the machine. A plasma blast blew off a panel of armour and heavy bolter fire chewed through wood and metal. Lysander could hear the low stuttering of the heavy bolters over the engines, and then the sudden hot crack of cannon shells cooking off inside the tower. Burning timbers rained down like the giant shell casings had moments before. A sheet of pitted steel fell like a guillotine blade, landing a few metres from Lysander and embedding itself corner-first in the paved ground.

'Breach!' yelled Gorvetz over the vox. 'We have a breach!'

'On my way!' replied Lysander. 'First Sergeant!'

'Brother Lysander!' replied First Sergeant Kaderic. The sound of chainblade through bone and metal buzzed away over the vox as he spoke.

'With me! We go up!'

Lysander ran for the half-collapsed building where Gorvetz was set up. Brother Givenar followed him, and other Imperial Fists from Squad Kaderic. He spotted Lycaon duelling with another servitor, a creature twice his height composed of several bodies wrapped around a steel frame to form its muscles, giving it a hunched, gorilla-like profile. As Lysander watched, Lycaon's crozius flashed and one of the servitor's arms came away.

Lysander found a stairway leading to the upper floors of the building, marked with burning flares left there by Gorvetz. He ran up, half blinded by the billows of dust and smoke boiling from the impacts of the tower's cannon fire. The shapes of Gorvetz's Devastator squad loomed through the darkness and Lysander made out Gorvetz himself, gnarled old face screwed up in a grimace as he joined his squad in hammering gunfire at the siege tower.

A huge hole had been torn in the side of the tower, three floors up. Inside, lit by the strobes of gunfire, Lysander could make out only a sifting, seething blackness.

'Kho! Break cover!' voxed Lysander.

Dorn's Dagger and the *Talon Blade* buzzed down from their positions hovering out of sight above the chasm walls. Lysander could see the red armour of Techmarine Kho as he guided his Land Speeder down through the eddies of smoke towards Gorvetz's position.

The priority was Kho. Anyone else who made it inside was a bonus, but Kho had to get inside and he had to survive. Otherwise the whole mission on Malodrax would be lost.

The *Talon Blade* thrummed past the position first. Sergeant Gorvetz and Brother Antinas, carrying the squad's heavy flamer, jumped down onto the running plates of the Land Speeder. A Land Speeder was not a troop carrier, but if needs be a couple of Space Marines could hold on for a short ride. The *Talon Blade* swept around close to the breach in the tower's side and Brother Antinas jumped, disappearing through the black gash in the armour. Gorvetz made ready to leap but a falling chunk of debris forced Gethor, at the *Talon Blade*'s controls, to swerve away from the breach, and Gorvetz had to hold on.

The *Dorn's Dagger* was close now. Lysander shouldered his bolter and jumped, hitting chest-first against the Land Speeder's engine cowling. He found a handhold and clung on, feeling the impact as Brother Givenar landed alongside him.

The crossroads whirled below him. Lysander could see Captain Lycaon and the Imperial Fists of his squad forming a rough battle line, fending off the combat servitors surging at them through the rubble to be cut down by bolter fire or drawn onto the point of a chainblade.

Lycaon was directing as if conducting a symphony.

Gunfire rattled against the underside of *Dorn's Dagger*. The Land Speeder lurched, and Techmarine Kho wrestled with the control yoke. The servitors below had realised that the Land Speeders were a target and those that could were firing up at them.

Lysander's left hand came away with the shift of weight and he was hanging by one hand over the crossroads, feet kicking out over nothing. The Land Speeder levelled and Lysander found another handhold, clutching tighter to the cowling.

'Brother Givenar, if you will,' voxed Techmarine Kho. Lysander saw *Dorn's Dagger* was level with the breach. Kho put the vehicle into a steady hover and clambered up out of the cockpit, the servo-arms of his harness spread to grab out at anything that might support him. Kho leapt from the Land Speeder and vanished through the breach.

Givenar pulled himself over into the cockpit. 'Go, captain!' he voxed, swinging the Land Speeder around. His touch was not as fine as Kho's, but like every Imperial Fist he had basic training in all the Chapter's vehicles including the Land Speeder. Lysander braced his feet against the side of the engine housing as the yawning mouth of the breach swung closer.

Lysander waited for another half-second, sure that he would get no closer. Then he pushed off with both feet and propelled himself through the torn armour and into the siege engine.

Darkness swarmed around him. Even through the filters of his armour's faceplate he could barely breathe through the stench of death, intensified and concentrated inside the siege tower. Toxin warning runes flickered, projected against his retina by his armour's autosensors. Lysander tried to make out his surroundings, but the darkness clung and the shape of the interior was sketched out as black on black.

'The *Dagger*'s hit!' voxed Givenar. Lysander could hear the Land Speeder's engines shrieking over the rumble of the siege tower.

The shape of *Dorn's Dagger*, with Givenar behind the controls, loomed in the tear in the armour behind Lysander. With a lurch the speeder crashed into the breach, its nose ripping through the ragged edges of armour as the engines fragmented and threw chunks of burning metal in every direction.

Lysander leaned over the nose of the speeder and grabbed Givenar's hand. He pulled Givenar out of the cockpit and into the siege tower. *Dorn's Dagger* stayed lodged where it was, the burning engines casting a flickering light through the tower's interior.

'Then we are on our own,' said Techmarine Kho levelly.

'Givenar!' exclaimed Antinas. 'Glad you made it! You're sure to make the rest of us look good.'

'Not hard with children like you,' replied Givenar.

'I meant by comparison,' said Antinas.

In the guttering light Lysander could make out the

beams of the siege engine criss-crossing the space inside. It was no surprise by now to see them hung with human skins, each one cured and tattooed to form a banner in the heraldry of the Iron Warriors. Lysander saw the steel face mask of the Legion and bold patterns of yellow and black like the warning flashes on their armour. He recognised the book, tower and hands of Kraegon Thul's personal heraldry, hanging high on a vast pelt that must have been cut from one of Kulgarde's brute-mutants.

'Up or down?' asked Lysander. Below was the churning of the tower's engines, and up was the chamber where the troops would wait for the siege engine's drawbridge to open.

'Down,' said Kho.

Lysander, Givenar, Antinas, and Techmarine Kho. Ideally more would have made it through the breach, but there were worse bands of Imperial Fists to take on this mission. Givenar took the lead heading downwards, and Lysander could see on him the wounded pride from having crashed the Land Speeder and closed up the breach. He had, at least, held on to his bolter, which he was playing through the shadows. The lower levels were choked with bodies, long-dead and dried out, stretched between the wooden beams and forming a dry, crackling layer underfoot. Huge cogs turned and pistons thrust through the gloom, choking oily smoke mingled with the stink of death.

'Movement!' shouted Brother Antinas. Before

Lysander could focus on the scuttling that came at them out of the dark, Antinas was opening up with his heavy flamer, spraying a long gout of liquid flame over a spider-servitor leaping at him. It was engulfed in the flame and landed on him, fire catching in the greasy joints of its armour and on the dried-out flesh of its human torso. Antinas slammed the servitor into the floor and clubbed it flat with the butt of his heavy flamer. The massive weapon crunched through the ribs of the human component and flattened its skull.

Another servitor leapt from the churning mass of cogs and gears right at Lysander. It was a maintenance device, its torso low and mounted on wheels so its lower jaw dragged along the floor, with countless small manipulator limbs fused to its spine. Lysander met it with his chainsword and sawed it in half, from shoulder to hip, colourless blood spraying over him.

There were few combat servitors down among the engines – most were maintenance devices, which fought with tools and plasma cutters. Techmarine Kho wrestled one to the floor with the mechanical arms of his servo-harness and blasted it apart with his plasma pistol, while Brother Givenar tore the leg off another and shot it to pieces with a burst of bolter fire.

'The tower's defenders are still outside,' said Kho as he threw the ragged remains of the last servitor aside. 'But they may not remain so for long if they realise the tower is invaded. We must move quickly. Go lower.'

The engines were huge and in many ways crude in

construction, but they had a solidity that explained how the tower had continued to function in the proving grounds on its own. A ruddy glow came from an open furnace door, and Lysander spotted charred bones in the maw of the furnace among heaps of black ashes.

'It fuels itself with the dead,' said Lysander.

'No shortage of those on Malodrax,' said Givenar.

'Most insightful, Brother Givenar,' said Antinas.

'Are you two done?' snapped Lysander. 'You can batter one another bloody when we are done with this world. For now we have work to do.'

Beyond the furnace was a huge chunk of black rock, shot through with veins of silver. Radiation runes were flickering on Lysander's retina as the Imperial Fists approached it. Metal fittings connected cables and pipes to the rock, which had a pitted, cratered appearance – Lysander guessed it was a meteorite, perhaps captured by Malodrax's own gravity, perhaps brought from another world. Even lacking any psychic ability himself, Lysander could feel the malice coming off it, a moral sickness given form, the sense of it clinging to the inside of his skull like an uncleanness trying to seep into his soul.

The controller of the siege tower could have been one of two possibilities. The first was a machine-spirit, similar to those present in ancient cogitators helping command the most venerable starships and war engines of the Imperium, albeit corrupted and malevolent. The second possibility was a daemon, summoned and compelled to possess the siege tower by sacrifices made at the moment its engines were started. The air of malice surrounding the tower had suggested from the start that the latter was more likely.

Techmarine Kho stood before the meteorite, the end of one servo-arm cycling to present the nozzle of a plasma cutter to the stone. The cutter's flame ignited, casting a harsh white light against the edges of the engines on either side. 'You who have called this machine your home,' said Kho calmly, 'you are now to be evicted. Flee to the warp. Stand and fight. The outcome will be the same.'

Kho's plasma cutter scored down through the stone, etching a glowing molten line down through the meteorite's surface. The meteorite was hollow and it cracked in two, the sound like a gunshot.

A gnarl of burning light bled out from the broken meteorite. It took a form – a coiled snake, turning in on itself, forming dizzying patterns with the coils of its body. From the centre of the sinuous body emerged a head, something like a snake's but with several pairs of human eyes. A long, glowing blue tongue flickered between its fangs.

Long slits opened up down its elongated body and vestigial arms reached out, the skin translucent, with malformed bones and fingers.

'This is mine,' hissed the daemon. 'And it is glorious. You are filthy. Burn in my glory!'

The daemon's form changed. A halo of burning gold

surrounded it. Reflections of itself spread out behind it, filling the tower's engine block with visions of tangled serpentine flesh. It was accompanied by a rising note, a clashing mix of atonal noise that raked through Lysander's skeleton as it washed over him. He heard the awful daemonic music again, as played by the orchestra that had accompanied Captain Hexal during his destruction of the *Shield of Valour*.

Anger burned in Lysander. The daemon's aura could not dampen it, and Lysander took a hold of it as surely as if it were the hilt of a sword. This daemon might addle his mind and overwhelm his senses, but the anger would see him through.

Lysander charged on through the blaze of light and colour. He felt writhing flesh slamming against him. He drew his chainblade and plunged it in deep, hearing the chainteeth finding purchase in scale, muscle and bone. The daemon whipped its body into Lysander and threw him back, impacting against the side of an engine housing.

Chunks of machinery fell around Lysander. A huge cog rang against the floor. The snake-daemon reared up, its mouth yawing wide to reveal an endless tunnel of boiling fire down its gullet.

Lysander lunged with his chainblade and cut right into one of the snake's fangs. The blade chewed through the fang and venom spurted. The daemon reeled backwards, the coiling of its bodies slamming into the remains of the meteorite that had housed it.

Through its coils forged Techmarine Kho, tearing at it with his servo-arms, the plasma cutter carving slices from its body.

Antinas and Givenar charged into the opening made by Lysander in the daemon's swirling coils. Antinas sprayed liquid fire up into the daemon's face while Givenar laid about him with his chainblade. Gouts of multicoloured blood erupted everywhere. Givenar leapt up onto the daemon's face, grabbing its remaining fang to haul himself up and ram his chainblade into the roof of its mouth.

Lysander unshouldered his bolter and rattled off the magazine into the daemon's skull. Eyes rolled back and burst. Lysander felt the hammer fall on nothing and charged, driving his shoulder towards the daemon's throat. Flesh parted under his feet as he threw his weight into it, ribs crunching in its neck as he impacted.

The daemon's head crashed to the floor onto Lysander's leg. Lysander kicked it away with his free foot and stood over the daemon. Its glory was gone now, its reflections dissolved, the only light coming off it bleeding out of its body along with its lifeblood.

'I told your kind I would return,' said Lysander. 'When daemons have nightmares, I am what they see, and I always keep my word.'

The daemon hissed and coiled back as if to strike. Lysander grabbed it by an eye socket, sinking his fingers deep into the spongy mass inside its skull, and dragged its head forwards again. He rammed his chainblade down into the back of its skull, sawing left and right through the gristle of its spine.

Techmarine Kho appeared through the flailing coils. A servo-arm held the head down while his plasma cutter joined Lysander's blade in its gory work.

The daemon's head came away and a mass of iridescent sludge oozed from its severed neck onto the floor of the engine block.

'The daemon is down,' voxed Kho.

'Report your situation!' came Lycaon's reply. From the sound of it his squad was still embattled outside the tower.

'Looking for the controls,' replied Kho. 'Stand by.' He turned to the other Imperial Fists, still smeared with gore from the daemon. 'Locate the cockpit, or whatever passes for it.'

'Well killed,' said Brother Antinas, looking down at the daemon's severed head. 'Who shall claim it?'

'Not you,' said Givenar, 'unless we grant the kill for flailing around on the floor.'

'Split up,' said Lysander. 'Lycaon needs the tower opened up. We're still fighting out there.'

The black heart of the siege tower churned between the engine blocks, with thundering pistons clashing overhead and exhaust pipes glowing dark-red with the heat. As Lysander clambered lower it got hotter and denser, with dust-dry bones flaking apart under his feet where they had fallen from sacrifices long before.

Down there in the tower's depths was a cogitator

of ancient mark, with thousands of valves filling a contraption of glass and pitted steel. The glass was discoloured as if by disease and reams of punchcards lay around it like a snowdrift. It was Antinas who found it first, and Givenar expressed gratitude that Antinas had not flamed it at first sight.

While the two swapped insults Techmarine Kho reached the cogitator and levered its casing open, exposing the clacking mass of valves and levers inside.

Lysander stood guard, ready for any remaining servitors to scrabble out of hidden corners to defend the cogitator. Kho plunged a servo-arm into the cogitator and wiring slithered out, datajacks finding places to interface with the ancient machine.

'It is insane,' said Kho as the data probes worked their way deeper into the machine. 'It was once proud and noble, but it was stolen by servants of the Dark Gods and implanted in here, under the command of the daemon. It has become corrupted and is beyond help, I fear.'

'Can you control it?' asked Lysander.

'I can,' said Kho. 'But for how long I cannot say. And its machine-spirit has become an abominable thing now, and must be destroyed when it is no longer useful.'

'I doubt that will be a problem,' said Lysander. 'What about the servitors?'

'I can cut the connection,' said Kho. 'They will revert to their simplest behaviour routines. I cannot control them directly or shut them down, not without a great deal of work.'

'That will have to do. Can you open us up?'

'I can lower the drawbridge.'

'Lycaon!' voxed Lysander. 'Get to high ground. The drawbridge is opening up.'

Far above the jaw of the daemon's face ground open, revealing the upper levels where the tower's complement of troops was to wait to reach the enemy battlements. Lysander listened over the vox as Lycaon's squad made for the upper levels of the surrounding ruins.

Lysander met Lycaon's men and the rest of Squad Gorvetz halfway up the siege tower, among the bones and dried-out hides of the tower's countless sacrifices.

'Excellent work,' said Lycaon.

'What losses?' asked Lysander.

'Wounds received,' said Lycaon. 'None dead, and all can fight.'

'Then we have been fortunate.'

'Kho!' voxed Lycaon. 'Can you move us?'

'I have full control over our motivator functions,' came Kho's reply. 'I hope to have weapons online soon. The machine-spirit is not cooperative but I am working to subdue it.'

Already the siege engine was changing direction, its engine blocks complaining as they turned the huge front wheels. The sound of falling rubble thudded against the exterior as the siege tower took on its new course, crushing the remains of the dismantled servitors that had served it a few minutes before.

'Your plan worked, Captain Lysander,' said Lycaon.

'So far,' said Lysander. 'And I imagine that was the easy part.'

15

'It is not for me to say whether my heresy was the correct path. I can say only that for me, there could have been no other. Is it for one man, even an inquisitor, to say what the universal truth of our species is, the one road that all humanity must walk? Some of us no doubt think it is, but I have not yet scaled those heights of arrogance. I chose to wield the knowledge and weapons of the enemy against him. Others say that makes me the enemy. When all history is played out and we look back from the end of time, perhaps we will know who is right.'

– Inquisitor Corvin Golrukhan

THE JOURNEY FROM the outskirts of Kulgarde's hinterland to the city of Shalhadar had seemed to take Lysander forever, struggling through the storms of that broken wasteland. Now, on the way back in the great procession Shalhadar's court had assembled, the landscape of Malodrax seemed to slide by almost without effort. It felt as if Malodrax was letting this silken, many-coloured monstrosity wind across its surface, eager to see what chaos would ensue when it reached its destination.

A hundred carriages were pulled by dozens of citizens each. They had lined up in the streets for the right to be yoked to the carriages, and they had scrambled over one another to be shackled to the one carrying Lysander – for he was the Executioner, one of the lead roles in The Chant of the Changing Ones. Their joy at serving Shalhadar had not dimmed even as they had dropped from heatstroke and exhaustion, to be dragged away by the outriders from Shalhadar's army who ranged ahead of the caravan on their strange bipedal mounts. Each carriage carried performers for the play – the principal actors, the dancers and singers of the chorus, the musicians who were to accompany the performance on stage, the dressers and the stagehands. Valienne had a carriage to herself, covered against the sun, from which she had not emerged throughout the whole journey. Talaya had another, and Lysander wondered if she would take on a role herself or was just there to help ensure Shalhadar's grand plan went off smoothly.

Lysander had to swallow down his disgust, like bile in his throat. Somehow the luxury of it seemed the worst. He had a carriage to himself and it was large enough for a dozen to live in comfortably, upholstered in silk and velvet, with hardwood chests of narcotics and peculiar devices of leather and steel he did not try to guess the use of. It was obscene that he should be feted by the people of Shalhadar's city, and granted such luxury when they were literally dying of exhaustion outside. If he had the option he would have torn it all down and laid waste to the caravan, ripping its painted foulness apart. But he did not have that option. Not yet. As pleasing as it would be to him to see the trappings of Shalhadar's arrogance tattered and burning, Kraegon Thul would still be alive and Malodrax would have won.

He had a copy of Valienne's play, too, which he had memorised. He did not pretend to understand the intricacies of drama, but fortunately the role of the Executioner required little more than a commanding physical presence which a Space Marine had no trouble mustering. Shalhadar's plan was simple in essence, and it played off the need of creatures like Thul to be worshipped and obeyed, and to have their enemies offer them supplication. Shalhadar was disgusting in every way, but he was clever. The plan would work, up until Lysander himself was required to play his part. Then, so much would be in the hands of chance.

'There!' came a cry from up front. Lysander pulled a curtain aside and looked out across the wasteland. 'Upon the horizon!'

Lysander saw it too. The battlements of Kulgarde, dark grey, fluttering with banners in the yellow and black of the Iron Warriors. There were so many emotions sparked in him by seeing the fortress again that he could pick none out. He recognised the blooms of filthy smoke from the forges behind the walls, and the scars covering the hinterlands from the battles of war engines let loose to prove themselves while Thul watched from the battlements. He saw, as clear as if they were in front of him, the bodies of his captive battle-brothers paraded and then cut down to be dragged to the Isle of the Bone Sculptors.

And yet he could not purify himself with battle. He could not lay about him and exterminate the filth that fawned at the altars of the warp, and burn the uncleanness away. Not yet.

'Send the call!' cried out one of the gang leaders who commanded the citizens hauling the carriages. 'Bring the riders in close! We enter the Warsmith's realm!'

Talaya stalked along the top of one carriage, watching the battlements. 'Send the heralds!' she commanded.

One carriage broke away from the column. Its occupants pulled down the coverings and revealed dozens of men and women there, each carrying a musical instrument. Another carriage followed, this one carrying a choir, to provide the fanfare that would accompany Shalhadar's offering through the gates of Kulgarde.

How many armies had tried to breach Kulgarde? The ground below its walls showed the scars of plenty of battles, and the skeletons choking the spiked rollers of the fortifications had come from somewhere. How many thousands had died trying to climb or breach those walls? And now it turned out that all it took to open the gates of Kulgarde was a song and a dance.

* * *

THE GATES INDEED opened, enormous blast doors stained with blood and machine oil. A squad of Iron Warriors stood on the battlements above the gate, carrying enough heavy weapons to turn the caravan's carriages into splinters. The choir and the musicians had gone ahead and played swooning, hypnotic music to accompany the entrance of Shalhadar's gift into Kulgarde. Evidently the Iron Warriors were willing to take his token of supplication, for they did not open fire and instead the caravan passed into the fortress.

Lysander was back among the brutal killing architecture of the fortress, every block and step designed to make the place impossible to take by force. An army might make it onto the walls but would find itself facing a sheer drop on the other side, with only a single-file stairway giving access to the lower levels. Passages barely wide enough for a single Space Marine allowed one Iron Warrior to fend off dozens of attackers alone. The wide, high-ceilinged passageway through which the caravan entered was itself a trap, for when the gates were breached and an enemy force swarmed in they would be covered on all sides by murder-holes and gun emplacements. They would be herded into the wide space which ended suddenly at a second gate protected by barricades and heavy weapons bunkers. The second gate itself consisted of several single-file doors, portcullised with bars so defenders could shoot through them.

Captain Hexal greeted the convoy at the second gate. His squad was with him, the same Iron Warriors who had attacked the *Shield of Valour* and taken Lysander's squad.

Talaya approached the gate, flanked by heralds playing a fanfare. She dismissed them with a gesture and let her mechanical limbs lower her delicately to the floor, where she bowed low.

'Lord Shalhadar the Veiled One acknowledges your lord's requests,' she said, 'and grants them. They shall be fulfilled as quickly as the suns move across the sky. He asks but one boon from Warsmith Kraegon Thul, that he accept this gift in humility. A performance of *The Chant of the Changing Ones*, an act of obeisance to the gods of the warp. For we all stand before the eyes of the gods, and by their will we yet breathe.'

Two things could happen. Hexal could open the gates and let the performers through, so that Shalhadar's act of supplication could unfold before the eyes of Kraegon Thul himself. Or Hexal could shoot Talaya and have a hundred Iron Warriors guns appear at the murderholes, and massacre every living thing in the convoy. Lysander had thought about the odds of each eventuality, and had concluded the chances were roughly even.

Hexal gestured to the Iron Warriors of his squad, and they stood aside. Mutant slaves hauled the gates open. Talaya waved forward those essential to the performance, the actors, musicians and stagehands. Lysander jumped down from his carriage.

Hexal had decided not to kill them all out of hand. That was something. But he might still recognise

Lysander, or at least realise he was a Space Marine. It was impossible for Lysander to hide his bulk and the crimson armour he wore only made him more prominent. He joined the crowd of bizarrely-dressed performers heading through the second gate, and tried not to meet Hexal's eyes as he walked.

The broadsword on his back could cut through power armour if Lysander struck just right. Hexal's head could be parted from his shoulders, or his spine could be severed by a blade through the abdomen. But Lysander's mind had hosted those thoughts before, and they were choked down as he remembered that Kraegon Thul was still somewhere inside Kulgarde, waiting to die.

He swore for the hundredth time that Hexal would die. He passed by Hexal and his squad, through the gate, and into Kulgarde.

THE DUELLING GROUND took up a significant stretch of the fortress interior. It was a great circular chamber of stone with galleries for the senior Iron Warriors to watch their fellow traitors drilling in close combat techniques or settling differences. This was to be their stage, the expanse of bloodstained stone scored with the marks of old blades. Their audience would be the Iron Warriors of Kulgarde, among them Warsmith Kraegon Thul himself.

Lysander watched motionless in what would become the wings as the stage was set. Sections of scenery were brought in representing a castle, a palace, a battlefield strewn with painted corpses and the fanciful clashes of colour and shape that represented the warp. Valienne, no less bedraggled and filthy than the moment Lysander found her, was arguing with the set builders and costumers about every detail. The rest of the cast were meditating or praying, each making their own form of appeal to the gods of the warp.

Pestilence was played by three youths in a costume that linked them together into a lumpen, shambling monstrosity, its lolling mouth operated by one of the actors while another rolled its bloodshot eyes and a third its malformed claw. The three were sewn into half their costumes and were blooding themselves, marking their skin with intricate bladed implements that left precise patterns of wounds on their skin. They glistened already with blood, and sang with high, wailing voices. Fate was played by a woman of improbable height and thinness, her face obscured by long white hair, her body made up to resemble a walking skeleton, accentuating her protruding ribs and sunken stomach. She was kneeling, throwing her head back and forth, barking like an animal as some spirit of the warp coursed through her. Perhaps the spirit was really there, perhaps it was a product of the woman's diseased mind. It did not matter. She was quite mad, and it didn't matter whether it was true spirit possession or a lifetime in Shalhadar's insane city that had broken her.

A chorus representing the remorseful dead were praying together, partaking in a feast of raw flesh the origin of which Lysander chose not to guess at. Musicians were anointing their instruments in fresh blood.

The sets were taking shape, dividing the duelling ground into stage, backstage and the audience. A few curious mutants were peering from doorways or from beneath the gallery railings, watching bemusedly as the outlandish scenes were assembled ready to be rolled out onto stage.

Lysander had his own costume, of course. A heavy black robe hung over his armour. He had changed the armour's helmet for an executioner's black cowl which, thankfully, still hid his face. Less fortuitously, his role called for him to give up his well-balanced blade in favour of a huge single-bladed axe for lopping off heads. It was a reasonable weapon, but limited compared to the sword – its balance was off and the single cutting edge reduced his options in a fight by half. It could still kill well enough, though, and a Space Marine had to be ready to fight with whatever came to hand.

The stage was complete. The cast were assembled in the wings, and Lysander found himself surrounded with those fanatics of Shalhadar's reign who had competed their whole lives for this moment. Their eyes shone with joy and an overwhelming gratitude, for they had finally been chosen to perform in the name of the Veiled One. Lysander was again grateful his face was hidden, because that was a look he could not have faked.

Lysander heard the sound of armour on stone and

knew Kraegon Thul was being accompanied into the chamber by an honour guard of Iron Warriors. The musicians struck up the overture, a nauseous skirl of rising and falling tones. The actors muttered their final prayers, and as the music reached a crescendo, the first of them took the stage.

'My fate on Malodrax did not lie among the court of Shalhadar. Malodrax had misled me, and I had almost fallen for its lies. But the willpower and intellect of an inquisitor was an obstacle this world had never come up against, and the truth became apparent to me even at the last moment.

'I had to get out. Through the system of emergency dead drops I made contact with Agent Sildyne, who met me by a spot in the city walls where some of the city's poorest dregs had quarried homes out of the stone. He led me and the remains of my warband, numbering Grun, Thol and Maskelin, through the warrens there and out of the city. Of all the acolytes who accompanied me to Malodrax, it was Sildyne who proved the most steadfast of purpose, the most driven to fulfil his duty.

'This world had failed to draw me towards its false goal. Instead, as we made our way out of the city's hinterland, I sought to understand what my purpose here really was. Though a heretic I be, still I feel the eyes of the Emperor upon me and His hand guiding me. Fate, and the Emperor's will, would not have brought me to Malodrax, would not have seen me witness so many horrors and survive, without a reason. I merely had to understand it.

'It was Thol who suggested to me the truth. Thol and his brother had been no better than animals when I found them, survivors among a tribe of killers and cannibals. I saw in them the viciousness of which an inquisitor must sometimes make use, but also the loyalty to one another that I felt I could turn into a dedication to the work of the Holy Ordos. As we ate a paltry meal of lizard and insect caught by the brothers, he said to me, "Lord Golrukhan, what this world wants is to be ruled."'

'"Indeed?" I said. "It seems to me that it wants nothing less."

'"But," continued Thol, "have you known that type of dog who bites and growls at everyone, but when you earn his respect, he will never leave you?"

'"I found two such dogs on your home world," I replied.

'"Or a woman," said Grun with a smile, "who wants a man, and so who curses and scratches her nails at every man she meets, so that she knows whoever can stand to keep pursuing her is good enough for her?"

'"I have not the knowledge of such things as you do, Grun," I replied, "but I understand what you mean." Grun was always the earthier of the two, and the crudeness of his language was enough to make me suspect possession when I first encountered him.

'"Malodrax wants a ruler," continued Thol. "But it doesn't want just any backstabber who can lie his way to a crown and a throne. So it sets up its trials to weed out the weak, and make sure that whoever makes it to the top is a worthy king."

'I was struck then by the truth of Thol's words, and even

of Grun's. Malodrax was not unusual in being cruel to those who lived there, for any world touched by the warp must be so. But it had a purpose behind its cruelty. Not for Malodrax the callous, random cruelty that blossomed so readily wherever the warp intruded on reality. No, what I had seen thus far, while obscene, had a purpose behind it, a design that only my superior inquisitor's mind could perceive.

'How many on Malodrax had lived and died under its suns, never knowing they were pieces in a plan concocted by the will of this corrupted world? Believing they were the masters of their fate, while Malodrax had determined the time and manner of their deaths from the moment they first breathed its air? It was quite the revelation, for which I thanked Thol and Grun, and immediately set to meditating upon what plan I should now enact to understand more about what Malodrax wanted and how it set about getting it. Could it ever be ruled? What qualities would be necessary in a man to pass its many trials and become its lord?

'There was one man who might qualify, of all those I had heard of on Malodrax. It was not the daemon prince of the city we had just left. Shalhadar, the Veiled One, was powerful indeed, but could a being of such infinite arrogance and self-absorption ever perceive this world's machinations that churned away beyond him? Malodrax must have laid a thousand traps for the Veiled One, any one of which Shalhadar might walk into, blinded by his inability to imagine anyone might out-think him. No, Shalhadar was not my goal here, I understood that now more clearly than ever.

'There was one man. I had heard his name, and I had

learned much of the history that created him. A traitor to mankind, to the Emperor himself, one whose willpower had seen him defy the God-Emperor when that divine being still walked the galaxy in the guise of a man. A member of a Legion whose discipline bound its hatred in iron bands, and whose ambitions include nothing less than the mastery of all the armies of the warp and revenge against the whole human race.

'Kraegon Thul, the Warsmith of Kulgarde. The garish sights of Shalhadar's city had blinded me to the possibility that Thul was my true objective here. And now, I was certain. What better machine for turning Kraegon Thul into the ruler of his own warp-born empire than Malodrax?

'The possibilities were dizzying. Was I witnessing the genesis of the next great lord of Chaos, the chosen of the Dark Gods, forged through the trials of Malodrax into a great figurehead to lead the next Black Crusade against the Imperium? The Emperor's will had put me here, and it was surely His will that one such as I be there to stop Thul taking over Malodrax, and from there, rising to become Warmaster of Chaos.

'"We head for Kulgarde," I said to my warband. Though they looked grim to hear it, none objected. Perhaps they felt instinctively, as I did, that our own trial had seen us successfully evade the traps of Shalhadar's court and that our final test was to stand against its chosen.

'And what plan did it have for me? Malodrax could surely not tolerate an inquisitor on its soil without planning a fitting fate for him. Perhaps it wanted me corrupted, or broken, or *merely dead. Or perhaps it wanted me to sit upon its throne. Whatever Malodrax wanted from me, it would not get it, for I was sworn to greater powers than any in the warp.*

'Our meal finished, we set out across the wastes in the direction of Kulgarde. Whatever fate awaited us, my acolytes showed no fear of it. They had seen what happened to those who strayed from the Emperor's path, and that held for them more dread than any death Malodrax might inflict.'

WHEN LYSANDER STEPPED from the wings, he was almost overwhelmed with hate at the sight of the Iron Warriors, a small retinue of them at the back of the seating, with aliens and mutants arrayed in front of them. Lysander saw right past the xenos horrors, as if they weren't there. Instead, he saw nothing but Kraegon Thul.

The Warsmith was wreathed in oily smoke. Lysander could hear the grinding of the cogs on his shoulder-guards even from the stage, even above the crooning of the choir who kneeled before the front row. Behind the clouded lenses of Thul's helmet were eyes watching Lysander at that very moment, and Lysander imagined a film of filth crawling over his skin as the Warsmith's corruption touched him. Thul's air hose sprayed spurts of white vapour from its ancient seals.

Beside Thul was the skinny, atrophied form of a type of mutant Lysander recognised – a Navigator, a bearer of a stable mutation that granted him a third eye with which he could see into the warp without being driven mad. That third eye was hidden behind a band of cracked and embroidered leather wound around his forehead. His face was emaciated and his frame, tall by unaugmented standards, was bent and hunched beneath the heavy dark-blue robes. He must have been the Warsmith's personal Navigator, who directed his fleets when he left Malodrax. How long would it be before Kraegon Thul gathered his legion of war machines and took off from Malodrax, to crusade against the Imperium he betrayed?

And on Thul's other side stood the creature Lysander had learned was named Karnak, Thul's alien head scientist. It was the first time Lysander had really seen Karnak clearly, the sharp and swooping lines of his elaborate armour, the half-moon shoulder guards and tall plume of the helmet that hid his face from view. Lysander could still not tell Karnak's species – under that armour he could be of any species of roughly humanoid size and shape, which might be one of thousands of hateful aliens the Imperium had encountered.

Lysander hated Karnak as much as he hated Thul, he realised then, but it was a different kind of hate. What he felt to look on Kraegon Thul was hot and intense, a relentless, volcanic emotion that filled him with fire. Thul was everything Lysander's Chapter stood against, an ancient enemy whose existence inflamed the anger of every Imperial Fist. But his hate for Karnak was cold and detached.

The worst sight of all was of the Imperial Fists, shackled to stone blocks just before the stage. Skelpis, Halaestus and Vonkaal were chained there. The stump of Skelpis's leg had been cauterised and was now a red-black mass of scorched scar. Halaestus's skin had been removed in geometric patches all across his body. Vonkaal's torso was torn open, his organs visible through the sawn-out sections of his ribcage. Lysander could not see the hearts beating or the lungs drawing breath. Vonkaal was dead, displayed as a monument to Thul's power. The arrogance of the display spoke of the very heart of the Iron Warriors. They had stood against the Emperor in the Horus Heresy and their Primarch Perturabo had locked horns with Rogal Dorn. They were driven by jealousy of the Imperium and the Loyalist Legions that had triumphed at the Battle of Terra. Now they displayed their captive Imperial Fists as war trophies, flaunting the possession of their deadliest enemies' defeated.

The play was already half-done. A corpse lay at Lysander's feet, of a cultist picked to play the personification of innocence slain by Fate. The actress who performed as Fate had killed him for real, razor-sharp needles on her hands clawing through his face to shred the brain matter behind. The mess of blood and gore pooled around the black leather boots of Lysander's Executioner costume. Another two bodies lay sprawled at the front of the stage, one killed during the play's opening to consecrate the stage to the Dark Gods, the other shot through with arrows representing the random cruelty of Pestilence.

'Behold!' called out Lysander as he followed the lines

of Valienne's play. 'For every sin there is a punishment, and though a man might cheat it for a lifetime, in death it will find him. Though he flee into the realms of the Immaterium, yet in madness it will find him. Though he seek to hide at the end of time, in infinity it will find him. Witness the sinner! Witness his folly!'

Lysander had never spoken to the cultist who was to play the victim he executed. The scene was impossible to rehearse fully. This was not a play that could be rehearsed, only unleashed when everyone knew their part. The cultist playing the Sinner danced from the wings, spreading blood from the devotional wounds on his arms and legs. He wore the leather straps of Shalhadar's pleasure-cult, and his skin was livid with old scars.

The sinner's monologue followed. Lysander had it memorised – it was a long mockery of Chaos, of fate and the randomness of the warp, and one of the centrepieces of Valienne's work.

Lysander watched for signs of life among the captive Imperial Fists. These were the battle-brothers he had come so far to save, and if they were just corpses hanging there, then Kraegon Thul would have won. The awful possibility, though Lysander had always known it was such, was a weight in his stomach that wanted to drag him down into the earth.

Brother Halaestus's eyes flickered, barely enough movement to be noticed. Lysander met Halaestus's eyes as they opened a slit, and with an equally subtle nod Halaestus acknowledged Lysander. He knew. Of course he knew a battle-brother. Halaestus had not given up hope here, he had not abandoned the belief that Lysander would return.

'Freedom is my religion!' the cultist cried. 'So shall I do what I will, and the fates be damned!'

The mutants in the audience spat and heckled. Among them Lysander spotted the creatures who served as orderlies in the medical wing, and whose species counted the Bone Sculptors among their number, with their faces like long animal skulls and their fingers tipped with syringes. Lysander felt his fingers tightening on the headsman's axe.

'I will make water on every altar!' cried the cultist who was to be Lysander's victim. 'Make every temple's threshold my soiling-place! And the gods can chase me if they will, for I have wrought spells and magics that blind their sight! See now the wards I have created, proof against daemon and witch. That is what I think of fate! I would walk in the warp if I could, and spit at every god I saw!'

Handfuls of filth spattered the stage from the audience. The cultist grinned as he saw his words getting to them. There were brute-mutants and forge-workers among them, and others besides – exotic xenos, witches bound in chains with steel cages bolted around their heads, celebrants tattooed from head to toe with the sigils of the warp, and followers of a corrupted machine-deity with industrial crushers and saws grafted to their skeletons.

The chorus rose up to grab the sinner and drag him to the back of the stage, chanting the profane names of the warp gods. The audience cheered, screaming for the sinner's head. A light fell on Lysander, and they realised the Executioner's axe was about to swing. One of the chorus dropped to all fours to serve as the executioner's block.

The sinner, by now battered and bloody, grinned up at Lysander. He had waited his whole life to die this way. Whatever he might have been, whatever existence he might have lived, had been stripped away from him by Shalhadar and replaced with a mindless fanaticism. More than anything, this man wanted to die to glorify his lord.

Lysander raised the axe. Valienne had written that the Executioner, personification of all who do fate's work, would slice off the sinner's head with a single stroke. She had specified that the blood would spray onto the stage and the chorus would smear themselves with it and tear the body apart, throwing the chunks of the corpse into the audience and turning the whole gathering into one celebration of death.

The music rose. The audience screamed and bellowed. Only Kraegon Thul, Karnak and the Navigator were still. Lysander's eyes met the lenses of Thul's faceplate.

The axe came down. It was not aimed at the sinner's exposed neck. Lysander let go of the axe as it swung down and it launched from his hands, tumbling end over end towards the audience.

The performers of the chorus were the first to realise

Lysander had deviated from the script. The closest, a woman with her head half shaved and her face open with deep bored pits that revealed the cavities inside her skull, turned to follow the axe's path.

Lysander knew he could not penetrate power armour at this distance, not with a mundane weapon. He could not kill Kraegon Thul this way. But he could win an ally for himself in the fight sure to follow.

The axe slammed into the stone block to which Halaestus's hands were shackled. The blade cut right through the chain and embedded itself in the stone. Halaestus's hands fell free.

The woman beside Lysander screamed. The rest of the chorus took up the cry as they realised this holy moment had been profaned.

The cultist playing the sinner kneeled up and gawped, expecting to be dead by now. Perhaps he thought he was, and was wondering why the afterlife looked the same as the one he had just left.

Lysander ran towards the front of the stage, throwing the other performers aside. The audience only realised something was wrong when he vaulted into the front row.

Mutant hands clawed at Lysander, tearing at the leather overcloak of the Executioner's costume. Lysander cracked a malformed skull with a backhand and grabbed one of the skull-faced menials by the throat, smashing his forehead into the face that leered up at him.

A knife arrowed at him. Lysander parried it with his forearm, grabbed the wrist that held it and broke the assailant's arm. He snatched up the knife and with a weapon in his hand he cut himself faster through the pressing ranks.

It was bedlam. A thousand things were happening at once. On stage the chorus were running wild, tearing at their hair and at each other. The other performers were rushing from the wings, the personifications of Pestilence, Fate, Malice and a dozen others weeping with horror that the performance had been destroyed. Some were trying to make their way towards Lysander, furious he had broken from the script, but were swamped by the mutants surging forwards to storm the stage. In the crowd, leaders of the mutant forge-gangs were standing and pointing down at the stage, bellowing orders for their underlings to avenge the insult of the aborted stage play.

Halaestus had extricated himself from his chains. He had snatched the axe from where it had become embedded in the stone block and was hacking at Brother Skelpis's chains, breaking from the task for long enough to cut the head off the brute-mutant bearing down on him.

Talaya was leaping over the scenery, her mechanical legs sending her flying over the stage in pursuit of Lysander. Kraegon Thul stood and turned aside, his Navigator cowering in his wake. Karnak stepped into Thul's place to cover the Warsmith's escape.

Lysander cut off an arm, a head, carved through a spine. The knife broke off in his hand and he rammed the stump into a skeletal eye socket, carrying on bare-handed. He clasped an equine skull in his hands, lifted and twisted, and threw the lifeless body aside.

Karnak was waiting for him, willing to let him tire himself out battering his way through Kulgarde's vermin. Karnak drew a long silver blade with a rapier point as sharp as the scalpels in his anatomy theatre. A spiked mace arced down at Lysander, but it just gave him something to snatch from his assailant and use to forge on faster.

Behind him somewhere, Talaya was struggling through the mutant horde. She was faster than Lysander and more mobile, but Lysander was stronger. He was making better progress than she was. He just had to keep her off him for a few more minutes, and then it wouldn't matter.

Lysander shattered a mutant's shoulder and trampled an alien orderly underfoot. Just one more row of seating remained between him and Karnak. It was occupied by one of Malodrax's native xenos, deformed and discoloured like the surgeon Lysander had killed on his last stay in Kulgarde. Lysander broke the haft of the mace over its skull and it crumpled underneath him.

He was face to face with Karnak.

Karnak swept his sword in an arc. On the surface it was intended to cut Lysander in half at the waist. In truth it was a feint to draw Lysander into a defensive motion, so Karnak could spear him through with the dagger he concealed in his other hand.

Lysander did not move. He caught the blade on his forearm, trusting the super-dense bone of a Space Marine to hold against the edge of the sword. The impact jarred through him and the blade bit deep into the bone, but it did not cut through. Lysander turned out of the path of the dagger's point as it punched towards his abdomen.

Karnak's eyepieces were centimetres from Lysander's face.

'I told you,' snarled Lysander, 'I would return.'

He rammed an elbow up into Karnak's jaw. The alien's head snapped back and Lysander locked the elbow of the arm carrying the alien's sword, bending it the wrong way as far as the armour's joint would allow. The armour kept the limb from breaking but the sword came loose and it was suddenly in Lysander's hands.

Karnak dropped back into a guard. Lysander swept the sword around his head to knock back any mutant getting too close. This was their fight now, no one else would interfere. Perhaps the mutants understood that, for none of them clawed at him now, or tried to grab him and weigh him down.

Karnak's eyepieces glinted. Lysander vowed he would tear that helmet off and look into whatever face Karnak sported below, before he took the alien's head.

* * *

'Malodrax has won.

'I am going to die. Nothing I can do or say will change that now. Has my heresy finally been punished? Is it the Emperor's will that put me here, and shows me my manner of death before it falls upon me? If so, I accept it. My Emperor has always been my guide, but in following Him I have strayed from the path laid out by His clerics and scriptures. If that choice was wrong, I am responsible for it, and thus should I suffer. But on Malodrax, it is not the Emperor's will. It is Kraegon Thul's.

'I entered Kulgarde as a slave trader, seeking to purchase the stupid and the worthless from Kulgarde's forges at a premium, to be sold on as drudge labour and sacrifices elsewhere. To do this I had items of value and currency salvaged by my acolytes in Shalhadar's city, for while I had not succeeded in entering Shalhadar's court I had moved among its highest echelons and the trappings of such society had not been completely stripped from me during my flight. Grun and Thol were my pack-mules, lugging these goods, while Sildyne and Maskelin were the slave masters who trained and disciplined my human stock. I had run this identity a number of times, and they were well versed in their roles.

'Thus did I gain entry to Kulgarde. I was assured by the Iron Warrior serving as castellan that there would be scant business for me, for Kulgarde needed all its bodies to run its forges and construct its war engines. Nevertheless I was given leave to visit the forges and see their need for good, new bodies, so I might return in the future bringing slaves for them to purchase. I knew that this ruse would not gain me an audience with Kraegon Thul, Warsmith and lord of Kulgarde, but it was enough to get within the walls.

'Firstly, Thol died. I cannot say from whence the blade came that slit his throat. Among the vast anvils and molten pits I was observing the brutal economy of Kulgarde, the raw materials it devoured and the suffering that fuelled it, and for a moment I was awed by the scope of the war that Kraegon Thul could wage. But when I next turned, it was to see Thol stumbling and clutching his throat, gurgling crimson as his blood filled his lungs. His brother Grun caught him, trying to get to the wound and stop the blood flowing, but Thol died not a minute after he hit the ground.

'Sildyne and Maskelin were at my side with their guns ready, hunting for the assailant. But how Grun howled! Like the wild beasts of his home world, a keening from the world's end. I cannot imagine anyone felt such sorrow as he did then, and my mind turned again to Talaya and the strange emptiness left in me to see her taken away. That was a chill, shivering sorrow – Grun's was a fire ripping through him, scorching away his insides and leaving nothing but a vessel full of grief.

'Could I have stopped Grun? Not without killing him, certainly. Not, perhaps, without dying myself. Perhaps it was that I did not think quickly enough, or that these old bones, able in combat as I may be, did not have the speed to match a furious feral worlder thirty years my junior. Before I had my hand on the hilt of my sword, Grun had snatched up a pair of glowing hot tongs from the nearest forge and with it had clamped the lower jaw of the nearest forge-slave. While the blade was still half-drawn he had thrown the slave into the forge, his body vanishing beneath the embers in a bright flower of flame.

'I called for Maskelin and Sildyne to stop him, but already Grun had leapt over the closest anvil and run towards an enormous forge-pit where a slave master was calling the rhythm to a gang of slaves operating the bellows. Grun went straight for the slave master, ramming the tongs into the huge mutant's belly and taking the barbed whip from his hands before the mutant's guts had hit the floor. He wrapped the whip around the scaly bull-neck and used it as leverage to break its spine.

'Already, a clamour had broken out. Orders were yelled and more mutants rushed from all corners of the great forge fields. We were seized by muscular soot-stained arms and though I could have fought, I knew myself outnumbered.

'I have not seen my acolytes alive from that moment. Grun I am certain must be dead, pulled apart by vengeful hands. Of the others, I can only guess. I reside now in a cell below the foundations of Kulgarde, hundreds of metres below the ground, where the heat is stifling and the darkness total. My ocular augmentations give me the capacity to write these words but all is the deepest blacks and blues. I shall die without ever seeing even Malodrax's sickly suns again. But not, at least, without getting some of what I came here for.

'The Warsmith descended to this level of the dungeon after three days of my incarceration. Surely most prisoners would have been raving and desperate by now, with their lower extremities immersed in the noisome water that covered the floor of the cell, the nibbling creatures and waterborne insects having stripped away the meat of foot and ankle. My internal painkiller dispensers were a crude augmentation and would not let me hold up to the most severe torment-ing, but they at least made that place bearable, even without food or light. Perhaps it was a disappointment that I was not begging for mercy by then, but I doubt the Iron Warriors expected me to have broken.

'The door to the cell was cut open, for it had been welded shut behind me. In the sparks from the cutting torch I saw the shape of the Warsmith Kraegon Thul. Like a walking tank, like an engine of war condensed into the shape of a Space Marine, he seemed the very image of industrialised killing. There is no battlefield on which he would not look at home, from the heartland of the Imperium to an embattled daemon world, be it as a general or a frontline butcher. I was looking into the mechanical face of war incarnate.

'"Your name," he demanded. His voice was like a distant landslide, accompanied by noisome smoke from the breath-ing hose and the machinery that whirled and thudded on the back and shoulders of his armour.

'"Lord Inquisitor Corvin Golrukhan," I said. "Of the Holy Ordos…"

'"Of the Emperor's Inquisition," interrupted the War-smith. "And you are the first inquisitor to tread the earth of Malodrax."

'"I am."

'By way of a reply, Kraegon Thul unhooked from his armour a trinket that I had not noticed among the machine parts and the jagged, pitted plates of his armour. It was familiar in form when I saw it clearly. A skull carved from ivory, set into a lacquered red sigil in the shape of a stylised letter 'I'. The Inquisitorial Seal, badge of an inquisitor's office. Simply showing it to any Imperial citizen, be he wasteland scavenger or Admiral of a sector battlefleet, can command unyielding loyalty unto the death. It is the symbol of an authority that can command the Exterminatus, place the seal on a decree of Excommunicate Traitoris, condemn a species to xenocide as Xenos Horrificus. This is what Kraegon Thul held before me.

'"Others will follow me," I said.

'"The others will die," he replied. "Unless they serve."

'"Serve you?"

'"Serve me."

'I chuckled at that. "Then that is why you are here? The Warsmith of Kulgarde wastes his time. Recall the words of the man you took that Inquisitorial Seal from, the ones he spoke before you executed him. Use them for my reply. I need not say them. My sentiments and his will be the same."

'"In this fortress," he said, "I have collected a war-staff that will one day accompany the stars of your Imperium with an army of war machines. One day soon. Among them are psykers born of this world who can strip a man's mind away and filter from the psychic sludge that remains any information on the innards of your Imperium I could want."

'"Then I shall savour one last struggle," I said. "Your psychic pets will have to fight to get into my brain. I wonder how many you will burn through before you can open me up?"

'"I have such vermin to spare," said Kraegon Thul. "You disappoint me. I had expected more of the Emperor's Inquisition. You came here for whatever prizes you could bring back and with them win the renown of your fellow inquisitors, all hollow, corrupted men who hide in shadows and play games of life and death to give themselves the sham veneer of a god. The sooner it all burns, the better. Mankind will thank me when your kind are gone."

'Thul did not stop for further conversation. He dropped something heavy and wet into the water around my feet, turned, and let the door be swung closed behind him. A welding torch flared to reseal my cage and in its staccato light I saw that Thul had dropped the head of Maskelin, my pilot.

'Maskelin's eyes had been put out, those keen eyes that could pick out a landing strip through a low-atmosphere firestorm. I had chosen him from among the Ghoul Stars smugglers, where he had learned to survive among haunted spaceship graveyards and dealers in the forbidden who would kill and skin a man as soon as take his money. He was faithful and brave, and I had met few like him. Those brilliant eyes had been torn from his head and for the most fleeting moment, I was overcome with grief at the knowledge he must have suffered. I shrugged off the feeling, for it was not becoming of an inquisitor, and when the darkness was complete again I let my augmentations recover enough to write these words.

'The volume in which I write is hidden beneath a loose stone at the back of my cell. I am certain the warders of

Thul's dungeon must know it is there. It suits them to let me continue to write in it, perhaps in order that I will come to rely on it for my sanity, so it will be all the keener cut to have it taken away. Then when I am quite mad, they will drag me to some gutter to drain away my blood, and slit my throat, and throw me to the mutants.

'This is the death I accepted when I took the vows of the Emperor's Ordos. We do not die young, or well. We die in the depths of a tyrant's fortress, stripped of our sanity, broken in body and mind but never in will. We take with us the satisfaction of never giving in to the interrogations of whatever imprisoned us. Everything else, we lose. And so I welcome this death, because it is the death of an inquisitor. I will go to join the Emperor in his final battle, if He will have this old heretic.

'And, of course, an inquisitor does not die as a normal man does. His mark on the galaxy is never fully erased. He has left his signature on the universe, he has dealt it wounds whose scars will remain. I have left my own scars, and they will not heal before my purpose is done.

'I will die knowing my duty will still be done. That is why I will live forever.'

16

'I swear I can feel the glee with which Malodrax tells its lies. If the sky could smirk down, the wind laugh at us, the mountains spit upon our despair, they would. It wants more than to make us suffer. It wants us to look down on our hands and see the blood of our own, to understand the lies which have driven us to destroy what we hold most dear, before it crushes the life from us.'

– Inquisitor Corvin Golrukhan

'THAT'S A WEAK spot?' asked First Sergeant Kaderic, peering through one of the firing slits in an upper level of the siege tower. Through the dust kicked up by the tower's rollers, Kulgarde's walls loomed as a brutal black horizon up ahead. Lysander had drawn his attention to the place where several storeys of scaffolding had been set up, spanning enormous new-quarried blocks that had been hauled into place to cover the hole left by the shattered roller at the wall's base.

'It is the only one,' said Lysander. 'Anywhere else the grinders will chew us up and the gates are a trap. That is where we will break through.'

'I feel I must thank you, Captain Lysander,' said Kaderic with a grim smile. 'I am used to being the least sane Imperial Fist around. But this plan to storm Kulgarde is crazier than anything I could come up with.'

'Leaving our brothers unavenged is insane,' said Lysander. 'Letting Thul build his war engines and launch his crusade is insane. This? This is the sanest thing I have ever done.'

Far below, among the siege tower's engines, Techmarine Kho was driving the tower across the torn-up ground of Kulgarde's hinterland, through the enormous shell craters and between the hulks of fallen war engines. The lookouts on the walls would have spied them by now and even if they had first thought the tower was another feral war engine wandering the proving grounds, they would have realised by now it was heading towards the fortress with a purpose. At Lysander's instruction, Kho was aiming for the place where Lysander had driven the siege idol through the wall when he first escaped from Kulgarde – it had been partially rebuilt and workers scrambled through the rigging and scaffolding even now. The spiked roller at its base had not yet been replaced, which gave the siege tower a chance – just a chance, not a certainty – of breaching deep enough to let the Imperial Fists disembark into the fortress.

This had been Lysander's plan of attack. It was the only way into Kulgarde – use one of Thul's war machines against him and hope the breach in the wall was still vulnerable enough for the Imperial Fists to get in the way Lysander had got out. It was, indeed, an insane plan, but on Malodrax it seemed the only thing that made sense.

'Five minutes,' voxed Techmarine Kho above the din of the engines.

'Battle rites!' ordered Chaplain Lycaon over the vox-net. 'Let your prayers be your bullets! Let your faith be your armour!'

The strike force was gathering in the upper levels, murmuring ancient prayers to the machine-spirits of their weapons and armour. Lysander spoke those words to his own wargear – his was new to him, for he had left his original wargear on Malodrax the last time he had seen Kulgarde. He prayed for the souls of their previous owners, for few items of the Chapter's wargear did not have components previously carried by another Imperial Fist. The armour was from a Brother Kalithrax, who had been slain by corrosive tyranid spores in the crusade against Hive Splinter Karkinos, and had been altered to fit Lysander in the forges of the *Phalanx*. The bolter had been carried by Sergeant Thornas, who had replaced it with a storm bolter crafted by the Chapter's artificers. The chainblade was built from components returned to the Chapter after the Imphalian Massacre.

Lysander asked his armour to be resolute and bold.

His chainblade he asked never to relent, whatever foe it might find beneath its teeth. His bolter he asked for accuracy and the smoothness of its action. He had said such words a thousand times before, and he felt his mind bedding down into the ways of war, the ways of the soldier taking him over as the world around him turned into a battlefield. He remembered the prayer he has spoken on the *Shield of Valour*, and for a moment he was back there in the chill recycled air of the ship, the Iron Hands about to launch their ambush from the warp.

He looked up from the bolter in his hands. The other Imperial Fists were finishing up their own rites, Lycaon ministering to his crozius arcanum and Antinas to his heavy flamer. Only Halaestus was silent and still, crouched by one wall, eyes closed.

'Brother Halaestus,' said Lysander quietly. 'We are at the eve of battle. We must observe our rites. I will lead them for you, if you wish.'

'Why?' asked Halaestus. 'What benefit is there? War is war. Praying for a better outcome will not change it. If it wants us dead, we are dead.'

'These are not the words of an Imperial Fist.'

'Then I am not an Imperial Fist!' snapped Halaestus. 'What does it matter if my armour holds? If the Iron Warriors aim a bullet at my heart then I would be glad of it! I would beg for it! I would plead to Kraegon Thul to end me himself! Throne knows I begged for it often enough when the Bone Carvers had me.'

'Then take revenge!' said Lysander, grabbing Halaestus by the shoulder. 'Thul must die. His Iron Warriors must die. Hold on to that if you care nothing for your own survival. Pray for your bolter! Pray for your blade!'

'And what does revenge mean?' Halaestus jumped to his feet. 'What will I get from Thul lying dead before me? I feel nothing. I am hollow. Revenge is the right of every Space Marine, but what does that mean to me?' Halaestus unhooked the clasps of his breastplate and pulled it away from his chest, revealing the tattered patchwork skin on his chest. He pointed at the long red scar leading from below his chin to the top of his sternum. In spite of a Space Marine's accelerated healing the scar had not healed and was still livid and weeping.

'I am not a Space Marine!' shouted Halaestus. 'I am not an Imperial Fist! I am not even a man!'

Lysander could not look away from the scar. There had been the seat of the gene-seed, the genetic material of Rogal Dorn and the organ that had regulated the many augmentations when Halaestus was turned into a Space Marine.

It was gone. The gene-seed had been cut out by the Bone Carvers and taken to Kraegon Thul's armoury, to be implanted into a new Iron Warrior. And though none of them had spoken of it directly, every Imperial Fist in the strike force had known what that meant.

The strike force had all heard Halaestus's words. Their rites completed, they were silent now. Normally one or two would be swapping boasts about the kills they would take in the coming battle, or reciting a parable of the Chapter's heroes, but Halaestus had stopped that.

Lysander picked Halaestus's chainsword off the floor of the siege tower and pressed it into Halaestus's hand, and left anything else unsaid.

'One minute!' came the vox from Techmarine Kho. The walls of Kulgarde filled the murder-holes, hung with banners and corpses, streaked with old blood and pitted with bullet scars from a thousand failed sieges past.

Bolter shots cracked against the armoured front of the tower, ranging shots from sentries on the walls. They would be no danger to the tower in themselves, but that was not the purpose. The Iron Warriors had the range. What followed would decide if the tower even made it to the wall.

On top of the battlements, with a great grinding of metal on stone, emerged a hemispherical structure of rust-streaked iron. The dome slid open to reveal a huge and ancient weapon, a massive laser cannon such as might be found in the batteries of a warship or wielded by one of the Imperium's Titan war engines.

'They still think we're feral,' voxed Chaplain Lycaon, 'and wish only to put us down like a rabid pet. But they will not believe that for much longer. This is where the battle begins. This is where we decide the fate of this world! Techmarine Kho! Do it!'

The engine note rose as the siege engine accelerated, the whole tower juddering as the rollers crunched through the broken ground. On the huge siege gun scrambled dozens of labourers, menials of Kulgarde working to dial in the focusing lenses and check the connections to the fortress generators that would create the massive laser pulse. The cannon was large enough to spit the siege tower on a lance of laser, and its elevation was being lowered so the shot would go right through its engines and the axles of its rollers. The engine would be crippled in a single shot, and the subsequent shots would blast it apart floor by floor until it was one more heap of wreckage in the shadow of Kulgarde.

The cannon was sighted. The siege engine kept accelerating as the Iron Warriors on the walls came into sight, hulking figures in their black iron armour, mutant labourers cowering from them wherever they went.

Lysander detected another note in the engine din of the siege tower, a higher, rising tone like the buzzing of a giant insect. He saw the reaction of the Iron Warriors on the walls as the Land Speeders zipped out in front of the siege tower, emerging from their concealed positions hovering just behind the tower's rearmost rollers.

Brother Gethor manned *Dorn's Dagger* with one of Squad Kaderic, Brother Glaven, on the multi-melta. With Techmarine Kho needed to drive the siege tower, the *Talon Blade* was flown by the strike force member that Kho judged most able at handling the controls – Brother Shovarn of Lycaon's command squad, with another of his squad, Brother Kaelon, on the heavy bolter. The Iron Warriors opened fire as the Land Speeders hurtled towards the gun emplacement, sprays of bolter fire arrowing around them.

Dorn's Dagger swooped down level with the gun emplacement as its guns opened up, and bright fire stuttered around the emplacement. Broken bodies were blasted apart, mutants torn to pieces by the heavy bolter shells detonating against the gun housing. Bodies fell, tumbling down past the front of the wall. The *Talon Blade* swept around to attack from the other side, stitching its assault cannon fire along the top of the wall. An Iron Warrior threw himself out of the way as another fired a volley up into the Land Speeder's underside.

More Iron Warriors were arriving on the walls. The alarm had spread quickly, the discipline of the Iron Warriors' chain of command kicking them into action. Already, a few seconds after the Imperial Fists played their hand, Kraegon Thul would know they were there. He would know Lysander had brought them.

Thul must have been waiting for them to come back. He must have had a plan for when they arrived, a plan kicking into action even now.

The *Talon Blade*'s multi-melta fired, a bright orange bolt of superheated particles ripping into the mechanism that controlled the attitude of the laser cannon's barrel. Molten metal spat fire as the whole gun shifted to one side, old metal screaming in protest. Menials ran for cover. A power cable came loose, spraying sparks as it whipped out of control.

Dorn's Dagger banked around for another pass, more gunfire falling around the emplacement. Something detonated inside it and white-blue flames erupted as the whole emplacement fell back, collapsing into its housing within the wall. Fuel cells cooked off and lightning raged through the destruction, throwing rubble and bodies everywhere. Debris rained off the front of the siege tower and chunks of burning masonry crashed through the scaffolding cladding the front of the wall.

'Ten seconds!' came Kho's vox through the din.

'Positions!' ordered Lycaon. The strike force stacked up behind the tower's drawbridge.

'I'm hit!' came Brother Gethor's voice over the vox. 'We're coming down behind the wall!'

Lysander saw *Dorn's Dagger* trailing smoke and flame as it spiralled out of control, disappearing behind the mass of burning wreckage that remained of the gun emplacement. The *Talon Blade* banked away from the destruction, keeping clear of the showering debris.

The siege engine rode up alarmingly, tipping back until Lysander was sure it would topple over backwards. But the moment passed and it pitched forwards again.

With a terrible impact, the top of the tower smashed into the wall. The sound was impossible to think through. Imperial Fists were thrown to the floor – Lysander kept his balance and saw the portcullis dropping open, crunching through the battlements.

The siege engine was several metres too short to deliver its payload directly onto the wall. The downed portcullis formed a bridge that sloped sharply upwards.

'Onwards!' bellowed First Sergeant Kaderic. He had taken up position at the front of the strike force, and none had questioned his right to be the first through.

Kaderic's squad followed him as he ran up the portcullis and vaulted over the edge. Lysander went with Lycaon's squad, who followed him and Squad Gorvetz followed up the rear.

The bullets were already flying as Lysander ran up the portcullis. His vision was full of the plume of flame billowing up from the shattered laser cannon. He leapt over the edge and the top of the wall rushed up to meet him.

He let his knees buckle under him and he dropped into a crouch. To his left was the enormous blocky structure of the gatehouse. Below it was the main way into the fortress, through the gates, and that structure could be filled with Iron Warriors pouring bolter fire into anyone who got past the outer gates and found themselves trapped below. To his right was the gun emplacement, still spewing flame.

A squad of Iron Warriors had made the top of the wall before the siege tower had hit. He recognised that gnarled bare metal power armour of long-obsolete marks, with faceplates mirroring the iron mask symbol of the Legion. Kaderic's squad had dived into them with fury that would be reckless in anyone else but which was a Space Marine's most dangerous weapon, marshalled and unleashed as precisely as a sniper's bullet.

Kaderic bowled an Iron Warrior to the floor as one of his fellow Imperial Fists hammered a volley of bolter fire at point-blank range through the Traitor Marine's chest. His armour burst open and hot blood rained up.

The Iron Warriors sergeant, a monster a head taller than any other Space Marine there, waded into the fight, swinging a two-handed power maul to a brutal rhythm. Lysander saw Brother Givenar charging at the sergeant, rattling off bolter shells as he closed.

Givenar crashed into the sergeant. The sergeant spun with impossible quickness for a man of his size, knocking the barrel of Givenar's bolter away. Givenar's combat knife was in his hand, blade aimed down to punch through an eyepiece or into the sergeant's throat.

The sergeant drove a knee up into Givenar's midriff and threw him over his head, slamming him down onto the ground. He raised the mace, head downwards, and drove it into Givenar's stomach.

Lysander felt the shockwave of a power field discharging. In a burst of blue light, the mace's head hammered down through Givenar and smashed a crater into the floor.

'Givenar!' yelled Lysander. 'Brother!'

Without seeming to will it, Lysander was running. He vaulted a fallen Iron Warrior as he sprinted for the sergeant. He thought he heard the sergeant laughing, a deep, metallic grating sound.

Lysander ran within the arc of the power mace. Sure enough the sergeant brought it up and whirled it over his head, bringing it round to smack into Lysander at chest height. Lysander brought up his chainsword and the two weapons clashed.

The power mace shattered the chainsword, sending its teeth flying in a steel hail. Lysander dropped to one knee as the mace was deflected over his head. He could feel the buzzing of the power field in his ears as it passed over him.

His sword gone, Lysander rammed a fist into the sergeant's knee. The Iron Warrior stumbled back and Lysander had his opening, leaping on the sergeant and knocking him onto his back. Lysander drew back his gun arm and slammed the butt of his bolter into the Iron Warrior's faceplate, over and over, a dozen hammering blows striking home in a handful of seconds.

The faceplate came apart. The face beneath had not seen sunlight for a long time. It was the colour of ash, of dead wood, dull and lifeless save for the black-irised eyes set way back in their scorched pits. Sharpened teeth were bared beneath a nose that had been cut away to a pair of slits. Another volley of blows slammed home, shattering jaw and cheekbone.

The Iron Warrior got a leg underneath him and tried to force himself up. Lysander let him, using the sergeant's own strength to bring him up and carry him higher, up over Lysander's head. The mace swung at him but Lysander was already stepping towards the front edge of the battlements, where the crenellations gave way to the sheer drop to the shattered ground far below. Lysander roared with a final effort as he hurled the sergeant out over the edge.

The Iron Warrior reached out to grab at a handhold on the wall's edge, but Lysander kicked his hand away and the Iron Warriors sergeant vanished over the edge, his cry of anger and shock receding as he fell.

Lysander turned. Their sergeant gone, the last Iron Warriors on the wall were fleeing through trapdoors and narrow entrances to the interior of the wall, into the upper levels of the fortress where the Warsmith ruled. Lycaon's crozius was smoking and well-blooded. Lysander counted three Imperial Fists dead – Givenar, one from Kaderic's squad and another from Lycaon's. He did not have time in the bedlam to name all the dead. With luck, the strike force would be back for them. Without it, the bodies would never leave Kulgarde. Nobody had leave to worry about that now.

'We press on,' said Lycaon, walking through the carnage towards Lysander. 'Kraegon Thul marshals his defences even now. Can you lead us onwards?'

Lysander paused to make sure of his bearings. Along the wall, past the gun emplacement, was a landing pad for a small spacecraft. It was now empty but Lysander recognised the landmark and pieced the structures below it together in his mind.

'Yes,' replied Lysander. 'I know the way.'

ANY OTHER MILITARY force in the Imperium, perhaps even a force from any other Chapter of Space Marines, would have been lost within seconds of entering the fortress of Kulgarde. Every corner led to a dead end, every intersection was a crossfire with murder holes and gun emplacements located to criss-cross the open ground with chains of gunfire. Each stairwell led not to the next level down, but to a pit without an exit where the defenders could pour fire down at the trapped attackers at will. Every trick that existed to bewitch invaders and lead them astray was employed among those cramped corridors of dark stone, the chambers of armouries and side chapels built to create killing zones at every turn.

But Perturabo, the primarch of the Iron Warriors and their tutor in the ways of fortress-building and the art of the siege, was a contemporary of Rogal Dorn. The two had learned from one another as rivals, and then as blood enemies. The two primarchs were mirror images, using the same pool of knowledge to pit their warriors against one another. The Imperial Fists knew the siege as well as the Iron Warriors did, and every trick the Iron Warriors employed to keep Kulgarde inviolate, Rogal Dorn had taught to his Chapter thousands of years before.

Lysander followed the path down towards the fortress's heart, at every step thinking what the next trick would be. Lycaon and Kaderic were beside him, and they knew the art as well as Lysander. They ignored the obvious pathways and aimed instead for the half-hidden passages the Iron Warriors themselves used to move about the fortress. They knew, as if by an

Emperor-given instinct, which levels were actually half-floors where they would be forced heads bowed into killing rooms with spears thrust down from above, and which archways concealed nothing more than a dead end into which they were being herded.

At an intersection, Sergeant Gorvetz brought Antinas forward to flood the corridors with flame, and Antinas did so with Givenar's name on his lips. The Devastator squad fought the gunfire of a dozen Iron Warriors with their own massive firepower, buying an opening for Kaderic's and Lycaon's squads to get past. Lysander voxed for Gorvetz to disengage and follow – Gorvetz replied that he could not turn his back on the enemies flooding the area or they would all be lost. And so the strike force left Gorvetz behind and forged on.

The fortress's design had robbed the Imperial Fists of a third of the strike force's strength, but any other force would not have made it that far at all. Lysander led the way through a chapel to dark gods, heaped high with sacrifices of bleached bones and the battle-dead. A hall crammed with mutants gathered to worship there was but an obstacle to be crashed through – with volleys of bolter fire followed up with a chainsword charge the hall was swept clean and the Imperial Fists rampaged through over the bodies.

At the far end of a long, broad corridor lined with statues of Iron Warriors from centuries past, Lysander recognised the armour and bearing of Captain Hexal.

'Brother Lysander!' called Hexal. 'We knew you would

return. You have kept us waiting too long! Let us get acquainted anew, for I have almost forgotten how it felt to make you kneel.'

'He seeks to distract us,' said Captain Lycaon. 'A fight to settle our honour here will give the Iron Warriors time to cut us off and trap us.'

'He has distracted me well enough,' replied First Sergeant Kaderic. 'If there is one here who should give this creature the duel he seeks, it is I. Go on, Lysander, go on! Hexal will have to take my head long before he tests his blade against yours.'

'I need you with me,' said Lycaon to Lysander, as more Iron Warriors burst into the passageway behind Hexal. 'Let Kaderic have this fight. He can keep Hexal off our heels. We must go on.'

'Then I go on with you,' replied Lysander. 'First Sergeant! Let Hexal know that he is dying! Let him feel what our lost brothers felt!'

Kaderic was already charging, his squad in tow, yelling the Chapter's oldest battle-cries as he closed with Hexal's squad. Any reply Kaderic made to Lysander's words was lost in the clash of chainblades and bolter fire, and Lysander and Squad Lycaon crashed down a stairwell and further into the fortress.

Lycaon and Lysander entered the sweltering heart of Kulgarde, where the reservoirs of molten rock boiled as they fed the forges above and below. Gangs of mutants, skin evolved thick and leathery against the heat, hauled enormous slabs of war engine armour from gigantic forges. The high ceiling was obscured by banks of smoke and lengths of massive chain looped down, hung with titan-sized weapons for fitting onto Kulgarde's war machines.

The mutants swarmed from their work posts, taskmasters bellowing orders to charge and butcher the Imperial Fists. Squad Lycaon met them with volleys of bolter fire, short and disciplined, shredding bodies as they surged forwards. With a terrible cry more mutants were arriving on the same level, sent by Kraegon Thul's orders to swamp the area and slow the Imperial Fists down until the Iron Warriors could force them to battle.

Like a sea of flesh at high tide, they flowed through their own dead. The taskmasters rose like warships on that tide, ordering forward the new arrivals of pallid medical orderlies and emaciated dungeon keepers, shambling labour-brutes and bloated chapel attendants. Thousands of them were flooding the forges, some pushed into the molten pits as they were crowded too close, others vanishing beneath the feet of the larger mutants around them. Their lives meant nothing as individuals – together, as one raging mass, they were an unstoppable force.

'Brothers!' ordered Lycaon. 'Stand and fight! I shall take Kraegon Thul's head. Lysander, can you get us to the throne forge?'

'I can,' said Lysander, snapping off his own shots into the tide of screaming mutants. 'But we do not have long.'

'It must be you and I,' said Lycaon.

'Then it shall be.'

Lycaon led the way into the burning darkness, where billows of smoke from the forges masked the way ahead. Lysander glanced behind him to see Halaestus fighting alongside Squad Lycaon, jaw set as he rattled off a magazine of bolter fire into the enemy. Then the darkness grew around them and Lysander lost sight of them.

So IT WAS that two Imperial Fists made it as far as the vast circular door, its two halves meeting at a massive combination lock. The lock's concentric circles were marked with sigils taken from the Iron Warriors heraldry, mounted over a mass of clockwork connected to the hydraulic rams that could swing the doors open or slam them closed.

The sound of the approaching horde rang against the pitted iron of the walls. Lysander stepped up to the lock and ran his hands across it.

He hauled the rings around until they lined up a hand, a shattered tower, an open eye and an eight-pointed star. With a hiss of spurting hydraulics the doors boomed open and a fiercer heat rolled out, a blistering gale heavy with sulphur and ash.

Ahead was the spherical chamber that Lysander had seen once before, when he had first come to Malodrax and was dragged by Captain Hexal through the halls of Kulgarde. He and his battle-brothers had been brought here, the forge throne.

The lower half of the sphere was full of churning molten iron, bubbling up plumes of flame. The walls were hung with weapons and armour, each one a unique masterpiece with blades of diamond or polished ivory shining in the yellow-orange glare. Hundreds of them hung there, still glowing, for the heat of their forging had never dissipated.

Suspended over the molten fires, connected to the doorway by a narrow walkway, was the circular platform on which stood the anvil. It looked like it had been hauled from some distant temple-forge, ancient and gnarled, scarred with the marks of a million blades hammered into shape.

Kraegon Thul was waiting. He stood before the anvil, smoke coiling around him, his outline shimmering in the heat. He was every bit the monster Lysander remembered, as if the industrial magnitude of war was distilled and poured into the shape of that ancient, age-corrupted armour. Kraegon Thul raised a hand and from the ceiling fell a familiar shape – the Fist of Dorn, Lysander's thunder hammer, taken from him when he was first brought to Kulgarde. Thul caught the hammer and swung it as if testing its balance.

It was obscene to see a relic of the Imperial Fists in the hand of an Iron Warrior. The machine-spirit of the ancient weapon must have been crying out in misery and anger. A wave of shame came over Lysander, for he had lost the weapon and placed it in the armoury of his Chapter's greatest enemy.

Chaplain Lycaon stepped forwards, crozius arcanum in hand. There had been no question that he would be the one to face Kraegon Thul. In ages past it was a law of the Chapter that the Commander's Right be respected on the battlefield, and that any Imperial Fist who tried to usurp it and face the enemy's champion himself would be punished with the nerve glove or cortical scourge. That was no longer the case, but the tradition was still strong. Though Lysander had brought the Imperial Fists here, it was Lycaon who should take the Warsmith's head back to the *Phalanx*.

'Kraegon Thul!' called out Lycaon over the scalding gale swirling around the crucible. 'You owe us many deaths, but to my shame, I can grant you only one! Kneel and I will take your head. Fight and I will cut you to pieces upon your own anvil, and the history of my Chapter will sing of your suffering! Make your choice, Warsmith, and die!'

17

'When I look upon death, as I know I shall, it will be with the knowledge that I have changed the universe around me. How many men can say that? A man might live two or three hundred years among the Imperial nobility, but what of it? A hundred more and it will be as if he had never existed. Not I. If nothing else, the enemies of mankind will remember me as a deadly foe, a lesson against underestimating my species. And so when I look upon death, I will welcome it.'

– Inquisitor Corvin Golrukhan

THE STAINED-GLASS WINDOW that dominated the chapel displayed a saint of Chaos, a prophet of the warp, dozens of storeys high, surrounded by the ruins of a once-great city. She was shown as a warrior, her skin bright red, horns on her brow, a golden bow in one hand and the severed head of a greenskin alien in the other. She wore a gown of flame with thousands of worshippers burning at her feet. The sky behind her was streaked with falling stars and shattered moons.

Lysander smashed through the window, the saint of Chaos disintegrating beneath him. The chapel whirled as he fell and he reached out, groping for his foe. His hand closed on the plume of Karnak's helm and he dragged the alien with him.

They had fought from the duelling ground through the temple, as Shalhadar's faithful battled the scum of Kulgarde everywhere around them. The surroundings had been a blur until Karnak got the upper hand for a split second, catching Lysander's blade on his own and hurling him through the window.

Lysander hit the ground hard, knocking the air out of his lungs. He had come down in a great clockwork monstrosity, an ancient engine that drove a production line hammering out segments of machinery and armour. Belts of articulated steel ran back and forth across the vast space as hammers and mechanical welding arms swung between the columns of cogs and pistons. The sound was deafening and Lysander's head swam with it.

Karnak had landed a short distance away, on one of the conveyor belts among the machine components. He still had his sword on him and he didn't look as winded as Lysander.

Karnak was already on his feet. Lysander's body complained as he snatched up his axe and circled, picking his way through the machinery grinding overhead. The axe was a crude weapon snatched from a brute-mutant moments earlier, a similar size to the executioner's axe with a notched and blunted blade. Karnak loosened up his shoulders, switching his sword back and forth. Lysander's armour was scored all over by the tip of the sword and his cloak was in tatters.

Karnak sprinted at Lysander. Lysander sidestepped behind a huge cog – Karnak dived through the spokes of the cog and whipped the blade at Lysander's leg. Lysander brought the haft of his axe down in time to deflect the blade but the sword cut straight through his weapon. Lysander dropped the useless halves of the axe as Karnak rolled to his feet.

'Kneel,' hissed Karnak in a hoarse whisper of a voice. 'Obey. Take a warrior's end.'

'You know I will not,' replied Lysander. 'You waste your breath.'

'Quite so,' said Karnak. 'But I must ask. It is how it is done.'

The exchange had bought Lysander the seconds he needed to think. Karnak was faster. Lysander was stronger. The Codex Astartes made much of how a Space Marine had to accentuate his strengths, never seek to compensate for his weaknesses. Rogal Dorn had taught that an Imperial Fist should be a master strategist when it came to planning the battle, but become a brutal savage when it came to fighting it. Lysander would not beat Karnak in a fencing match, but he had tricks this alien could never match.

Lysander grabbed the spokes of the cog beside him.

Metal screamed as the cogs around it disengaged, stripping teeth. He ripped the cog free of its mountings – it was three metres across and solid iron. Lysander spun like a hammer thrower, letting the force come up from his feet, through his legs up to his abdomen and chest, and out through his shoulders. The cog scythed into Karnak, smacking him square in the midriff and throwing him back through a bank of spinning clockwork. Shards of brass and steel rained down. The conveyor belt ruptured under the impact and threw links as it spooled into the air, scattering a fountain of scrap metal.

Lysander leapt the distance between himself and Karnak. He kicked the alien's sword away and was on him, putting all his weight on the armoured chest. He slammed a fist into Karnak's throat, feeling the alien buck and squirm under him, trying to wriggle out, but Lysander was too heavy and strong.

'You should have just killed me,' snarled Lysander.

Karnak forced an arm free and clutched at Lysander's face, trying to get his fingers through the eyeholes of the executioner's hood. The hood came free and Lysander grabbed Karnak's wrist, trapping his arm against the floor. Karnak was left looking up at Lysander's exposed face.

'You're Lysander,' said Karnak.

Something in the moment of recognition threw Karnak's focus. He stopped struggling for a moment and Lysander smashed a fist into his faceplate. The armour split and Lysander's fist came away with fragments of the eyepieces embedded in his knuckles.

Karnak grabbed a shard of broken metal, a strut snapped off from the clockwork he had crashed through. He stabbed it at Lysander's neck but Lysander knocked the hand away, spotting a great spear of jagged metal stabbing out from the wreckage. He hauled Karnak off the floor, taking his whole weight – as furious as he was, Karnak seemed to weigh nothing at all.

'Wait…' gasped the alien.

Lysander lunged at the wreckage. The jagged spike punched through Karnak's back and speared out through his chest, just off-centre. Lysander let go and Karnak was left hanging there, skewered through like an insect on a scientist's wall.

Karnak convulsed and coughed. Lysander tore the broken helmet off him, ready to look into the alien's eyes before the killing blow went in.

He had wondered many times since he had been on Malodrax just what kind of alien Karnak was. The elaborate armour and the air of arrogance suggested one of the eldar, an ancient and cruel race for which Lysander had nothing but disdain. Perhaps Karnak was one of Malodrax's natives, who had kept the civilisation and learning of his people in return for becoming a slave to Kraegon Thul. Or maybe he was from one of the numberless xenos species with whom humanity had not yet had any contact, brilliant but deviant creatures who planned mankind's downfall in the galaxy's shadows. All these had been possibilities, and Lysander would have been happy to kill any of them.

But he was not looking at an alien now. He was looking into the bloodied face of a human. It was long and lean, the hair shaved back close, the eyes deep-set and grey.

'They got you…' said Karnak, a dribble of blood running from the corner of his mouth. 'They used you. But it is not too late…'

'Who are you?' demanded Lysander.

'Sildyne,' came the reply. 'My name is Sildyne.'

Lysander stepped back a pace. 'Sildyne? Golrukhan's assassin?'

Sildyne smiled weakly. His teeth were broken and bloody. 'Who did you think made sure the scalpel would break? I would have done the same for your brothers, but Thul sent them to the Bone Carvers before I could… before I could do anything. I feel no pain, you know. That is how we can tell we are dying. My spine is cut.'

Lysander's thoughts were spinning. He seized onto the one thing he had – the reason he was there, the man he had come to kill. 'Where is Kraegon Thul?' he asked.

'Somewhere safe,' said Sildyne. 'You are here to kill me. You will not get at him now. But…' Sildyne groped at the belt of his armour, where several compartments were built into the plates around his waist. One of them slid open and he took out a long, thin-bladed dagger, its hilt a vial of colourless liquid, wound round with filigree gold. 'Golrukhan gave me one last task to perform if he was ever killed or taken alive. To kill Kraegon Thul. This was to be my weapon. The venom in it will seize the gene-seed's genetic markers and turn them against the host. A Space Marine can survive most anything, but not this. I put myself close enough to Thul to use it, but that... that monster... he never took off his armour.' Sildyne laughed at that, the sound a ragged bubbling from his torn lungs. 'One glimpse of exposed skin and I would have killed him. But there was none.'

Sildyne held out the weapon. His fingers went limp and the weapon fell – Lysander caught it before it hit the floor. He saw now the channels in its stiletto blade, through which the venom would course when the blade was pushed home and the vial shattered.

'What must I do?' said Lysander, looking down at the weapon.

'Leave here. Escape. Come back with friends. But remember, Lysander. This was not an accident. They sent you here to kill me. Malodrax sent you. They are all slaves to its will. Do not follow them. Do not let this world use you any more...'

Sildyne's eyes rolled back and his mouth lolled open. His hands fell nerveless by his sides. For a moment Lysander could only stare at the man he had killed, the man who had engineered his escape, had dedicated himself to killing Kraegon Thul, and who had been rewarded with an execution.

'My tome has been taken from me and I write this on a scrap of parchment in the blood of my torn fingers, in a code that only an acolyte of mine could ever read. I am not such a fool that I believe anyone will ever read it, but the Emperor's sight is upon me and I will set out these thoughts even if He is the only one who will ever see them.

'I am to die. I have been left to the warders of this dungeon. The door has been removed from my cell and they will come for me when I am weak, so that I will in those final moments consider myself no more than prey. Not an inquisitor, not a servant of the Emperor, nor even a man, but a cowering, feeble prey-creature fit only to be devoured by a superior organism. Before that final breaking comes, I will make my testament.

'I have broken with the codes of the Inquisition and sought out profane knowledge instead of its destruction. I made terrible bargains for such knowledge, and paid for it in the lives of brave and loyal acolytes who deserved better. I betrayed all that should ever matter to a man to follow this path and gather a greater understanding of our foes, against every teaching of righteous men. But I did this for my Emperor, because I only ever believed that to know our enemy was to defeat it, and that to defeat it was to best serve Him On Earth. I die, perhaps, as punishment for my heresies, but as all of Terra is my witness if I were to live my life again I would make those same choices, betray those same brethren,

and commit those same heresies. For me, there was never any choice.

'Malodrax has claimed me, as it has claimed billions before. Perhaps I should never have come here, for the very fount of knowledge it promised served as a trap to draw in flawed men like me. But though my body be torn apart by the jackals that gather even now outside my cell, I am not yet done here.

'Agent Sildyne lives. He contacted me in secret, in the guise of one such warder, at great peril to his own life. He has with him that archeotech weapon for which I paid so much, and I have instructed him in the manner he will kill Kraegon Thul. If I cannot plunder Malodrax for its secrets, I can at least see to it that its most dangerous inhabitant dies. Thus is discharged the final duty I will perform as an inquisitor.

'They are coming. If they find this note they will be unable to read it, unless Sildyne has broken and given them the code – if so, it does not matter what they know, for they know it already. If you are one such creature of Kulgarde reading this, know that the Emperor will have his revenge against you even if I do not.

'I have a rock prised from the wall of my cell and I shall break a skull or two before they are done. In the name of my Emperor, I go to my death still fighting His fight.'

– Inquisitor Corvin Golrukhan.

'LORD SHALHADAR WILL be most pleased,' came a familiar voice from high above. Lysander looked up to the rafters and there, among the pistons and noisome steam, clung Talaya by her spider's legs. She clambered down slowly, savouring the moment, as if every drop of Sildyne's blood on the floor was her own victory. 'And Thul as well. He planned to kill Karnak for years, but one blow from that weapon and any Iron Warrior facing him would die. It was too great a risk even for the Warsmith. But when you walked through the gates of my lord's city, the problem was solved.'

Lysander picked up Sildyne's sword. 'At least I can kill one soul today who deserves it,' he said.

'Kill me?' said Talaya. 'What a ridiculous idea. I just came to make sure you did your job.'

She scuttled back up a brass column, towards the darkness among the rafters.

Lysander sprinted at the column. He hit it so hard he felt his shoulder crumple with the impact, bone and joint crushed against the metal. The column buckled and bent, ripped free from the ceiling. With a sense of satisfaction that blotted out the pain, Lysander heard the clatter of Talaya falling to the ground behind him, thrown off her perch by the unexpected impact.

'Did you truly believe I would not kill you?' said Lysander as he rounded on Talaya. 'Do you have so poor a view of fate, to think it would not pit us against each other? From the first moment I saw you, I knew it would end with me taking your head.'

Talaya picked herself up, losing her customary grace as she scrabbled across the floor. 'Malodrax will have its blood,' she said. 'Either's will do.'

Talaya was fast. Lysander already knew that. When she leapt at him, propelled through the air by her back legs, it was exactly what he expected. The rain of blades that fell from her he had not anticipated. Slits opened up in her armoured body and arrowhead-shaped shards sprayed out, hundreds of them. Lysander threw out an arm in front of his face as they rained against him, embedding themselves in his skin, finding purchase in bone and sinew. A dozen slashes of pain flashed against his consciousness. Power armour might have turned them away, but not the mundane armour he wore now.

Lysander dived forwards, avoiding Talaya as she came down talon-first on the spot where he had stood. Lysander tore off the vambrace now impaled with six or seven shards, feeling the hot blood flowing down his forearm as they were pulled free, and threw it to the floor.

'Did you like that trick?' said Talaya with a smile. 'I have more.'

Lysander lunged at her, reaching for one of her mechanical legs. If he could twist it from its mountings, he could use it as a weapon. Talaya flitted out of reach, skittering to one side and spearing him through the left calf with one of her talons. Lysander yelled and fell to one knee, and Talaya leapt onto his back, grabbing on with her other legs – one speared into his chest, another into the side of his abdomen, a third down through the meat of one shoulder.

Talaya leaned forwards so he could see her face

upside-down in front of his. Though Shalhadar had left her form mostly human, there was nothing human now in that face. Her eyes seemed to grow, pupil and iris merging into a swirling, star-scattered vision of the warp, smile wide and manic.

'You too shall serve,' she hissed.

A gunshot sounded and the upper half of Talaya's face was gone, replaced with a great red-black crater.

The force pinning her to Lysander relented. Lysander grabbed her by the scruff of the neck and threw her down to the ground, her talons tearing free of him. The shot had hit her in the back of the head and the exit wound had blasted away everything from forehead to nose. She had been dead before she hit the floor.

Lysander followed the path the bullet must have taken. Leaning against a pillar, still aiming down the sights of an Iron Warrior's bolter, was Brother Halaestus. Brother Skelpis leaned against him in turn, tottering on his single remaining leg.

'You live,' said Lysander.

'After a fashion,' said Halaestus. 'We are not alone.'

'Come forth!' shouted Skelpis behind him. From the shelter of a pillar emerged a thin, sorry figure – Thul's Navigator, fresh bruises swelling one side of his face. He looked terrified.

'Can he get us out of here?' said Lysander.

'I can!' said the Navigator hurriedly. His voice was dry and whispery. 'Thul has a ship, a personal transport. I can take you there. And I know the way through the orbital reef. Without me you will surely perish. Do not kill me, for your own sakes!'

'Do you trust him?' asked Lysander.

'Would you?' replied Skelpis. 'He's scared right enough, though. For now he speaks the truth.'

'You know what will happen if you lie to us?' said Lysander to the Navigator.

'You'll kill me.'

'I would have hoped you'd credit us with more imagination than that. Brothers, you did well taking him alive. We may yet survive this.'

'Don't thank me, captain,' said Halaestus. 'It was Skelpis's idea. I was just going to shoot him.'

THE NAVIGATOR KNEW Kulgarde well, and had been primed with the quickest routes to the fortress's landing pad. The sounds of battle reached them as he led the three Imperial Fists through the labyrinth of passages and side rooms, through the upper levels and onto the fortifications. The few menials and mutants they encountered were shot down or had their necks broken – most were flooding the levels below, where the riot sparked by Lysander had become a pitched battle between Shalhadar's players and the inhabitants of Kulgarde. No doubt Shalhadar's people would be butchered to a man down there, and everything in Kulgarde wanted to tear off a piece of flesh for itself.

Thul's ship resembled the older marks of shuttle used by the Adeptus Astartes, ancient and complex in design, its hull armour left bare metal with the black and yellow flashes typical of the Iron Warriors around the engines and gun ports. The iron mask symbol glowered down from the side of the ship. It was substantially upgunned compared to newer ships of its type, with ranks of rotary cannons lining the underside and twin laser turrets either side of the tail.

The Navigator led them onto the landing pad and pressed his hand against a panel hidden among the geometry of the hull. A slice of the hull slid out to form a ramp into the ship.

'One more thing,' said the Navigator.

The note in his voice – not of fear this time, but of certainty – told Lysander to look away. The Navigator spun around and ripped the embroidered band from his face.

Lysander threw Halaestus to the floor. Skelpis, unbalanced, fell with him. Lysander covered his eyes with his forearm so he would not see what the Navigator had just revealed.

The ship's crews of the Imperium, the voidborn who served on its battleships and the craft of the Chartist Captains, were a superstitious people, and few topics carried as many dark tales and warning parables as the third eye of the Navigator. Navigators were essential to long-distance space travel, but they were mutants, and hence, while their existence was tolerated, they were hated, feared and avoided by right-thinking people who told tales of the terrors contained in that third eye.

It allowed a Navigator to look upon the warp and not only keep his sanity, but chart a path through it. But most of all, it could kill. The reflection of the warp that remained in the third eye would annihilate a man's mind if he looked into it. It could leave his body a dried-out husk, all life and moisture driven from it. It could blast him apart from the inside, leaving him smeared across the deck. A look from it could make him burst into flames or freeze his blood solid. Every tale had one thing in common – a Navigator may look feeble and broken, but a glance from that eye will kill.

Lysander had heard enough such tales, and he knew they were true. The Navigator's eye would destroy even a Space Marine's mind, if he let it. Lysander did not.

He rammed his forearm into the Navigator's face, and felt the cold fire of the third eye as his arm smacked into it. The Navigator was thrown against the side of the ship, withered frame crumpling. Lysander had pulled the blow but even so he had felt a cheekbone break, maybe the socket of one of the Navigator's mortal eyes. Lysander kept his arm pressed against the third eye as he looked the Navigator in the face.

'Did you think you could outwit Imperial Fists?' snarled Lysander. 'Do you think we are children? Even if one falls, even if all the fates align and you can take one of us down with that cursed eye, the others will avenge him on that withered husk you call a body! I run low on reasons to let you live.'

'Forgive me!' yelped the Navigator. 'I can help you!

You need me! Look!' the Navigator shrugged off his robe and Lysander saw, on his scrawny chest, swirls of old ink that formed the lines of a star map. The Navigator's whole torso was tattooed with it. 'Malodrax is surrounded by an orbital reef,' he said, 'and you will never find your way through without me.'

'Without your skin, maybe,' said Lysander.

'The lock!' said the Navigator. 'The lock to the crucible! You do not know how to open it. I do! I know!'

Lysander held out a hand behind him. Halaestus put the Iron Warrior's bolter into it and Lysander pressed the barrel up underneath the Navigator's chin.

'The hand, the eye, the tower, the star,' gasped the Navigator. 'It is the combination. I know more, much more. Let me live, that is all I ask of you. A small favour. I mean nothing to you.'

'You're right there,' said Lysander.

'We have no time, captain,' said Skelpis, getting back onto his remaining foot and leaning against the hull. 'I hear Kulgarde's forces approaching. They must be done with your players.'

'Get on board and start it up,' said Lysander, pushing the Navigator up the ramp into the ship. Inside the vessel was functional and grim, its utilitarian interior broken only by an altar to the Chaos Gods set back from the cockpit. The altar was a slab of stone, with hundreds of figures depicting the countless warp powers standing over it in niches cut into the steel bulkhead. Thul's heraldry covered a banner hanging in the berths further back into the body of the ship – Lysander tore it down and threw it over the altar. He could destroy it properly once they were off the planet.

The Navigator sat in the pilot's seat and worked rapidly at the many gauges and control runes. The ship's engines started, a loud, shuddering growl. Halaestus helped Skelpis up the ramp and the two strapped themselves into the grav-restraints in the berth section. The ship lifted up off the pad, vertical thrusters howling, and through the cockpit viewshield Lysander could see the walls of Kulgarde and the distant horizon tilting as the ship banked over the front of the walls.

The ship angled upwards, nose to the diseased sky. The main engines kicked up a note and hurled the ship upwards.

Lysander dropped into a place on the grav-bench, buckling the restraints around him. He caught Halaestus's eye and for the first time realised what he must look like to his battle-brothers – Lysander wore not a Space Marine's armour but ornate crimson plate forged in Shalhadar's city, and he had fought with an executioner's axe instead of the bolter and chainsword. But there was nothing to say – the sound of the engines would drown out any words. Lysander looked away from Halaestus and watched the clouds give way to the dirty black of Malodrax's orbit, as the planet was finally left behind them.

18

'The secrets this world promises are many and powerful. Here is an opportunity to study such a world in detail, not as conqueror, but as a student of its ways. I shall bring back to my conclave a wealth of such knowledge that shall furnish the armouries of our minds for generations to come. I give thanks that I was born with the qualities to serve in the Holy Ordos of the Emperor's Inquisition, for to know the exhilaration of such a moment is something the great masses of the Imperium shall never know.'

– Inquisitor Corvin Golrukhan

IT WAS THE way of the Imperial Fists to capture such moments in sculpture and fable, and even then, in the very moments it unfolded, Lysander could imagine the forms this history would take.

Lycaon was the model of an Imperial Fists Chaplain – unyielding, a complete stranger to doubt, impossible to dismay. Kraegon Thul might have been crafted to be everything the Imperial Fists hated, an Iron Warrior with the blood of Lycaon's battle-brothers on his hands, a harvester and corrupter of the Chapter's gene-seed, a monster with ambitions to bring down another great Heresy upon the Imperium.

Kraegon Thul saluted mockingly, raising the Fist of Dorn as if this were a duel between brothers to decide the better swordsman. Chaplain Lycaon made no such gesture. The two circled the great anvil, keeping the altar of blackened steel between them. This was how it would be remembered, the two matching wits before the first blows, icons of the war that had begun when the Warmaster Horus broke from the rule of the Emperor, and that had never ended.

This was the moment the Chapter's artisans would render in memory of the event. Because the moments that followed could never be.

Thul brought the Fist of Dorn down against the anvil. The hammer split the anvil in two with a thundercrack and from it spilled the trapped souls of a thousand sacrifices, all those in whose blood the anvil had been anointed. Lycaon was thrown off his feet by the eruption of dark magic and Lysander was thrown against the frame of the crucible's door behind him. Thousands of teeth gnawed at Lycaon's armour, tearing away chunks of black-painted ceramite. The gale ripped away the Chaplain's helmet and one side of his face was torn to shredded pulp, blood welling up and hardening into a gnarled half-mask.

Lycaon arrested his fall before he plunged over the

edge into the fires. He squared back up to Kraegon Thul, but the Warsmith strode through the two halves of the shattered altar and was within a hammer swing of Lycaon now. Thul thrust the head of the hammer at the Chaplain, who was barely able to turn the blow away with his crozius. A mundane weapon would have been shattered by the power field, but the Fist of Dorn was forged to withstand the fires of hell and the chill of the warp, and it would not be so easy to disarm the Warsmith.

The released sacrifices swirled around the upper half of the crucible, weaving between the weapons and armour hanging there, howling as if they still felt the pain of their deaths.

Lycaon ducked a swing of the hammer and rammed a shoulder into Thul's chest. But Thul was not knocked back one step and wrapped an arm around Lycaon's shoulder, pinning the Imperial Fist's crozius arm to his side. Thul picked Lycaon off his feet and hurled him against one half of the anvil.

Lysander charged across the walkway. He could already see in his mind Thul's follow-up blow, a swing of the hammer into the prone Lycaon's stomach, crushing him against the anvil. The only thing between Lycaon and that fate was Lysander.

Thul turned to face Lysander. Lysander snapped off bolter shots into Thul's chest – the Warsmith's power armour was proof against them and the shots did little more than grab his attention, but that was Lysander's plan.

'Captain Lysander,' said Thul. 'You come for me again. Did you not learn from your last lesson?' Thul lunged and swung at Lysander, the blow aimed at his head.

Lysander's bolter met the Fist of Dorn. The bolter shattered as Lysander knew it would. He let go of the wrecked weapon and grabbed Thul's wrist with both hands, trying to bend it down and force the head of the hammer to the ground.

Thul had been a warrior for thousands of years. The Traitor Legions spent most of their lives on worlds wholly or partially within the warp, where time did not flow as it did in real space. That meant some of them had been alive since the Horus Heresy, and had fought in hundreds of campaigns over millennia of warfare. Thul had fought every kind of fight there was hundreds of times over. Lysander's gambit was the best one for the situation – lock the opponent's weapon and use the split-second opening to get in a headbutt or a kick to the front of the knee, enough to send the enemy reeling and open for disarming and a killing blow with his own weapon. Lysander himself had practised it countless times in the sparring halls of the *Phalanx*, and had executed it often enough in battle. But Thul had run those same drills and fought those same battles, only more so, and he was ready.

The heel of Thul's hand smacked into the side of Lysander's head. Lysander's helmet was dented and wrenched sideways, the eyepieces unaligned and his vision suddenly obscured. Thul spun and dropped to a knee, driving his elbow down onto Lysander's thigh. Lysander's femur snapped and the ceramite of his armour buckled, and suddenly he was on his back with a leg folded the wrong way in front of him. Thul wrenched the Fist of Dorn back out of his grip.

'Very disappointing,' said Thul. 'All these centuries I seek to make your kind understand, and what is your response? You break your bodies against us as you have always done. As it was ten thousand years ago, so it is today.'

Lysander tried to roll away but Thul stepped on his shattered leg and the pain that shot through Lysander was too much for even a Space Marine to bear. It blinded him, a white bolt of searing cold slicing from his leg up through his whole body. His thoughts were drowned out by the blank wall of agony.

His armour dumped its reserve of painkillers into his bloodstream and his vision swam back. Thul had the Fist of Dorn up ready to drive the head into Lysander and crush his torso flat. Behind him appeared the shape of Chaplain Lycaon, armour scored and dented from the punishment Thul had dealt out. Lycaon brought up his crozius above his head like a woodcutter about to split a log, the blade positioned to come down against the crown of Thul's head and cut it in two down to the collarbone.

Thul did not even look round. He reversed his grip on the hammer and drove it into Lycaon's shoulder. The power field blew the armour open, revealing torn bone and muscle. Lycaon reeled backwards and Thul spun around, bringing the full force of the hammer blow into Lycaon's chest.

Lycaon was smacked back into the remains of the anvil, and the spirits released howled a crescendo as his chest was blasted open by the discharging power field. The ceramite of his breastplate was split and splayed out like bloody metal wings. His head lolled back, mouth open, eyes rolled back, in the unmistakeable attitude of death.

Lysander might have cried out. It was hard to tell through the haze of pain and the keening of the spirits overhead. It was not the shock or the sorrow that hit him. It was the obscenity of that sight, of a man like Lycaon torn open. He could not fall – he was the image of an Imperial Fist, resembling a statue of Rogal Dorn more than a man. And here he was, turned into nothing more than meat and blood and ruptured armour, by a creature like Thul.

Lysander groped for the remains of his broken bolter.

'I have lived for millennia,' said Thul as he turned back to Lysander. 'I have seen this galaxy and the truths of it. Do you think we do what we do for the sake of it? Because doing evil is its own end? If you put just a fraction of that zeal into understanding what is truly right, Imperial Fist, you would join us in a heartbeat.'

'While one of us lives...' gasped Lysander, feeling his guts twisting with the shock of his broken leg. He could not walk, but he could fight.

'While one of you lives,' said Thul, 'the fight will never end, you will be avenged. Is that not it? I have heard the sentiment many times. You, who have lived within your Imperium, among its corruption and hatred, you still rail against those who would change it. I thought perhaps you would understand, Lysander. You have been more than a Space Marine. Malodrax saw to it you were something very different, for a while. But you are the same as the rest.'

Thul kicked the shattered bolter away from Lysander and stamped down on his ruined leg.

The shame was as bad as the physical pain. To be laid helpless by the enemy was, some said, worse than death – to permit him to do whatever he wished and not be able to fight back. It was inimical to the very existence of a Space Marine. If he died here it would not be as a warrior. It would be as a victim, his duty left undone.

But Lysander was not dead yet. There was always a way any battle could be won. The chances might not be high, but they were always there. There was something in Thul that was a weakness – he just had to find it before Thul finally took his head off.

Thul believed. That was the one lesson Lysander could be sure he had learned in all his pursuit of Kraegon Thul. The Warsmith believed absolutely in his cause.

'Malodrax wanted me,' said Lysander. 'It changed me.'

Lysander wished he could see Thul's face, so he could gauge some reaction. 'It took you and it used you,' said the Warsmith. 'Just as the Imperium forged you into a weapon to use against its own, to murder and oppress your own people. Chaos is freedom, Imperial Fist! Let your experience on Malodrax break you from the cage of your mind. Abandon what you were. You have bargained with daemons and assassinated the foes of the Iron Warriors. You are an Imperial Fist no longer.'

'I do not know...' slurred Lysander, fighting to stay conscious, 'what I am any more.'

Kraegon Thul kneeled over Lysander. 'You can be a crusader for the freedom of the human race,' he said. 'We will take our war to the stars. We will strike at the Imperium, at its underbelly, for it is ancient, corrupted and soft. One swift strike with the war engines of Kulgarde and we will be at the gates of Terra.'

'And what will you do then?' asked Lysander. 'With the Imperium at your mercy?'

'Burn it down,' said Thul, and Lysander was sure that behind that faceplate he was smiling. 'Bring the human race to extinction, and rebuild it in the image of the warp.'

Lysander reached up towards Thul, like a leper reaching for the hem of a saint's cloak.

He grabbed the back of Thul's helmet. Thul believed in his cause so completely that, given the chance to convert a new follower, he had let his guard down. It would be the only chance Lysander would get.

With the few remaining drops of strength he had, Lysander tore the helmet off Kraegon Thul's head.

Thul's head resembled a planetoid bombarded with

meteors and scoured by solar fire. It was impossible to tell between skin, bone and the pitted dark iron of his armour where the collar merged with the flesh of his neck. Corroded implants surrounded one eye socket, reaching up over his battered, hairless scalp. His mouth was lipless and narrow, his cheeks split open by age and decay to reveal the teeth in his jaw. His nose and chin were scarred by the constant application of the rebreather hooked up to the hose that ran down the front of his armour.

'Look into my face, my new brother,' said Kraegon Thul. 'Mankind will fall. We shall found its new age. To none but the warp shall we bow. This I swear.'

Lysander reached down to the ammunition compartment at his waist. Normally this held spare magazines for his bolter. He opened it up and took out the device inside.

Thul's eye glanced down and in that moment, he knew. He had lowered his defences and Lysander had brought him in with the promise of a rare prize – an Imperial Fist turned from the righteous path.

Lysander drove Sildyne's dagger up into Thul's face. It punched through the eye and into the socket, sinking its long, thin blade into the front of his skull. The crunch of the glass vial in the handle was impossibly satisfying – feeling it break, Lysander forgot the pain for a moment. The venom inside was injected through the microscopic holes in the blade, into Thul's cortex.

Thul reeled away and fell against the anvil. He put a

hand to his face, the dagger still sticking out of his eye.

'Still…' he slurred. 'Still, Imperial Fist, you disappoint…'

The venom coursed through his Space Marine's enhanced circulatory system. His organs, forced to peak efficiency by the gene-seed, were thrown into overdrive. Heart hammered, lungs pulsed, and brain spun. Thul clutched his head as blood, discoloured to a dark purple, spurted from his nose and between his teeth.

His slid down the anvil as the organs in his chest ruptured. More blood ran from the joints of his armour. The skin of his scalp writhed and bubbled as his brain boiled in his skull. The skin peeled away from his face, a blackened mask of gore all that remained of his features. The Fist of Dorn dropped from his fingers and clanged against the side of the anvil.

The sound of the spirits died down as they vanished, leaving the weapons and armour sections above swinging from their chains.

For several long minutes Lysander lay there on the platform before the anvil, and more than anything he would have dearly loved to let his mind fall into unconsciousness. Warm waves of dull pain were washing up and down him from his leg and shoulder. But he was not quite done yet.

He rolled onto his front and dragged himself towards the body of Kraegon Thul. The pain was worse and came in sharp, hot bursts, but it was good because it meant he could still feel something. He pulled the dagger back out of Thul's eye. Thul's head lolled to the side as what remained of his brain leaked out through the socket.

Lysander rolled to the edge of the platform. The waves of heat coming up off the molten steel hammered at him, but like the pain, it was good to feel something at all. He dropped the dagger over the edge and it vanished in the fire.

He took *Being A Description Of Malodrax And Its Foulness* from its compartment at his waist. He turned the book over in his hand and wondered if it could ever have been a coincidence that Malodrax had put the book in his path. Malodrax wanted to be ruled, but no ruler ever came up to its standards. Had it been testing Shalhadar and Kraegon Thul, by putting an Imperial Fist into their hands who might be manipulated into serving them, but who might return to destroy them? Perhaps the daemon prince and the Warsmith had been puppets, just as they had made Lysander their puppet, and Malodrax had been the real adversary all along.

Lysander dropped the book, too, into the molten cauldron. It disappeared in a lick of flame. Only then did he let himself pass out.

HALAESTUS WAS LAID out among the dead in the Chapel of Dorn. Not all the Imperial Fists in the Malodrax strike force had left bodies fit to be displayed on the *Phalanx*, beneath the gaze of Dorn's golden statue and the icon of the Emperor looking on from the altar. Not all had been recovered. Halaestus had left an intact body, though the mutilations from his imprisonment stood out starker than ever against the greying skin of his corpse.

Lysander had not attended the main service for the lost. He had been in the apothecarion of the *Phalanx*, undergoing treatment for the ruptured organs suffered beneath his own hammer. Now Lysander had made the necessary journey to the Chapel of Dorn to pay his respects.

First Sergeant Kaderic stood among the funeral slabs. Battle-brothers from his squad were among the dead. He paused by the body of Chaplain Lycaon, the fatal wounds concealed beneath the body's golden shroud, and looked up at Lysander's approach. Kaderic had led the strike force after Lycaon had died, having defeated Hexal in their duel and cut the Iron Warrior's head off. He had led the Imperial Fists to the battlements where the *Breaker of Darkness* had sent down its gunships to pick them up. Kaderic had fought off the wretches of the fortress until the gunships could leave, carrying Lysander's unconscious body over his shoulders the whole time.

'You walk, Captain Lysander,' said Kaderic. 'In Kulgarde I had not known if I would see you living again.'

Lysander looked down at Halaestus's ruined face. The shroud did not quite cover the top of the scar in his throat where Kraegon Thul's Bone Carvers had torn out his gene-seed. 'Have you heard how he died?' he asked.

'With valour and fury,' said Kaderic.

Lysander wondered if there could have been a reply that meant less. An Imperial Fist was expected to fight and die with valour and fury – it would be an obscenity if he died any other way. Halaestus could have died a whimpering wreck and the same would still be said of him. Lysander had little doubt that Halaestus had gone into Kulgarde with no intention of walking out again. An Imperial Fist would never speak ill of the Chapter's battle-dead, of course, but that did not mean Halaestus had died well.

'They are your men now, Lysander,' said Kaderic. 'The First. When we saw it was you who killed Thul and avenged Lycaon and all our dead – we knew you were our captain, then.'

'It will take them time to accept me,' said Lysander.

'Time, maybe, but nothing else. Whatever there was to prove has been proven.'

Lysander looked from one end of the chapel to the other. Many had died. Many that could not be replaced. And Lysander had brought them to Malodrax.

Malodrax had come close. He could not deny that. The deals he had made with daemons, the lies he had told, even if only lies of omission, to his fellow Imperial Fists, and the part he had played in the plan to assassinate Sildyne – that had been almost enough. Thul's words had reached deep into his soul, but not quite deep enough.

It was the anger that had kept him true. That had

411

BEN COUNTER

never died down. That hot focus on revenge had kept the corruption from him, even when he was steeped in it. Malodrax thought it knew how deep a creature could hate, but it had never encountered Lysander before. What compromise and doubt still clung to him, the hatred would burn away. Malodrax had come close, but no one would ever come that close again to turning Lysander into something an Imperial Fist should never be.

'I wonder,' said Lysander, 'how far would be too far, in the name of victory.'

'How many dead would be too many?' said Kaderic.

It was not what Lysander had meant. He had been thinking of all the deeds that had brought him so close to the abyss, the deals and the alliances with the powers of Malodrax. But Kaderic, like all the Imperial Fists, did not need to know how close Lysander had come.

'How many dead,' agreed Lysander. 'How many of our Chapter's futures erased before they happen? To take command means many things, but above all it means making that choice. If a path leads to victory, but is littered with the dead, do we take it? That is what a captain of the Chapter must decide.'

'Then when the choice must be made,' said Kaderic, 'what will you do, Lysander, for victory?'

Lysander looked again at Halaestus, then at Lycaon, and all the faces of the dead on Malodrax.

'Anything,' he said.

* * *

412

THE IMPERIAL FISTS had sabotaged the forges and war machines before they left Malodrax with their dead and wounded. The Iron Warriors, leaderless, had retreated from the main fortress and by the time they retook it when the Imperial Fists were gone, the place had been rendered useless for Thul's plan of sending a legion of war engines to fuel a Black Crusade and drive to the gates of Terra. It was overrun with mutants and xenos dregs who rose up in rebellion against the Iron Warriors, for with Thul dead the Iron Warriors seemed vulnerable and mortal as they never had before. Kulgarde was consumed by war. In the corpse-choked passageways and underground warrens, it seemed the place had been built to maximise the death of its inhabitants.

Shalhadar's city had begun to tear itself apart before the Imperial Fists even reached Kulgarde. Many of the population fled into the rocky desert, there to die of thirst or starvation, or to form a feast for Malodrax's predators that descended following the scent of death. Some of Shalhadar's courtiers overcame their grief and began battling to see who would become the new lord of the city. Their followers slaughtered one another in the streets as the devastated citizens continued to tear at their flesh and enact ever fouler sacrifices to the gods for deliverance. The city became an ever more monstrous vision of madness, worthy of the warp itself.

Malodrax wanted to be ruled. Two beings had arisen who wanted to be lord of the planet, but each one had been undone by a common plan to divide the world among them and to use a lone Imperial Fist to serve them. That plan had killed them both. And so they were unworthy of the crown.

Malodrax wanted to be ruled. It was patient. Another would rise, and perhaps this time he would prove up to the planet's standards.

For now, Malodrax would wait.

ABOUT THE AUTHOR

Ben Counter is the author of the Soul Drinkers and Grey Knights series, along with two Horus Heresy novels, and is one of Black Library's most popular Warhammer 40,000 authors. He has written RPG supplements and comic books. He is a fanatical painter of miniatures, a pursuit which has won him his most prized possession: a prestigious Golden Demon award. He lives in Portsmouth, England.

Available from

and blacklibrary.com